CONSUMED
The Deep in Your Veins Series

Suzanne Wright

For Mae

CHAPTER ONE

(Ava)

It wasn't often that I found myself scowling. In general, I was a happy, upbeat, animated person. Even when I was a toddler, I'd always had a ready smile on my face. Always had more energy than I knew what to do with. My father had called me 'dippy'. My mother had called me 'neurotic'. Whatever. Both sounded fun.

I knew I was a little too...easily excitable...for most people's tastes. Knew I was quirky with the whole 'humming at random times' thing, my refusal to eat anything green, and my aversion to all things luminous yellow – it was a weird colour and I didn't trust it. But I didn't see the point in changing to please others, it was a thankless job. And it seemed totally dumb to let people or their behaviour get to me. But when it came to a certain blond Pagori vampire, I didn't seem to have much choice in the matter.

It was a few months ago, before Samantha Parker and Jared Michaels had ascended to become the Grand High Pair, that my brother and I had come to The Hollow – a gated community set on an off-the-map Caribbean island. The previous ruler, Antonio, had agreed to help me and Cristiano locate some of our missing nest. Sam, Jared, and their personal squad had accompanied us during the search, and that was when I'd first met Salem McCauley.

Confident. Focused. Reserved. Fearless. Dangerous. Private.

Salem was a complex character. He also had a very unapproachable air about him; his posture seemed to scream 'stay the hell back'. Most vampires did. Maybe I should have been one of those people who gave Salem a wide berth. I didn't, though…because his tall, trim build and his confidence and intensity always sparked a primal need to build inside me, twisting my stomach. It was too basic and elemental for me to make any sense of it, so I'd stopped trying to.

Normally, only one thought raced through my mind when I was around him: *He is so freaking hot.*

Right now, a totally other thought was zooming through my brain: *I'm going to kill him.*

The conversation I'd had an hour ago with Fletcher, Sam and Jared's PA, replayed in my mind once again:

"Fletch, you should see the new member of Evan's squad, he is so cute. We talked for a while, and he seems really nice – smooth, too."

"You know that he won't ask you out, though, don't you?" Fletcher said carefully.

Offended, I frowned. "Why not?"

"Well…he wants to live."

"Okay, you've totally lost me."

"If he touches you, Salem will kill him."

I shook my head. "He wouldn't."

Fletcher's smile was almost pitying. "Ava, you're on an island where the ratio of men to women is something like 60 to 1. Don't you find it a bit weird that not one bloke has come onto you? Salem put the word out that if any man touched you, he'd kill him."

I ground my teeth. "He has some fucking nerve."

Fletcher shot me an impatient glance. "Oh, come on. Did you really expect anything different? I don't know why you two haven't got together, but I do know he won't let anyone else have you."

And so, I was going to kill the shithead.

Said shithead was currently beside me at the long, glass conference table with the rest of his ten-man squad. I didn't have a clue why I'd been asked to sit in on their meeting with Sam and Jared in the main building of The Hollow. Until the pair finally entered, I wouldn't know. I might have been excited if it wasn't for one thing…*I'm going to kill him.*

It had been a week ago, when he'd cornered me outside the restrooms of a bar, that he'd quite unexpectedly kissed me. No, 'kissed' wasn't the right word – it was too tame. Salem hadn't kissed my mouth, he'd taken it, plundered it, left me aching for more. But he hadn't given me more.

Another conversation replayed in my mind…

Off-balance by the way he'd so abruptly pulled away, I stumbled, breathing hard. Every part of me cried out for him, and I knew by the bulge in his pants that he wanted me too…So why was he standing all the way over there?

As if Salem had seen the question in my eyes, he stated, 'I'm not going to fuck you. I don't want a one-night stand or a fling.'

'What do you want?'

His eyes flared. 'Everything.'

The unexpected response made my stomach clench – whether that was in anxiety or excitement, I didn't know. Probably both. But there was one thing I did know: 'I don't do relationships. I can't give you more.'

His mouth curved slightly. 'Oh, but you will.'

Since then, he hadn't kissed me again. But he'd teased me with subtle, light touches –brushing against me as I past, his hands lingering in places they had no right being. Each time, the memory of him devastating my mouth while his hands kneaded and teased would slam to the forefront of my mind. And the bastard knew it. He was attempting to wear me down. But it wasn't going to work. Nope. Not at all.

Relationships never worked well for me. Guys liked me well enough until they realised just how quirky I really was. The cheeriness, the humming, the giggling, the optimism, and the 'being a morning person' thing – or 'dusk person', in my case – would begin to wear on them.

Eventually, they would get frustrated with me all the time, would try to change me, and then I'd have to punch them in the dick until they vomited. It just seemed practical to avoid all that and stick to flings, where everything was superficial and casual.

It had been so much easier to resist Salem when he'd been a hot and cold motherfucker: talking to me some days and then blowing me off on others. Even then, though, I'd never been able to stay mad at him for long. There was a deep sadness in Salem; a well of pain. He was good at hiding it, and I probably wouldn't have sensed it if I hadn't known someone like him – my brother.

From minute one, Salem had been oddly protective and possessive of me for some unknown reason. In actual fact, I wasn't sure that *he* knew the reason either. He seemed confused by his behaviour, seemed to be a person who didn't trust his own feelings. Or maybe he just wasn't good at understanding them.

That protectiveness and possessiveness had hit a whole new level in the past week. Every ounce of his natural intensity and determination was focused on me. It was scary and, well, kind of hot. But hearing that the cheeky fucker had literally ordered the other males on the island to stay away from me, thereby stopping me from having a fling with anyone else...not so hot. If he thought he could—

"What's wrong?" Salem quietly rumbled.

So deep in thought, I nearly jumped out of my skin. His gaze was piercing, searching, concerned. Oh, I had every intention of answering his question, but now wasn't the time or the place. And it would be fun to torment him a little anyway, particularly since he could be quite adorable when he was irritated.

"What's wrong?" he repeated.

I sniffed. "Nothing."

"Ava..." It was a warning.

A warning I snorted at. The red ring to his irises that marked him as a Pagori vampire began to glow, which meant he was either thirsty, angry, or horny. Pagoris were the most powerful of the three breeds; they easily became aggressive and were incredibly strong and fast, but the downside was that they had an overpowering bloodlust. Kejas, who were marked by the amber ring to their irises, all had hypnotic beauty to lure in their prey, but the poor things also had fangs.

I was a Sventé. My kind were the weakest of the three breeds; considered tame in that we didn't have a strong bloodlust, which allowed us to easily blend in with humans. Also, our gifts tended to be defensive and mostly boring. However, once in a while, there were Sventés with offensive gifts, just like me and Sam.

Sam, who had once belonged to my nest – a nest I might soon leave – had later become a mix of all three breeds, but I wasn't sure exactly how it happened. It was a story that only a select few knew.

"Ava...What. Is. Wrong?" Salem growled; that deep rumble did strange things to my insides. But I'd ignore that, I'd ignore my body's responses to him, and I'd ignore his demand for an answer. Instead, I'd do what I always did when he annoyed me.

I smiled sweetly as I gently – and a little patronisingly – patted his rock-hard chest. "Just breathe." And, yep, his face turned a disturbing shade of red. Ooh, such fun.

CONSUMED

(Salem)

The female drove me fucking insane, and I was pretty sure she knew it. I wasn't usually the type to care about other people's problems. Just like I wasn't usually attracted to petite women, and just like I ordinarily found bubbly, ridiculously happy people to be highly annoying. Yet, Ava Sanchez…She did something to me, brought out reactions that I was done with overthinking.

"Stop petting me like I'm a warm, cuddly bear." She often did that when I scowled or snapped at her, all the while smiling indulgently at me…like a parent might do to a back-chatting toddler. I *wasn't* warm. And I *wasn't* cuddly.

But then, she knew that. We'd fought alongside each other; she'd seen me use my vampiric gift to kill, seen me enjoy using it. Yet, she apparently didn't have the common sense to be wary of me. It was satisfying, since it got kind of old when everyone looked at you like they feared you wanted to eat their spleen. But it was also frustrating, because it would be impossible to keep someone safe if they didn't experience fear. And she clearly didn't.

Since she'd first appeared at The Hollow, I'd become increasingly fascinated with Ava. The hot little body, the innate grace, the combination of sweet and deadly, the beautiful fucking smile, and the fact that she smelt like sex, jasmine, and black liquorice – the impact of it all had hit me like a damn freight train.

I didn't like seeing her pissed and subdued. In Sam's words, Ava was 'like the energizer bunny'. She was fast-moving, fast-talking, and always wearing that big cheery smile that I should have found irritating. Now, though, she was acting like…well, me: surly, irritable, and distant. I didn't like it. She was unusually upset and I wanted to fix it. But she was playing dumb.

I wanted to collar her throat and force her to tell me what was bothering her.

I also wanted to slam her edible body onto the table and shove my cock deep inside her.

It was a struggle not to do either of those things. I was obsessed, and I knew it. Knew that it wasn't good, because I was always intense and aggressive in going after what I wanted. It was never good for someone like me to be obsessive about anything, to want something as badly as I wanted Ava Sanchez.

The reality was that I had absolutely no right to want her. I was tainted and jaded, had too many stains on what was left of my soul. Ava, with her cheery and mischievous nature, couldn't have been more different from me. To be with her would feel like I was touching something I had no right to touch. Christ knew I'd tarnished enough things in my life.

For a short time, it had made me hold back from her. But I was too selfish to be noble and self-sacrificing. I never denied myself what I wanted, and I wouldn't deny myself Ava. Nor would I settle for a fling. No, we were going to be much more than that. Because I always held tight to what was mine. Whether Ava liked it or not, that was exactly what she was.

Needing to know what was bothering her so I could quickly deal with the problem, I growled into her ear, "Ava, tell me."

Again, she flashed me a sweet little smile and patted my chest. "Easy, big guy. We don't want you hyperventilating."

I ground my teeth. "What makes you feel the need to drive me insane?"

"Do you want a list?"

Just then, Sam and Jared entered the room with their Advisor, Luther. That couldn't be good. All vampires had a gift of some kind, and Luther's was precognition. Many meetings had started with "Luther had a vision", and things had often gone to shit after that.

My voice was low when I spoke again. "We'll talk after the meeting." The minx sniffed, dismissing me. Oh, she'd pay for that.

Although Sam and Jared had been the Grand High Pair for a few months now, it still felt weird to have meetings without Antonio being present. He was the one who had designed The Hollow, wanting a safe place to reside, since he'd had to worry about attempts on his life by those who coveted his position.

Sam and Jared now faced that danger, but unlike Antonio, they didn't remain sequestered on the island. The Bound couple came on all assignments with my squad, just as they had when they had been commanders. If I was right, we were about to be given a new assignment. I had absolutely no idea why Ava was present at the meeting, but something told me that I wasn't going to like the reason.

"Evening all." Sam wasn't much for pleasantries. She leaned forward in her seat, flicking her long brown hair over her shoulder.

"Luther had a vision last night." Everyone groaned, which pulled smiles from the couple and Luther.

"No offense, Luther, but you make it hard to like you." Damien was smiling as he said it. The others laughed.

"Please tell us it's a *good* vision this time," pleaded Harvey. "Like Coach is finally going to dump Jared and Bind with me." Despite that Sam had ascended, we would always think of her as 'Coach', first and foremost.

Sparks of electricity suddenly shot from the fingers that Jared had been drumming on the table and hit Harvey smack-bam in the forehead. The impact made his entire body shudder. A glint of satisfaction lit Jared's hazel gaze.

Sam rolled her eyes, complaining in her British accent, "All right, all right, pull your big-boy pants up and stop moaning. What we're about to say is serious, and you need to take it that way. I'll let Luther tell you what he saw."

His posture regal, the Gandalf-lookalike cleared his throat. His grave, solemn expression made me tense. Yep, things were about to go to shit.

"It was a large manor of some kind," he told us. "Luxurious. Elegantly furnished. But there was such evil – it was in the air, in the walls. You were all there, searching the numerous bedrooms. I could *feel* that you were disgusted, enraged. Some of you were carrying female vampires, all of whom were malnourished, scantily dressed, and drugged to the point of unconsciousness."

There was complete silence for a moment. Then Max asked, "A brothel?" Luther nodded.

"You don't think the females are there willingly," I guessed, my voice hard with anger at just the very idea of it.

"No, I believe they are being held against their will."

Profanities rang throughout the room.

Denny shoved a hand through his scruffy dark hair, appearing lost. "What you're saying…is that someone's running a brothel for vampires?"

Luther sighed. "It would seem so."

"The brothel keeper will probably be female, since that's how many human brothels work." Reuben suddenly flushed, clearing his throat. "Not that I would know from personal experience or anything."

"One thing is for certain." Sam's smile was a little on the malevolent side. "I'll enjoy whipping the living shit out of her just before I burn the place down." I liked that idea. Being a Feeder, Sam was able to absorb and manipulate the surrounding energy. She liked to shape the energy into different things – bolts, beams, balls – but she much preferred her energy whip.

"But...I don't get it." Chico was stroking his Johnny Depp style moustache and goatee, as he often did when thinking hard about something. "Vampires are naturally sexual creatures; we can get sex easily enough without paying for it."

"Yeah," agreed Stuart, "there are clubs we can go where we'll find that willingly, and it happens right there on the dance floor."

"There'll always be a market for illegal brothels," Sam pointed out, her aquamarine eyes sad. "Maybe this brothel exists to cater for certain...tastes."

"When do we leave?" Butch's eerily dark eyes were eager. If there was one person who enjoyed assignments more than I did, it was Butch. The fact that his gift was defensive rather than offensive didn't make him any less dangerous. He was an asset to the squad with his ability to deflect or negate anything that came at him.

"I'll teleport us all there soon." Jared had three gifts, thanks to Antonio's ability to impart power: teleportation, electrokinesis, and telepathy. He wasn't able to read minds, but he could hear any thought that was directed at him. "Luther gave me the coordinates for the place; it's in New Hampshire."

Sam's gaze came to rest on Ava. "We'd like you to come along."

I stiffened. *Oh, the hell no.* "No disrespect, Coach, but shouldn't this be handled by the legion?"

Sam shrugged, unconcerned. "If Ava accepts my offer to join the female squad I'll soon be forming, she will be part of the legion. This will be good experience for her."

Okay, I couldn't deny that, but..."You don't think this is a bit much for her first assignment?"

"Clearly you're missing the fact that *this is none of your business*," Ava sang at me. I chose to ignore her remark on the grounds that it simply didn't suit me.

"We're going to be invading a brothel. It's not going to be pretty." I'd come to learn that Ava had a big heart and was highly empathetic.

She would no doubt be sickened by what she found there; the images would stick with her. I didn't want that.

Stifling a smile, Jared raised his hand. "Salem, take it from someone who has a lot of experience with independent females, you don't want to say another word."

Oh, but I did. I knew Ava could take care of herself, knew she was strong. Her gift of muscle memory meant that she could memorise and perfectly replicate any combat move she saw. It also made her faster and stronger than other Sventés, and it gave her better reflexes. But, dammit, that wasn't the point.

"Your concerns are noted, Salem," said Sam. "But she was in Luther's vision, she was at the brothel with us. Taking her out of the equation might alter things in a bad way. We can't risk that."

Fuck. That wasn't something I could fight.

"I'm happy to be on board." Ava ignored my scowl.

"Good." Sam rose from her chair, and everyone followed suit. "You all have ten minutes to tank yourselves up on NSTs. I want us at full-strength."

NSTs, or Nutritive Supplemental Tonics, contained blood and vitamins. They were developed by Antonio, so that he didn't need to move thousands of humans into The Hollow to feed on. The NSTs provided a boost and quickly satisfied the thirst, but they never quite quenched it. Only pure blood did that.

As everyone piled out of the conference room and into the pristine corridor, I kept my eyes on the tiny female in front of me…who was starting to pick up her pace, like she was trying to get away from me. *Not gonna happen.* Fisting my hand in the back of her t-shirt, I lifted her – ignoring her kicking legs – and shoved her inside the nearest empty conference room before closing the door behind us.

Ava spun on her heel to face me. "I'm not a ragdoll."

Even glowering at me, she looked cute and sweet. How was that even possible? I advanced on her, pleased when she didn't back up. "Tell me what's wrong."

Hands perched on her hips, Ava lifted her chin. "Aside from the fact that you're an interfering bastard who thinks you have some say in my decisions?"

"Yeah, aside from that."

She blinked, surprised. Apparently she'd expected me to resent that statement. "Tell me it isn't true that you've told the males on this island

I'm off-limits." When I didn't deny it, she said, "You are unbelievable."
She folded her arms, her innocent little face scrunched up in outrage.
"Take it back."

"No. Even the thought of another guy touching you makes me
want to kill – and we both know I'd do it without hesitation." And I'd
enjoy it. Probably a little too much.

Her arms flopped to her sides. "Are you high?"

"You know I want you, Ava. So I don't get why you're so
surprised."

She massaged her temples. "We don't have time for this. Just take
it back." Head held high, she tried to march past me. Oh no, I wasn't
having that.

I collared her throat and slammed her against the wall, crowding
her, trapping her there. She didn't struggle or object. Instead, she froze,
looking up at me with eyes that were glinting with need. It was a need
that mirrored my own.

As the smell of her lust and her mouth-watering scent snaked
around me, I groaned inwardly and breezed the pad of my thumb over
her bottom lip. "Do you know why I resisted you for so long? Because
I knew that if I had even one taste of you, you'd never be free of me.
I thought I could do the right thing and stay away. You're sweet and
kind and everything I'm not. I've done a lot of bad things. Things I
don't even regret. You can do a hell of a lot better than someone who's
as fucked up as I am. But I'm a selfish prick. I've never let anyone keep
me from what I want. Ever."

She licked her lips. "I told you, I don't do relationships."

Unease flashed across her face, taking me by surprise. I fought to
soften my voice, drawing circles on her throat with my thumb. "What
are you so wary of, Ava? Me?" She shook her head, but I wasn't
convinced. "I'll never hurt you. Tell me you know that." I'd kill for
her, but I'd never hurt her.

"I know."

I scraped my teeth over her pulse, barely resisting the urge to bite
down hard and feel her blood flowing into my mouth. I badly wanted
to know how every part of her tasted. "Then why are you nervous?"

She quickly shook her head in denial. "I'm not."

My lips curved as realisation dawned on me. "You know how tight
I'll hold you to me, don't you? The thing is, baby, I've had a taste of
you now." Recalling how her mouth had felt beneath mine in the bar,

I almost groaned. "There's no going back. As far as I'm concerned, you already belong to me. Every single inch of you. And what's mine stays mine." Reluctantly releasing her, I stepped back. "Accept it, Ava. The sooner you do that, the simpler things will be."

CHAPTER TWO

(Ava)

"It doesn't look like a brothel."

I had to agree with David on that. Situated on a long stretch of land a hundred feet away from us, the large manor was beautiful, modern, and contemporary – the kind of house you would expect to hold cocktail parties or charity functions. But behind those colourfully stained windows and red brick walls lay a sight that I wasn't looking forward to seeing. "They obviously aim to attract upper-class clients."

I was surprised my voice was steady, considering Salem was pressed up against my side; his body taunting mine merely by being so close. Damn the bastard. After his little declaration, I'd scampered from the conference room, unsure and off-balance. A part of me wanted to give in to him, because the hard thing about resisting a guy like Salem was that...well, that he was as hot and deliciously dominant as Salem. But another part of me was determined to stand my ground. If I was to give him what he wanted, Salem would eventually try to change me like others had before him. I was surprised by just how much the thought of that hurt.

Squatted at my other side, Butch ran a hand through his bronze hair. "It sure guarantees them discretion, being all the way out here in the middle of nowhere."

Damien turned to Sam and Jared. "By all rights, you could storm in there and demand they surrender. You're the Grand High Pair now."

"Yeah," agreed Sam, "but they might have a teleporter in there, someone who can get the girls out of the manor before we even have the chance to help them. We can't risk that."

Max shuffled forward. "So what's the plan?" I noticed Max was crouched close to Sam – no doubt to irritate Jared purely for his own amusement, as he often did. Going by Jared's scowl, it was working.

"I need my spies." Sam looked to Denny who, as an animal mimic, was able to reduce his body to liquid just like the sea cucumber. "I want you to scout the perimeter, find out if there are any guards for us to play with, and check out how many entrances there are. Stuart, I need you to take a look around inside; we need to know how many vampires we're dealing with and exactly where they are." Being a Shredder, Stuart exploded into molecules just as Denny melted into a puddle of mush. Then they were both gone.

"Okay, so there are three floors, plus the attic." Jared pursed his lips. "It's possible that there's a basement too, so we have to be prepared to search five floors."

Sam nodded. "We'll need to split up for that."

"Depending on how many girls are in there," began Max, "it could take quite a few teleporting trips to get us all back to The Hollow. Where will we put them?"

"The infirmary is ready for them," Jared informed him. "If they're as bad as Luther described, they may each need to be put on a drip of blood for a while."

"What drugs do you think they're using in there?" Harvey's face was twisted in confusion. "I mean, Luther said we were carrying the girls in his vision, so they have to be pretty out of it, right?"

Sam turned to Harvey. "I've been thinking about that and…it makes no sense that they would be sedated. Drugs flow in the blood. If a vampire fed from a sedated person, they'd be quickly sedated themselves."

David tilted his head. "Huh, I never thought of that."

Damien shifted closer to Sam. "Another reason it doesn't make sense is that if the girls are totally knocked out, what good are they to clients who like them to be active participants?"

Harvey clicked his fingers. "Exactly. It just doesn't add up."

"We have to consider, though, that if the girls *weren't* kept sedated, they'd get out." Chico had a valid point. "They're vampires, they will all have gifts."

"Maybe they're not drugged at all," I mused. "Maybe whoever runs the place or one of the staff has a gift that allows them to put people under sedation. Or maybe it's some kind of mind control."

Salem frowned thoughtfully. "You could be right there." I didn't hold his gaze for long, not wanting him to see just how emotionally off-centre I was.

"Here's Denny," announced Reuben.

Returning to his usual form, Denny came to squat in front of Sam and Jared. "There are no guards outside."

"None?" Jared exchanged a surprised look with Sam.

"There are security cameras everywhere, though. At the back of the manor is a parking lot. I tell ya, these clients aren't average Joes. Some of the cars are Porches and Bentleys. There are even three limos. The chauffeurs were outside, talking; I got the impression from what they said that limo-service is something the brothel provides."

"What about the entrances?"

"There are three. The front door. The patio doors – which seem to be the general entrance for the clients to use. And there's also a set of steps that lead to a basement, but it's boarded up." He exhaled heavily. "There's a large annex behind the house, surrounded by barbed wire, like a huge aviary or something. Not sure if that's where the girls are taken to eat or sleep, but there's a row of empty beds in there."

A thought occurred to me. "It could be where the captives were taken when they first arrived."

"I heard things. Cries. Whatever's happening in that place, it isn't good."

Wisps of the surrounding energy seemed to suddenly attach themselves to Sam and slithered over her skin, as if responding to her livid state. "Bastards," she bit out.

Butch spoke then. "Stuart's on his way."

Once he'd reformed into his human self, Stuart crouched beside Denny, his eyes troubled. "Brace yourselves. You're going to see things in there you'll never forget. Luther was right: the place is fucking evil."

As if he'd picked up on my anxiety and wanted to ease it, Salem placed his hand on my thigh and squeezed lightly. "How many are we dealing with?" he then asked.

"There are ten staff in total; two receptionists, the guy monitoring the cameras, three chauffeurs, a bartender, two maids, and a woman who hovers around, overseeing things. She must be the brothel keeper.

All of them are Pagoris."

"Motherfuckers." Reuben sighed and rubbed at his stubbly jaw, probably appalled that his own breed was so deeply involved.

"Any clients in there?" Sam asked Stuart.

"Nine. Four of them are Pagoris; two are upstairs, but another two are sitting in the waiting area, laughing and joking while reading the 'menu' of services. There are also three Kejas and two Sventés upstairs."

"How many captives?"

"There's one in every bedroom, and one in the attic. In total, that's nine girls. And six guys." Surprise lit many people's faces.

"Guys?" Damien's dark skin paled slightly.

"It probably should have occurred to me that both genders were targets." Sam scrubbed a hand down her face. She went to say something else, but when her gaze landed on a squirming Stuart, she narrowed her eyes. "What is it?"

It was a short moment before he responded. "They're not all vampires."

"There are *humans* in there?" Jared's shock was shared by all of us.

"Two, actually." Stuart squirmed once more. "But there are other kinds of preternatural beings, too."

Sam's brows flew up. "Say again?"

"I don't know exactly what they are, I just know they aren't vampires. I think one of them might be an animal shifter – they all have a musky scent like her – but I'm not sure. I haven't been around many other species."

"Shit," muttered Jared.

Sam clenched her firsts. "It would seem then that these vampires are running a brothel for those who might want to fuck and snack on other beings as well as their own kind."

"That's certainly a niche in the market." Cold as those words were, Butch was right. Preternatural species didn't mix often, preferring to stick to their own kind.

Jared nodded. "Vampires will pay good money for the opportunity to feed from other species – especially since some are rumoured to increase strength and power." He looked at Sam. "You said it was possible the brothel was catering for certain tastes. You were right."

She didn't look pleased to be. "Talk us through the layout, Stuart."

"The basement is empty of people."

"What's down there?"

"It's some kind of dungeon. Like a sadistic playroom."

"The ground floor?"

"If you go in through the front door, you'll find yourself in an open-plan apartment. If you go in through the patio doors at the back, it's like walking into an office reception area. There's a desk with two smartly dressed females behind it. On the left is a lounge with leather sofas, mahogany tables, antique furniture, and even a bar. On the right of the reception area is a room which is filled with monitors. The security system is top of the line. There's one male watching the cameras."

"Is he vigilant?" asked Jared.

"Not really. He alternates from watching the monitors to reading a newspaper."

"That's good." Jared looked at the manor. "What about upstairs?"

"There are seven bedrooms on the first floor. Another seven on the second floor. And one in the attic."

"Only one?" Sam frowned. "It has to be pretty spacious. Weird they haven't tried to make it into more than one room."

"I'm guessing they didn't because they intended to use it as some kind of torture chamber." Stuart puffed out a long breath. "I thought the basement was bad. Two guys are with the girl and...fuck, we have to get her out of there."

"Yes, and we have to do it before the clients leave," agreed Sam. "But if we rush in, we'll fuck it up and people will get away. Where are the other upstairs clients situated?"

"Two are on the second floor, and three are on the first floor."

"What about the staff?"

"They're all on the ground floor, except for the maids – they're in one of the rooms on the first floor; one is changing the bed-sheet while the other gives the girl a shower in the adjoined bathroom, getting her ready for the next customer. She can barely stand."

The mercury glint to Sam's irises were glowing fiercely. "Reuben, do your thing for David and Chico."

"Sure thing, Coach." Reuben briefly touched each of their shoulders. Like that, David's psionic blast and Chico's poisonous darts were fatal – thanks to his gift of power augmentation.

Salem frowned. "Not me?" Usually, Sam ordered for Reuben to make Salem's psychic punch fatal.

Sam shook her head. "Not this time. I want the brothel keeper alive so I can question her, but I need you to knock the bitch out first. If Ava's right and someone has the gift to put someone under sedation, it could be her. I can't afford for her to be conscious and have the opportunity to send us all to dreamland or, for that matter, use any other gift on us."

"We're going to need to separate the moment we get in there." Jared was clearly raring to go, but his tone was calm and even. "If we deal with the staff first, we might give the clients a chance to slip away, and vice versa. That's not an option."

Sweeping her gaze across us, Sam spoke. "Salem, Denny, and Max will take the ground floor with me. The rest of you hit the stairs. David, Stuart, Butch – take the first floor. Chico, Reuben, Harvey – check the second floor. Jared, Ava, Damien – head for the attic. First we eliminate the clients and the majority of the staff, then we free the captives."

Salem's hand clenched on my thigh, and I knew what was coming. "Coach, Ava is—"

"Once the brothel keeper is out cold, you're free to join Ava. In the meantime, Jared and Damien will be with her, so don't whine."

It was obvious to me that he wanted to argue, but Salem was nothing if not loyal; he followed orders, even when those orders galled him. "Do we let anyone live?" he asked.

"Only the keeper. I've got a lot of questions for her. I particularly want to know how many others are involved and where we'll find them."

"Stuart, which side of the manor gives access to the stairs?" asked Jared.

"The back. They're behind the reception desk."

"Then we go in through the back."

"Don't teleport us inside," Sam told Jared. "Not yet."

His brow furrowed. "Why?"

"Denny said there are three chauffeurs in the parking lot. If we can get rid of them first, the bastards will be down by three. Three might not sound like much, but if those three have substantial gifts, it'll make a big difference."

"Then I'll teleport us all behind the manor, a safe distance away so we won't be seen." A moment later, we were among the trees at the side of the annex. The chauffeurs were leaning against the limos, laughing.

Max rubbed his hands together, blue eyes glinting with anticipation. "Who's doing the honours?"

Jared looked at Sam. "There is one problem you haven't considered while bloodlust is running through your veins, baby. The second we kill those fuckers, the security-guy will see, and he'll alert the others."

"We can't destroy the cameras. It would make the guard suspicious." Harvey seemed to like to point out the obvious.

Twisting her lips, Sam tapped her chin. "If we lure the bloke out first and deal with him in a spot the others won't see, we can take him out of the equation quickly."

Reuben tied his shoulder-length brown hair back with a rubber band. "How do we lure him out?"

"Denny, any chance you could shoot some of your green slime onto the camera at the side of the manor?" asked Sam. "On the black and white monitors, it'll look more like some kind of bird shit to him. He won't be worried, but he'll most likely come out to check and clean it off."

Denny rolled his shoulders. "I can do that." Another of his animal mimic abilities was to ooze slime out of his pores like Hagfish. In vampire-speed, he'd rounded the corner of the manor. Still hidden in the trees, he shot a small stream of ooze into the sky. We all watched as it flew down and landed on the camera with a splat.

Once he was back, Sam and Jared nodded their approval at him. Soon enough, a burly Pagori dressed in a black suit stalked out of the patio doors, briefly greeting the chauffeurs and moaning about fucking birds.

"Well, what do you know, it worked." Harvey sounded astonished and amused.

Offended, Sam glowered at him. "Of course it worked."

As the guy reached the camera, Jared spoke. "Chico, take care of this one. Your method makes less sound than ours, and we don't want the chauffeurs to hear anything."

"No problem." A millisecond later, Chico stood where Denny had previously been; holding his hand out, palm up. Three darts imbedded themselves in the burly Pagori, making him soundlessly explode into ashes.

"One down," Harvey quietly sang when Chico returned.

"Now for the chauffeurs." Jared turned to Max. "You first. Then

Sam, Chico, and David can do their thing."

Once Max had paralysed the chauffeurs' senses – leaving them unable to cry out for help or see their enemies to defend themselves – Sam, Chico, and David attacked; Sam threw an energy ball, Chico shot more darts, and David splayed his fingers wide and sent out a psionic blast. Like that, all three Pagoris were ashes.

"Four down," sang Harvey.

Chico sighed at him. "Okay, that could get annoying real fast."

"Time to go inside," declared Jared.

Sam danced her gaze along all of us as she spoke. "Do what you always do: attack first, and attack hard, because you never know what gift the vampire facing you will have. And remember: I want the keeper alive."

Gripping my chin, Salem gave me a hard glance. "Stay alive."

I nodded. "You, too."

And then Jared teleported us all inside.

The receptionists gawked, their eyes wide. Before they had a chance to call for help or react in any way, Max paralysed their senses. A psionic blast from David and an energy ball from Sam destroyed them a mere millisecond later.

Turning to the left, we found that the bartender, the keeper, and two clients had jumped to their feet. Salem, Sam, Max, and Denny attacked just as the keeper starting screaming orders, the bartender doubled in size, and one of the clients conjured a spear of frost. As others from the squad raced up the stairs, Jared teleported me and Damien to the attic.

We appeared outside the door just as two naked Pagori males rushed out, obviously having heard the commotion. As one took a swipe at Jared with a set of steel claws that he barely evaded, the other lashed at me with a long leather barbed whip that was stained with blood – and I had to wonder if he'd been using it on whoever was in the attic. *Well, shit.* The whip caught my face, and one of the barbs slashed my skin. Fucking ouch.

"Whatever you do, don't let those claws touch you!" shouted Jared.

A brief glance at them told me why: they were dripping with luminous yellow liquid. Poison, I knew. See, you should always be wary of anything luminous.

Hearing the shouting, crashing, and roaring that was coming from the floors below us, I knew the battle was in full flow. And was that the screech of a hawk?

The whip came at me again, but I dodged it just as Jared aimed a bolt of electricity at its owner. The bastard slammed up a gleaming shield that looked much like glass. He smirked tauntingly, earning himself a growl from Jared.

As if he thought I would be the easiest target, Claws struck out at me. So dumb. Thanks to my gift, I could take out a vampiric version of Jackie Freaking Chan. Moving so fast that the action was a blur, I dealt him a solid palm strike to the nose. The sickening crunch made me wince inwardly. Before he had a chance to retaliate, I swiftly followed it up with a blow to the kidneys, a punch to the solar plexus, and a kick to the kneecap. The pain seemed to ripple down his body, making me smile in satisfaction.

I was peripherally aware that the other Pagori had just wrapped the whip around Damien's ankle, whose astral-self had been darting around in an attempt to distract the fucker. But said fucker unfortunately wasn't stupid. Before he could drag Damien's body to him, Jared aimed yet another bolt at him. Once again, the shield saved him. Taking me by surprise, though, it cracked slightly. Huh. So it wasn't unbreakable. That meant Jared could –

Suddenly we all dropped to our knees as a deafening, ear-splitting sonic boom of sound seemed to echo throughout the building. Pain pounded through my head, making my vision blur and my ears bleed. Knowing I was close to passing out, I forced myself to breathe and think through the pain. My vision cleared…just in time to see that Claws was quickly recovering, the asshole.

Standing now, blood pouring from his nose, he again came at me. I jumped to my feet and managed to dodge his claws, but I knew that if it hadn't been for my gift, poison would be streaming through my veins right then. He launched himself at me, and I retaliated with blows to the jaw, ribs, shoulder, face, and temple. Disorientated, he blinked and staggered. A punch to the throat followed by a kick to the groin had him stooping, cupping his balls and dick.

"Get up!" Damien's astral-self yelled at Jared, who was still on his knees.

Whip Boy laughed, dropping his arms – and inadvertently dropping his shield. That was all the opening Jared, who was apparently faking, needed. He projected a powerful lightning bolt hard enough to make the bastard explode into ashes. Ha.

Instinct made me return my attention to Claws, who was back on his feet and charging at me. Before I even had the chance to react, psychic energy rippled through the air and crashed into his head…knocking him out cold. *Salem.* As Jared happily reduced Claws to ashes with a bolt of electricity to the heart, I turned to Salem, who was then at my side. "Thanks."

Salem's eyes did a quick head-to-toe study of me, presumably looking for injuries. "I'll stay with her and Damien," he told Jared. "Go to Sam."

Jared didn't argue, clearly anxious to get to her, even though he would know through their bond that she was alive.

"We need to get the girl." Salem took my hand in his and led Damien and I into the attic.

We stopped dead at the sight. Holy shit, Stuart hadn't been exaggerating when he called it a 'torture chamber'. Dark and bleak with blood-stained walls, it stank of fear and despair. It was empty apart from some medieval-looking devices, a bed with cuffs attached, and a table that…Fuck, I didn't even want to know what half of the sadistic implements on it were.

The girl was naked, blindfolded, gagged, and bleeding from several places. In addition, she was hanging limply from the fucking ceiling by a rope that bound her wrists.

Moving closer, I was able to see that though her injuries were closing due to her preternatural-enhanced healing, they had been painful and horrific. Her breasts, groin, and the soles of her feet had been thrashed with a barbed whip – no doubt the one belonging to the bastard Jared had just killed. Her Achilles tendons had been sliced, and holes had been drilled into her arms and legs. Additionally, it seemed that someone had tried to literally bite a chunk out of her bruised face. It looked like she'd also been brutally raped, going by the blood on her inner thighs.

I swallowed hard, tasting bile. "Oh. My. God. W-why would someone ever do that? Why?"

Salem squeezed my hand in comfort. "Because people can be evil, Ava."

"We have to get her down." Damien's voice was vibrating with anger.

"Is there a blanket or something we can wrap around her?" Salem asked me as he and Damien moved to free the girl.

"I'll look."

Damien moved behind her and untied the gag and blindfold. "She's unconscious – either she's still sedated, or she passed out with the pain or blood loss."

After a quick search around the room, I sighed. "There are no clean sheets or any clothes."

"We'll have to use the one from the bed." Salem eyed it with distaste. Understandable, since it was stained with blood and semen. But it was better than nothing.

"Can you hold onto her while I untie her wrists?" asked Damien. Nodding, Salem gently took her weight while Damien freed her, and I quickly helped him wrap the sheet around her.

"Take her," he told Damien. That was when her eyelids flipped open. "We're not here to hurt you, we—" Salem broke off as her eyes bled to black. Then it was like a wave of energy splayed out of her and sent he, Damien and I careening into the walls.

I coughed, getting to my feet. "Fuck. You guys okay?" Hearing grunts of affirmation, I turned my attention to the girl who had crumpled to the floor, her black eyes honed on me. "Demon." *Well, shit.*

Having met demons before, I knew to be scared. They weren't evil like the stories said. Just like other species, they could be good or they could be bad. But the entity that lived inside them – the one looking right at me through black eyes – was a whole other matter.

"Only one thing is fucking stopping me from hurling a psychic punch in your direction, which is that you've been hurt bad enough," Salem snapped at the demon as he stood upright. "But if you attack her again, I won't hesitate." The demon didn't react in any way.

Indicating for the others not to move closer, I spoke to the demon, my voice clear and steady. "I know you can hear the shit going on downstairs. You could hear it before we came inside, couldn't you? You waited. Knew this was your chance to get out."

The black eyes just stared at me blankly.

"We were helping you."

"You're one of them." The voice was flat, toneless, and tired. "I don't want your help."

"You're not too fond of vampires right now. I get that. Personally, I'm ashamed of what my own kind have done. That's why we're here. To make them pay, and to burn this place to the ground. I don't think you want to be here when that happens." Demons could control and call on fire, but not if they were as weak as the one before me. "You dug deep and used what energy you had left to fight whatever is sedating you and fight us. But we both know that little act drained you."

"I'm not going with you."

I couldn't exactly blame her. If the situation had been reversed, I'd have said the same thing. If we took the demon to The Hollow, she would bring hell on us the moment she was fully recovered. "There's a teleporter with us who can take you wherever you want to go."

A brief pause. "How can I trust him?"

"You can't. I wouldn't expect you to. But if you stay here, you'll die. What do you have to lose at this point?"

Another pause, this one longer. "Get the teleporter."

"Damien, astral project your ass to Jared, please. If the danger's died down, ask him to come up here." With a nod, he did as I asked.

It was a few minutes before Jared appeared, just as Damien returned to his body. The demon was barely hanging on to consciousness at that point.

Before I could say anything, Salem asked Jared, "Everything under control down there?"

"The clients and staff are dead, except for the keeper. She's hog-tied with Denny's slime, so she isn't going anywhere. We're starting to free the captives. What's going on here?"

"I need you to teleport her away," I replied. "She doesn't want to come with us, but she can't leave by herself." Seeing his confusion as he met those black eyes, I explained. "She's a demon."

"You want me to touch a demon?" His expression said, 'Are you fucking crazy?'

"We owe her. For what our kind did, we owe her."

For the first time, Jared seemed to really *see* the room, see the signs of torture. Sighing in resignation, he gently scooped the demon up off the floor. The guy was no coward. "Where do you want to go?"

"The Underground," she slurred.

"Ha!" I barked. "No fucking way." Both Jared and the demon double-blinked. I knew about The Underground. "If he appears there with you looking like that, every demon there will dive on him. And a whole lot of them will die, because he's no easy target. Try again."

Respect and a hint of impatience flashed in the demon's eyes. "My apartment." She gave Jared the address.

"If I get there and find myself surrounded, I'll teleport us *both* back here. Understand?" His voice wasn't harsh, but it was firm and brooked no bullshit. The demon gave him a curt nod. Sweeping his gaze across Salem, Damien, and I, he then said, "I'll meet you guys downstairs in a minute."

Once Jared disappeared, Salem turned to me. "You handled that well. Later you can tell me how you know about demons. Right now, we need to make sure everyone's okay."

It turned out that a few were badly hurt, but all would heal soon enough. Max had a fever, which was apparently a side effect of having a spear of frost penetrate his chest. Stuart was absolutely covered in deep claw marks, courtesy of hawk talons belonging to a shapeshifting vampire. Reuben's eardrums had burst as he'd been right next to the vampire who'd released the sonic boom of sound. Also, Denny was barely conscious after being attacked by one of the captives he freed; the guy turned out to be a psi-vampire, and after taking a huge amount of Denny's energy he'd managed to escape.

As for the other captives, only nine of them were vampires – one of whom was killed by a maid who had teleported from room to room, picking off captives. In addition to the vampire, she'd killed two humans, a coyote shifter, and a witch before she was destroyed.

Apart from the demon and vampires, the only other left to live was – in Harvey's words – 'a guy whose skin turned to scales as he grew wings and flew the fuck away'. Most were speculating that he was a dragon shifter who hadn't had enough energy to fully transform.

It was shortly after Jared teleported the last of the survivors and the injured squad members to The Hollow that the brothel keeper finally woke. She looked nervous as all shit to find herself surrounded by several vampires, all of whom were glaring at her with pure hatred.

When her gaze settled on Sam and Jared, she swallowed hard. Sweat beaded on her brow as her pulse began to pound – I could hear it from where I stood with Salem.

Clasping her hands behind her back, Sam grinned. "Hi, remember me? I'm the one who caught you with my whip when you tried to make a run for it. Not before you ordered your bartender to kill me, of course."

Nervously, the woman peeked at Sam. "I'm sorry, your Grandness. I didn't realise it was you when I made that order."

Sam groaned in annoyance. "I hate that title." She sighed, taking a step toward the woman. "It's really not my authority that you need to worry about. It's the fact that I'm a homicidal bitch who's balancing on the knife-edge of 'insane'."

"Balancing?" snickered Jared.

"All right, maybe I fell off the edge some time ago." She shrugged. "It makes life more interesting."

"You knew who we were." Jared's eyes were drilling hard into the keeper, his irises glowing red, as he clenched his fists. "You knew *exactly* who Sam – *my mate* – was when you screamed at your bartender to kill her. So I think it's a little late for respectful words, don't you?"

I mock whispered to Salem, "Uh-oh, Jared's gonna lose it. Do you think he'll do what he did to the last vampire who wanted Sam dead?" My voice was hopeful. The vampire I was referring to had infiltrated The Hollow and tried to destroy everyone in it.

Sensing that I was trying to make the woman panic by confirming a rumour that had spread throughout vampirekind, Salem played along. "You mean hit every single vulnerable spot of her body, one by one, with a high charge of electricity? Maybe. Jared did seem to enjoy the guy's pleas for mercy before he eventually killed him with a high voltage bolt to the chest." The rest of the squad nodded.

"Since you know who we are," began Sam, "I think it's only fair that we know your name."

She cleared her throat, looking a little sick. "Marge."

"Well, Marge, I thought we'd have a little chat." Sam sounded pleasant and friendly, but the glow to her mercury irises made it perfectly clear that she was totally pissed. "Maybe you could explain to us why the shit that's gone on under this roof is acceptable."

"I-it's not a-acceptable."

"Very good. Gold star sticker for you. Maybe you could explain something else to me. See, I noticed a few things while you were snoozing. Ava and I went snooping, found some interesting stuff in the closet in your bedroom. We were looking for appointment books, hoping to get the names of some clients. We didn't find them. We found something else instead. I think you know what I'm talking about."

Marge didn't speak, just gulped.

"We found a collection of DVDs. And not just any DVDs. Recordings. It seems that you planted secret cameras in each of the rooms. My guess is that you blackmail the clients afterwards. Am I right?"

Eyes wide with fear, Marge nodded.

"I have to hand it to you, I didn't see that coming. Mostly because the whole thing is bad enough. I mean really, Marge, why own an *establishment* such as this?" The word 'establishment' was made to sound like a profanity.

"I just run it, I don't own it." Ah, trying to shift responsibility and escape punishment.

"Who does?"

With that question, Marge's expression closed down.

"Don't, Marge. Don't do that 'I can't tell you' routine. It's really not worth it. I want answers. If you don't give them to me, I *will* hurt you, and I *will* do it with utter pleasure. And then *Jared* will hurt you, and we'll all clap and urge him on. Give me a name, Marge."

"I *can't*. Even if I could, you'd never find her."

Jared's brow rose. "Why exactly is that?"

"She's untraceable. Literally. She has no scent. Never leaves even a hair fibre or footprint behind. It's her gift. Part of that gift is that she never leaves a clear memory of herself anywhere – no image, no name, nothing. There is truly no way to track her down."

Salem stiffened beside me. I cast him a curious glance, noting the thoughtful frown on his face.

"Then how do you know she's a 'her'?" Jared was clearly dubious. "There's obviously a loophole in that gift if you know that."

"The only memory of her appearance she leaves behind in your head is an impression…like a shadow, a silhouette."

"Maybe Ryder could help," Chico suggested.

Ryder was their top interrogator as he had a psychic hand – could rifle through people's minds, access their thoughts and memories. The reason he wasn't yet a member of the legion was that, being relatively newborn, he wasn't yet in total control of his bloodlust or his gift.

"Not a bad idea. We have a few empty cells." Sam gave Marge a winning smile. "I'm sure you'll be thrilled to know you're coming back to The Hollow with us."

On the contrary, the woman looked like she was about to hyperventilate. "There's nothing more I can tell you."

"Sure there is. Like if there's more than one brothel. Like how you managed to keep the captives sedated. Like where they were kidnapped from."

"I don't remember every name, don't remember every—"

"You don't need to. I have someone who can rummage through that brain of yours and tell me what I need to know."

"Are you going to kill her after that?" I asked excitedly, clapping a little. "Ooh, can I watch?"

"Watch? You can join in. If anyone deserves a little pain, it's this heartless bitch right here."

I grinned. *Damn fucking straight.*

CHAPTER THREE

(Salem)

"Okay, here's our issue," began Sam, pacing outside the infirmary wherein the survivors and the injured squad members were settled. "The minute all those involved in the brothel learn it's been destroyed, they'll panic and worry that the staff or survivors gave up their identities. They'll hide."

"Maybe not," argued Butch. "They don't know we have someone like Ryder. They might be positive that Marge won't talk."

"None are more convinced that they are being pursued than those who are guilty," said Antonio, who had come to speak to Sam and Jared on hearing about the brothel. The elegant ancient Keja was one of the calmest and most intelligent people I knew.

With a nod of agreement, Sam continued. "That means every single one of them will go to ground. Remember, they don't just have *us* to fear. They know that if there are any survivors to tell the tale, they'll also have the other species of preternatural on their arses. They won't want to risk it. Which means the moment Ryder finds out their names, we act – hopefully it will be in time to locate the fuckers before they do a runner."

"It should not take more than a few hours for our researchers to match the names with addresses," Antonio assured her.

"Which means you all have a few hours to recover," Jared informed the squad members. "Max, Denny, Stuart, and Reuben won't be coming, since they need more time to recuperate from their injuries."

"We'll take Alora, Jude, Paige, and Imani in their place," announced Sam. The four females had joined the battle to defend The Hollow against the attack a few months ago. Sam had then offered them a place in her upcoming female squad, and all four had gratefully accepted.

Jared smiled. "Evan won't like it." Evan, who happened to be Jared's twin brother as well as Alora's partner, was seriously overprotective of her. Almost as bad as I was with Ava…who had slinked away from me a few minutes ago, the minx.

Sam blinked at her mate. "You say that like it matters." Jared just snorted. "Ava will be coming too," she then told me.

Ignoring the 'there's no point fighting me on this' expression on Sam's face, I said, "She saw a lot of shit tonight. A break would be good for her."

Sam slid me a look of complete disgust. "Either you're underestimating her – which I strongly doubt – or you're just being your interfering, overprotective self. She's part of this now. She'll want to see it through. Bloody deal with it or she'll end up ramming the heel of one of her stilettos right up your arse."

Antonio bowed his head, making his wealth of thick, shoulder length coal-black hair shield his face, and I knew he was trying to hide a smile – unlike everyone else, who openly showed how amused they were at my expense. Assholes.

Damien folded his arms across his chest. "Speaking of seeing the assignment through…What will happen to the clients, Coach? Are they next on the list?"

"Thanks to the fact that every DVD was marked with the client's name, they'll be easy enough to find and kill. We'll assign the task to some of the other squads, send them hunting straight away." All in all, there were ten squads in the legion. "The rest of us will concentrate on locating and destroying everyone involved in the making and running of the brothel."

"Go eat, drink some NSTs, and wait for our call," ordered Jared.

Wanting a quick word with Sam and Jared, I stayed behind as the rest of the squad left. Antonio also remained, but I didn't mind speaking in front of him. "You got a minute?"

"Sure," said Sam.

"The owner of the brothel...I think I may have met her before."

Surprised, Jared asked, "When?"

"Before I joined the legion. My Sire ran a fight club." Will had made me into a vampire forty-eight years ago; had given me a chance to get revenge on the bastards who –

I quickly shut the door on that memory. "Many vampires went there and fought against others for money. I was one of my Sire's fighters. He ran the business, but he didn't own it."

"A woman did," guessed Antonio.

"I saw her plenty of times; she was often a spectator at the fights. But when I try to remember her face, try to bring that image to my mind, it's just as Marge described: vague impressions. Even though I know exactly where I saw her, exactly what she was doing, I can't see her profile clearly in my head."

Sam and Jared exchanged a look.

"It might not be the same vampire," commented Antonio. "It could just be one with the same gift, or even something similar."

"Maybe, but I thought it might be worth mentioning."

"Would you be all right with Ryder scanning your mind?" asked Sam.

Not really.

She quickly assured me, "He won't snoop where he's not invited. He'll just look for your memories – vague though they may be – of her."

Nonetheless, I wasn't comfortable with anyone poking around in my head. In truth, it wasn't a good place for anyone to be. But this was too important to ignore. "All right."

"At the moment, he's visiting dear old Marge. I sent Harvey to keep her immobile, since it's possible she's able to put others under sedation. It might be that she needs to touch people in order to do it. We weren't prepared to take the chance." Sam glanced at her watch. "Meet me at my office in an hour. Ryder will be done with Marge by then."

"Will do, Coach." In the meantime, I'd go shower and then find out why my little Svénté thought she could run from me.

(Ava)

Standing under the hot spray of the shower, I sighed. I'd needed this; needed to wash off the blood of the survivors and the smells of death and despair from my skin. Needed to have this space and time to properly assimilate everything I'd seen at that manor.

Was the horror I'd witnessed discouraging me from joining the legion? Maybe it should. I had no problem admitting I had a soft heart and was nowhere near as emotionally tough as Sam. But I wasn't discouraged, I wasn't thinking of walking away. Quite the opposite, actually.

For weeks now, I'd been struggling about whether to accept Sam's offer. Cristiano had assured me that he wouldn't view me leaving him as disloyal, and he'd even encouraged me to stay at The Hollow for a little while; see if it was a place I could imagine myself being happy. It turned out that I could, but leaving him would be hard.

We had been inseparable growing up, thick as thieves. He had always been extremely protective of me, just as I had always been extremely protective of him – which was a good thing, since our parents hadn't given a shit about either of us. They were both crack-heads that were wrapped up in their own little world and did nothing but argue. Only one thing kept them together: their addiction.

I was eight when the social workers came and took me and Cristiano away. First we were given to our maternal grandmother, then later to our maternal aunt, and then we pit-stopped at a few foster homes. Why had we moved around so much? Because no one found the package of a little girl with a mild case of Attention Deficit Hyperactivity Disorder and a boy who had anger management issues to be all that attractive or rewarding.

Back then, Cristiano had had so much rage in him, so much suppressed violence. It had made him irritable, withdrawn, and unable to bond – always on the attack as a method of defence. I, on the other hand, had always been my usual upbeat, energetic self. At first, our new caretakers had liked that I was chatty and open; it made them feel good about themselves, I now understood. They felt like we were bonding, like they were good at the parenting stuff.

Later, though, they'd become irritated with my endless amount of energy; with the restlessness, the edginess, the difficulty keeping quiet, and the habit of misplacing things. I'd received a lot of tired sighs, eye rolls, groans, curses, and punishments. Whenever it got bad, Cristiano had leaped in and defended me – often in a violent way. Then the social workers would return and we'd be moved again.

Compared to what a lot of kids went through, it wasn't at all a bad experience, even though there had been that one sickeningly perverted guy that had very soon deeply regretted what he'd done. But it was a constant cycle of rejection: being welcomed, being accepted, and then having both of those things ripped away.

I'd never truly felt 'necessary'. Not to anyone. Not even to Cristiano. We were close, and he loved me, but he was a very self-sufficient person. He didn't allow himself to need people, not even me. This lack of feeling important to anyone was probably a dumb thing to be upset about, but the hurt was there all the same.

Becoming a member of the legion would give me a sense of importance, make me something *more*. The existence of the legion was necessary. The assignments they went on were necessary. And if I was part of that legion, *I* would be necessary on some level. I could play a part in ending some of the shit that went on in the world. I could –

Hearing a knock on the front door of my apartment, I groaned. No doubt it would be Salem. I'd spent two hours trying to shake him off. But it was hard to get away from a six foot mountain of persistence. Each time he'd sensed me trying to slip away, he'd picked me up by the back of my t-shirt and returned me to the spot beside him. Eventually he'd been distracted enough for me to make a sharp exit.

Despite his incessant knocking, it wasn't until I'd triple-tied the belt around my robe that I opened the door. And there he was: his powerful stance alert, his feet braced shoulder-width apart, and his hooded eyes honed on me. He looked as indomitable, imposing, and unflappable as always. He'd also changed and showered.

Stepping right into my personal space, he kicked the door shut behind him. "You ran from me." He sounded a mixture of annoyed and amused.

Refusing to defend my actions, I shrugged carelessly. "I wanted a shower."

"So I see." He took in my apartment with a quick glance, his expression blank. But he was no doubt shuddering inwardly at the very feminine atmosphere. Despite that I hadn't been sure I'd remain at The

Hollow, I'd picked up some accessories to spruce up the place and give it some colour. Mostly pink.

"Why are you here?"

"I wanted to make sure you were okay." He smoothed the wet locks away from my face. "It was a tough night." He was as gruff as always, his tone empty of sensitivity. Anyone else might have mistaken that for apathy, but I knew him well enough to know that this was simply how Salem talked. Besides, he didn't waste words, didn't say anything he didn't mean, so the fact that he'd bothered to check on me showed that he cared.

And that got to me. The fucker was good at this wearing-me-down thing. Cristiano had been sure to warn me away from Salem, of course. He was dangerous, Cristiano had said. He was a trained killer, he'd said. Yes, well, he was also freaking hot.

"I'm fine," I assured him. His expression was doubtful. "Really, I'm fine."

"Hmmm." Burying his face in the crook of my neck, he groaned. "You smell good. Your scent makes me hard every time. I want to wear it on my skin." His voice was thick with need. "And I want my scent on you."

His tone, his words, and his body heat were all beating at my defences. "Salem." It was supposed to be a warning, but it came out breathless and needy. Dammit, he wasn't even touching me and I was melting for him. "You want something I can't give you." I was reminding myself as much as I was him.

"What I want" – he licked a line along my throat – "is you beneath me. Moaning my name." He sucked at my pulse, nipping it lightly. "What I want is my teeth in your skin, and your taste on my tongue. Don't you want that, Ava?"

No, I didn't…Right?

He sucked on my earlobe before biting down gently, but not enough to draw blood. "Don't you want to know how I taste?"

Oh, I did want that. I'd wondered about it more times than I could count.

When he went to open my robe and found the huge knot, his mouth curved in amusement. "You thought you could keep me out?" He *tsk*ed. "Ah, Ava, you can't keep me away from what's mine."

As if to prove that, he brought his mouth down hard on mine, stabbing his tongue inside and seeking out my own. A large hand snapped around my throat as another slid under my robe and palmed my ass, pulling me to him. His cock, long and thick and hard, dug into my stomach. Like that, my nipples tightened and a fierce ache began to build deep inside me. *Ah, crap.*

I should have struggled, I should have hit out at him. But I seemed to have no willpower when it came to Salem. He'd eaten up every inch of my personal space…and yet I liked it. That wasn't normal, right? I wasn't sure – it was hard to think past the way my entire body burned for him. It reflexively responded to him, craved him, and was soothed by him.

Abruptly he froze, cursing. It was only then that I realised someone was knocking rhythmically on the door. "It seems you have a visitor."

I swallowed hard, doing my best to look cool and composed. This could *not* happen again, because I was pathetically weak when it came to him. "Listen, Salem—"

He put a finger to my mouth. "You kissed me back, Ava. You want this as much as I do. If you deny it, you're just insulting your own intelligence. Others might think you're dizzy and flaky, but we both know that's not true."

That was probably the nicest thing a guy had ever said to me.

With that, he stalked to the door and opened it wide…only to find Alora there, her fist raised and ready to knock again. Clearly taken aback, she simply stared at him.

"What's up?" asked a familiar voice. Then Jude was bumping Alora aside. Her eyes widened at the sight of Salem. "Oh."

And Salem being Salem, he just grunted at them. Then he glanced at me over his shoulder. "Expect a call from Sam and Jared in the next few hours. We're not done with the assignment tonight. I'll be seeing you soon."

Once he was gone, Alora and Jude both rushed inside, talking at once.

"Well, well, well," drawled Jude, closing the door.

"Now I know why you didn't turn up at the café for lunch." Alora grinned.

"Oh shit," I muttered. I'd arranged to meet them at one of the cafés. The Hollow contained plenty of cafés, stores, bars, and even a nightclub and a bowling alley. It was surrounded by a tropical rainforest, and had a man-made beach in the centre for all the residents – vampires and humans – to use. Only Sam, Jared, their immediate staff, and the legion had access to the private beach behind the mansion.

"Sorry, I should have called to say I couldn't make it. You heard about the brothel, right?" Nothing remained secret on the island for long.

Jude's upper lip curled as all three of them settled on the sofa. "Sickening, isn't it?"

"I went along."

"So *that's* what Salem meant." Alora's expression softened. "Aw, sweetie, that must have been hard. No wonder your mind was elsewhere."

I told them about the assignment, filling in the gaps in the account they had been given.

"Why did Sam and Jared ask you to join them?" asked Jude.

"She said it would be good experience for me, and that I was in Luther's vision so it was important that I went. It occurred to me that she might have been hoping that taking me on an assignment, showing me the good the legion do, would convince me to join. If so, it's worked."

Alora's face lit up. "Yay!" With her quirky clothes, she often came across as hippy-like. It was true that the female was free-spirited, but she was also bold and daring.

Jude grinned. "I knew you'd cave eventually. But this good news is not going to distract me from asking what the hell's going on between you and Salem."

"Nothing is, and nothing will be."

Alora's mouth dropped open. "Dear God, why not? I mean, he's scary but he's also spectacularly hot. Just don't tell Evan I said that."

"He wants a serious relationship." I repeated the things Salem had said, including the possessive words he'd spoken.

Alora actually fanned herself. "I think I'm going to swoon." I laughed, shaking my head.

Jude leaned back, folding her arms. "Do you think by 'hold you tight' he meant he wants you guys to Bind?"

Huh. I hadn't even considered that. Binding was so much more than marriage – a powerful psychic connection formed between the two vampires, joining them on a level that far surpassed anything else. "I can't imagine Salem ever Binding with anyone." He was just too…Salem. Serious. Curt. Emotionally introverted. Too guarded to ever give that much of himself to anyone.

"But he wants a real relationship?"

I nodded. "And I just…I can't. I've told you about my unsuccessful dating life." It had been just like my childhood – a constant cycle of people unable to accept me as I was, trying to change me. "I've learned my lesson."

"You say that like it's going to be easy for you to keep resisting him." Alora's perceptive eyes were sympathetic. "Ava, nothing about this is easy for you. You've been drawn to the scary bastard since day one."

I'd never found him scary. "He makes me feel safe."

Jude seemed stunned. "Well, he makes *me* nervous."

Yeah, that was a typical reaction toward Salem. But I didn't think I was weird for feeling safe with him or for finding him kind of adorable. In my opinion, these people who feared him didn't see what I saw; didn't see the unfailingly loyal guy who put everything he was into everything he did, who was so invested in his job because he *cared* about the safety of his kind. They only saw the surface – the grunting, scowling, sullen surface that watched everything with a predator's eye.

Sure, he could be dour and growly. But just because he didn't bother to put on a polite pretence and smile pleasantly at everyone didn't make him a bad person. It made him someone who chose not to hide behind a front, who chose to be who he was and not let people's judgements bother him.

He was also a person who concealed a great deal of pain and guilt, who believed he deserved to suffer. That, too, wasn't the sign of a bad person. It was the sign of someone living in his own private, self-imposed torment who needed to damn snap out of it.

"Butch makes me nervous too," continued Jude. "I mean, have you *seen* him and Salem when they go on assignments? They love what they do." Ha! Like Jude was any more stable! She freakishly loved using that scary knife of hers to slice and dice. She was one of those people who seemed calm and polite but would soon as cut your throat than look at you. It didn't seem to bother her boyfriend, Chico, though.

"I once heard Salem say that killing was the only thing he was good at," said Alora. "It's so sad that he sees that as his only talent."

Well, he *was* good at it. He didn't hesitate, didn't give anyone an opening, didn't balk at anything he had to do, and didn't show an ounce of mercy. His ability to throw psychic punches suited his violent nature. But there was more to him than that, and it was definitely sad that he didn't see it.

"What are you going to do about him?" Jude smiled weakly. "I mean, it doesn't seem like he's going to take no for an answer."

"I can hardly blame him. One second I'm rejecting him, the next second I'm kissing him. Talk about mixed messages."

Alora waved a hand. "You're a vampire – a naturally sexual creature. It sort of makes you a sure thing."

I snorted. "That's the shittiest excuse I've ever heard. But I'll take it."

"Let's look at the situation outside the box." Alora crossed her legs. "Now that you've decided to stay here, it means you're going to live on an island where no guy is going to risk touching you, which means unless you want to start batting for the other team, your sex life is going to suffer. But here's this guy – hot, intense, and willing to be totally committed to you – who can give you what you want when you want it.

"Obviously it's worth noting that you find relationships tricky and uncomfortable. Based on your experiences with dickheads, you're sure that Salem will try to mould you into someone you're not. But is that fair to him? Maybe you should give him more credit than that."

Jude nodded. "He doesn't strike me as the type to make decisions lightly. For him to want more than just some fun with you, he must really like what he sees so far."

"Maybe," I allowed. "But being with Salem would be really hard for both of us. I mean, he's super, super intense. He'll walk all over me if I let him. Which I won't, so that'll cause lots of arguments because he likes to have his own way."

"He'd get bored with a woman who didn't push back." Alora sighed. "Evan's the same. He tries to take over all the time, only he's smooth and subtle about it. When I call him on it, he just shrugs and smiles. I can't get mad at him when he smiles at me like that."

"He still pressuring you to Bind with him?" Jude asked.

"Every damn day." Alora wasn't yet ready for that, since her last attempt at Binding went completely tits up. She wanted them to know each other much better first, and to be sure what they had was solid. I could understand that. "But if he gave up, he wouldn't be Evan."

I smiled at her. "Sorry, I know he's yours and everything, but I have to say Evan is, like, achingly gorgeous."

The redhead's smile matched mine. "Oh, I know. He's got a real talented mouth, too."

I leaned forward. "Ooh, do tell."

(Salem)

As Sam requested, I came to the office that she shared with Jared in the main building of The Hollow. Before the attack a few months ago, the mansion had been solely Antonio's home. He'd offered it to Sam and Jared when they ascended, but the couple felt that it was too much Antonio's, and they didn't feel right asking him to move out.

As such, the pair lived on the beach in a house that Antonio had had built for them. The mansion was now split into two, at his request; half was his 'living quarters', and half was office space – complete with conference rooms – for Sam and Jared. Antonio had felt that such space should be in the centre of the community, thus placing significance on the pair's role and status.

Sam and Ryder were in the office, sitting either side of her desk. When I entered, she smiled. "All right, Salem. Take a seat." She gestured to the chair next to Ryder.

I'd met Ryder only a handful of times, since his bloodlust wasn't yet under total control so he didn't mingle much. I'd liked him well enough...right up until I heard Ava describe him as 'pretty'. My jealous 'How the hell can a guy be pretty?' question had been met with 'He has such soft features and emerald-green eyes'. So now I kind of hated him, which was why I only gave him a brusque nod – something he seemed to find amusing.

"It turns out Marge was telling the truth about the owner of the brothel." Sam twirled her pen between her fingers in a fidgety movement. "All that was left in her memory was a vague silhouette; no features, no name, no hint of what breed of vampire she could be. Marge doesn't even remember how she came to be hired. I told Ryder everything you told me, so he's going to take a look at your memories."

Ryder turned to me. "If the weak silhouette in your mind matches the one I saw in Marge's memory, we'll know this is the same person."

"I strongly recommend you don't go looking anywhere else in my head."

He gave me a solemn nod. "I can assure you that I have no intention of doing so – if for no other reason than it takes up energy I'd rather not waste."

I grunted. "Fair enough."

"It'll be easier and faster if you can bring what memories you have to the forefront of your mind – even if they're unclear. Think about the times you glimpsed her, what she was doing."

Concentrating hard, I dug up my memories of the woman. I almost lost my hold on them when I felt Ryder's presence in my head. It didn't hurt, but it was fucking weird. Like having a hand inside my skull, rooting around.

After a few moments, Ryder pulled back. "It's the same woman."

Sam began fiddling with her pen again. "Salem, you say your Sire worked for her?"

"Yes."

"It's possible that we could track her through him."

"Could he really tell us anything about her that we don't already know, considering her gift protects her?" I somehow doubted it.

"Maybe he might not be able to tell us anything new about *her*. But he could remember anyone who worked alongside her."

"Marge has memories of two Pagoris who were the woman's – and this was Marge's word for them – lackeys," Ryder informed me. "Oddly, though, their faces were just as vague."

I frowned. "So if someone's with the woman, her gift protects their identity too?"

"Possibly," replied Sam. "It could be that she acts as a type of shield, like Butch. All she would need to do is touch or stand very close to them for her gift to protect them, *if* that's the case." She shrugged. "The thing is that the brothel has only been up and running for six months. I'm guessing your Sire's fighting club has existed for much longer."

I nodded. "Years."

"Then it's possible that at some point, she made a mistake. She didn't shield one of her 'lackeys' or sent them in her place. If so, your Sire would have their names and faces in his brain."

If Sam thought I could contact him and he'd helpfully tell us what he knew, she was going to be disappointed. "He and I parted on bad terms." I hadn't heard from Will since I left for the try-outs. He hadn't been too pleased about it, had taken it personally. There hadn't been any yelling. Will rarely lost his cool. But his rage and sense of betrayal had vibrated along our blood-link.

"You think he'll be difficult?"

I shook my head. "He'll give you information if you ask for it. But he'll want something in return. Will never does anything for nothing."

"Do you think it's possible that he had any involvement in the brothel?"

"No. Will's a lot of things, and he's capable of a lot of things. But although he's not big on following laws, he has his own set of principles and he sticks to them. He believes it's wrong to hurt women and children."

Sam thought on that for a moment. "I'll contact him later, see what I can find out. Right now, we need to go hunt down Marge's 'suppliers', as she thinks of them – the people who kidnapped and sold the victims to her. There were names and clear images of them in her mind. Our researchers should have their locations by now."

"How many are there?"

"Four, in total. It's a little group of Kejas who like to dabble in trafficking. Each of the bastards will have an entire squad from the legion tracking them. Hopefully that's enough."

A little while later, we discovered that, to everyone's utter fucking dismay, it wasn't enough. Each of the suppliers had done as Sam had suspected and gone to ground. Their apartments were empty, and it was clear that they had left in a hurry. The vampires from their small nest – who made their dislike of the group of four very clear – claimed to have no knowledge of where they were or how to reach them. They promised to get in touch with Sam and Jared if the group made contact.

Back at The Hollow, Sam threw a series of energy balls at the sea, and it was clear then why Jared had wanted to discuss the issue outside – he'd sensed that she was on the verge of exploding.

"Either they found out what happened to the brothel, or the owner warned them to lie low," growled Sam, pacing.

"She could have killed them," suggested Harvey. "She wouldn't want any witnesses, right?"

"Considering what her gift is," began Ava, "I doubt that she'll be worrying about that. It will have made her overconfident."

I'd been thinking the same thing. "She's likely to think she'll never be caught, or she probably wouldn't have opened the brothel in the first place."

Chico sighed. "So what now?"

"Now we place our trust in the researchers." Jared didn't move his eyes from a severely pissed Sam as he spoke. "They're going to search through what records they have on Pagori lines, find the names of vampires who have a gift that allows them to be untraceable."

"You could put bounties over the heads of the suppliers," proposed Paige. "You could even make a statement over V-Tube about the brothel. It will quickly go viral." V-Tube was the vampiric version of YouTube and was often used as a way for Sam and Jared to post messages.

Sam paused in her pacing. "That could work."

"It proved effective when you wanted Paige found," Imani chipped in. "She'd managed to maintain a low profile for a long time until then."

Beside Imani, Butch nodded. "If nothing else, it will make the suppliers panic even further, could rob them of any allies they have."

Sam turned to Jared, a smile forming on her face. "I like this idea."

Jared took her hand. "Then let's do it."

CHAPTER FOUR

(Ava)

Hoping to catch Sam before she started work the next evening, I headed to the beach house a little after dusk. It was Jared who opened the door, his hazel eyes widening in surprise. "Ava," he greeted simply. "Come on in."

"Thanks." I'd been inside many times before, and I was totally jealous. The place was bright, relaxing, and homey. And it had great eye candy. Honestly, Jared was like the personification of sex. But I preferred Salem's rough, hard looks to Jared's pretty face.

Taking in my wide smile, he groaned. He looked exhausted. "You're a dusk person, aren't you?" I just giggled, which made him groan again. "You know where to find her." He disappeared into the kitchen while I went into the living area, where Sam sat on the floor, cursing at the T.V.

"Evening," I sang.

Without turning, she held up her finger. "One sec, Ava. Give me one sec." She was playing on her PlayStation; she was literally addicted to the thing.

"Ooh, can I play?"

Suddenly, Jared was between us, having moved in vampire speed. "No. No. No. The last time that happened, the pair of you were on it for two hours." He handed me a cola-flavoured NST and pointed to the sofa. "Over there. And stop smiling. It's too early for chirpiness."

"Killjoy." I went to sit beside Sam's snake, Dexter. As I greeted him and lightly stroked his white scales, they turned a brilliant blue. Dexter had been a gift from Antonio's Sire, who had the ability to make his pictures come to life. After Wes drew a snake on Sam's arm, it instantly became a tattoo that could become a live snake. He was a mix of a rattlesnake, the black mamba, spitting cobra, and a garter snake – a breed Wes had termed 'Strikers', and I badly wanted one. Dexter's colouring actually changed with his mood. To go from white to brilliant blue meant he had gone from relaxed to happy.

Jared sighed tiredly at his mate, who was again cursing at the T.V. "Baby, get off the damn thing! You haven't even touched your breakfast!" Actually, to be fair, it looked like she'd nibbled on her toast and possibly had one swig of her NST. "*Sam…*"

"Fine." Ending the game, she turned to face us and shot me a bright smile, though it was strained. She was calmer than last night, more composed, but she was still seething inside. "Evening, Ava. Please tell me you're here to accept my offer."

I returned her smile. "Actually, I am."

Her expression smug, she pointed at Jared. "Ha. Told you."

"I said that you'd refuse the offer and go back to your brother," he explained to me. "Not because I didn't think you had it in you to join the legion, but because I know what it's like to be really close to your sibling. I'd hate to leave Evan behind."

Ah, well that really did explain it. "I called Cristiano last night and told him I'd decided to stay. He admitted he'll miss having me around, but he wants me to be happy more than anything else. He said if this makes me happy, I have his support."

Sam smiled at Jared. "See, he's not all bad."

Jared snorted, and I had to laugh. It was true that Cristiano got some perverse joy out of pissing people off – me being the only exception – and he'd certainly pissed off Jared by flirting with Sam. She didn't realise that Cristiano wasn't just dicking around; he really did care about her. But Jared saw that, and he hated it.

Sam took a swig of her NST. "What made you decide to stay?"

"Going on the assignment, seeing what kind of fucked up shit goes on in the world, made me realise just how important the legion is. I want to be part of that. And it's always fun to watch you work, Sam. No one does interrogations quite like you."

She bowed. "Why, thank you."

Jared gave her an indulgent smile. "I can agree with Ava on that one."

"Have you heard anything about the survivors yet?" I asked them before taking a gulp of my NST.

"Mary Jane phoned half an hour ago," replied Sam. Mary Jane, who had been a nurse in her human life, liked to act as one at The Hollow. "Denny, Stuart, Reuben, and Max have all recovered. The survivors are looking better after being on a drip of blood. They're healing and not as gaunt, but they're flitting in and of consciousness. They can move a bit and sometimes they even talk. But they can't get up, and they're not making sense. Like someone who has a fever."

I had to wonder if the survivors even realised they were no longer in the brothel. "Maybe they're not fighting for consciousness because they're worried they're still in that place. This all has to seem dream-like for them."

"You could be right." Sam drank the last of her NST and reached for her toast. "Enough on that topic or I'm going to lose my shit again. Let's talk about you and Salem."

"Um, let's not."

Sam stared at Jared, who narrowed his eyes. I had the feeling they were communicating telepathically. "Fine." He stomped out of the room, throwing over his shoulder, "You've got five minutes."

When Sam looked at me expectantly, I shrugged. "There's nothing to tell."

"Not even about the kiss a week ago?"

I gawked. "How do you know about that?"

She smiled. "I have my sources. And really, Ava, you know nothing remains secret on this island for long."

Fair point. "He totally sprung it on me. As I was walking out of the restrooms, his hand shot out from the shadows, grabbed me and pulled me to him. Then he was kissing me."

"Very Salem. He speaks more with actions than with words. So there's nothing more to report? No more kisses?" I shook my head. "That's funny. When he came to my office last night, he smelt of two things: soap, and you."

"All right, fine." I told her everything that had happened in the past couple of nights.

Sam's smile got increasingly wider as I spoke. "Salem certainly knows how to knock a girl's equilibrium. Determined little sod, isn't he?"

"Hmm. Well maybe he could go knock another girl's equilibrium and leave me in peace."

She cocked her head. "Is that really what you want?"

"He pulls faces at me all the time."

"Because you drive him insane."

"He's bossy and controlling."

"But you're no pushover."

"He picks me up by my t-shirts!"

"And it's absolutely hilarious every time," she chuckled. "This is the way I see it: you can keep on saying no, keep rejecting him, and insist he back off. Eventually, he probably will. Blokes and their egos never cope well with rejection, do they? Then he'll give you the space to move on. But it also means that *he'll* move on.

"You'll have to watch him with someone else. And it's not like you'll be able to leave. Being part of the legion is a life-long position. Maybe he'll go back to one of the humans I've seen him with in the past" – oh, he'd been with some of the women here, had he? – "or maybe it'll be one of the new female squad members. Will you be able to handle that?"

"Yes."

"Correction, will you be able to handle that without causing grievous bodily harm to both him and his girlfriend?"

"No."

Sam shrugged. "They're the only two options open to you. You can give him a chance instead of making him pay for what other blokes have done to you, or you can stick to your guns and then watch him with someone else. It's all a matter of which you prefer."

Strolling back into the room, Jared glanced at his watch. "Baby, we have to go or we're going to be late." Sam's eyes lit up. At my inquisitive look, he explained. "We're holding the first round of try-outs for Sam's new female squad. They're probably starting to enter the arena as we speak. Sebastian found us twenty potential members."

"Ooh, can I watch?"

"No. Because if we let you watch, the others will want to watch too and—"

"Please?" Flashing them my brightest, most innocent smile, I vowed, "I won't tell anyone, I swear. I never went to any try-outs, so it would be fun to see what they're like." I could tell they wanted to say no again, so I pouted a little. *"Please?"*

Jared sighed in defeat, shaking his head at me. "How do you do that?"

Sam shared his exasperation, but she was smiling. "No one can resist those kitten eyes." Rising to her feet with a clear plate in one hand and an empty bottle in the other, she nodded. "All right, you can come. But don't invite anyone."

I placed my hand over my heart. "I won't, I promise. Who are acting as the interviewers?"

"Us and Evan." That made sense. Evan was not only a commander within the legion, he was also Sam and Jared's appointed Heir. That meant he would replace them when they were ready to step down – and probably with Alora at his side, since it seemed that Evan had no intention of letting her go.

"We're holding most of it in the arena. Go get yourself comfortable in the VIP box."

So that was exactly what I did. The enclosed arena was located a short distance away from the beach house. The interior resembled a large horse paddock, and each wall was marked from A – D, which represented north, east, south, and west. A large seating area surrounded it, featuring a VIP box on the middle tier. I waited there, watching through the glass as the four females already there fidgeted and exchanged nervous looks.

One by one, another sixteen females piled into the arena, forming a line, looking just as anxious as the others. I was able to tell by the coloured tints to their irises – or, in the case of Sventés, the fact that there were no coloured tints – what breed of vampire they were. Nine were Pagoris, six were Kejas, and the final five were Sventés. Some were having whispered conversations, but their eyes continually darted to the door as they nervously waited for the interviewers to enter. Hell, I was nervous for them.

"Ava, it's a pleasure to see you."

I'd smelt Sebastian before I heard him. As usual, the tall Keja was wearing an Armani suit that complemented his athletic build. I flashed him a warm smile. "Hey, Seb. How's it going?"

"All is well, thank you."

"Come to see how your recruits perform?"

"Of course. Do Sam and Jared know you're up here?"

I nodded. "I begged them to let me watch."

His eyes narrowed. "You gave them that pouty 'don't hurt me, I'm an innocent kitten' look, didn't you?"

I laughed. "If I didn't know any better, I'd think you're implying that I'm manipulative."

Sebastian opened his mouth to speak again, but then the whispers abruptly died, garnering everyone's attention. Sam, Jared, and Evan had entered the arena.

It was Sam who spoke first. "I'm sure you all recognise the three of us, so I don't think we need to introduce ourselves. As Sebastian will have explained to you, our intention is to form a female squad of ten. We already have five. This does not mean that fifteen of you will be going home. It could be that you all leave. It depends on your capabilities and resilience. We can't afford to be lenient or give chances. We need to be sure that you can handle being part of a squad. It's not easy. It's not pretty. You will go on assignments that make you feel sick to your stomach. You will see things that haunt you."

I could vouch for that.

"You will be trained to kill, and you'll be required to kill. Because the rest of your squad have to know that someone has their back. If you can't deal with any of that, you need to leave now." When no one moved, she gave a nod of approval.

Jared stepped forward. "Something about each of you caught Sebastian's attention. It could be your combat skills, it could be your strength and endurance, or it could be your individual vampiric gift. It could even be all of them. But if you can't control your bloodlust, all of that is irrelevant." He nodded in our direction, and I realised he was giving a signal to someone above the VIP box.

Moments later, gas was being released from the hoses that were protruding from the roof. "Why gas?" I asked Sebastian.

"It's not gas," he replied. "It's a special cocktail."

I frowned. "Of what?

His grin told me I'd like his answer. "Different scents of blood."

Ooh, clever.

"This is exactly what happens in battle," continued Jared, his gaze boring into each of the recruits. "Various blood scents surround you, rousing your bloodlust. It is absolutely essential that you can think clearly through that bloodlust; that you can remain vigilant, focused, and in total control."

That was when a bare-chested human entered the arena, blood

dripping from a bite on his neck. Like that, the females turned restless and appeared to be trying to hold their breath. The human sidled up to Evan, who then commanded each of the girls – one by one – to step forward. I watched closely, wondering if any of them would cave to temptation. Maybe that was why I didn't sense the vampire behind me until a strong set of arms curled around my shoulders.

"Hmmm. This brings back memories."

Sebastian glanced my way, sighed at the sight of Salem, and returned his attention to what was happening in the centre of the arena. Apparently he didn't see the point in trying to send away the obstinate Pagori who was perched on the seat behind me, curving his body over mine.

"I'm pretty sure you shouldn't be up here." My words came out embarrassingly shaky, since he was running the tips of his fingers along my collarbone. I felt him shrug one shoulder carelessly.

"I wanted to see you."

I gestured to the sight below us, wincing in sympathy as a Pagori was sent away. "Did that happen at your try-out?"

"Yes. Two of the recruits gave in to their bloodlust and tried to have a taste of the human's blood."

By the time the test currently taking place was over, two more Pagoris had been sent away. It was no surprise, really, since the breed had an overpowering bloodlust. "Poor things."

Sebastian exhaled a disappointed sigh. "I had such high hopes for them. Shame." He left the room in a blur, most likely intending to wish them well.

"The second part of the try-out will test you physically," Jared announced as he, Sam, and Evan led the females outside.

"What happens out there?" I asked Salem, since we couldn't follow.

He brushed his nose against the sensitive spot behind my ear. "Several Pagoris from the legion are waiting at the fringe of the rainforest. Each recruit will have to reach the end of the forest in the fastest time they can. But…it's not as easy as it sounds. They won't be allowed to step on the ground – they can only use trees, rocks, and logs. Also, they won't be allowed to use their gifts, because this is all about their physical abilities. As if that doesn't make it tricky enough, they'll also have one of the Pagori squad members chasing them."

I gaped. "What? But that's crap. I mean, these girls aren't trained."

"That's why they get a ten second head start. But if they're caught, it's game over. And they go home."

I sighed. "I feel kind of...guilty."

"Why would you feel guilty?"

"Because I got offered a spot in the legion without having to go through all this."

"That's because you proved you can cope. You controlled your bloodlust during the battle to protect The Hollow. You showed that you're damn fast—"

"Yeah, but that's only because of my gift."

"Doesn't matter. Yes, your gift gives you an edge. But it's about more than speed, or all the Pagoris would win this test at every try-out, wouldn't they? It's also about agility, about using every physical strength you have. Agility is a strength of your breed."

"How did you know I was up here?"

He nipped the tip of my ear. "I followed your scent when I caught it outside." He inhaled deeply. "I smell it, and I think 'mine'. Have you accepted the reality that we'll be 'more' yet, Ava?"

I twisted in the seat to face him. Instead of dropping his arms, he clasped them around me. "Look...I don't think we'd match well."

"Explain."

"We're different."

"Explain harder."

I knew just how to make my point. "I've accepted Sam's offer to join the legion." His eyes narrowed the *tiniest* bit, and I smiled. "Don't like that, do you?"

"I want you safe."

He wanted to lock me in a tower where I'd never come to any harm. "Aw, ain't you sweet," I cooed, patting his chest. A muscle in his jaw ticked as a scowl surfaced. Ooh, he was offended again. How amusing.

"No, Ava, I'm not. Never mistake me for a good guy."

I rolled my eyes. "I know, I know: you're the biggest, baddest, scariest thing out there."

He tilted his head. "You're not afraid of me at all, are you?"

"You're too sweet and cute to be scary."

His scowl deepened. "I'm *not* sweet, and I'm *not* cute."

"Cutely manly, then."

A growl seeped out of him. "No. Now, you were saying why you think we don't match."

"You'll try to take over, Salem. My independent streak will drive you crazy."

He arched a brow, unimpressed with that argument. "That all you got?"

I lifted my chin. Fine, I'd give him the whole truth. "I'm not easy to deal with. I'm cheery. I fidget. I like singing. And dancing. And watching girly movies. I'm a dusk person. I giggle a lot – which annoys even me. I hum for no reason and usually don't know I'm doing it. Most people fear normal things like spiders. I have an illogical fear of dying in an elevator. I can handle blood and gore, but if you show me anything that's luminous yellow, I'll freak the fuck out. I—" A finger against my lips cut me off.

"How about you let me talk now? I *should* find you annoying. Happy people generally get on my nervous. You don't. Maybe that's because I know there's more than one side of you. You're not flaky and flighty. You're smart, you take shit seriously, and you're dependable. And you can kick ass like no one's business. Yes, I'll probably try to take over. It's in my nature, just like being chirpy is in yours. But I've noticed that you're quite capable of taking me on. So I really don't see the problem."

He honestly didn't see the problem, I realised. Nothing I'd said made any difference to him. "You are so ridiculously stubborn."

"This isn't stubbornness. This is me knowing exactly what I want and being determined to get it." He cupped my chin. "Look me in the eyes and tell me you don't want me."

"Will you leave me alone if I do?"

"No." His gaze pierced mine as he whispered, "Lie to me, baby."

I couldn't. I wanted him, whether he was good for me or not. Whether I was good for him or not. And it *was* wrong to reject him purely based on what others had done before him. But…"I need to know a couple of things first. I heard that you've had some fun with the humans round here. If you think that's going to keep happening—"

"There hasn't been anyone for me since you got here. I don't want anyone else." The stark sincerity in his voice made it impossible for me to doubt him.

"One more thing. You're very guarded, Salem. You keep a part of yourself locked away. It's not bad. But I need to know if it's something you'll do with me. You can't ask someone for everything if you're not prepared to give everything back."

Releasing my chin, he brushed his knuckles down the column of my throat. "My head…It's something that's better left alone. If you go digging in there, you won't like what you find."

The shadows in his eyes made my chest ache. "I want everything."

"Then you'll get it. But when you go looking for things best left alone, when you find out what you want to know and then try to leave, I won't let you go. Know that now. Decide if 'everything' is *really* what you want. Sometimes ignorance is bliss."

Maybe. "Everything or nothing, Salem."

A hint of humour flashed in his eyes. "And you thought you couldn't take me on." He licked along the seam of my mouth and I opened for him, moaning when he drove his tongue deep inside. Damn, the guy could kiss. It was raw, consuming, and dominant. Sealing a deal with a force that said there was no going back. "Later, when we're alone in my bed, I'm finally going to find out how every single part of you tastes."

"Presumptuous bastard."

His mouth curved slightly. "It will happen. I'll be so deep inside you, it'll almost hurt."

"I get to taste too."

"If you're good."

Picking up movement in my peripheral vision, I noticed that the interviewers were leading the recruits back inside. Returning my attention to the try-out earned me a nip to the neck. "I want to watch. You can have my undivided attention later."

Another nip. "I'll hold you to that."

"The final test is combat," Sam informed the females, who had reformed into a line.

Only eight remained out of the seventeen recruits that had progressed to the second task. Three Pagoris, three Kejas, and two Sventés. Naturally, I was rooting for my own breed, so I was pretty disappointed to find that there were only two left.

"Now you get to dazzle us with your gifts. It's not about if you win or lose. It's about showing us what you've got. If any of you have a gift which is fatal on impact, you need to step forward now. I'll have one of my squad members temporarily weaken it."

Three of them claimed to have gifts that could badly injure, but none were lethal.

"Then let's begin," proposed Jared. He matched up two Kejas, who wasted no time in attacking. The first had a gift similar to Butch's, which allowed her to 'repel' what came at her as opposed to deflect. Even her opponent, whose ability was to secrete ash, couldn't get close to her. Naturally, the first female therefore won.

Next Sam paired a Sventé with a Keja. The Sventé had enhanced reflexes, allowing her to stay out of reach. The Keja was pyrokinetic and rather impressively created a baton of fire. But no matter how hard the pyro attacked, she couldn't reach the Sventé. She did manage to clip her once or twice with a fire ball, but not enough to cause any real damage. It was an example of how defensive gifts could be more effective than offensive gifts at times.

As such, the Sventé won, which severely pissed off the Keja so much that she threw a tantrum and demanded a rematch. The other breeds of vampire could be quite prejudiced against Sventés, and it obviously hurt this particular Keja's pride that she had been defeated by someone she viewed much weaker than her.

I gawked. "What an uptight little bitch."

Sam actually laughed at the Keja. "I think it's time you went home. I need people who'll follow orders. I've ordered you twice to get back in line. If you can't even do that, then you're no good at all to me." Her back ramrod straight, the Keja stormed out of the arena. Knowing Sam, I was betting she would have seen the potential in the Keja and still considered her for the squad if she hadn't just blown her chances.

A Pagori and a Sventé were then set against each other. The Sventé had a seriously impressive gift. Simple and defensive, but impressive. Her skin was impenetrable. That meant that no matter how many weapons the Pagori conjured out of thin air, nothing harmed her. Obviously, then, the Sventé won. Unlike the Keja, the Pagori didn't go postal.

The remaining two Pagoris were then paired up. The first Pagori attacked instantly, shifting into a black jaguar and launching herself at the other Pagori...who strangely didn't move. Then, just as the jaguar neared, the animal suddenly halted, shaking her head. Even more shocking, it then started doing the freaking mamba.

"Mind control," whispered Salem. I realised he was right. The panther was under the complete control of the other Pagori. "Impressive."

"Totally. But so is the jaguar."

I felt Salem nod. "They'll both have Coach's attention."

Calling an end to the duel, Jared instructed the females to return to the line. Interestingly enough, the jaguar-shifting Pagori didn't appear to remember a single thing about the other female taking control…It sort of left a gap in her memory.

Sam approached the Sventé who had impenetrable skin. "It's clear that you're protected against physical objects, but are you protected against psychic attacks too?"

The Sventé shook her head sadly, clearly sensing how much her acceptance into the squad might hinge on that answer.

Sam just gave her a quick nod before addressing all of the recruits. "Please remain here while we" – she gestured to Jared and Evan – "have a quick chat." The females turned to each other and began talking quietly, most likely wishing each other good luck.

I turned my attention to Salem. "Do you think any of them will be chosen for the squad?"

Salem's expression was pensive. "It's hard to say. Coach never does what I expect her to do."

"She'll badly want to choose another Sventé," I predicted. Sam hated that our breed wasn't acknowledged as strong.

"Yes. But she'll pick who deserves to be picked. She won't let herself see them as Pagoris, Kejas, and Sventés. She'll just view them as potential members of the legion."

He was probably right. From what I'd heard, Jared – who had once been prejudiced against Sventés – had denied her a place in the squad at her try-out, despite that she'd been much more powerful than the rest. She wouldn't repeat such an injustice.

It was a few minutes before the interviewers made their way back to the line. The chit-chat among the recruits immediately stopped.

Jared spoke. "You all performed excellently – even those of you who lost the duels. But as my mate said earlier, we already have five. Being a member of the legion is gruelling and requires discipline, control, and a damn strong stomach. There will be two more rounds of try-outs after this, meaning there will be another forty vampires for our consideration at a later point. From this particular round, we have selected two."

I frowned. "Just two?"

Salem propped his chin on my shoulder. "Seem harsh to you?"

"I just feel bad for the others."

"People's feelings can't be taken into account. If Coach, Jared, and

Evan don't feel one hundred percent sure that the recruits can cope – physically and emotionally – in the legion, they can't accept them. Not just because they won't be effective members, but because one of two things can happen: they'll psychologically break, or they won't live long."

"I know you're right." Hiring someone who wasn't tough enough could, in effect, sentence them to an early death.

Having done a slow prowl along the line, Jared stopped on reaching the Pagori with the ability to control minds, and gave her a congratulatory smile. "Welcome to the new squad."

Excitement flashed in her eyes, but she took it totally in stride, giving him a simple nod of thanks.

Jared moved on until he came to the shape-shifting Pagori. She looked totally stunned when he pointed at her – possibly because she'd lost her duel.

"I can understand why they chose her," said Salem. "The combat task isn't about winning or losing. It's an opportunity to demonstrate what you can do. Her gift is pretty substantial."

While Sam talked a little with the unsuccessful applicants, I turned to Salem. "I want to go down there and meet my new squad members."

"You'll have to wait until later. First, they get a tour of The Hollow. Then they'll be taken to their new apartments to get settled in. I heard that Sam's planning to throw a beach party later…a sort of 'welcome party', since she hadn't felt particularly welcome when she first got here. So you'll have to wait until then."

I sighed in disappointment, wrinkling my nose. "Okay."

"But we won't be at the party for long."

"We won't?"

"No. You and I have business. And it's been a long time coming."

(Salem)

It was when I'd followed Sam's order to meet her outside the arena that I'd caught Ava's scent. I'd known about the try-outs, known I should remain outdoors, but I hadn't been able to resist the lure of that scent. Hadn't been able to resist having some time with the person who had the singular ability to make me want to grunt, scowl, and laugh all at once. And now, I was glad I hadn't resisted. Because she'd finally let down her defences, and we'd be celebrating that fact much later in bed.

For now, whilst Ava was off to meet with Alora and Jude for lunch, I'd find out why Sam had asked me to meet with her. Only when the arena was empty apart from her and Jared did I finally approach. "Everything all right?"

Sam folded her arms across her chest. "I spoke to your Sire."

"What did he say?"

"He claims to know a few things that could help us. He wasn't very specific, though."

Sounded like Will. "What was his price?"

"He wants permanent residence here with his mate and guard."

That did *not* sound like Will. "I was expecting him to ask for something outlandish, like using your personal squad to do his dirty work on occasion." Which wouldn't have happened. "I wouldn't have expected him to be prepared to leave his business and nest behind."

"He knows I'll be closing down his fight club, since I refuse to support the running of anything that that bitch is involved in."

"You're taking away a lot of her income," I noted.

Jared grinned crookedly. "Oh yes. She no longer has money from the brothel, and I doubt she's succeeding in blackmailing her clients any longer, now that the evidence is gone."

Very true. "She'll be pissed."

"Angry people make mistakes." And that was obviously what Jared was hoping for.

"What did you tell Will?" I asked Sam.

"I told him I'd think on it. I wanted to speak to you first." She sighed. "I despised my Sire, Salem. He was a conscienceless twat, which was why I happily ended his pitiful life. If Antonio had asked for Victor to live here – a place I consider a haven, as well as my home – I'd have found it extremely fucking difficult."

"Will isn't like Victor. He's not what anyone would call a good guy, but he's not all bad."

"I don't trust him. You remember when I was first made a commander and your entire squad was being arrogant, high and mighty, and got stuck in a 'we don't want or need your help, we're perfect' zone?"

Yeah, we'd all been ignorant bastards to her; certain we didn't need coaching because we'd passed the try-outs and been picked for the legion. We'd gotten all wrapped up in the honour of being selected, and had pretty much forgotten who we were.

"I contacted vampires from your lines, got personal, painful information about your pasts and hit you all with them. I wanted to snap you back into reality and make you realise that being accepted into the legion didn't mean you got to forget all the experiences that made you who you are and gave you your strengths."

It had worked. It had hurt, but it had definitely snapped us out of our zone.

"It was Will I spoke to about you, Salem. He sang like a fucking canary. Told me all about what happened to your parents that horrible night a long time ago before you became a vampire. If someone had called me, asking for that kind of info about you, I'd have told them to fuck themselves with a plunger."

My mouth twitched into a half-smile. Much like Ava, Sam never failed to amuse me. "Thanks, Coach."

"For that reason, I don't like him, and I don't trust him. But this whole matter is a lot bigger than me. Still, if it will be too hard for you, I can turn him down."

Having Will around could be awkward, given that he was controlling and believed that, as my Sire, he had influence over what I did or didn't do. At one time, I hadn't cared. Now, though, things were different. "I'll be fine if you accept his offer. Just as long as he doesn't think he has authority over me."

"You answer to only me and Jared. If he doesn't like it, he'll just have to learn to bloody deal with it."

Jared stuffed his hands in his pockets. "His mate and guard, what are they like?"

"Blythe is exactly what Will needs: someone he can control, someone who'll follow him blindly. His guard, Todd, is a quiet guy. Deadly, though."

Jared twisted his lips. "We'll do background checks on all of them before we agree. I just wanted a brief idea." He cocked his head. "You're sure you can deal with your Sire living here?"

I'd dealt with worse. "Call him. Accept his offer."

"Be absolutely positive, Salem, because we can't go back on our word," said Sam.

"Accept his offer," I repeated. "I'm fine with it."

It was when I was at the exit that Sam called out, "Oh, and Salem? About Ava…She's been hurt a lot, made to feel like she's not good enough exactly how she is."

"Who the fuck made her think that?" I demanded, totally pissed – which weirdly seemed to please Sam.

"Only Ava can answer that. Just make sure you're one hundred percent serious about her, that you're willing to take her just the way she is, before you attempt to start something with her. I don't want her hurt again."

"Neither do I." And I'd ensure it didn't happen.

She nodded. "Good. Now sod off, I'm busy."

My mouth twitched again. "Right, Coach."

CHAPTER FIVE

(Ava)

I doubted that anyone had experienced the kind of beach parties that happened at The Hollow...purely because they didn't have Fletcher and his boyfriend, Norm, to organise them.

Sam told me that the guys had thrown beach parties before, but she claimed they had outdone themselves this time. And they had certainly succeeded in making the new squad members, Maya and Cassie, feel welcome.

A lot of people were under the huge marque, which was decorated by colourful lanterns that lit up the evening. Under there was a DJ, a bar, a table of finger foods, pool tables, and a makeshift dance floor – a dance floor on which Antonio and his mate, Lucy, were swaying together while frowning at a very drunk Max, who was dancing with an inflatable palm tree.

Most of the girls, including me, were relaxing in the large luxury cabanas or on the cream rattan sun loungers that were surrounded by tiki torches and had a huge bonfire as a centrepiece. Most of the legion, however, was either swimming, surfing, or making use of the jet skis. Of course, the more immature members – sadly this included Harvey and Damien – were building obscene sand-snowmen.

"Where's Salem?" asked Alora.

Lifting my head from the rattan lounger, I took a sip of my cocktail, careful not to spill it on my beach dress. "Reuben soaked him with a water gun that was loaded with curry-flavoured NSTs. So Salem chased him into the rainforest. Where's Evan?"

"Swimming. Or, more accurately, taking turns with one of his squad at trying to drown Denny. Kind of impossible for them to do that, since Denny's gift lets him mimic both sea cucumbers and hagfish."

"Guys are such odd creatures," muttered Jude.

"Where's Chico?" I asked her.

She tipped her head toward a group of guys who were attacking each other with water balloons. "Being an idiot."

"I really can't believe the DJ's playing *Club Tropicana*." Paige, who was sprawled on the lounger next to mine with Imani, shook her head.

From her bed on the porch of a cabana, Sam laughed. "Fletcher's playlists are always hilarious."

"Does he dress up at every party?" asked Imani. Paige was very protective of her, and since Paige's gift was to take an injury and give it to someone else, she was perfectly capable of doing so. Imani needed protecting, since her gift was to sever blood-links, making it possible for her to destroy a vampire's connection to their Sire or even their mate. Such a gift could be misused, as we'd all learned the hard way...but that was a whole other story.

"Nope," replied Sam. "Not sure what inspired Fletcher to dress up as Captain Jack Sparrow, and I'm not sure I want to know."

"I have to say," began Maya, our new resident shapeshifting vampire, "I wasn't expecting this."

Sam cocked her head. "What?"

"When you said there would be a party, I imagined some sort of ballroom with classical music and champagne."

Cassie nodded. "Yeah, I was panicking about it, because I'm not good with formal gatherings. Hell, I'm not good at any gatherings."

"I know what you mean," chuckled Sam. "I'm the same, and I promised that any parties I threw would be fun, not pretentious. But Fletcher's the mastermind behind it all."

Hearing Evan laughing hysterically, we all turned to see that Salem was now pursuing Reuben at the far end of the beach – only this time, Salem was in possession of the water gun loaded with curry-flavoured NSTs. Both Reuben and Salem looked like they'd been dunked in a sewer.

I giggled. "I never thought I'd say this...but I think Salem is having fun."

Studying him, Sam said, "It's hard to tell from all the way down here."

"It's hard to tell even when he's up close," Alora quite rightly pointed out. "He always looks so serious."

"So the tall, surly – and, I have to say, totally hot – blond is yours?" Maya asked me.

My smile was wide and proud. "He is."

Cassie looked from me to Salem. "Considering the size of him to the size of you, I'm surprised he hasn't broken you." I laughed.

"They haven't done the dirty deed yet." Alora drained her cocktail.

"That's for later," I chuckled.

"He won't hurt you," Paige assured me. "I mean, I don't know him well. I don't think anyone knows him *well*. But I've seen the way he is with you. He's like freakishly overprotective. He'll be gentle."

I shot her a horrified look. "Why in the holy mother of fuck would I want him to be gentle?"

"I don't think you have to worry, Ava." Sam shook her head. "There's nothing gentle about Salem."

She was right. Even his feather-light touches weren't tender. They were teasing, seductive, and possessive – promises of what was to come.

At that moment, Jared approached with two snow cones. Having handed one to Sam, he laid on the lounger beside her.

"Where'd you get them?" I asked him.

"There's a snow cone machine under the marque."

"I have to get me one of those." I rose to my feet, stretching. Then I frowned. "Who are they?" Three vampires were just removing their shoes to cross the beach.

Sam followed the direction of my gaze. "That must be Salem's Sire. I agreed for him to move here permanently in exchange for information on the brothel's owner. I didn't think he'd arrive so soon."

"He has information on the brothel's owner?"

"Salem didn't mention it?" When I shook my head, Sam quickly gave me a rundown.

"Wow." I was a little put-out that Salem hadn't told me, despite knowing he wasn't a guy of many words. At the very least, it would have been nice to know that his Sire was coming with his mate, since it was much like 'meeting the parents'. "Who's the other female?" The very attractive female with long dark curls, an hourglass figure, and a very sensual walk. She fairly oozed sex, despite that she wasn't dressed seductively. Her outfit was very 'Lara Croft'.

Sam shook her head. "I have absolutely no idea. They asked to move here with their guard, but Salem said it was some bloke called 'Todd'."

Alora planted a hand on her hip. "I think it's safe to say that isn't Todd."

"I see Salem's disappeared again. Good." Sam put a hand on Jared's arm. "Don't telepath him just yet. I want to talk with his Sire a bit first."

That was when I sensed something. "You don't like him."

"I don't trust him."

Well if Sam didn't trust him, I didn't trust him. She'd always had good instincts. I would have asked for more details, but they were almost within hearing range. The rest of us took our cues from our Grand High Pair and stood, waiting.

Obviously recognising Sam and Jared, the three Pagoris headed straight for them – all wearing pleasant, gracious smiles. They bowed, which almost had Sam grinding her teeth. She really hated the bowing thing; it made her feel uncomfortable.

"It's an honour to meet you both," said the dark-haired male, smooth and confident. "As you may have guessed, I'm Will. This is my mate, Blythe. And this is my first-born, Gina."

Jared raised a brow. "You requested to bring your mate and your guard." It was a reproach. The Grand High Pair liked to pre-approve their visitors and residents.

Will gave a weak smile. "As I said, Gina's my first-born, we're very close. She didn't want to be left behind, and I didn't feel I could deny her, so I brought her in Todd's place. I hope this won't be a problem."

Sam twisted her lips as she studied Gina. "A background search will be done on you."

Gina nodded respectfully. "You have to be careful about who you allow on your island. I understand. To give you a brief summary…I've been a vampire for over one hundred years. Will is my Sire, and I've served him for the whole duration of my existence as a vampire. I worked with him to help Salem attain the level of control he now has. It will be good to see Salem again."

Instantly, I stiffened. There was too much intimacy in the woman's voice as she spoke of Salem for my liking. And when she said his name, it dripped with ownership. More annoyingly than all of that, though, was the scheming glint in her eyes that told me she didn't just want to 'see' him.

And just like that, I had Alora, Jude, Paige, Imani, Maya, and Cassie gathered behind me…like I was facing an invading army and we were all going into battle. I would have laughed if images of Gina and Salem weren't flicking through my mind, pumping anger and resentment through my system.

Thousands of petty questions popped into my head: 'Had Salem been serious about Gina?', 'Had he cared for her?', 'If yes, did he still care for her?', 'Will Salem be glad to see her?', and 'Can I kill her without pissing anyone off?'

My inner jealous harpy was urging me to introduce myself as Salem's girlfriend and make it clear to Gina that he was off-limits. But instinct told me to wait. If I was going to learn more about her and her intentions toward him, I would need her to believe she could talk freely.

"These are members of the female squad," Jared told the Pagoris when they looked at us expectantly. I didn't greet them, since I didn't trust myself to speak. The other girls didn't greet them either, and I knew it was a show of support and loyalty toward me.

"You're forming a female squad?" Blythe grinned, a little *too* animated. "That's fantastic. It should have been done a long time ago. There are too many chauvinists out there." Clearly she hadn't watched Sam and Jared's ascension on V-Tube or she would have heard Sam announcing her intention of forming this squad.

"There is," agreed Gina. "I never understood it. Particularly the prejudice against Sventés."

Oh, come on! It was obvious that they were sucking up to Sam by making a point that all of vampirekind knew was close to her heart. It seemed that Sam saw that instantly, because she regarded them with a sceptical gaze.

"There's plenty of food under the marque, if you're hungry," Jared told them.

"Thank you." Will smiled. "I was hoping to speak to Salem first. I've been looking forward to seeing him again. It's been a long time. We have a lot to catch up on."

"Where is he?" Gina glanced around. Her expression was cool, but anticipation swirled in her eyes. And I didn't like it.

"Around," Jared answered vaguely, taking Sam's hand in his and squeezing lightly. The act was soothing, and it made me wonder if Sam's mood was turning a little sour. After all, she knew exactly what it was like for her partner's ex to show up. And she was no doubt protective of Salem, as he was a member of her personal squad.

Blythe's smile faltered. "He does know we're relocating here, doesn't he?"

"Of course," replied Jared. "But I don't think he expected you to turn up so soon or he probably would have been on the lookout."

"I'm sure he'll be here in a few minutes," said Sam. "He never leaves Ava alone for long."

I quickly sent a thought to Jared: *Tell Sam not to formally introduce me yet.* He acknowledged that with an almost imperceptible nod.

Gina's head whipped round to face Sam. "Ava?"

"His girlfriend," Sam elaborated with total delight.

Gina ran her eyes along me and the group behind me, suspicious. But the suspiciousness quickly faded, and she looked to the marque, straining to see the people inside. Apparently she'd dismissed us as possible choices for Salem and was assuming his girlfriend was over there. Someone behind me snorted.

"Girlfriend?" Blythe rocked back on her heels. "Well that's a surprise. Salem was never much interested in relationships. Other than with Gina."

Hearing footsteps, I turned my head to see Chico, Butch, and Stuart – all of them looked fierce and watchful. "Hey," greeted Chico carefully as he sidled up to me, "everything okay over here?"

Sam didn't move her gaze from the newcomers. "We have some new residents. This is Salem's Sire, Will, and his mate, Blythe. Oh, and that there is Will's first-born, Gina."

"She's Salem's ex," I murmured only loud enough for the guys to hear. Instantly, they shifted behind me – more support. Will cast the slowly growing crowd an odd look but seemed to shrug off his confusion.

"These are members of our personal squad," Jared told the visitors. He then suddenly added, "And so are the vampires on their way over."

I saw then that Harvey, Damien, David, and Max were fast approaching; most likely in response to the gathering of our vampires. Max was looking much more alert now, possibly sobered by the prospect of trouble. Jared exchanged looks with the four of them, and

I had the feeling that he was communicating with them telepathically. My suspicion proved correct when, appearing a little pissed, the guys joined the mass at my back.

Will spoke then. "Salem's part of this squad, correct?" At Jared's nod, Will's smile seemed to shrivel. There was no happiness or pride there, despite that, in vampire terms, Salem was his 'son'. Apparently he didn't like Salem being a member of the legion. Well, well, well.

Blythe did her best to make eye contact with the male squad members who had planted themselves behind me. "I don't suppose any of you know where Salem is?"

"Not a clue." Chico's voice was close to a growl.

"Maybe he's with Ava," mused Blythe before asking Sam, "Is he serious about her?"

"Very."

"Have they Bonded?"

Sam reluctantly bit out, "No."

Gina's expression turned calculating, and I barely held in a hiss of warning. My inner jealous harpy dug out her crossbow – she had an arrow with Gina's name on it.

"But it's only a matter of time," added Sam, obviously trying to rile Gina.

Will shook his head. "Salem will never Bond with anyone." It was an echo of my own thoughts.

"I wouldn't be too sure about that. He's very possessive of Ava."

Gina tittered. "Salem's possessive by nature; that means nothing. I know him inside out. Trust me, he will never fully commit himself to anyone." It was said with approval, as if she was someone who didn't believe in love or the need for commitment; perhaps saw those things as weaknesses. "If this girl thinks any differently, she'll be massively disappointed." The word 'girl' was spoken dismissively, like I was something to be pitied, like I was nothing – certainly no threat to her. "The girl is a delusional fool if she thinks she can hold onto Salem."

Growls, hisses, and profanities sounded throughout the crowd behind me. I glanced at them over my shoulder, seeing then that Evan, Denny, Fletcher, and Norm had also joined us. "Relax," I mouthed at the mass. It didn't have any effect. Irises were glowing, a snarl was fixed on every single face, and they all appeared ready to pounce.

Jude had her beloved knife out, clearly desperate to slice the bitch up. Max was flexing his hand...as if barely resisting the urge to close his fist and temporarily deprive Gina of her senses. Hearing a high-pitched squeaking sound, I peered up to see a harpy eagle circling over us; I had to wonder if Alora – who had the ability to communicate with animals – had called it here, ready to sic it on Gina.

I turned around in time to hear Sam very bluntly ask Will, "Why are you here?"

He blinked. "You want information—"

"But you didn't need to move here. That was your price, and I'm wondering why."

"Who *wouldn't* want to live in the most secure place on Earth for vampires?" Good point.

"Just remember that your stay here is conditional. If the information you have is worth shit to us, you'll be leaving immediately."

Will bowed slightly. "Understood. But I believe you'll find my information very—" His sentence halted abruptly as, much like the rest of us, he heard a familiar sound: Salem's voice. He was walking along the beach toward us with Reuben, coming from the direction of our apartment building; they had both showered and changed into fresh t-shirts and jeans.

One glance in our direction had Salem's shoulders tensing. In a blink, he and Reuben had joined us.

"Salem, we've been waiting rather impatiently for you." Will's smile was wide and genuine.

Other vampires might have rushed over to their creator and greeted them warmly, but Salem wasn't the gushy type. He simply nodded politely. "Will, Blythe." As his attention shifted to the third Pagori, he frowned. "Gina." His unwelcoming tone soothed my jealous harpy a little. As he took in the supportive group at my back, his frown deepened.

Arching a sardonic brow, Gina said, "Don't I get a hug?" It was a provocation, a taunt.

Still, if he touched her at all, he was *so* dumped. And maimed.

Ignoring her, Salem came to my side, searching my eyes. "You okay?"

Maiming exercise cancelled. I gave him a winning smile. "Of course." He curled an arm around me…and I watched as realisation hit the three visitors. Will and Blythe shifted uncomfortably. Gina, on the other hand, flushed a weird shade of purple – seeming both stunned and livid.

With an expression of total and utter joy, Sam spoke. "Glad you could join us, Salem. We didn't get a chance to introduce her to them."

Salem tightened his hold on me. "Will, Blythe, Gina" – her name was said with a frown again – "this is Ava."

I turned my smile on Gina, adding a little self-satisfaction to it. "Or, as you put it, the delusional fool who thinks she can hold onto Salem."

(Salem)

Shit.

You didn't need to be someone who worked with psychic energy to sense the riot that was brewing. The air was snapped taut with tension, anger, and unease. Menace literally emanated from the residents of the island – particularly Ava and Sam.

Not the diplomatic type, I didn't even bother attempting to defuse the situation. Instead, I stood there trying to work out what the fuck had happened to make two squads gather behind Ava; the act was both supportive and protective. Each individual looked ready to not only leap on Gina, but to literally fight for the pleasure of being the one to deliver the killing blow.

The expression on Ava's face…it was one I'd seen on Sam's face countless times when she'd dealt with Jared's ex, Magda. Which had to mean three things: One, Ava knew Gina and I had history. Two, Ava was pissed about it. Three, Gina had blurted out some bullshit. *Fuck.*

Abashed, Will smiled at Ava. "I don't suppose you could forgive our ignorance…? I would imagine that some of the things we said weren't pleasant for you to hear."

Will had blurted out bullshit too? What the fuck had they said?

The questions must have been clear on my face, because Jared's voice was suddenly in my head. *They basically called Ava – not knowing she was right there – stupid for thinking you'd ever fully commit to her. And they claimed there's no way you'll ever Bind yourself to anyone. You should know that Gina seems intent on getting into your pants.*

I silently snorted. Like there was even the slightest chance of that ever happening.

"If we had known who you were," began Blythe, "we would never have…"

"Talked so freely," finished Ava, her smile bland. "That doesn't change what you're thinking." In other words, apologies were pointless because they were nothing but efforts to placate her. Ava moved her attention to Gina then. "But there are some things you *shouldn't* be thinking. Like whatever it was that made you look at Salem like he was living, breathing candy."

Gina's face hardened. "Don't think you can—"

"Ava's right." Will placed a hand on Gina's shoulder. "Salem's clearly happy. What we want is to make things right, not to widen the rift that exists between him and ourselves." He gave Gina a meaningful glance that made her mouth snap shut. But I knew Gina, I knew that wouldn't be the end of it.

It wasn't that Gina would be jealous of Ava. No. But she had a very strong sense of entitlement, believed that not only was she due whatever she wanted but that it should remain hers and *only* hers. She was possessive in a venomous, spiteful way. She would choose to keep something purely so that no one else could have it. Like a spoilt brat who refused to share her toys just to be cruel to others.

As such, she would get a kick out of fucking things up for me. Out of playing with Ava like a cat with a mouse. Which meant I'd probably have to kill her at some point.

Ava and I were new; we were treading a fine balance, and I didn't need anything tipping the scales into 'this won't work' territory. I doubted that Gina's presence or behaviour would make Ava withdraw from me, she was strong enough to deal with this and anything else. But she shouldn't have to, and I didn't want her to.

"How about you and I take a walk, Salem," proposed Will. He took a few steps, obviously expecting me to follow.

"Maybe tomorrow." I sensed through our blood-link that my words both shocked and offended him, and it was clear then that he believed he still had some authority over me. I'd be happy to correct that assumption, but that could wait. Right now, Ava was angry and upset. There wasn't a chance I was going to leave her alone like this. And I had a pretty strong feeling that it would go very badly for me if I did.

Will went to speak again, but Jared overrode him. "Salem's right. It's probably best for you all to get settled into your apartments first. Let everyone cool down." The authority with which he spoke couldn't be ignored. Will, Blythe, and Gina all nodded respectfully – albeit reluctantly. "Sam and I will show you to the residence hall you'll be staying in."

"Tomorrow evening, then, Salem." Affronted, Will cast me an odd glance before he, Blythe, and Gina – who shot Ava a hard look – were escorted away.

Once the visitors were out of hearing range, Ava looked at her supporters. "Thanks, guys."

"Gina's going to be a problem," predicted Jude. Fletcher nodded fiercely in agreement – no doubt the Empath had picked up a lot about Gina.

Alora's narrowed-eyed stare was focused in the direction that Gina had left. "We'll keep an eye on her." The other girls nodded.

I closed my hand around Ava's wrist, needing to be alone with her. "Come on." She hesitated. "I know you're pissed, but it isn't really me you're pissed at, is it?"

Alora literally shoved Ava at me. "Go have fun with Salem. Don't let that bitch ruin a night of hopefully hot sex." Evan laughed, kissing Alora's temple.

As Ava and I were leaving, I heard Chico's voice behind me. "Jude, put the knife away. She's gone now. We've talked about this before: your Michael Myers vibe freaks me out."

That got a giggle out of Ava. "So where are we going?"

In answer, I scooped her into my arms and travelled at vampire speed to my apartment, making her giggle again. Finding herself standing in my bedroom, she arched a brow. I shrugged. "Like you said earlier, I'm a presumptuous bastard." I went to thread my hands through her hair, but she stepped back.

"You know, it would have been nice if you'd given me a heads up about all this shit with your Sire."

"Coach only discussed him moving here earlier. I didn't rush to tell you because I didn't think he'd show up so quickly."

She raised a hand to ward me off when I moved to close the small distance between us. "Wait. We need to talk."

Talk? "I'm not a talker. You know that." And I certainly didn't want to talk when I finally had her here, where she belonged.

"Yes, I know that. But this is important."

The anxiety in her eyes kept me where I was. "All right, what is it?"

"I need to know what happened between you and Gina."

Way to kill the mood. I didn't know much about relationships, but

I was pretty sure that discussing your ex with your current partner couldn't go well. "Ava…"

"I'd prefer not to waste time out of my life talking about her either. But this is what she's going to do: every chance she gets, she'll say a little about your relationship with her; she'll tell me things that she thinks will hurt me or make me doubt you. And she'll believe it gives her some sort of power over me; some power over *us*."

Okay, she had a point. I'd seen Magda do the same to Sam…which was a big reason why Magda had eventually ended up dead.

"If I already know what there is to know, there can't be any surprises. I'll know whether the things she says are lies or truths. I'll be prepared for what she might try to use to hurt me. I need that if I'm going to keep from smashing her nose into her brain. Besides, if this was the other way around and *my* ex was here—"

"He'd be dead by now." And I was totally serious.

She rolled her eyes. "Just tell me so we can forget about her and get to the good stuff."

"Okay, we'll talk…but I have a condition." At her questioning – and pretty suspicious – look, I explained. "Here's the thing, Ava: you're right here, in my bedroom, so close I can practically taste you. There is no fucking way I can get through this 'talk' without touching you." I backed up until I reached the bed, and then perched myself on the edge. "Get your hot little ass over here and straddle me. Then we'll talk."

She narrowed her speckled brown eyes. "If I do that, you'll try to distract me and we'll never see this conversation through to the end."

"We will, I swear." Because I wanted it over with as quickly as possible. "Come here." After a few moments, she came to stand between my legs. I lifted her by her tiny waist and positioned her to straddle me; making her dress ride up her thighs. "That's better. Now…what do you want to know?"

Hands resting on my shoulders, she asked, "How did you and Gina meet?"

"Through Will. She's one of his vampires."

"And?"

"And we were together for a while."

Impatience flashed across her face. "Typical of you to be so vague," she grumbled. "How long were you together?"

I traced her collarbone with one finger. "A year, maybe. I don't know."

She blinked. "A year? Then it must have been serious."

"It was the opposite of serious, which was why we were together for that long." Ava waved her hand, encouraging me to elaborate. "We were both very work-focused, and neither of us wanted 'serious'. I guess you could say we were together out of convenience."

"Why did you break up?"

"Because I came here."

"And she was fine with that?"

Recalling the tantrum Gina had thrown, I snorted. "No. She has a very high opinion of herself. For me to even think about leaving her was not only a shock, but the ultimate insult."

"So the relationship ended badly?"

I nodded, combing my fingers through hair that looked like liquid chocolate. "She was pissed that I planned to go to the try-outs. She went running to Will and Blythe, who were just as pissed at me. Will said that if I walked out, he'd no longer consider me part of his nest."

"Harsh."

"I don't think he really expected me to pass the try-outs. I don't think any of them did."

"What's her gift?"

"She's able to release sexual pheromones; it's known as 'the sex call'."

Ava froze. "In other words, she can make people *want* her? Desire her?"

I cupped her face, pinning her gaze with mine. "It won't work on me, Ava. Physically, it might have an effect – that's not something I can control. But she can't get into my head, she can't control me mentally. It's a case of mind over matter."

I could see that she was doubtful, but she nodded. "Did you love her?" The question was quiet, hesitant; hinted of insecurity. She had absolutely no idea of the hold she had on me. I'd have to work on changing that.

Slowly, I slid my hands up Ava's thighs, snaking under her dress; loving the velvety feel of her ivory skin. "No."

Her breathing stuttered as my thumbs traced the edges of her silk panties. "You're sure?"

"Positive. Now enough about her. She's not important. Is she?" I wanted Ava to say it, to believe it.

"No."

I bit her earlobe. "No, what?"

Ava shuddered. "No, she's not important."

Rewardingly, I cupped her hard, wrenching a soft moan from her. "Who is important to me? Who?"

Her eyelids fluttered shut as I slipped my thumb under her panties and flicked her clit. "Me."

"That's right. You don't have any reason at all to be insecure. I want you more than I've ever wanted anyone. Say it." Snapping off the scrap of silk, I slid my finger through her folds, finding her slick. I groaned. "Say it, Ava." It was a clear warning: if she didn't repeat it, I'd torment every inch of her.

Pupils dilated, face flushed, she licked her bottom lip. "You want me more than you've wanted anyone."

"Good. Now don't forget it." I plunged my finger inside her. *So fucking tight.* "Ride it, Ava. That's it. Get yourself ready for me." Wanting more of her skin, I whipped off her dress. No bra. Just a perfect set of perky breasts that made my mouth water. She moaned and bucked as I palmed and squeezed one breast, thumbing the nipple. Fuck, I wanted a taste.

"Up. I want you on your knees." That put my mouth level with her breasts. I latched on to one taut bud just as I drove another finger inside her. I groaned at the feel of her – so wet and hot and mine. She tried to ride my fingers, but I held her still, scissoring them inside her, preparing her for what was soon to come.

She squirmed. "Don't tease."

I fucked her hard with my fingers. Every moan and gasp she made seemed to stroke my cock; it was thick and aching, ready to take her. When I knew she was about to come, I withdrew my fingers. In a blur of movement, I had her spread out on the bed with my head between her thighs. Parting her wet folds, I blew out a long breath, making her shudder. Then I finally took a long lick. Christ, she tasted good. Over and over, I lapped at her, occasionally pausing to torment her clit.

She writhed and jerked, moaning. "Salem, don't stop this time."

I *couldn't* stop. Not when I finally had her where I wanted her. She couldn't imagine the amount of times I'd thought about feasting on her like this; stabbing my tongue inside her, swirling it around, and then moving to suckle on her clit. Soon enough, she exploded.

As I gave her a minute to recover, I stripped off my clothes.

Looking down at her delicate body as I fisted my cock, I knew there was no way I could avoid hurting her. I was thick and long and painfully hard, and she was so small. Not that she seemed concerned at all – she eyed my cock with greed and curiosity.

When she reached out to touch me, I pinned her hands to the bed. "No."

She pouted. "I want to play."

If that happened, I'd come there and then. "Next time." I stood at the end of the bed and gripped her thighs, dragging her toward me until her ass was hanging off the edge. Tilting her hips, I positioned her to take me. "Look at me, Ava." As her gaze locked with mine, I began to slowly sink inside her. *So tight.* When a hint of pain flickered in her eyes, I paused.

"I'm okay," she panted.

Taking her at her word, I fed her another few inches.

Her eyes flashed impatiently when I stopped again. "I'm not going to break."

"No, but you are going to get so ruthlessly fucked that there's a good chance you won't remember your name. I want to be sure that every moan that comes out of your mouth is of pleasure, not pain. So we're going to take it easy for a minute." Still slow, I smoothly sank inside her to the hilt. Her back arched and a gasp flew out of her as her inner muscles clamped around my cock. "Ava?"

"I'm okay, really. It's just that no one's been this deep before."

"You'll get used to me." Curling over her, I sucked a nipple into my mouth and plucked at it with my teeth. When she started squirming and *ordering* me to move, I released the nipple with a pop. Slipping my arms around her thighs so they rested in the crook of my elbows, I slowly withdrew before sliding back in, wanting her to feel every inch. I couldn't move my eyes from the sight of her body taking my entire length again and again.

"I don't want gentle, Salem."

"And I don't want you in pain."

"Yes, you do. Because then even once it's over, I'll still be able to feel you every time I move." A mischievous smile curved her lips. "And you like that idea."

My nostrils flared. Yep, that appealed to the possessive streak in me more than I cared to admit. She was playing a dangerous game here. I nipped at her mouth punishingly. "You shouldn't push me, Ava."

"Aw, you're so sweet to warn me." And, yes, she patted my chest. I growled. "Careful."

Clenching around my cock, she whispered against my mouth, "Make me feel you."

And then I was hammering into her; it was rough, fierce, and wild. She arched into every thrust, her nails digging into my back. I'd needed this since laying eyes on her three months ago. Needed to feel her around my cock, needed to hear her moaning my name, needed to wipe away every memory of any other guy from her mind.

Right now, I needed to make her come so hard, I'd be burned into her skin.

I adjusted my angle slightly, so that I was hitting her g-spot with every thrust. Her eyes widened and her legs tightened around me. "I hope you like the feel of me inside you, baby, because there'll be no one else after me. You'll never take another person inside you. You'll never feed from anyone but me. And no one will ever drink from you but me. Only me."

Without warning, I bit down hard on her neck, feeling her blood – so potent and rich – flood my mouth. She tasted so fucking good, it made my head spin. She screamed as her body clenched and pulsed around my cock, milking me. My come literally exploded out of me.

A small set of teeth suddenly sank into my shoulder. *Fuck.* I'd heard that Svente saliva was powerful enough to throw someone into an orgasm, but I hadn't imagined it would be like this: heat and need slammed into me, seemed to fill my cock until I thought it would burst. And then it did, and I emptied myself inside her again as I growled her name into her throat.

As I waited for the aftershocks to ease, a deep sense of satisfaction settled in my gut. I'd finally claimed her. We'd exchanged blood; she was in me now, and I was in her.

It wasn't until I'd settled us both into my bed that her eyelids flipped open. "Sleep, baby." Holding her close, I watched as her dreamy post-climax high began to wear off and discomfort filled her. She was used to keeping things casual, didn't know quite what to do now. It was almost funny. Her mouth bobbed open, as if she needed to say something to dispel the awkwardness but wasn't sure what.

Eventually, she spoke. "Hey, I heard that after sex, some female spiders—"

"You don't need to feel awkward, Ava," I told her softly, amused in spite of myself. "You don't need to say anything. All you need to do is sleep. Okay? Sleep."

It took a few minutes for her body to finally relax, and it was at least another five minutes before she dozed off. I brushed her hair away from her face, deeply content to have her exactly where she belonged. She looked even more innocent while she slept.

To me, it was no little thing that she had allowed herself to fall asleep beside me. It was a sign of trust. People were vulnerable in such a state, but Ava was not only trusting me not to take advantage of that, but to keep her safe. And I would.

CHAPTER SIX

(Ava)

"Sex with Salem is like being at a concert," I told Fletcher as we browsed through the clothes in one of the stores; he hadn't stopped questioning me since we met outside our apartment building. "There's the buzz of anticipation, the thrill of knowing you're about to experience something amazing, the agonising wait for the show to begin, and then suddenly everything goes wild and you never know when it will end."

Fletcher sighed dreamily. "I had a feeling all that intensity of his would make him a rock star in bed." He added another skimpy dress to the pile hanging over my arm. He was truly a fabulous shopping partner – or 'wardrobe assistant', as he preferred.

As I'd made the decision to remain permanently at The Hollow, I now needed to stock up on clothing. Everyone knew that if you wanted help shopping, you went to Fletcher. It was like he hunted the clothes, sniffing out the right styles and sizes. He was also brutally honest without being insensitive, and he could help you look racy without appearing slutty.

"I'm glad you two finally had a tumble," said Fletcher. "All that longing and sexual frustration that rolled off both of you like fumes was giving me migraines."

I rolled my eyes at the drama queen who, like Sam, was a Brit.

"Is it something you intend to repeat, or was it just a nice jump to keep you going for a while?"

"It wasn't a one-night stand."

"Really?" he drawled. "So are we talking a fling or something serious?"

"Serious."

He narrowed his eyes. "Why is doubt and anxiety fairly wafting from you? Are you having second thoughts? Because I really don't think he'll back off."

"No, it's just…I worry that we'll clash a lot. I'm very independent, and he's seriously overprotective to the point of being interfering."

"True. And that won't stop or ease off," he warned.

"Why do you say that?"

"Salem's the type of person who expresses himself with actions. So if he cares about someone, it's only natural that it will manifest itself into protectiveness. For him to let go of that would be like cutting off his avenue of expressing his feelings. Does that make sense?"

"Yeah. I never thought of it that way. What else do you sense around him?"

Fletcher went back to browsing. "Not much. In fact, most of the time, I can't pick up anything from him – which gets on my bloody nerves, because I don't like being thwarted. But sometimes there's a crack in his walls. Like when he's around you."

I halted, surprised. "Really?"

Fletcher pursed his lips. "I suppose you could say he softens around you."

"There seems to be so much sadness in him."

"The glimpses I get of his emotional state are very fleeting," began Fletcher, his voice serious, "but I can tell you that there's a lot of guilt there. Guilt, grief, and a need to atone."

Naturally my curiosity spiraled. "This guilt isn't something to do with me, though, right?"

"No, it's a deep-seated guilt. It's been festering within him for a long time. But it's all background noise for him when you're there; his surface emotions are different then. Around you, he always feels fascinated. Inflamed. Desperate to own. I have to say, he's not going to be an easy person to be with."

"Why do you say that?" Not that I disagreed.

"That possessiveness he feels – it's dark, Ava," he cautioned. "Not destructive or something that would hurt you. But it's a 'he'll-do-absolutely-anything-even-kill-to-keep-you' possessiveness. It's not something that will fade. There's this...*need* inside him to be sure nothing bad happens to you, that you're safe and happy. Any person who dares to harm you by word or deed is at serious risk of being annihilated."

I blew out a breath. "I don't get it. Don't get why he'd care so much. I mean, he hasn't known me long."

"That's not why you're confused that he cares, I can sense it." Fletcher shook his head. "I have no idea who has made you feel that you're not good enough – although I'm guessing the seed of that idea was planted in your childhood, and idiots have only made it worse. But that's just dumb. You have no need to feel so insecure or to doubt your own appeal."

I shrugged, mumbling, "I'm annoying."

He slipped an arm around my shoulders. "Not one person on this island has had a bad word to say about you. Yes, it can be tiring to be around people who are constantly wired. But you're just too adorable to be annoying."

I snorted at that, which earned me a slap on the shoulder. "Ow."

"A very special thing about you, Ava, is that you accept people as they are – you don't judge, you don't expect things from others, and your friendship doesn't come with conditions. That's rare. There are so many judgmental sods in this world. But you always look for some grain of good within the bad. I have to warn you, it's doubtful that you'll find any good in Gina."

I swallowed hard. "The idea of her living here, of seeing her everyday..."

"It hurts you to be around her, knowing her history with Salem," Fletcher guessed. "That's understandable."

"What's her game? What am I dealing with?"

"Being around people like her makes me feel ill." He shuddered. "She's a bloody vortex of need. There's a hole inside her that will never be filled; that stops her from being satisfied. So much vanity, greed, arrogance, and selfishness. She doesn't have any feelings for Salem – I doubt she cares for anyone but herself. She sees him as a possession."

That made me bristle. "Yeah? Well she can fuck off."

"She doesn't seem to feel threatened by you," he informed me with amusement. "She was enraged at the beach party, but there was no unease. I'm guessing she feels very confident that she has some claim to Salem."

"I think one of the reasons she doesn't feel threatened is that her gift gives her some control over men. She releases sexual pheromones."

Fletcher's face fell. "The sex call? Oh bugger. She's going to try to seduce him with it."

"Salem says he can resist it; that it's possible his body will respond whether he likes it or not, but that it's a simple case of mind over matter." I snorted. "There's nothing simple about the sex call. If she can get him under her thrall, she can make him vulnerable to suggestions – we both know what she'll *suggest* he do." Hop straight into her bed.

"And he'd hate himself for it later." Fletcher was silent for a moment. "But maybe it *could* be a case of mind over matter. I mean, he felt absolutely no yearning for her at the party. And he was truly livid when he saw her there, infuriated that she'd upset you. Maybe those negative emotions will be enough to help him fight the sex call. And don't forget that Salem's very strong-minded. If anyone can stand firm against her gift, it's him."

"Yeah, but she'll be aware of that. Which means she'll wait before she strikes, wait for the right moment – one in which he'll be vulnerable on some level. If it works, he'll be pretty much under her total control. Just the idea of that makes me sick."

"Same here." He sighed, rubbing my arm comfortingly. "We'll just have to put our complete faith in Salem. "Look on the bright side—"

"There's a bright side to the fact that my boyfriend could be seduced into cheating on me against his will?"

"If it does work, Sam will end her. The bitch will be gone, and you'll never have to deal with her again."

"Sam wouldn't kill her." My smile was feral. "You can't kill someone who's already dead." If Gina succeeded in seducing Salem, the bitch was mine.

Laughing, Fletcher pinched my cheek gently. "I often forget that behind this innocent exterior lies a bloodthirsty banshee. The contrast is fascinating."

"Well thanks. Now let's move on from this rather depressing subject and I'll go try on all this stuff."

"We haven't been to the lingerie department yet."

"Lingerie? Sam was right – you know no boundaries. I love it."

(Salem)

For the second time over the past few evenings, I was summoned to Sam and Jared's office. This time, only the pair was inside.

"I take it this is about Will."

Sam nodded. "I had Ryder scan his mind."

"I'm surprised Will agreed to that." He'd always been very secretive and cautious.

"He wasn't happy about it, but he couldn't say no, since he needed to *prove* that what he knew was worth anything."

"What exactly was his information?"

It was Jared who answered. "Much like Marge, he doesn't recall the woman or even remember how he came to work for her, but he once met with her assistants without her. Their appearance match the silhouettes in Marge's mind of the woman's 'lackeys'."

"Does he know their names?"

"Unfortunately, no," mumbled Sam. "But the conversation he had with them was interesting. They referred to the woman as their Maker. That means she has a nest of some size, so we're not dealing with a few rogue Pagoris working alone. Also, the blokes were smartly dressed and rode in a Mercedes. These vampires aren't like my old Sire, struggling to have money, power, and influence. They already have it. People like that can't keep a very low profile."

Jared stuffed his hands in the pockets of his knee-length leather jacket. "When Will asked them why she wasn't present for a meeting, they responded with: 'she's visiting her Sire in Manhattan'."

"All of that will definitely help the researchers narrow down their search," I mused, but I wasn't as appreciative as I should have been. A part of me had selfishly hoped Will had been lying and would be quickly sent home.

"You're disappointed," observed Jared.

"Gina's going to make things hard for Ava."

Sam snorted. "She'll try. There isn't a person on this island who won't jump to Ava's defence, if necessary. Not that Ava needs anyone to defend her in any way. I'm willing to bet she can handle that petty little bitch quite well."

"I agree. I'd just prefer it if she didn't have to." I turned to leave, only to have Sam speak again.

"One more thing. I agreed for Will and his two chosen vampires to come here. But I didn't promise that they'd live."

Jared smiled. "She leaves a loophole in every promise."

I nodded. "I'll remember that."

Sure that Ava would have returned from her shopping spree by now, I made my way to her apartment. She was chatting on her cell phone when she opened the door. Her welcoming smile hit me right in the groin. I couldn't resist planting a brief kiss on her very tempting mouth. As a gesture of invitation, she moved aside to let me pass, mouthing 'Cristiano'.

I hated that asshole. Mostly because he'd warned me away from Ava; even went as far as to conjure a knife and hold it to my throat. So I'd effortlessly wrestled it out of his hand and flung it aside before ordering the useless bag of shit to stay out of my fucking business.

As Ava babbled about the brothel-situation to Cristiano, who had apparently seen Sam and Jared's announcement on V-Tube, I walked into the living area. I would have taken a seat on the sofa if it wasn't for the fact that there was no space. "That's a lot of bags."

"What? Um, yeah, that was Salem you heard. Why is he in my apartment?" She began worrying her bottom lip, looking panicked. "Um. Well...that's kind of a long story."

I heard Cristiano then: *"Tell me you're not seeing that psycho! Didn't I warn you to stay clear of him?"*

She bristled. "I'm not sure I like your tone."

"Jesus, Ava, are you fucking clueless?"

I snatched the cell from her. "Hello Cristiano," I drawled. My voice sounded dangerous even to me, which was most likely why Ava made a try for the phone. I dodged her move, shaking my head. That didn't stop her from lunging for it again.

"You'd better have a damn good platonic *reason why you're in my sister's apartment."*

"Really? I'm devastated that I can't provide you with one."

"You fucking psychopathic bastard!"

"There's no need for that kind of language."

"I told you not to touch her!"

"And I told you this has nothing to do with you," I stated firmly, voice hard.

"It has everything *to do with me!"*

"Wrong. What happens between me and Ava is our business."

A growl. *"End it! She can do better than a born killer!"*

"I won't dispute that she can do better. But I can't and won't give you what you want. Ava's mine." She was also amusingly hanging from my arm, doing her best to reach for the phone. I transferred it to my other hand, earning myself a smack on the chest.

"You'll hurt her—"

A spike of anger shot through my system. "That's one thing I'd never do." Apparently there was enough conviction in that statement that not even Cristiano would doubt it, because he instantly quieted.

When he spoke again, his voice was calmer. *"Put Ava back on the phone."*

"All right. But if I hear you trying to talk her into walking away from me, I'll end the call."

"Interfering bastard," he muttered.

I grunted. "So she often tells me." I held out the phone, and she grabbed it with a haughty sniff before backing away.

Her voice was quiet and hesitant. "Hello?"

"Are you sure about this, Ava?"

She looked at me for a long moment before answering. "Yes."

Good, because she wasn't going anywhere.

"Why couldn't you have picked someone...sane?"

She smiled. "He has lucid moments, though they're few and far between. And he's a warm, cuddly bear at heart."

I arched a reproachful brow as I advanced on her. She backed up, giggling. "You'll pay for that, Ava."

"What did he say?"

Still backing away, she giggled again. "Nothing. Look, I'm going to have to go."

"Wait, I'm not—"

I struck quickly, snatching the phone and ending the call. "Warm and cuddly? I don't fucking think so."

"The land of denial is a toxic place to live." She squealed as I suddenly slung her over my shoulder and began striding toward the bedroom. A giggle burst out of her as she demanded, "What are you doing?"

"Demonstrating that I may be many things, but cuddly isn't one of them." I dumped her on the bed, and she squealed again. I stared at her, lips pursed. "I wonder if I can get you to make that noise when I'm inside you. Let's find out."

CHAPTER SEVEN

(Ava)

"So let me get this straight." I placed my empty NST bottle on the counter in front of me as I leaned forward in the breakfast stool. We'd migrated into his apartment just before dawn, since he hadn't wanted to sleep in a bed adorned with pink, glittery covers. "You not only want me to give up my apartment and move in here, but you want me to do it tonight?"

Salem didn't even look up from his breakfast. "Yep." To him, this was a foregone conclusion.

It truly was a shame that I couldn't reach far enough with my legs to kick him under the counter. "No."

That made his head snap up. "Why?"

With anyone else, it would have been easy to explain – mostly because it was totally obvious. Our relationship was a few nights old; it made sense to give it some time before taking such a big step. But Salem didn't think like other people. He didn't think in terms of what was normal or what was reasonable to others. He thought in terms of what *he* wanted and what made sense to *him*.

To Salem, it made absolutely perfect sense for me to move in here. It wasn't even arrogance. It was that he genuinely didn't see the problem. "Look, I can't just give up my apartment."

"Why?"

"Because we don't know for sure that our relationship will be a permanent thing."

"Yes, we do." Like it would be achieved by the power of his formidable will.

"Just because you *want* it to be permanent doesn't mean that it *will* be."

"Yes, it does."

I suppressed the urge to bang my head on the counter. "Life isn't full of guarantees. There's always a possibility that we could mess this up."

"No, there isn't." He punctuated that by shoving a forkful of egg into his mouth.

This time, I *didn't* suppress the urge to bang my head on the counter. In fact, I did it three times; all the while digging deep – really, really deep – for patience. I didn't find any. "It would be stupid to rush things."

"Rush? This thing between us started three months ago."

"Yeah, in your head."

His brow very slowly slid up. "Are you saying it didn't?"

"I'm saying that you like to think I've been yours all this time because you're ridiculously possessive." I wagged a finger. "Having someone blow hot and cold with me for three months does not constitute a relationship in Ava's world."

"That wasn't me blowing hot and cold. That was me fighting with myself." He took a sip of his coffee-flavoured NST. "In any case, it doesn't change the fact that what's between us all began the minute you arrived on the island. This was inevitable, Ava. It was just a matter of us both accepting it."

"I'm willing to concede that this has been building between us for a while. But I don't see how this means we should push things. No, we should wait; get to know each other better." And slowly get him used to my hyper ways.

"We've spent the past few months doing that."

"I would have thought the last thing you wanted was to share your personal space with anyone." The guy was just so cagey and private.

He pushed aside his empty plate. "You're not 'anyone'. You're Ava. You're mine. You belong here, with me."

The girly part of me actually liked the caveman thing, which was severely frowned upon by the independent woman in me. "Look, we shouldn't try to sing before we can talk, or we could fuck things up."

"Isn't the phrase 'don't try to walk before you can crawl'?"

"Not when I say it."

The corner of his mouth kicked up into a quarter of a smile. "Why fight me on something you want as much as I do? And you *do* want it."

"Because, *as I've already explained numerous times*, it's too early in the relationship for this." I jerked in surprise as he suddenly appeared at my side in less than the time it took to blink.

Swerving my stool to face him, he cupped my chin, pinning me with his frustrated gaze. "You're talking like this is one of your casual flings, Ava. It's not. It's far from fucking casual."

"I never said it wasn't."

"You gave yourself to me. What's more serious than that?"

"I'm not saying this isn't serious—"

"You knew how tight I'd hold you. You knew just how possessive and domineering I'd be." Releasing my chin, he cocked his head. "How old are you, Ava? Human and vampire years in total."

I shifted in my seat, suddenly and inexplicably feeling a little defensive. "Twenty-eight."

"So young." He ran the tip of his finger from my temple to my jawline. "I've walked this Earth for over eighty years. When you reach that age, when you have such a long history of memories, experiences, mistakes, and regrets, it's much easier to be introspective. Much easier to know what you really want, just how important it is. And just how hard you'll fight to keep it. We take it for granted that the people around us will always be there. That's not how it works."

"You lost someone very close to you." This was the grief that Fletcher had mentioned.

"One minute someone's there, the next minute they're gone. Just like that." He clicked his fingers. "You and I both have very dangerous jobs. Jobs that can take us away from each other so very, very easily."

I understood what he was getting at. If something happened to him in the future, if I lost him, I would feel that I had wasted time with the whole 'let's wait a while and see how things go'. And I would hate that I'd wasted it.

Fletcher hadn't been wrong when he said that Salem wouldn't be an easy person to be with, that he was darkly possessive. But then, I'd already known that. Known that I'd thrown myself in the deep end with someone who would demand everything from me, who would become my second skin if I let him. It would have been scary if it wasn't for that odd ability he had to make me feel safe.

Even now, with him looming over me, tension radiating from him, and his face a mask of frustration and torment, I felt safe. I also felt myself losing the battle to be mad at him. How could I, when there was no much pain in his eyes? I wanted it gone.

Slumping in my stool, I sighed in defeat. "You're good at this."

"What?"

"Getting your way."

The shadows left his eyes and his mouth curved into a *full* smile. I nearly fell off the stool in shock. Moving to stand between my legs, he threaded his fingers through my hair. "Remember that next time you think about fighting me on something."

I snorted, amused. "You'd be bored if I always let you have your own way." I wanted to ask him about the loss he'd hinted at. But I didn't want to dig up the pain again, didn't want to lose that panty-dropping smile. I'd shelve my questions for now.

"You could never bore me." His mouth was mere inches from mine when there was a knock at the door. My entire body seemed to sigh in disappointment. "Later," he promised me with a growl.

I followed him out of the room, expecting it to be Will, or maybe even Gina. As such, I was surprised to see Sam and Jared at the door. "Evening," Sam greeted with a smile as she entered. Salem and Jared exchanged curt nods.

"We stopped by your apartment first," Sam told me. "When you didn't answer, we figured you'd be here."

They'd been looking for me? A lifetime habit kicked in, urging me to instantly declare…"It wasn't me. I wasn't there. I have no idea what you're talking about."

She chuckled. "You're not in any kind of trouble. If you were, you'd probably be able to use that sweet, innocent face of yours to get out of it. We just have some questions that we hope you can answer."

"Oh. Not a problem, then."

Salem came to my side, curling his fingers possessively around my wrist. "What's going on?"

"Like Sam said, we just have some questions for Ava." Jared's intense, hazel gaze then locked on me – it was hard not to squirm. "When we were in the brothel, the demon we found in the attic mentioned The Underground. You knew what she meant." I nodded. "So you know about demons?"

"A little. One of the people I was friends with when I was human...Well, it turned out she was a demon. I didn't find out until after I Turned. Since I was preternatural too, she felt comfortable enough to reveal what she was."

Salem spoke to Jared then. "Why the interest in demons?"

"An hour ago, we were contacted by a vampire from Sebastian's line," he replied. "He was instructed to pass us a message from a demon named Knox Thorne." Jared looked at me. "You know him?"

"I wouldn't say I *know* him. I met him once, but we didn't really talk much. My friend belonged to his lair before she mated into another one, so I saw him at the celebration of her mating."

"Well, it seems that the demon who was held captive in the brothel belongs to Thorne's lair."

"What was the message?" Salem asked Jared.

"Thorne wants to meet with us. According to the messenger, the guy's pissed and he wants to know about the vampires behind the existence of the brothel."

Sam's expression was grim. "We can't afford to give him any intel. It's one thing for us to track and destroy the bitch as punishment. But if another species was to attack her, the woman's entire line would want to retaliate, despite that she deserves whatever comes her way."

Jared nodded. "If a war then begins, we'll be forced to choose a side. I wouldn't want to defend her, but it wouldn't be good to side with demons over our own kind. We'd no longer be trusted to protect vampirekind."

"A war between vampires and demons could even make other preternatural species nervous and worry they're next," Salem pointed out. "They could decide to attack us first, considering it the best form of defence."

"Exactly," said Sam. "We've agreed to meet with Thorne. If we hadn't, it would not only have been considered an insult, but it would have made him think that we aren't taking all this seriously. The problem is that I don't know much about demons, and I don't want to go in there blind. All I could find out about Knox Thorne is that he's a ruthless businessman who runs a chain of hotels, casinos, restaurants, and nightclubs."

"He wants us to meet him at one of his hotels," revealed Jared. "But we need to know what we're dealing with here. Demons are pretty insular and private – it's hard to understand them. The last thing I would have expected to learn was that a demon is a fucking billionaire who mingles in perfectly with unsuspecting humans."

"That's the thing about demons," I began, "they hide in plain sight. You won't find them dressed in leather, holed up in bars. Demons like power and control and challenges. A lot of them are CEOs, politicians, bankers, lawyers, police, and people in the media."

"What's The Underground?"

"A subterranean location that's apparently like Vegas on steroids. I've heard that they've got casinos, bars, fighting rings, bistros, and clubs down there. My friend said they even hold concerts in The Underground."

"And if I had teleported to their personal playground with an injured demon, they would have pounced on me," Jared realised. "What about demons themselves? What are they like?"

"They aren't naturally evil, if that's what you mean. They can be good, bad, or something in between. They're notoriously sexual, they have addictive natures, and they enjoy adrenalin rushes. Like with us, there are different breeds. I'm talking *lots* of different breeds: reapers, harpies, incubi, succubae, hellcats, hellhounds – the list goes on."

Appearing pretty fascinated, Sam tapped her chin. "Which breed is the most powerful?"

"From what I learned, none are more powerful than the other. Whether a demon is powerful or not depends on the individual."

"You said they're not evil, but the thing we saw in the attic – that was fucking evil," maintained Salem.

"Demons are a lot like shifters; they have a dualism to the soul. Whereas shifters share their soul with an animal, demons share their soul with an entity which is – essentially – a psychopath. Their eyes turn black when the inner demon surfaces; that's what we were dealing with in the attic. Some do hand over full control to their inner demon, become rogue, but they're quickly dealt with. Demons police their own pretty well."

Jared took a moment to digest that before speaking again. "What about their hierarchy? Where does Thorne sit in it?"

"Their hierarchy isn't like ours, they don't have an overall leader. Demons belong to different 'lairs', and each lair has a dominant figure. Thorne's the leader of his lair, which is a pretty large one. That means he has more influence than most. He's widely respected amongst his kind."

"Great," mumbled Sam. "We couldn't have pissed off a lowly lair, could we?" She sighed. "What's he like? I want to know who I'll be meeting."

"In a word, daunting. Seriously, I'm not easily intimidated or freaked. But that guy scares me – mostly because he's not trying to be scary. He's really smooth and charismatic, but you can just *feel* that his calm can change in the blink of an eye. And he's really…" I hesitated, knowing this wouldn't wash down well with Salem.

"What?" Sam prodded.

I turned to Salem. "Don't get mad, I'm just objectively stating a fact." He narrowed his eyes but said nothing. I returned my attention to Sam. "Thorne is devastatingly good-looking." As I'd expected, Salem growled. "I'm just saying so she'll be prepared! Demons are like vampires, they have natural sex appeal. His is really potent – enough to throw someone mentally off-balance. You should probably also know that a lot of people believe he's one of the most powerful demons in existence, but no one seems to know what type of demon he is."

Jared ran a hand through his hair. "This keeps getting better and better."

Sam frowned thoughtfully. "I think you should come to the meeting with us, Ava."

Yay! "Happy to."

Of course, Salem's entire body went rigid. "You can't be serious, Coach."

"It makes sense. Ava has a better understanding of these creatures than we do. She's met Knox Thorne before, and the presence of a mutual acquaintance might help keep things calm. Besides, she's part of the legion now. We'll call it 'work experience'."

A muscle in his jaw ticked. How cute. "For all we know," growled Salem, "the meeting could be a trap."

"I've already considered that, which is why we'll be taking plenty of back-up. Obviously we won't take all of the squad into the hotel itself – that will look like a challenge. But we'll keep them close by. And Jared can teleport us out of there if necessary."

I soothingly patted Salem's arm, knowing it would swing his focus to me. "Big guy, if we've got any hope of making this work, you need to stop interfering when it comes to my assignments."

"She's right," said Sam, amused.

Salem moved his gaze back to Sam. "I stay with her every minute. She doesn't leave my side."

At her nod of agreement, I clapped a little. "This is going to be fun."

Growling, Salem turned to Jared. "The female has no fear. It's not natural."

Jared sighed, sharing a look of understanding with him. "Welcome to my world, Salem."

The hotel, which was situated in the heart of Vegas, was absolutely amazing. And it was swarming with demons. What made them stand out to us was their preternaturally alluring sex appeal – all demons were built for sex, sin, and seduction. The doormen, concierge, receptionists, and general manager were clearly sentries. While some of the guests were demons, others were totally clueless humans.

Sam, Jared, Salem, and I waited at the reception desk to be 'given clearance' to go further. Chico, David, Denny, Max, and Butch were ordered to remain in the sitting area, but they weren't happy about it. They couldn't be more pissed than the rest of the squad, though, who Sam had told to sit in the restaurant opposite the building.

"You're humming," Salem told me. Oops. He cupped my elbow as he then whispered into my ear. "Remember to stick close to me."

I might have teased him, but this wasn't a time to be glib. We were surrounded by potential enemies, and the meeting could go either way. "Okay, okay."

"Mr. Thorne is ready to see you now," the receptionist suddenly announced, signalling for the concierge.

Without a word, the concierge escorted us through a 'staff only' door to the far right, and then led us down a long hallway. On reaching an unmarked door that seemed to pulse with power, he knocked and announced, "I've got your visitors."

"Then you'd better let them in," called out a deep, throaty voice that I recognised. The concierge opened the door, but he didn't come inside.

Knox Thorne stood between his desk and the window, his powerful build accentuated by his black suit. Dark eyes measured every one of us, giving away nothing. His body language was cool, relaxed. It was probably genuine. I'd gotten the impression that he wasn't fazed by much. Considering he was without any guards despite being in the presence of four vampires, I was most likely right.

Of course, he was as compelling as always. He projected a raw sexual magnetism that could ensnare any female and reduce her thought processes to mush. However, I wasn't as affected as the first time we'd met. Maybe that was because Salem's arm was brushing mine; the skin-to-skin contact had my body attuned to him and him alone.

I was guessing that Sam's metaphysical bond with Jared made her immune to Thorne's natural appeal, because she was the image of composure. No one spoke for a few moments, too busy sizing each other up. It was Jared who, being a fairly impatient person, broke the silence.

"Demon," was all he said in greeting.

"Vampire. Quite an entourage you have." Thorne slid his gaze to the restaurant across the street where the rest of the squad waited. He was no idiot. Sadly.

If Sam was surprised, she didn't show it. "Would you expect us to go to unfamiliar territory without back up?"

Thorne didn't answer her. Instead, he moved his attention to me. "Miss Sanchez…good to see you again."

I guessed that the only reason Salem didn't bristle was that there hadn't been anything suggestive in the demon's tone. Despite that Knox made me uncomfortable, there was one thing I liked about him: he wasn't a flirt. Oh, he was charming when he wanted to be, but not in a way that was designed to provoke or taunt; he didn't seem to play those kind of games. "It is," I said.

"You've come up in the world since we last met, if you're working directly for your Grand High vampires. I'm betting they hoped that a 'friendly face' might help keep things calm."

"People don't come much friendlier than me."

Amusement very briefly glinted in his eyes. "True." Thorne shifted his gaze to Sam and Jared, stuffing his hands in his pockets. "Now that the preliminaries are over" – yeah, that was about as polite as it was going to get between the two species right now – "you can tell me why one of my demons ended up in one of your brothels." His rage seemed to thicken the air, but he appeared totally composed.

"It wasn't *our* brothel," denied Sam sharply, her distaste clear in her voice.

"But it was run by one of your kind."

"And now it's burned to the ground. We're no happier about this than you are. We dealt with it as soon as we discovered its existence. And we won't leave the matter unpunished."

Cocking his head, Thorne narrowed his eyes at her. "What are you? You're not like any vampire I've seen before."

Sam's smile was flat. "I'll tell you what I am if you'll tell me what you are."

Apparently he wasn't that curious, because he returned to the matter at hand. "What do you know about the owner of the brothel? My demon met her, but for some reason we don't understand, she has no real memory of this female vampire. Why is that?"

"It seems that this vampire's ability is to remain untraceable," revealed Jared. "It protects her identity to the extent that a person is left with only a vague impression of her in their memory."

"What about the staff? What did they have to say?"

"The only one we allowed to live is the keeper. Nothing she told us will help find this vampire."

Thorne's eyes seemed to bore into Jared. "You're not telling me the entire truth are you, vampire?"

"Did you expect us to?"

"No. In your position, I'd deal with the matter myself."

"So you understand."

"I understand. It doesn't mean I won't track down the vampire responsible and give her exactly what she deserves." Thorne's eyes briefly bled to black: his inner demon was seriously pissed, and it wanted us to know that.

"We'll find her, and we'll deal with it," Sam assured him.

"No, vampire. *We'll* find her, and *we'll* deal with it. We have our ways of finding things out."

"Let us handle it." It wasn't a plea from Jared, it was a demand. "I can guarantee that she'll pay for what she's done."

"I want blood, vampire. The only reason I'm not gunning for yours is that you saved my demon's life and returned her home. But I *will* have vengeance on the person who deserves it. You don't know the havoc I'll reek to make sure she pays."

Sam slowly shook her head. "We can't let you have her."

Thorne's smile was pitiless. "I guess then, it will be all down to who finds her first. Don't expect there to be anything left of her by the time we're done."

Due to it being a somewhat unproductive evening, nobody was happy as we later discussed the matter in one of the conference rooms at The Hollow. It was clear that both Salem's squad and mine were feeling the pressure of finding the bitch before the demons did.

Having dismissed everyone at the end of the meeting, Sam called out, "Ava, can I talk to you for a second?"

I halted midway through the room while the others continued to file out. Salem unsurprisingly remained, the nosy bastard.

Sam smiled at him. "You can wait outside."

I had to bite my lip to stop from laughing at the disgruntled look on his face. The fact that I was amused only seemed to aggravate him more. Such fun.

"We won't be long," Sam assured him, shooing him away with her hands. After a moment, he grunted and left, but planted himself by the door to wait for me. How cute.

Sam turned to a very amused Jared and said, "You too." That wiped the smile from his face and, sighing heavily, he went to stand with Salem outside the room. Only then did Sam round the table and come to stand before me. "I just wanted to check if you were all right; that Gina hasn't been bothering you."

"Actually, I haven't heard or seen anything of her." Which had surprised me.

"Good. I can't promise that will last. Some people seem to take extreme delight in taunting their exes' new partners. It's weird and pathetic, but it manages to achieve the desired effect and drive you insane. Gina had that same glint in her eyes that I often saw in Magda's."

"I heard Magda was bad." She'd even given Sam up to her enemies, which was undoubtedly one of the reasons why Sam had eventually killed her.

"She was Jared's Maker as well as his ex, so she thought she had a very big claim on him. She was determined to stop me from Binding with him out of sheer spite. I don't think Gina sees you as a threat."

"That's what Fletcher said."

"Then I must be right. The thing is, once she realises she's wrong and that Salem's serious about you, then you'll have some problems. It will all be petty and vindictive crap, but it will often hit you where it hurts. If it gets too much, come to me. Personally, I think you'll be able to handle it just fine, and *that* will piss her off much more than you coming to me."

I smiled. "That's what I'm thinking."

"Then feel free to torment her in your own special way."

My laugh was embarrassingly close to a cackle. "Oh, I will."

"Nothing will piss her off more than you and Salem Binding."

I snorted. "That's not going to happen."

She frowned at me...like I was a little slow on the uptake. "Why would you think that?"

"Um, because it's true." Did she even *know* Salem?

"It's obvious that you two are serious. You're moving into his apartment, aren't you?"

"Is *nothing* private on this island?" I groused.

"Not much." She cocked her head, her gaze now studious and daring me to lie. "Don't you want to Bind with him?"

I shifted uncomfortably. "We haven't been together long enough to be talking about Binding."

"That's a human answer, Ava. We're not human anymore. It doesn't work like that for vampires. We're immortal. Time comes to mean something different when it's not running out. How many times in your human life did you stress over something because 'the time's not right', or 'it's too soon', or 'it's too late'? None of that applies now. So, I'll ask you again: don't you want to Bind with him?"

"No, I don't." At her doubtful look, I added, "It's not something Salem would ever be comfortable with. I couldn't yearn for something that would make him unhappy."

"Fletcher's right; you are too nice," she mumbled, making me giggle. "I have another question. What makes you think that it would make him unhappy?"

Surely that was a rhetorical question. But when she looked at me expectantly, I explained. "Salem's not the type to expose himself. You know that Binding with someone means being completely naked to them; it's about being willing to share every single part of you, including your soul. Salem guards his soul, and refuses to be vulnerable to anyone." I shrugged, trying to seem aloof about it when in reality the emotional distance hurt. It wasn't something I took personally, though – it was just the way he was. "And let's face it, he's not the romantic type."

"No, but neither is Jared."

"What made you so sure about Binding with Jared? From what I heard, you two hadn't been together that long when it happened."

"Well, like I said, we're not on a timescale anymore. When it comes to making decisions about taking huge steps, there's no timescale to measure against. It forces you to rely on your instincts. We're predators now. Predators possess and guard what's theirs. I just...felt like Jared was mine. And I accepted it." She paused. "For the record, I happen to think you're wrong. I think Salem would feel good about Binding."

"As you often say...bollocks."

She laughed. "You were right in all the other things you said about Salem. He's very self-contained and private. But he's open to *you*. He treats you differently than other people – he has since minute one."

"You mean he acknowledges me as an actual person," I joked. Sam seemed thrilled with the answer, though.

"Yes, that's exactly it. See, Salem's only interested in the people who he considers important to him on some level. In that sense, everyone else is pretty much interchangeable to him, so he finds it easy to keep them out and ignore them.

"But you're not the kind of person anyone could fail to notice. You're pretty, and shiny, and loud. You grabbed his attention straight away. It was strange to watch his reaction to you. Like a kid that's spotted something new, interesting, and possibly fun to play with, but who's too unsure to reach out and touch it – still, he ain't gonna let anyone else touch it." Her smile widened. "Trust me, it's only a matter of time before you two are Bound."

Yeah, and I would start farting rainbows.

Not gonna happen.

CHAPTER EIGHT

(Ava)

I sighed tiredly. "They're just cushions."

Salem was looking at them like they were ticking bombs. "They're pink. And they have sequins. And they have diamonds. And they're frilly."

"What's your point?"

"They're girly."

"*I'm* girly." I wondered if I should point out that the current flush on his cheeks perfectly matched the shade of the cushions. It had appeared the moment he entered my apartment to find all the things I was taking with me stacked in the living area.

"I'm *not* putting them on my sofa."

"Why not?"

"Ava, they have 'I'm a princess, bow to me' printed on them!"

I placed my hands on my hips. "Tell me something. Is your apartment going to be *my* apartment too? Or am I just a lodger?"

A muscle in his jaw ticked. Ooh, how amusing. "You're not a lodger."

"Don't you want me to feel comfortable in my own home?"

"I already compromised by agreeing to bring that plastic coffee table that's shaped like a cat."

"Only because it was black."

"And the weird bird-cage lamps."

"Only because I agreed to put them in the bedroom so no one else will see them."

He pointed at one of the boxes. "Why do you need all these fucking candles? We're vampires, we have perfect night vision."

"They're scented candles." He just stared at me blankly, like I was speaking in biblical Hebrew. "I light them when I take a bath."

"And what the hell is that?"

"A French sofa." I ran my hand along the sloped, intricately carved back of the pink single-ended sofa. "I kept this in my bedroom so I could relax on it when I wanted to read, or do my nails, or play Minion Rush on my iPad." He dug the heels of his hands into his eyes, and I had to smile. "Reconsidering the moving thing yet?"

"No." He actually looked shocked that I'd assumed that. He scooped me up, curling my legs around his waist. "I want you with me. Besides, I'm pretty sure I could fuck you on that sofa."

"You could probably fuck me while I'm sitting on one of my bean bags too." I gestured behind him, and he tensed. I realised then that he hadn't noticed them yet.

He seemed genuinely afraid to look. "They're pink, aren't they?"

"At least they match the rest of my stuff."

His response was a grunt.

With the help of Reuben and Damien – who were clearly biting back laughter at the situation – we moved my things into Salem's apartment. The expression on his face as his very manly space was increasingly invaded by pink was absofuckinglutely priceless. I honestly thought he was going to snap when he saw my 'Hello Kitty' coasters.

Once we were alone, I shrugged at him. "I warned you I was girly."

Staring at what I personally believed were serious improvements to his living area, he nodded. "You did."

"At least I haven't scattered colourful, exotic plants everywhere. Poor Evan was devastated that Alora insisted on taking them with her when she moved in with him." Salem exhaled a long breath, looking in actual pain. "If you want me to leave, just say so. I won't be mad." I'd be upset, but I'd understand. Salem was like the manliest guy I'd ever met – so manly that even 'pink' couldn't chip away at his masculinity. But he was comfortable in dark colours and simple designs. I'd literally bedazzled his fucking home.

His brows pulled together. "Why would I want you to leave?" He grabbed my wrist and yanked me to him, making me crash into his chest. "I knew what I was letting myself in for when I asked you to move in. I've seen your apartment and your scarily feminine style, remember."

"And you thought you could talk me into leaving most of the scarily feminine stuff behind," I accused with a smile as his arms snaked around my waist.

Unrepentant, he shrugged. "It was worth a shot." His mouth took mine, ate at it, as his hands slid down to cup my ass and lift me. He seemed to like carrying me.

When I came up for air, I smiled. "Thank you."

"For what?"

Accepting me as I am. "Well, although you whined and grumbled over me bringing this stuff here, you weren't half as awkward as what you could have been. And I know you kept most of the swearing inside your head."

He brushed his mouth against mine. "Thank you."

"For what?"

"Not insisting on bringing the glittery clock or the cardboard cut-out of Yogi Bear."

I giggled. "I don't need Yogi when I have my own bear right here." I rubbed his chest. "So cute and cuddly."

Here came the deathly scowl. "I'm not cute. And I'm *definitely* not fucking cuddly."

The sudden ringing of a cell phone stopped me from teasing him any further. "That's mine." He set me down so I could grab my phone from the table. "It's Sam," I told him before answering. "Hello?"

Then there was Sam's voice. "Ava, I could do with your help. Meet me outside the infirmary as soon as you can."

Both startled and concerned, I did exactly that. Of course Salem came along, claiming he just wanted the pleasure of my company. I was pretty sure his main motivation was to protect me from Gina, suspecting the bitch might try to get me alone at some point. And, of course, there was the whole 'nosy bastard' thing.

Sam and Jared were both waiting outside the infirmary; his front pressed to her back and his arm curled around her shoulder. She seemed tense and nervous.

"Is everything okay?" I asked. "Please tell me none of the survivors died."

Sam shook her head. "Mary Jane called me half an hour ago. One of the survivors is fully conscious."

"That's good news, right?"

"It's bloody brilliant news." A pained look took over her face as she added, "I have to go in there to speak to her, but I'm sure you're well aware that I don't have a way with words. You're good with people, you make them smile and stuff."

"You want me to come with you?"

"I don't want to take Jared, since I doubt she'll be comfortable around blokes right now, considering what she's been through."

"Understandable." The survivor would probably also be less inclined to talk about what had happened if a guy was present. "I'm ready when you are."

Sam turned to Salem. "You can either wait out here with Jared or—"

"I'll be here," he stated, his gaze on me.

I gave him a smile. "I won't be long."

I followed Sam into the infirmary and over to a bed at the far end of the room. I was pretty sure that if Fletcher had been with us, he would have passed out from the strength of the emotions that seeped from the vampire lying awake on the bed. Fear. Despair. Pain. Anxiety. And – totally breaking my heart – shame.

I wanted to tell her that she didn't have a single thing to be ashamed about; that nothing that happened had been her fault, but I was guessing that wasn't a conversation the girl would want to have with a perfect stranger. I smiled gently, keeping my voice soft but empty of pity. She didn't warrant pity, she deserved a fucking medal for surviving. "Hi. I'm Ava."

The thin, pale redhead gave a tiny nod, swallowing hard. She couldn't have been more than sixteen when she was Turned. I wondered if that had been a factor in why she'd been chosen for the brothel. Some people were sick enough to prefer young ones.

When the redhead's eyes examined Sam, she cleared her throat. "You're the Grand High—"

"Yeah," Sam quickly confirmed, still uncomfortable with all the formalities that went with her position, including the very 'posh' title.

"I'm a member of the legion," I told her. "Can I ask what your name is?"

She swallowed hard again. "Rosa." Her gaze returned to Sam. "The nurse said you rescued us, that you destroyed the brothel. Thank you."

Not good at accepting thanks or praise, Sam said, "With the help of my mate and squad. Ava was also there."

Rosa's expression suddenly turned fierce. "Did you kill the bastards?"

"We killed the staff and the clients that were there that night. The legion has been picking off the other clients, one by one."

"Good."

"Did you know that Marge didn't own the brothel?"

"There was another woman." Rosa grimaced. "I think. I don't trust my mind right now. It's cloudy."

Sam's voice was careful as she spoke. "I have someone who could search your mind if you—"

"No. I don't want anyone else inside me."

The panic and agony in her wide eyes made my chest ache. "That's fine," I softly assured her.

Sam shifted from foot to foot. "I'm sorry to have to do this, Rosa, but I need to ask you some questions. We're trying to track down the owner and the others involved, but it hasn't been easy. What do you remember?"

"I remember being kidnapped. I was on my way home from my friend's house. A van pulled up in front of me, and two guys in black jumped out of the side door and dragged me inside. I fought them, but then one of them touched my forehead and, just like that, I couldn't move. Couldn't even scream. When the van finally stopped, the door opened and there was this woman with Marge. I don't remember much about the woman." She squinted, rubbing her temples.

"That's okay," I quickly said. "Don't hurt yourself trying to remember. Her gift protects her identity."

After a short moment, Sam asked Rosa, "What happened then?"

"The woman and Marge discussed me like I was a cow at a market. They decided they wanted to buy me, paid the guys who kidnapped me, and then I was transferred to another van. Marge touched my arm and...it was like I was drugged. When I next woke up, I was tied to a bed. I'm sure you know how things went after that." She averted her gaze, her face flushed with a fresh bout of shame.

Again, I was tempted to tell her she didn't have any reason to feel such an emotion. Instead, I distracted her with another question. "Did you ever meet the owner again after that?"

"I think I did once. Everything's kind of jumbled." Rosa ran a hand through her slightly matted hair. "She was talking to me, told me there was no point in crying or begging them to free me. She said I wasn't going to get out of there. Not unless someone was prepared to pay the high price of draining me dry – then I'd only leave as a pile of ashes. Every time someone came into my room, I prayed that would happen."

Hearing the defeat in her voice was painful. Every single one of the motherfucking assholes deserved to rot.

"Did you ever hear any names?" Sam asked.

"Only Marge's name, and the maids – Mona and Penny."

Sam nodded. "Thanks for answering our questions. I know you must be eager to get home, but I'd like it if you would stay until all the players in this game have been eliminated. They might not like the idea of anyone living to tell the tale; I don't want them to come after you."

"I'm not in any rush to get home." Her smile was bitter. "The guys in the van...I heard them talking about my Sire. He *sold* me. My own Sire sold me."

"Oh, is that so?" Sam's voice had dropped into 'I'm going on a killing spree' territory.

It would make a sick sort of sense that the players would be willing to buy the vampires from their Sires – it was assurance that the line wouldn't try to track the victims down or retaliate.

"What's his name?" Sam ground out.

Rosa studied her carefully. "You'll kill him."

"Yes." No hesitation there. Rosa seemed pleased by that.

"Stephan. He doesn't use a surname."

"That's fine. Just tell me where to find him." After Rosa rattled off an address, Sam nodded. "He won't be a problem anymore."

(Salem)

I leaned against the wall, waiting very impatiently for Ava to come out. I knew her well enough to know she'd walk out of there with tears in her eyes, and I was going to be here when that happened. Her heart was too big for that tiny body.

"You don't like it that she's joined the legion, do you?" It wasn't a question from Jared, it was a confident statement.

I shrugged. "I can't trust she'll be safe, she has no fear." It meant I couldn't relax on assignments if she was out of my sight.

"Then you're not going to cope well when she's going on assignments with her squad and you're not around to protect her."

Definitely not. "And you're much better with Coach?"

"Not at all," admitted Jared non-defensively. "Especially since my mate has a habit of putting the safety of other people before that of her own," he grumbled. "The Binding link helps."

"How?" Since I didn't have a romantic bone in my body, I'd never wondered what Binding was like.

"The connection lets me know if she's hurt, if she's conscious, her emotional state, her location. It's like having another sense; one that's completely attuned to her. It stops my imagination from running wild, worrying if she's okay." Jared cocked his head, studying me. "Is Will right? Is Binding something you would never do?"

I hated personal questions. "Why do you ask?"

"You're pretty intense with Ava. Demanding. I'm just wondering if she gets as much of you as you demand of her."

I stiffened. "That's between me and Ava."

"Just be careful with her. I'm not saying I think you'd ever hurt her physically. But you could hurt her emotionally, even though it might not be intentional."

"What the fuck does that mean?"

"You're hard, Salem. Self-contained. I'm not much different, though I tend to talk a lot more than you do. Trust me when I say that unless you give instead of just taking, it won't work between you and Ava. I held things back from Sam, and it came back to bite me on the ass because she found out from other people. That hurt her. But not as much as the fact that I was keeping her out."

They were good points, but…"My head's not a place Ava should go poking around in."

"Maybe not," he allowed. "But if you want to be with her, you have to let her see what's there."

"I told her I would."

Jared gave me a knowing grin. "Just like I promised Sam I'd tell her, but I was hoping it wouldn't come to that. Hoping she'd drop it. And so are you."

Perceptive bastard. "Remind me why we're having this conversation."

"Sam considers her a friend. And I happen to like Ava. We'll look out for her."

Okay, that sure got my back up. "*I'll* look out for Ava." She was mine to protect.

"I hope so. Because if you hurt her, Sam will be pissed and she'll take it out on me – probably with her whip. Then she'll hunt you down and do the same to you."

"Ava wouldn't let her."

Jared smiled at that. "Believe it or not, I'm trying to help you here. I like you, and I don't like many people. I trust you to not only watch *my* back but to watch *Sam's* back – that's no little thing; she's everything to me. I don't want you to screw it up with Ava because I think you make a good couple. You balance each other out. She sometimes doesn't take things seriously enough, you take everything *too* seriously. She's loud and dynamic, while you're quiet and reserved. You're very work-focused, and she's always out to have fun. She's impulsive and has no fear, while you're cautious and level-headed. She's good for you because she enjoys life and makes you live it. And you're good for her because you protect her from herself and everything else without stopping her from being who she is and trying to change her."

I was about to ask why the fuck I would ever want to change her, but then the infirmary door opened. As I'd anticipated, Ava's eyes glistened with misery. She walked right into my open arms, and I locked them tight around her.

"The bastards need to die." Her voice was shaky, but her words were strong.

I nodded. "They will."

"Each and every one of them," vowed Sam. She then related everything that Rosa had said, making both Jared and I curse repeatedly. "Stephan's going to be hunted, just like the clients and suppliers."

"Do you think it's possible that the other survivors were sold by their Sires?" I asked.

Sam ground her teeth. "Yes. If so, their Sires die too."

By the time Ava and I got back to my – no, *our* – apartment, she had pulled herself together. The woman had a spine of steel. But thanks to the frustrating and, to be honest, slightly confusing conversation I'd had with Jared, I wasn't in the best mood.

Still, after some time with Ava, who never failed to amuse me –

which was an achievement in and of itself – my mood had been close to improving, despite that the colour theme of my apartment was now black and pink. And despite that I had weird princess cushions on my sofa, which I naturally had every intention of getting rid of somehow.

Then Will, Blythe, and Gina had to go and fuck up my recovering mood by appearing on the doorstep.

"What do you want?"

The huge smile on Will's face didn't falter at my unwelcoming tone, but irritation rippled down our blood-link. "I know things ended badly between us, Salem. But let us mend the rift. After all, we're going to be neighbours now."

"Who is it?" Ava appeared, all smiles. Remembering her upset expression at the beach party, I reflexively shifted her ever so slightly behind me but without obstructing her view. Blythe noticed the protective move and quickly turned to Ava. "Do you think we could forget what happened at the party and start afresh?"

Ava, the image of perkiness, nodded. "Well of course." Her voice sort of…tinkled, like a bell. "We're practically family."

What? But then I saw that her beaming smile hadn't quite reached her eyes.

The 'we're practically family' comment pulled a low hiss from Gina.

Blythe suggested, "Let's start over, Ava. I'm Blythe, Will's mate."

"I'm Ava. It's a pleasure to meet you." And she sounded so sincere, I almost believed it.

"And you remember Gina."

Ava's expression softened…like Gina was an injured animal. "I know it must be hard for you to see Salem with someone else. I don't blame you for being jealous. After all, he's pretty fabulous."

I tensed as Gina's face morphed into a deadly glare. She went to say something but was quickly silenced by a sharp look from Blythe.

Will released a long sigh, looking very pleased with the situation. "Now that that's all over and done with, maybe we could all go inside and talk."

We *could*…but I didn't want to invite them inside mine and Ava's apartment. I didn't want them in our personal space, and I didn't trust them around Ava, especially Gina.

Ava must have sensed my struggle, because she proposed, "How about we all go have dinner together at the new Italian restaurant? Have you guys eaten yet?"

Blythe smiled winningly. "That would be lovely."

So we edged around the man-made beach as we made our way to the restaurant, passing stores, cafés, bars, other restaurants, the bowling alley and nightclub. Ava, her hand in mine, was practically skipping – a bundle of unlimited energy. She chatted non-stop about absolutely nothing… *That store over there sells the best shoes. I love shoes. Especially stilettos. My favourite pair are red. Isn't red a great colour? It's not my favourite colour, though. My favourite's yellow. Or maybe blue. Hey, isn't the water a gorgeous blue?'* On and on it went.

When she wasn't talking, she was humming. Or singing totally off-key, getting the lyrics mixed up. Will, Blythe, and Gina no doubt believed she was kooky and whimsical. But I knew exactly what Ava was doing. Still upset about what happened at the party, she was getting some payback.

Who needed to argue and exchange insults when you could just annoy the hell out of someone by being overly friendly and bubbly? Only Ava could have pulled it off.

Finally inside the restaurant, I sat beside Ava, which placed Will, Blythe, and Gina opposite us. Gina was glaring hard at Ava, playing on every protective instinct I had. I shot her a 'back the fuck off' look, which she returned with a self-satisfied smile.

"Ooh, this looks good," Ava practically purred when the server set her ravioli in front of her. She shot him a grateful look that had him grinning at her like an idiot. So I growled at him. That got him moving. Ava just rolled her eyes at me. Humming, she then picked off what looked to me like little green leaves from her ravioli and put them on a napkin. Realising that Will was looking at her oddly, she said by way of explanation, "They're green."

I probably should have found it weird that she refused to eat anything green for no apparent reason, but I strangely found her little quirks kind of endearing.

Blythe took a bite of her pasta before speaking. "You must have impressed your Grand High Pair in the try-outs to earn a spot in the legion, Ava." It was a prompt for information. Clearly they hadn't watched the ascension over V-Tube. Sam had announced that she was forming an all-female squad and that Ava – among others – would be given a place.

Ignoring the prompt, Ava gave her a shy smile.

"I'm assuming you have a substantial gift." It was another prompt.

But I knew that Ava wouldn't reveal her gift to someone she didn't trust. The knowledge could be used against her; if a vampire ever decided to come at her and knew what her gift was, they would know that she needed bodily contact to harm them. As such, they would know to keep their distance and attack her from afar.

Gina sneered. "Being a Svente, I can't see *that* being possible. No offense, child, but vampires of your breed" – said with scorn – "tend to have defensive gifts."

Ava didn't seem in the least bit offended, but I knew any slight on her breed would gall her. I was also betting that being referred to as 'child' would annoy her. To a vampire as old as Gina, though, that was exactly what Ava was – something young, weak, and vulnerable.

Whatever her true feelings were on the matter, Ava just shrugged. "Even defensive gifts can be substantial." She held a forkful of ravioli to my mouth, dismissing – and thereby irritating – Gina. "Here, try some. It's *so* good."

Stifling a smile at her ability to piss someone off whilst looking the personification of innocence and pleasantness, I indulged her by taking a bite.

Blythe sipped her red wine-flavoured NST. "Where exactly are you from, Ava?"

"Originally, Seattle. But my brother and I did a lot of traveling and eventually ended up in London."

"Is that where your nest is?"

"Um-hm."

"Who is your Sire?"

Ava waved a flippant hand. "Oh, Victor's dead."

Blythe's brows flew up. "Dead?"

Ava nodded cheerfully. "Sam killed him when he wouldn't free her from his hold."

"Oh, you're both from the same nest?"

"Now I see how you got a spot in the legion." Gina snickered. "Doesn't it bother you that you didn't earn it, child?"

Ava gave her a fond smile and leaned in, as if about to tell her a secret. "I used to know a woman who's like you, putting people down a lot because she has low self-esteem. Anyway—"

"I do not have low self-esteem," growled Gina with a snap of her teeth.

The fond smile turned patronising. "Of course you don't." And now Ava was humming again.

"Gina, enough," Blythe quietly scolded.

If I didn't know Blythe as well as I did, I'd have thought she'd warmed to Ava and was defending her. That wasn't it at all. One thing Blythe loved to do was make alliances, become friendly with 'the right people'; people who could give her something, help her become friendly with more 'right people'. She'd seen how everyone had gathered supportively behind Ava at the party. She'd seen that Ava was well-liked here; that she would be a good person to have on side. And she was doing her best to win Ava's trust and friendship.

Sadly for Blythe, that wouldn't happen. Ava wasn't the flaky, oblivious girl she was showing them.

Will spoke then. "This is a very beautiful place. The Hollow, I mean. Very peaceful."

"It is," agreed Blythe. "The best decision we ever made was coming here. I can see why you didn't return to us, Salem."

"How do you find being part of the legion?" Will asked me.

"Good."

"Was it very long before your squad was sent out on assignments?"

"Ooh, that's classified information," said Ava. "We can't share stuff about assignments with anyone outside the legion." She rolled her eyes, as if it was pathetically dramatic.

"I see. Are there many trainers within the legion?"

Ah, so Will wanted a spot in the legion. I should have expected that, really. In truth, the legion didn't have 'trainers'. Each commander was responsible for the training of their own squad. As Ava had said, though, we didn't share anything about the legion with outsiders. "That's something you'd have to speak with the Grand High Pair about."

"Surely there's always room for more trainers."

"Like I said, that's something you should speak with the Grand High Pair about." A spark of frustration buzzed down our blood-link.

Blythe smiled. "It would be good for you to find work, Will. You're not the type to sit around. I'm sure Salem could put in a good word for you."

"If you want to be employed by Sam and Jared," began Ava, "you have to prove yourself."

Gina shot Ava a condescending sneer. "And what could *you* have possibly done to prove yourself? Or maybe you just giggled until their heads hurt." Her curt, abrasive tone caught the attention of a waiter and some of the other diners.

Ava snorted softly. "Who lit the fuse on your tampon?"

Eyes bulging in anger, Gina went to bark a retort when Will banged his fork to get her attention. He shook his head; making Gina grind her teeth.

Will turned to me with a smile, but I sensed that he was far from happy at that moment. "I'm guessing your interviewers were very impressed by your control at the try-outs."

"Salem does have very good control," remarked Blythe. "Thanks to you, Will, of course. You'd make a good trainer for the legion, without a doubt."

I was rapidly losing my patience with this conversation. "I can't imagine why you'd want to work in the legion when you didn't approve of me coming here."

His expression hardened. "I didn't support you coming here because I didn't support the idea of you punishing yourself."

"Punishing myself?" I echoed, confused.

"You blame yourself for what happened to your parents. The only thing that gave you the incentive to live was vengeance."

Gina spoke to Ava. "Has Salem told you why he became a vampire? How badly he wanted revenge? That the reason he joined the legion was to die? To die with honour, granted. But still to die. I cannot say I've met many suicidal vampires."

Shocked, I snapped, *"What?"*

"The problem was that once you had revenge," began Will, "you lost your sense of purpose. Even though I made you one of my fighters, it didn't help. You gradually deteriorated. Joining the legion was, in effect, a suicide mission for you."

He and Gina were so very wrong about that. Admittedly, the matter of whether I was dead or alive had ceased to mean much back then. But I never took the easy way out of anything. I had a number of reasons for joining the legion, but killing myself wasn't one of them.

"Threatening to cast you out of the nest was unforgivable of me," continued Will, his tone sad. "But I hated the motivation behind your leaving and…I just wanted you to live."

"I wasn't suicidal," I rumbled, "and you know it." And the fact that he was implying it in a public place – where people were deliberately listening to the conversation – pissed me off even more.

Will held up his hands in a placatory gesture, but his satisfaction was streaming down our link. "I'm merely trying to point out that I can see this is no longer the case; that the legion has clearly been good for you."

"No, you're not." Ava's tone was no longer cheerful and breezy. It was hard and glacial. And it had our three companions blinking in surprise. It also had some of the surrounding vampires on their feet, creeping toward the table.

"E-excuse me?" stammered Will.

"You're jealous," accused Ava.

"Jealous?" Will scoffed. But I realised that she was right; his frustration came from the fact that he was jealous.

"You practically reek of envy. And why shouldn't you be jealous? Here's this guy who you Turned, took into your nest, taught control, and trained how to fight. Did he stick around? No. He took all that and he did something huge with this immortal life you gifted him with – and he did it without you. If he deserves this success, surely then the person who trained him deserves to have it too, right?" She leaned forward. "Wrong. It takes a lot more than good control and the ability to fight well to be accepted into the legion."

Blythe cleared her throat. "Why don't we all calm—"

Ava raised a hand. "Blythe, we're not gonna be friends so you might as well switch off the sweetie pie act." She looked at Gina with utter distaste. "And you...don't you have a hole to crawl into?" Ava pushed out her chair, and I followed her lead. Before she could move to leave, however, Gina was around the table with her hand clamped around Ava's arm, fingernails digging into the skin.

Ava effortlessly shrugged off Gina's hand with a fancy move, and wagged her finger. "Nu-uh."

Gina looked shocked for a moment but quickly recovered. "You think you have him, child?" A devious, spiteful grin crept onto her face. "Has he told you how far back him and I go? I was there when he was Turned. I was the first person he fed from. His first sexual experience as a vampire happened with me."

Ah, shit. "Shut the fuck up." I planted myself between the two females, as if I could protect Ava from Gina's words.

"Good in bed, isn't he?" Gina's devious grin widened. "There's nothing better than when Salem lets go in bed. But I suppose you wouldn't know that. He probably has to watch his strength with you."

That would have been true if Ava's gift didn't give her a strength that matched mine, but obviously I had no intention of discussing our sex life with anyone else.

"Does it hurt you that you'll never have all of him, child? Does it hurt to know he'll always hold back with you – physically and emotionally?"

I turned to Ava, intending to lead her away. Her lips began to tremble, and her little face scrunched up in agony. "It hurts so badly." She threw her arms open wide at Gina. "Hug me." I'd honestly never seen anyone back away as quickly as Gina did then. Ava exchanged a heart-felt laugh with the vampires that had gathered around. She was still laughing when she strolled outside, shaking her head.

I looked at Will and Blythe. "We're done." And I meant for good, and I could see by their expressions that they knew it. "I've got nothing more to say to either of you."

Anger fairly radiated from Will. *"I'm your Sire."*

I snorted at him. "It doesn't mean anything to you that I'm one of your vampires, so why should it mean anything to me that you're my Sire?" I glared at Gina. "Stay the fuck away from Ava."

"And if I don't?"

"You must want to die."

CHAPTER NINE

(Ava)

"Did she really pop your vampiric cherry?" The shy question was enough to make Salem pause in his pacing. *Finally*. Seething, he hadn't said a word since we left the restaurant. He'd just grabbed my wrist, led me to the apartment, plonked me on the sofa, and then took to pacing in front of me. I'd said a number of things in the hope of snapping him out of his 'I'm gonna kill Will' zone, but nothing had worked. Until now.

"It doesn't mean anything," he eventually responded.

I snorted. "What a guy thing to say. I take it she was also telling the truth when she said she was the first person you drank from too?"

"Technically, Will's the first person I fed from."

"He gave you his blood to Turn you. That's not the same as your first feed. Was it Gina?"

"Yes," he bit out.

My stomach dropped. I didn't want those images in my head, didn't want to think about Salem drinking from her, or touching her the way he did me. But knowing the facts was better than not knowing. Maybe I should have given my jealous harpy full control and choked Gina with her own intestines. "What about the 'you becoming a vampire to get revenge' comment? Is that true?"

Salem looked at me helplessly, and I thought he wasn't going to answer. Then he cursed and quietly muttered what sounded like 'Jared was right.' Shoving aside one of my cushions, he slumped onto the sofa next to where I was sat, cross-legged. He didn't look at me as he said, "When I failed to pay off a gambling debt, the bookies locked up and barricaded every possible exit of my parents' house. Then they burned it to the ground. My mother and my stepfather were trapped inside." He'd spoken in his deceptively apathetic tone, but I could sense his pain and anguish.

Twisting in my seat, I took one of his balled-up hands in mine and propped my chin on his shoulder. "I'd say I'm sorry, but it's too inadequate." Was there really a right thing to say, something that could actually help, when someone was grieving?

"So, yeah, it's true that I wanted revenge and that I blame myself for their deaths. In theory, it wasn't my debt. But the blame still lies with me."

"What do you mean by 'in theory'?"

"It was my half-brother's debt. He was only seven-fucking-teen. He got into gambling because he was following in my footsteps. He ran up a big debt with the wrong person. When he couldn't pay it off, he bolted. So I was expected to pay it for him. I didn't have that kind of money, and the bookies weren't interested in it being paid in instalments. They put a gun to my head, told me I had forty-eight hours to get it. But there was no way I could do it."

In my opinion, then, the blame didn't belong to Salem. His half-brother had *chosen* to run up that debt. And the bookies had *chosen* to react by targeting his parents. I was about to say as much when he spoke again.

"I expected them to come after me. I was ready for that. Going after my mother was the worst thing they could have done. I found out who started the fire. I killed them both. But that made the others retaliate, and they almost killed me in an alley. Will found me there, dying. Maybe he smelled the blood. He offered to Turn me. All I was interested in was making the others pay. So I said yes."

"I hope they paid in full. With interest."

His expression took on a faraway quality. "I could hear her screaming."

Oh, God. I scrambled onto his lap, straddling him, and tucked my head under his chin as I leaned into him. His arm curled loosely around me.

"One of the neighbours called me when the fire started. I couldn't get inside. I told my mother that I'd get her out. She kept screaming for me, but when she stopped screaming...Shit, I'm not sure which was worse."

Now I understood what Fletcher had meant by Salem's grief and need to atone. He hadn't been able to save the people who he cared for, so now he was determined to save as many others as he could. It also explained the intensity of his protective streak. And I was obviously going to have to handle it, because it wouldn't ease.

"I told you I've done a lot of bad things. I meant it. One of the very few *good* things I've done is join the legion. And Will just took it, twisted it, and tried to make it into something bad."

I pulled back to meet his gaze. "But it didn't work. He just showed himself for the envious, spiteful shithead that he is. He wants what you have, and he resents you for that. He was goading and punishing you."

"Like Gina was goading and punishing you."

Yeah, and it had partly worked. Of course I'd been quite aware that he wasn't a virgin. But knowing Salem had a past and actually being face-to-face with that past – hearing the things he and Gina had done together – were two very different things.

My jealousy must have been apparent in my expression, because his eyes narrowed and he gripped my chin with his thumb and forefinger. "I told you the night of the beach party, she doesn't matter to me. Only you do."

I believed him, which was why her goading had only *partly* worked. "Good." I pressed a light kiss to his mouth, and it was like lighting a match – he immediately took control; cupped the back of my head and ravaged my mouth with his lips, tongue, and teeth. Nobody had ever kissed me the way Salem did, greedily feasting and claiming. He didn't coax or tempt, he demanded and took.

He was also pouring every ounce of his anger and guilt into the kiss, like I could make it better. I wanted to. As I shifted out of his hold and rose from the sofa, his hand snapped out to snag my arm.

"Where are you going?"

In answer, I grabbed one of the cushions he hated – and repeatedly tried to bully me into binning – and placed it at my feet. "I'm hungry." Then I kneeled between his legs.

As understanding hit Salem, heat and need began to emanate from him; buzzing against my skin and feeding my own hunger. Jaw clenched, he watched through hooded eyes as I leaned forward and exhaled heavily against the fast-growing bulge in his jeans. Keeping my movements agonisingly slow, I tackled his fly under his heated gaze. His cock, semi-hard and all mine, bobbed free. I licked from base to tip, and swirled my tongue around the head before dipping it into the slit. His rough groan made me smile.

"See, these cushions have their uses." Over and over, I licked and nibbled and teased, until he was so hard it had to be painful. When his warning growl told me he'd had enough of the teasing, I took him into my mouth and sucked hard enough to make my cheeks hollow.

"Fuck, that's good." Fisting a hand in my hair, he began guiding my movements – which was surprisingly kind of hot. "Keep that mouth wrapped nice and tight around me. Yeah, just like that."

Determined to bring him to the edge of his control, I sporadically danced my tongue around him, or grazed him with my teeth, or glided the flat of my tongue along his underside, or swallowed around him. I wanted him to lose himself, to forget all about what was haunting him. Soon, he was lifting his hips, surging into my mouth.

"I want inside you."

I was expecting him to pull me up, rid me of my jeans, and then impale me on his cock. Instead, I found myself kneeling on the sofa, my back to Salem, as he whipped off my tank top and ripped off my jeans. A hand on my lower back pushed me forward, and I grabbed the back of the sofa to steady me. I gasped as a finger shoved inside me.

"Wet and ready, just the way I like you." His bare chest plastered to my back, he looped an arm around me and lifted me slightly as he put his mouth to my ear. "Hold on." Then he plunged inside me, stretching me, causing the most exquisite burn. "All of it, Ava." His second thrust drove him balls-deep, giving me exactly what I wanted.

He rode me hard, forced me to feel every inch of him. His pace was frenzied, and each plunge of his cock was ruthless...building the friction until I was practically sobbing with the need to come.

Feeling his teeth nip my shoulder teasingly, I moaned. "Bite me."

Growling, he sunk his teeth deep into my shoulder just as his finger circled my clit. That was all it took for my climax to barrel into me, tearing a scream from my throat. He pounded into me once, twice, and then slammed himself deep as his cock pulsed inside me.

With a satiated sigh, I slumped; thankfully, his shuddering body held me easily. "Bastard, I'll be damned if I don't get to keep my cushions." His mouth curved against my neck.

At dusk, we were called for a meeting with Sam and Jared. They, along with the rest of Salem's squad, were already waiting inside the conference room when we entered. We had no sooner taken our seats than Sam was speaking.

"Evening, all. You will be pleased to know that our researchers came up with three possible suspects for the brothel owner. All are Pagoris, all are rumoured to have identity-protecting gifts, all have reasonably small nests of their own, and all have Sires that live in Manhattan – perfectly matching the profile."

Jared spoke then. "We could sit here and waste time by reviewing all three of them, or Sam and I could skip to the third suspect, who we are pretty sure is the woman we're looking for. Which option do you prefer?"

Chico frowned. "That all depends on how sure you are about this third suspect."

Sam's answer was immediate. "Ninety-nine percent sure."

The utter confidence in her voice was enough for me. I smiled. "Then introduce us to who's behind door number three."

"Diane Glass." Jared handed me a photograph.

I took a quick look at the brunette, noticing her prominent cheekbones and bow mouth, before passing it on. "Her gift didn't protect her from being photographed?"

"She was human when that was taken," said Sam. "According to our researchers, she's quite the business woman – has her hands in many pies, none of which could be considered legal or moral. But that's not why we're certain she's the Pagori we're looking for. During her human life, Diane worked in a brothel."

"As a keeper?" asked Stuart.

"No, as a prostitute." Sam gave a faint smile at the shocked faces staring at her.

Jared draped a possessive arm over the back of her chair. "Originally, Diane came from a prestigious family in Long Island. She ran away from home when she was a teenager. Considering her father was charged fifteen years later for sexually abusing his niece, it's not such a stretch to conclude that Diane left home because her father had been doing the same to her."

CONSUMED

"She was an easy target for pimps," I pointed out sadly.

Jared nodded. "This particular pimp was known for using emotional manipulation rather than violence as a way to recruit and control his employees."

"You can picture it now, can't you?" said Sam. "Here we have this lost girl who's been exploited, is all alone, and feels unloved. Some bloke comes along, tells her she's beautiful and pretends to care for her, making her the focus of his superficial charm. The pimp then makes himself the centre of her world, isolating her from others by convincing her that he's the only person who cares for her. He shelters her, feeds her, seduces her, and makes her totally dependent on him. Which only makes it easier for him to take control when he says, 'Hey, it wasn't all for free; now you owe me money and you'll have to work for me to pay me back'. Diane was a prostitute in his brothel—"

"Wait a minute, she was a victim of this shit, and yet she opened a brothel of her own?" Damien's voice rang with both disgust and bafflement.

"It's sadly not uncommon for prostitutes to attempt to recruit other prostitutes," Chico told him. His human years on the police force had probably taught him that.

"As for opening her own brothel..." Sam shrugged. "It could have been her way to reclaim the control she lost when she was exploited this way. The reversal of roles means she seized the power, isn't a victim anymore."

"And it's probably a little bit of that 'if you can't beat them, join them'," said Denny.

"She's angry at men." When everyone looked at me questioningly, I went on, "She lures her clients, who are mostly men, with this unique brothel, records their deeds, and holds it over their heads by blackmailing them – punishing them with what they've done. The people she forced to work there...they were just pawns to her."

Sam cocked her head as several emotions flitted across her face. "You're right. This wasn't about making money or trafficking. The brothel was just something that enabled her to punish the type of men she believes wronged her all her life."

"It would even explain why she owned the fight club." Jared rubbed his nape. "A primary result for the men – even the winners – was pain. By owning that club, she was the bringer of it, in a sense."

"It's looking like this Diane Glass is in fact the owner," said David.

115

"Please tell me the researchers have an address." Butch sounded eager to exact some retribution.

"Actually, they have two addresses." Sam's words made the entire squad smile. I felt the air change and lighten with anticipation and eagerness. Both emotions fairly radiated off Salem – typical.

"She has an apartment in Manhattan and a house in the South of France. We'll hit France, and one of the other squads will visit—" Sam paused as the door swung open and Evan entered, closing it behind him.

He held up a hand. "Sorry, but I knew you were having a meeting about the brothel, and I figured you'd all be interested in this." He took a seat before continuing. "My squad and I managed to track down one of the suppliers. The son of a bitch was already dead – nothing but a pile of ashes."

"Do you think Diane got to him first?" asked Reuben. "Cleaning house, so to speak?"

Evan sighed. "I don't know. But some of the clients were found dead too. Get this: all of them, just like the supplier, had some kind of red powder mixed in with their ashes."

I gasped. "Demons."

All heads whipped round to face me, but it was Salem who spoke. "What?"

"All demons are impervious to fire, but some can actually create and manipulate it. From what my friend told me, some exceedingly powerful demons can call on the flames of hell, though it's extremely rare. Ashes left behind from hell's flames are said to contain a red residue."

"And Knox Thorne is rumoured to be extremely powerful," mused Jared.

"He is," said Salem. "I could feel it at the hotel."

Sam nodded. "Me too. I also got the feeling he was trying to conceal just how much power lives inside him. But why would he do that?"

I shrugged. "Only he can answer that."

"And you've got no idea at all what kind of demon he could be?"

I shook my head. "It's possible that he's an incubus, since his sexual allure is off the charts." I smiled at Salem's growl.

"Whatever the case," rumbled Salem, "it seems like the demons are on the right track."

"That's definitely not good." Chico cursed. "God knows what the supplier told him before they killed him."

Max skimmed a hand over his military haircut. "Like finding everyone responsible for this shit won't be hard enough without racing against the demons."

"Yep." Sam shrugged. "But if the situation was reversed and one of mine had been kidnapped and forced to work in a brothel, I would do everything in my power to avenge them."

Harvey smiled. "That's why we love you, Coach." He blew her a kiss…and then jerked as an electrical charge from Jared zapped his chest.

"Back to the matter of our upcoming trip to France…Ava, I'm sure you've figured out that you're here because I want you to come along." Sam gave Salem a 'don't interfere' look.

After a stare-out with Sam that almost had me laughing, he grunted, resigned. "She stays with me every second," he stated, his tone non-negotiable.

Jared struggled to hide his smile. "Fine."

"When are we leaving?" I asked.

"As soon as Sam and I have talked to the squad who will be checking out Diane's Manhattan apartment." Jared got to his feet. "All of you expect a call within the next hour. And be ready."

(Salem)

"I have to say, I wasn't expecting this." Stuart's words penetrated the silence that had fallen the moment Jared had teleported us to France, only to find the sight in front of us.

"Maybe we should have, considering what Evan told us earlier," said David, which was a valid point.

I grunted. "The demons seem to be ahead of the race." Why else would the house be nothing more than a heap of ashes – ashes that contained red residue?

Jared tapped his temple. "I just heard from Evan. The interior of Diane's apartment has been destroyed by what could be mistaken for an average fire, if it wasn't for the red residue in the ashes."

"Hey, do you think someone's leaking information out of The Hollow?" Max asked Sam as we circled the scorched ground where the house had once stood.

Her brows drew together. "Leaking info?"

"Think about it," pressed Max. "The demons didn't seem to be on track. Then suddenly, they're going after the same people as us, and they've even beaten us here."

"As Thorne said, demons have their ways of finding things out," said Ava, who was walking in front of me; edging away from a large mound of debris.

Max looked at her. "Yeah, and one of those ways could be by corrupting one of our own."

Sam puffed out a long breath. "I hate to say this, but you could be right, Max."

Satisfied by that, Max continued. "It could even be that they've possessed the mind of one of the legion."

Jared turned to Ava. "Are demons capable of possession? Or is that a myth?"

"From what I've heard, it's rare," she replied. "Only enormously powerful demons can do it."

"Demons like Knox Thorne," reflected Jared, shooting her a meaningful glance. Ava shrugged.

"You could have Ryder search the mind of every legion member," suggested Damien. "He'd find the taint, right?"

"Yeah," allowed Sam, "but we're talking a *lot* of people. It could take days for him to find out whether our suspicions are right."

Jared squatted and scooped up a little of the red powder with his finger. "A better question would be: was Diane inside the house when the demons destroyed it?"

Sam halted next to him. "And we need an answer fast."

Butch stared at the remains of the house with an agitated glint in his eyes. "So how do we find out if she's alive or if she's part of the ashes we see here?"

Jared stood upright. "We visit her Sire. He'll know if she's dead, because their blood-link will have severed if that's the case. And if she is alive, he could lead us to her."

Denny grimaced. "I doubt he'll give her up easily."

"Of course he won't," said Sam. "She's part of his nest, and a blood-link has a strong effect on the mind. His loyalty will be to his nest, first and foremost, whether we like it or not."

"What we need to know is how far he'll be willing to go to protect her." Jared glanced at the cloudy sky. "It's one thing to be reluctant to hand Diane over; it's another thing altogether if he's prepared to hide her. He might even be prepared to fight us."

"You really think he might fight you?" Harvey sounded surprised.

"As the Grand High Pair, we're due respect and obedience. But it doesn't always work that way." Sam toed a small scorched rock. "There'll always be people eager to overthrow us, for one thing. And no leader of a nest is going to appreciate being *ordered* to do anything by anyone – especially to give up one of his own, thereby sentencing her to death. As such, there's a huge chance Diane's Sire won't help. That's assuming, of course, that she isn't already dead."

"You could speak to the vampires she created, too," Ava suggested. "They each have blood-links with her, they'll know if she's alive."

"I'll assign one of the squads to the task."

"In the meantime, we'll have our researchers dig up everything about Diane's Sire," declared Jared. "Then tomorrow night, we pay him a visit."

Butch arched a brow. "And if he doesn't do what you ask?"

It was Sam who responded, her expression blank. "He dies."

CHAPTER TEN

(Salem)

Conscious that we would be going on an assignment in a few hours' time, I went to pick up some NSTs at dusk, since our stock had ran low. I wanted Ava at top strength when we paid Diane's Sire a visit, particularly since there was a chance that a fight might break out.

It was as I was retrieving a crate of bottles from the walk-in refrigerator at the store that I heard people coming up behind me. The familiar scents told me exactly who it was. Ignoring their presence, I rounded Will and Gina and went to the counter. Annoyingly, they trailed after me.

Gina did her best to make eye contact, but I refused to look at her. "You're not angry that I hurt your little Svente's feelings, are you, Salem?" Like that would make me not only childish but touchy.

"I think he must be," said Will.

"Didn't I say we were done?" I muttered, dismissive.

"I'm your Sire, Salem. We'll never be 'done'." Will's smug tone made me want to smash my elbow into his throat.

Instead, I paid for the crate and then left the store. The fuckers continued to follow me.

"So it would seem that you're stuck with me."

I wanted to wipe away that self-satisfaction, and I knew one way to do it. "There are ways of breaking the blood-link, Will." I kept my answer vague, not wanting to reveal Imani's gift. I was betting that

120

Imani would be willing to break it if Ava asked.

"You would Bind with Ava?" Pure astonishment dripped from Gina's words.

Of course she would ask that since, as far as those who didn't know of Imani's gift were aware, the only way to break a blood-link was to replace it with another. Binding with Ava would destroy my link to Will. But that would mean forming a psychic, unbreakable bond to her – one that wouldn't permit any physical or emotional distance between us.

I waited for panic to set in at the very idea of it, but it didn't come. There was actually an appeal to having the tie with Ava that Jared had with Sam, to be that deeply connected to her. And it would mean Ava couldn't be free of me. Not that I'd ever let her go, but I was selfish and possessive enough to find the added assurance sort of...comforting. And if there was anyone who I was willing to allow so deep into my soul, it was Ava.

Will must have taken my silence as a reluctance to admit that I would never Bind with her, because I could hear the smirk in his voice as he then taunted, "You can't escape me, Salem. No matter what you do, you will never change the fact that I'm your Sire." Like I was stuck under his rule.

"You lost your authority over me the moment I joined the legion." Even he couldn't deny the truth of that statement.

"You owe me," he growled. "You would have died in that alley if it wasn't for me. The people who ordered the death of your—"

I had my hand around his throat in under a millisecond. "Don't say it." Apprehension flashed across his face just as a tingle of fear shot down our link. Will was strong and a good fighter, but I'd always unnerved him on some level. I'd seen it in his eyes, heard it in his voice, and felt it through the link a thousand times. Maybe part of his wariness was that my emotions weren't so clear to him; according to Will, he only felt 'tiny flickers' of emotion from me, as if I was too closed off.

"Let him go, Salem," urged Gina, gripping my arm. I shook her off.

"I gave you your revenge," Will reminded me. "Now you must repay that debt."

I released him with a shove. "I couldn't get you a position in the legion even if I wanted to. It doesn't work that way."

"But you can talk to Sam and Jared. You can put in a good word for me. I would make a valuable trainer."

Even if there were trainers within the legion, I wouldn't have done any such thing. Not after the devious shit he'd pulled at the meal. "If you're so confident in your suitability, you don't need my interference." I strode away, and they thankfully didn't try to follow.

"You broke the golden rule I gave you during your training."

I didn't turn at the sound of his voice.

"I told you never to allow yourself any weaknesses. But you have one now, don't you? Sventés are so fragile compared to us, aren't they? So easily breakable."

Halting sharply, I slowly turned to face him. "Are you threatening Ava?" I rumbled, sure my irises were glowing red.

"Of course not." He sounded genuinely offended, but his eyes glinted with amusement at my angered response. "I don't hurt women. You know that." But Gina would have no problem with hurting Ava. And if Will wished it, she happily would.

"Sam and Jared might have vowed to let you stay here, but I can promise you right now that if either of you hurt Ava, they will banish you all from this island faster than you can blink. But I'll get there faster, and I'll make sure you don't leave this place alive."

"You'd never hurt me." But Will didn't appear as sure as he sounded. He was right to be worried.

It was rare for vampires to harm their creators. Even if the vampires had no regard or time for their creators, they respected the fact that they had Turned them. Plus, not only was the blood-link overpowering for the mind, it was incredibly painful to break unless it was replaced with another.

All of that would make a vampire extremely hesitant to harm their creator. But I knew for a fact that none of that would keep Will alive if he did anything at all to harm Ava. "As you pointed out, I have one weakness. That weakness is the only being on this planet that's safe from me. Remember that."

"There are three entrances," Stuart told Sam and Jared after doing a perimeter check in his molecule form of the club opposite us. "One at the front, one at the back, and one at the side. The only entrance being used is the front."

From our spot on top of a twelve storey building across the street, we could see the line of people hoping to get into the club belonging to Giles Rowland – Diane's Sire. It was guarded by four Pagoris, all of whom were vigilant.

"We need to cover all three doors," Sam told us.

"In case Giles tries to flee?" Ava asked from beside me.

"Yes, and also in case he decides he wants a fight and calls for back-up. I doubt he will, but it's best to be cautious. Stuart, Damien – I want you covering the side. Reuben, Harvey – you guard the back door."

"If people start trying to get in or out," began Jared, "contact me." All they would need to do was direct a thought at him. "The rest of you will come through the front with me and Sam, watch our backs."

So that was what myself, Ava, Chico, Butch, David, Denny, and Max did. As we approached the club, three of the bouncers straightened to their full height, their posture confrontational. The fourth paled.

"There's a line," spat one of them.

The fourth bouncer bowed at both Sam and Jared. "It's an honour to meet you." That was when the other three realised that, hey, we weren't your average vampires. They also bowed as they opened the doors wide, allowing us all to enter. The place was dark, loud, and smelled strongly of sex and blood.

Ava leaned into me. "Do you think these humans know they're around supposedly mythological creatures?"

Noticing that one human had a set of fangs buried in her throat, I grunted. "Maybe. I think someone wipes those memories before they leave. A lot of Kejas can do that."

Jared tipped his chin toward the bar. "There's our guy."

I recognised the tall, grim looking vampire from the photograph the researchers had provided. I'd suspected then that I'd met him before, long ago. Now, I was certain I was right, but I couldn't recall where from.

There were three Pagoris either side of Giles, keeping others from getting too close. None of them were aware of our presence. Yet. It was really only a matter of time.

One of the nearby vampires accidentally bumped into Jared and swiftly turned – maybe to apologise. Then he gawped, clearly very much aware of who he was looking at. Without moving his eyes from Jared, he tapped the vampire behind him with the back of his hand. The guy turned, joined his friend in gaping at Jared, and then clicked his fingers at another vampire to gain his attention. On and on it went – one vampire wordlessly warning another, who warned another, who warned another, until eventually news of our arrival reached Giles just as the music abruptly switched off.

Giles snapped to full alertness, eyes searching for us. A wave of his hand caused the crowd to part, creating a path. We followed Sam and Jared as they strolled casually toward Giles.

Smiling graciously, he bowed at them; his guards copied the move. "It is a pleasure to meet you both."

I might have believed that if it wasn't for the apprehension that very briefly glinted in his eyes. I was betting he knew exactly why we were there.

"Same to you," drawled Jared. The civil exchange seemed to relax the crowd, and the music came back on.

As Giles introduced his guards, I briefly studied each of them, and was surprised to discover that I'd met one of them before. Going by the black glower he was wearing, he recognised me too. And that was when I realised why Giles was so familiar.

Why does that guard look like he wants to castrate you? Jared asked telepathically.

Back when I worked for Will in his fight club, I was pitted against this guy by Giles.

I take it you won?

Knocked him unconscious in under ten seconds – that was without using my gift.

Despite that glower, it wasn't that particular guard that was at risk of seriously pissing me off. It was the one who was raking a heated gaze over Ava. I shifted closer to her, gaining his attention, and shot him a 'don't even fucking think about it' glare. Wisely, he averted his gaze.

Rather than introducing each of us, Sam simply said, "We brought along some friends."

Giles did a very quick study of each of us, and his eyes lingered on me. "You're one of Will's vampires. Salem, isn't it?" I merely nodded. Giles then turned to the bartender. "Hal, please get our guests whatever drink they choose. It's on the house, of course."

Sam smiled as she perched herself on a stool. "I appreciate the gesture, Giles, but we're unfortunately not here to socialise." Jared sidled up to her, presenting a united front.

CONSUMED

"Oh?" Giles' smile wavered slightly. "Then what has earned me the honour of your presence?"

"I think you know. But let's pretend that you don't. Let's pretend that you didn't watch or hear of the announcement that Jared and I made on V-Tube. Let's even pretend that you didn't know we'd mentioned the involvement of a vampire who has a gift that protects their identity in that announcement. *Or* we could drop the pretence and have a straightforward conversation that doesn't insult anyone's intelligence."

Giles inclined his head, admitting, "I saw the announcement. You think the person you are searching for may be Diane."

He didn't say it may have *been* Diane, didn't say her name in the past tense, which would suggest she was still alive.

Sam shrugged casually. "We'd simply like to talk to her."

"Many vampires have gifts similar to Diane's."

"That they do, Giles. That they do. Which is why we need to briefly speak with each one of them."

"Hopefully it will be a case of crossing Diane off the list of suspects," said Jared. "Where do we find her?" His expectation of an answer was clear in his expression and tone.

"She has an apartment in Manhattan."

"Yes, one of our squads did pay it a little visit." Sam sighed. "It seems that there was some kind of fire. Does she have any other homes?"

"Not that I am aware of. But I do not know the business of each one of my vampires."

"Her entire nest has gone into hiding." Sam had been pretty pissed on hearing that from the squad she'd assigned to find them. "It's not looking good for dear Diane. It's important that we talk to her."

"I wish I could help, but—"

"Don't play games." Jared's voice was like a whip. Giles' guards tensed, ready to protect their Sire. My past opponent was focused totally on me, probably desperate for an excuse to attack.

"People of various species were kidnapped, sold, and forced to work in a brothel," continued Jared, his voice close to a growl. "The owner was also blackmailing the clients. It is imperative that we take care of this, because if we don't, another species might."

Giles' face fell. "Some survived?"

Jared evaded the question. "The trail will eventually lead back to a suspiciously absent Diane, which will then lead to you." And he'd pay for what Diane did.

"There was a demon in that place." Sam's revelation made Giles blanch. "She got away."

Giles swallowed. "I heard that a horde of demons has been hunting vampires." And it wasn't a stretch to conclude it had something to do with the brothel.

"It will only be a matter of time before they come knocking at your door, Giles," she pointed out.

"What do you want from me?"

"I told you, we want Diane."

His sigh was resigned. "I do not know her exact location. She told me she must go into hiding, but she refused to tell me where." That was not only an admission of her guilt, but a confession that he had withheld her guilt.

Sam's expression hardened. "You should have come forward, Giles."

"Would you give up one of your squad?"

"No. But if they did the sick shit that Diane did, I would – though it would pain me to do it – end their lives."

"You should know that she is infuriated by your interference. You have lost her a lot of money."

Sam's smile was crooked. "Trust me, Giles, she ain't more infuriated than we are."

Jared spoke then. "Your blood-link must give you some idea of her location."

Giles shook his head. "Her gift conceals her even from me. It is impossible to find Diane unless she wants to be found."

"Then you must get *her* to come to *you*," Sam told him. "And then you must give her up."

"I do not know where—"

"You can find a way to contact her," interrupted Jared. "And I'm sure you can convince her to come to you. You're her Sire, after all."

"Five nights." Sam hopped off the stool. "You have five nights to lure her to you or to find out her location. When we receive your call, we'll come for her. Don't disappoint me, Giles." The latter words were hard.

Panic glinted in Giles' eyes. "It will not be easy to find her."

Jared snickered. "Neither will what we do to anyone who stands in the way of us and Diane – that includes you."

(Ava)

"What do you think Giles will do?" Sprawled on top of Salem on a beach lounger, I propped my chin up on his chest, enjoying the feel of his fingers threading through my hair.

"If he's got any sense, he'll give Diane up. But my bet is that he'll try to cover for her, worried he'll lose the trust and loyalty of his nest if he gives up one of his own."

"Then it's a good thing that Sam and Jared have sent Sebastian to track her." He was an expert tracker; the best The Hollow had.

"There's no one that guy couldn't find."

"I called the infirmary earlier to ask Mary Jane how Rosa was doing. She's getting better. Turns out, though, that a few more of the survivors came around." I smiled wanly. "Despite Rosa's assurances that they were safe, the newly awakened banded together and tried to escape. Can't say I blame them for taking advantage of the fact that they were finally lucid. Thankfully, they calmed down once Mary Jane sent for Sam."

"Did they have any useful info?"

I shook my head. "According to Mary Jane, their stories were the same as Rosa's – even down to their Sires selling them. Sam and Jared are keeping them here for a while to be sure Diane can't get to them. Plus, there's a chance that the demons would track them down, hoping they know something. They're safer here."

"Do you think Max is right and there's a leak at The Hollow?"

I cocked my head. "I'd like to think not. But the more I think about it, the more it makes sense. I'd like to believe it's not intentional; that someone's not purposely betraying us."

He slipped a hand under my t-shirt, smoothing it up and down my back. "Coach and Jared will probably ask Ryder to search the minds of every member of the legion."

"The poor guy will be drained by the end of it. Why are you glaring at me?"

"Maybe it's because you said 'the poor guy' in a soppy voice," he grumbled, looking adorably petulant.

"You can't seriously be jealous."

His hand paused in caressing my back. "You called him pretty." He spoke like I'd committed mass murder.

I had to smile. "Yeah? Well I prefer rugged, moody, and mentally unstable."

"Mentally unstable?"

"Hey, I didn't say it was bad. I like you just the way you are. Whether or not you continue to feel that way about me, we'll soon find out."

Salem's eyes narrowed dangerously. "Who made you feel you're not good enough exactly as you are?"

I blinked innocently. "No one."

"Don't bother bluffing, Sam already mentioned it."

Damn Sam for blabbing. "Like I said, it's not a big thing."

"Then there's no reason why you can't tell me."

Crap, I'd walked right into that one. "When I was a kid, I had a mild case of ADHD. People found it hard to cope with me." I shrugged, like it was nothing. Apparently my blasé act hadn't worked, because that seemed to piss him off even more.

"What 'people'?" When I didn't answer, he growled, "*Ava.* I answered your questions when you asked."

All right, that was a fair point. "My parents. My grandmother. My aunt. My foster parents. The last set of foster parents weren't so bad, but that was because I got a little better as I got older. It was only Cristiano who accepted me as I was." Until Salem.

His arms tightened around me as he muttered, "Bastards."

"I really wasn't easy to have around. I've always been a naturally upbeat, quirky person anyway. Add in the mild case of ADHD and it was no wonder they got tired of me."

"They had no fucking right to make you feel so bad about yourself." A look of realisation crossed his face. "You're waiting for me to get tired of you, too, aren't you?"

I could see that hurt him, which was the last thing I wanted to do. "I moved in with you, didn't I?"

"But you still worry I'll eventually reject you, don't you?" My expression must have answered that, because he pinned me with a serious gaze. "It's never going to happen."

"You say that now, but—"

"There is no 'but', baby. Shit, if either of us will think about leaving at some point, it will be you."

"Why would I leave my cuddly bear?"

A muscle in his jaw ticked. "*Ava.*"

"You already told me about how you avenged the death of your parents by turning vigilante. I'm still here."

"There's a lot more." It was a warning. "But it's too late for you to run. I've told you before: what's mine stays mine." As if to punctuate that claim, he took my mouth with a force that almost hurt. Every flick of his tongue and every touch of his hands were sure and confident. And I was soon panting and desperate for more. Which, of course, was what he wanted.

I pulled back. "Okay, okay, I'm officially distracted. I won't push you to elaborate. But you'll have to tell me some time."

"Some time," he agreed rather reluctantly. And I knew that was the best deal I'd get.

CHAPTER ELEVEN

(Ava)

When Salem left for one of his squad's training sessions at dusk, I'd been green with envy. I knew Sam and Jared gave them combat training, and the idea of gaining better control of my combat-based gift was damn appealing. So when Sam had called me five minutes after Salem left and invited me to come along – and to bring the other girls with me – I hadn't hesitated.

Mere seconds after I'd entered the arena, Salem appeared at my side; his face a question mark. I gave him a bright, excited smile. "Guess what! Sam invited us. She wants us to undergo some training. Isn't that great?"

His entire body went rigid. "Training?" he echoed, incredulous and disapproving.

"Yes," I replied, stretching out the word. "Why are you scowling at me?"

Before he could respond, Chico was speaking as he headed for Jude. "Did I just hear that you've been invited to train with us?"

Jude nodded happily, which earned her a frown. "Is there a problem with that?" Her expression both dared him to say 'no' and warned him not to even think it.

Salem turned to Sam, who was strolling toward us. "You can't expect them to train with us, Coach." The words were firm without being disrespectful.

Sam shrugged. "Why is that?"

"Yeah," drawled Alora, crossing her arms over her chest. "Why is that?"

It was Chico who answered. "They've had no training whatsoever, Coach. We're at an advanced level; they could never keep up." The rest of the squad had gathered at this point, none of whom looked pleased by the presence of me and my not-yet-fully-formed squad.

"I'm well aware of that, Chico," Sam told him. "I'm also aware that there's trouble brewing over dear old Diane. Here's what you're all not getting. It's likely that one of two things will happen. Either Giles will call to inform us that he's lured Diane to his club, or he'll give us her location. In both cases, we'll be walking into a trap because it's clear that the bloke has no intention of giving her up.

"That means there'll be a battle at some point – maybe with Giles, maybe with Diane herself, or maybe even with both of them. I need these girls prepared for the battle. I need to know they feel confident enough to protect themselves. They won't be confident without some training. For the next few evenings, I need you all to help with that."

Chico took a step back. "I'm sorry, Coach, but I can't. Part of training is learning to deal with pain and keep on going, and I can't hurt women."

Cassie frowned, confused and frustrated. "You must have hurt women during battles."

"Yeah, but that was different. They were enemies; it was a case of my life or theirs. But *this*...you seven are under our protection, and I can't hurt any of you." The rest of the squad nodded, their postures rebellious.

Sam sighed. "Admirable, yet irritating."

I was in agreement with that. While their protectiveness was kind of cute, it was also annoying and even insulting.

"Chico, go stand against the eastern wall. Cassie, take a spot against the western wall so that you're directly opposite him. There should be at least three car-spaces between you."

Grinning like a Cheshire cat, Cassie followed Sam's order.

"Good," said Sam once the two vampires were in position. "Now Chico, hit her with some darts." He hesitated, clearly balking at the idea. "Come on. Reuben has reduced the effectiveness of your gift. The thorns will do nothing more than make her itch."

"Fine." Chico inhaled deeply, raised his hand…and nothing. Sweat beaded his brow, and lines of strain marked his face as it became a mask of frustration.

"Chico, *we're waiting.*"

"I can't," he bit out.

"Why? Because you're reluctant to hurt her?"

"No."

"Then, why?"

His upper lip curled. "Because I can't fucking do it. I want to, but it's not happening. I just…*can't.*"

"That's right. Would you like to know why, Chico?" Sam looked at me. "Should we tell him?"

"Oh yeah." I smiled at Chico. "It's really good."

Maya nodded. "You'll love it. Really."

"The reason you can't do it…is that Cassie won't let you," explained Sam. "Right now, she's in your mind – a presence so subtle you can't even feel it. She can stop you from harming her, can make you do absolutely anything, and there's nothing you can do about it."

"I could even take full control of your mind," Cassie revealed. "And if I wanted to, I could even remove your memory of this moment afterwards, so that you won't even remember it."

"Would you like that?" Sam asked Chico. "At least then your pride will still be intact."

"Point taken," Chico mumbled.

Reuben exhaled heavily. "Okay, Coach, I get it. This kind of gift will protect Cassie well. But they can't *all* control minds."

Sam tapped her chin with her finger. "Hmm. I tell you what, why don't you go get yourself comfortable in Chico's spot? Ava, you can replace Cassie."

I clapped a little. "Ooh, this will be fun." I stopped when Salem put a restraining hand on my arm. "Easy, big guy." I patted his chest, expecting him to scowl at me. But he was staring at Sam, shaking his head.

Reuben's huff was almost petulant. "This isn't necessary. I know what Ava's gift is, and I know she's good – I've seen her fight."

"But you still don't think she stands a chance against one of you super-duper blokes, do you?" fired Sam, crossing her arms over her chest.

"Not when I'm much bigger than her, and not when all I have to do is touch her *once* for her to be vulnerable to me."

"Fine. So show us."

Salem shook his head again. "I won't let him hurt her, Coach."

"He's not going to hurt her. All he needs to do is touch her to weaken her gift, thus proving his point." She motioned Reuben toward Chico's spot, and he practically stomped all the way there.

I smiled at the girls, shaking my head sadly. "Will they never learn?" A clever defensive move had me free from Salem's hold and moving to replace Cassie.

I heard Sam muttering to Salem, 'She needs your support right now, not coddling.'

Standing opposite my opponent, my feet shoulder-width apart, I arched a brow. "Ready, Reub?"

He grinned cockily. "Yes, let's—" Then he found himself zooming backwards, crashing into the wall, after a solid kick to the chest from me. He'd underestimated my speed – how silly. And entertaining.

Before he could even think about retaliating, I had my hands on his head. "In this teensy, weensy moment, I could have snapped your neck."

He bounced to his feet. "That wasn't fair! You gave me no warning!"

"Oh, and someone you face in a battle will give you a warning, will they?"

"She's right, Reuben." Jared sighed tiredly. "You should have known better."

I skipped to Alora's side, waving at a frowning Salem. So cute.

Sam scanned the rest of the squad. "Anyone else care to be an arse?"

The girls shot Butch looks of disgust as he stepped forward. "Look, Coach, I'm not saying that the girls aren't tough. They are. But..." He flicked an impatient glance at Imani, who I'd noticed he could be a little *too* protective of at times. "Imani's gift is substantial, but it's to sever blood-links. In a battle, what can that possibly –?" Abruptly, he cried out and dropped to his knees; his hands cradling his head.

The girls and I watched in morbid fascination as he groaned in agony through gritted teeth. I knew that Imani's gift allowed her to sift through a person's mind with a psychic hand. Unlike Ryder, she couldn't access memories or thoughts, but she could find and then snap any blood-link. And I wondered just what she was doing with that psychic hand at the moment.

"Looks like he wants to jump out of his own skin, doesn't he?" observed Paige, her voice detached and clinical.

Alora elbowed her gently. "You know, I was just going to say that."

"I'd feel bad if he wasn't such an ass," said Imani.

Jude patted her back supportively. "Some people have to learn the hard way."

Cassie sighed. "It's such a shame that he didn't just learn from Chico or Reuben's mistakes."

"When you think about it," said Maya, "this is actually his own fault."

I nodded. "Totally."

"Stop, stop, stop!" Butch growled, pounding the ground with his fist. Then suddenly he sagged, panting.

"What did she do?" asked David once Butch was upright.

"She strummed the blood-link in my head like a fucking banjo!"

Imani shrugged innocently. "You wanted to know how it could possibly help in a battle. I figured it would be easier to show you."

Maya looked at her. "So it's an ability that will not only hurt, but distract your attacker and make them vulnerable. I like it."

Scanning the squad, I almost laughed. Their shoulders were slumped, they were squirming uncomfortably, and they were wearing child-like pouts.

Sam released a cleansing sigh. "Now, I take it we're not going to hear any more of the 'but they're girls, we can't harm them' bollocks." When none of the guys spoke, she nodded. "Fabulous. Let all this serve to remind you that it doesn't matter how powerful you are, there'll always be someone who can better you. Look at Ava…Such a cute, harmless-looking exterior. But if I let her loose on any of you, there's a high chance she'd win. At the very least, you'd walk away with some injuries and a bruised pride – just like our Reuben."

Whatever a clearly embarrassed Reuben mumbled under his breath earned him a whack over the head from Salem.

Sam turned to me and the girls. "During training, there are three goals. One, to learn to channel all your energy so that there's none leaking from you. Two, to improve the use of your gifts so that you can not only improve as individuals but as a squad. And three, to know each other's gifts inside out.

"Unfortunately, I have a small number of nights to get you prepared for whatever happens next. That's why having these blokes here will help. The first thing I'm going to teach you is how to suck in all the preternatural energy that's leaking from you. You began producing this unnatural energy when you were Turned, causing your mind and body to evolve. If you can't hold it inside you, you won't be able to use your gift to its full potential, and you'll also be vulnerable. We can't have that."

Disappointed to find that I had energy leaking from me – only a little, but still – I was absolutely determined to fix it. I followed Sam's instructions to the letter. I got the hang of it pretty quickly, since I was determined not to show any weakness in front of the guys or give them ammunition to change their minds. I suspected that was why the other girls quickly got the hang of it too.

Once Sam was satisfied with our attempts, we moved on to improving our strengths while also tackling our weaknesses. The squad joined in for that, and they actually did it without grumbling. How shocking. Sam assigned one guy to each girl, wanting us all to have some one-to-one time before the session was over.

When it came time to assign me a helper, Sam said, "My concern with you, Ava, is that your gift can't protect you against psychic attacks."

I sighed. "Yeah, that's a bummer."

"But a huge strength that comes with your gift is that you're bloody fast. You can sense psychic energy rippling through the air, right?" At my nod, she continued, "That type of energy hits fast and hard. But so do you. So I'm thinking that with some training, you could learn to dodge the psychic energy with your enhanced speed. Want to try it?"

I smiled. "Let's do it."

"Salem, we need you for this. First, though, we need Reuben to weaken your punch so it's nothing more than a psychic slap."

Salem looked from me to Sam. "You expect me to –?" He shook his head. "No."

She gave him a weak smile. "Salem, I know it will be hard. But I also know that if anyone else here even *slightly* harms her, you will put them in a coma – happily."

He conceded that with a grunt and a slight tilt of the head.

"Plus, if you help her, you'll also have peace of mind that she's learning to better protect herself. That's important to you."

A muscle ticked in his jaw. "I'll do it."

As soon as Reuben weakened Salem's gift, we began. When the first slap hit, I was surprised. It actually *felt* like a slap across the head, but *inside* my head – acting as a jolt to my mental equilibrium and awareness. It didn't hurt as badly as I'd expected, though. Still, every time a psychic slap came my way and I didn't manage to evade it, Salem would wince or curse.

When Sam realised he'd started to go easy on me, she threatened to pair me up with David. The impact of his psionic boom when weakened apparently felt like a burning zap to the brain. Unwilling to allow David anywhere near me with that gift, Salem had relented.

Then he turned into a total bastard and attacked me without mercy. It should have pissed me off, but I actually did a lot better after that. Mostly because I knew that he would no longer pull his punches – no pun intended – so I'd need to move my skinny ass fast. Plus, I saw the guilt that flashed on his face each time I flinched at one of his slaps. It made me more determined to improve.

By the time the session was over, I was pretty good at it – even if I did say so myself. Not that it made Salem feel any better. He turned broody and growly, which I probably shouldn't have found cute or amusing, but I *so* did.

We had an hour long break for lunch, and then we were back in the arena. We repeated the same exercise again, which I was certain was going to make Salem explode with anger at some point. The only thing that kept him relatively calm was that what he was doing was actually working.

Near the end of the session, Sam gathered me and the other girls together. "Now it's time for me to pair you with someone from your own squad who will suit you during battle – who has a gift that can complement your own. Alora, you're with Maya."

I wasn't surprised by that. We'd discovered that Alora's gift of communicating with animals allowed her to fully understand Maya when she was in her jaguar-form – to understand the meaning behind each hiss, chuff, and growl. Not only that, they could communicate telepathically using pictures while Maya was in that form.

"Paige, you're with Imani," Sam then announced.

That wasn't much of a surprise either. Paige was extremely protective of her friend, and I'd seen them work well together during battle. Imani would disable her opponent as she'd done with Butch, and then Paige would use her gift of transferring injuries to destroy them.

"Lastly...Jude, I'll be matching you with Cassie."

I understood that, too. Jude's gift wasn't offensive, so it would be best if she worked with someone like Cassie, whose gift of mind control could help protect her. Also, Cassie wasn't the best fighter in terms of combat, whereas Jude was well-trained in that area so she would be good at watching her back.

Sam gave me a faint smile. "Unfortunately, that leaves you without a partner. But that's only for now. Three more will eventually join the squad, and one of those will be paired with you. During this battle, you'll have Salem as your shadow anyway."

That was true, so I didn't mind so much that I was without a partner. As such, I was in a damn good mood when I got home. Salem, however, was in a very foul one. "Must you be so miserable?" I asked with a smile.

He pulled me to him. "I hated hurting you. It goes against every instinct I've got."

Aw, so sweet. I looped my arms around his waist. "You wasn't hurting me. You were helping me learn to protect myself against someone who gladly will. That's important."

He rested his forehead against mine. "I don't know if I can do it again."

"Sure you can, because it's working. Besides, Sam was right. You'll go bat-shit crazy on anyone who hurts me, even if they are part of your squad."

He just grunted, clearly unhappy that I'd won that argument.

"I think Reuben's going to be mad at me for a while."

Salem's mouth twitched. "You could be right." His hands framed my face. "Such an innocent, pretty package for a deadly female."

"It's probably wrong that I'm more flattered by 'deadly' than 'pretty'." I smoothed my hands up and down his back soothingly. "Stop sulking."

A frown. "I don't sulk."

"You *so* do. It's sort of adorable."

"I'm not adorable."

"Ooh, here comes the growling. Makes me all gooey inside."

A glint of humour entered his eyes just as his mouth curved. "In theory, your teasing should further piss me off. But it seems you can weirdly calm me down this way."

"Does this mean we can leave out the arguing and skip straight to the make-up sex?"

His mouth curved a little more as he scooped me up. "Works for me."

CHAPTER TWELVE

(Ava)

"I think I have paint in my ear."

Alora gagged. "I think I have it up my nose. One thing's for sure, it's going to take me some time to get it all out of my hair."

"Same here. We must look like rainbow cookies."

As part of our training, Sam and Jared had taken us, the squad, and the rest of the girls to Sam's tactical training field deep in the rainforest. We'd played a few games of paintball, all of which were designed to help us learn battle tactics like how to best engage and eliminate an opposing team, and also how to defend and hold outposts.

Even though we'd worn camouflaged overalls, padded gloves, and safety masks, paint had still managed to make its way into places it had no right being. Our socks and the collar of our t-shirts were also stained with blobs of paint. Feeling some squish between my toes wasn't a pleasant sensation.

After the games were over, Sam and Jared had sent us and the other girls ahead of them so that the guys could engage in a few much more advanced games. Jude, Paige, and Imani were giving Maya and Cassie a tour of the rainforest. Alora and I, however, were returning to our apartments to shower and change, since we were due to meet with Ryder soon to have our minds scanned for 'demon interference'. I seriously doubted that my mind had been compromised, but I wanted to be certain.

It was as we neared the fringe of the rainforest that we noticed a figure lounging against a thick, vine-covered tree. Gina laughed cruelly on spotting us. Did anyone want their boyfriend's ex to see them in a bad state? I didn't.

"A fashion statement of some kind?" she asked.

"I still can't quite believe it speaks," I said to Alora, who chuckled.

The amusement vanished from Gina's almond eyes. She was beautiful – there was no doubt about it. But she was cold, and that tainted it. At a guess, I'd estimate that she had been in her thirties when she was Turned. Being so much older than me and with so much more life-experience, she made me feel unworldly, young, and naïve in comparison – especially since she persisted to call me 'child' and used that condescending tone when talking to me.

I offered her a blank look. "Excuse us."

"I see that you haven't gotten past what happened at the meal. Really, child, you're too sensitive."

"Whatever, old woman."

She almost snarled. Ooh, how fun. "I can't see it. I can't see what could possibly have drawn you and Salem together. You're nothing alike. You have nothing at all in common. Salem's always liked strong women. Not to mention that he's a breast man."

I adopted my airhead tone, knowing it drove her insane. "Yeah, but what I lack in breasts I make up for in pure awesomeness."

She ground her teeth so hard it was audible. And hilarious. "You can't honestly think it will last. Salem isn't going to join you in Munchkin Land."

"Sure he will. There's a wizard nearby and everything."

Ignoring that, she continued, "You have a lot to learn about men, child. Especially Salem, since—"

"Yeah, uh-huh, me too." I waved a hand dismissively. "I have stuff to do, so…" I went to pass, but she planted herself in front of me.

"You really do think you can hold onto him, don't you?" she sneered.

"And you really do think you can lure him away, don't you?"

"Astonishing," mused Alora. "Not to mention delusional."

"I can have any man I want, including Salem," Gina stated, adamant. "I can make even a Bound male into my very own puppet."

Fletcher was right; she saw Salem as a possession. To this woman, men were toys for her to play with and control. She liked that she could manipulate, seduce, and control them; that she could have a level of power over them.

"I'd wager I could even have Jared under my thrall."

Alora winced. "I'd advise you not to try it. If it worked – which I strongly doubt – Sam would kill you. And if it didn't work…well, Sam would still kill you."

I nodded. "Now, fascinating though this is, I have no intention of abandoning my schedule to give a shit about the petty crap that goes on in your head." Again I went to pass Gina, but she moved to block my path.

"You're not as blasé about this as you're acting," she insisted. "My presence here worries you. You know Salem will fall under my thrall, you know you could never forgive him for it, and you know part of the reason he'll so easily fall under my control is that he *wants* it."

Seriously, how could I not pity her? "Feel free to immerse yourself in that alternate reality if it makes you feel good about yourself. It would be cute if it wasn't so pathetic."

Ooh, that *really* pissed her off. She glowered as she advanced on me. "You little—"

A loud squawk split the air as a parrot came to land on the branch of a neighbouring tree. It bobbed its head as it squawked, "Gina's a slut, Gina's a slut, Gina's a slut."

I exchanged a knowing smile with Alora, who was looking suspiciously innocent. Sometimes I wished I had her gift.

Gina's glower turned deadly, and I expected her to cover the tiny distance between us with one huge lunge. Instead, she froze. And I quickly understood why. Jude, Paige, Imani, Maya, and Cassie were coming up behind me and Alora – presenting a wall of defence. Gina snickered and backed away. Her expression said 'we'll speak again soon'. Then, in vampire speed, she was gone. Good fucking riddance.

(Salem)

Ava laughed and smiled at people all the time, it was part of her nature. And they always laughed and smiled with her – it was the effect she had on people. It was fine.

Unless it was Ryder.

Entering Sam and Jared's office to find them laughing and joking like old friends, Ryder's hand on her elbow, made something dark and dangerous slither beneath my skin. I clenched my fists and ground my teeth as I attempted to get a hold on the fury, bitterness, and a strange black emotion I didn't recognise that began to curdle in my stomach. It was jealousy, I realised. Not something I was very familiar with.

Either Ava had sensed or scented my presence, because she turned with a welcoming smile. A slight crease formed between her brows as she took in my expression. Ryder instantly dropped his arm, recognising my possessive reaction.

Part of me wanted to storm over there, punch the 'pretty' little prick, and drag Ava out of the room. Evan and Alora, who were chatting in the corner, wouldn't prove to be a hindrance. Only two things stopped me from doing exactly that: one, Ava had stepped away from Ryder; two, there was no guilt in her expression. This wasn't the look of someone who had done anything wrong. She hadn't been flirting. She was loyal and good, and she didn't deserve my anger. It wasn't her fault that I could be a possessive and jealous bastard when it came to her.

That didn't mean I was going to leave her with the little fucker.

"Everything okay?" Ava asked, concerned, as I approached.

"Fine." I grabbed her hand and tugged her to my side, glaring at Ryder…who annoyingly seemed to find the situation funny.

"Ryder said my mind is like sunshine." She laughed.

Like sunshine? Was that supposed to be a pick-up line? Because if so, I might reconsider the whole punching thing.

"It's a refreshing place to be," elaborated Ryder. "Full of positivity and joy." There was no awe or longing in his voice, so I'd allow him to live. For now.

Ava dug her heels when I moved to leave. "Wait! I need to check if Alora's still game for movie night."

Movie night? As she flitted over to Alora and began a very animated conversation, Evan came toward me, drinking an NST.

"You had your mind scanned yet?"

I nodded. "Last night. No sign of demon interference."

"Good. I was telling Ava earlier that another supplier was found. Like the last one, he was a pile of ashes – ashes containing red residue. A high number of the clients we tracked were in the same state."

"So it's looking like there's a leak." And as much as I found that

CONSUMED

important, I couldn't give Evan my full attention; my gaze kept straying to Ava, and I was sure it was territorial.

"Sadly, yes." He exhaled heavily. "If that's true, I'd like to think the person has no idea what they've done. But it wouldn't be the first time that someone at The Hollow proved to be a traitor. The idea of it being someone in the legion…That's hard to stomach."

"Who else has access to the information?"

"Sam, Jared, Antonio, Sebastian, Ryder, and our researchers. I trust all of them."

I wasn't the trusting kind, so I couldn't say the same. But I found it hard to believe that any of them would betray The Hollow – particularly Sam, Jared, and Antonio.

Evan took a gulp of his NST. "I thought you might want to know that your Sire sought me out last night. He wants a position in the legion. Did he go to you about it first?"

I briefly glanced at Ava. "Yes. I sent him to Coach and Jared."

"He consulted them, too. When they blew him off, he came to me. He's persistent, I'll give him that."

"What did you say?"

"That there aren't any positions of any kind available right now." Another swig of his NST. "Even if there were, I would have turned him away. Sam doesn't trust him, and I respect her judgment. I know he's your Sire and that might offend you, but—"

"It doesn't offend me. When he came here, I saw another side of him." A side I didn't like or respect. I glanced at Ava again, frowning when I saw that Ryder had joined her and Alora.

"You don't have to worry about Ava and Ryder, you know." Evan sounded amused.

"I know." I realised right then that I trusted Ava. "Doesn't mean I like seeing him or any other guy touching her. And I'm not sure you're in a position to judge me on that." He could be just as bad with Alora.

"Oh, I know," he admitted with a smile.

"What the hell is movie night?"

"The girls get together once a month in one of their apartments. They watch a movie, eat crap, and do whatever things girls do. I don't know what those girl-things are, and I don't think I want to know." He shuddered a little, as if feminine things made him uncomfortable. Yeah, I could relate to that. His smile turned crooked and teasing. "I hear your new sofa cushions are nice."

143

I arched a brow. "How are all your plants?"

His smirk shrunk. "Bastard." There was no heat in the word.

"Clearly we're going to have to end their conversation for them." I went to Ava, picked her up by her t-shirt, and carried her out of the office.

She kicked her legs. "This is simply unnecessary."

Ignoring that, I zoomed to our apartment in vampire speed, only releasing her when we arrived in the living area.

She pivoted, glaring at me. "What was all that about?" Her confrontational posture slipped away as she then asked, "And why are you advancing on me like a feral wolf scenting prey?" She backed away, but there was no wariness in her expression as I stalked her.

Once her back met the wall, I placed my hands either side of her head. "You let him touch you."

Her mouth formed an 'O'. She patted my chest, and for once there was no patronisation in the act. "It was just my elbow. Nothing exciting or sexual or remotely important." Apparently, that was supposed to be a reassuring statement.

I brought my face close to hers, barely refraining from growling at her. "Not remotely important? *All* of you is important – inside and out." But thanks to the assholes in her past, Ava didn't see that, so she didn't see her importance to me. I'd told her several times, but she just wasn't hearing me. Insecurities still taunted her, and I hated that.

"You took what I said the wrong way."

"Whether it's your elbow, your ass, your breasts isn't the point – *every* inch of you matters." And every inch of her was mine. I slammed my mouth on hers, driving my tongue inside. Dominating, devouring, and consuming her with just my lips, tongue, and teeth. She softened under the assault, letting me lead. Pacifying me, I understood. I didn't want to be soothed. I wanted to fuck.

I unbuttoned and roughly shoved down her jeans. She kicked them off just as she pulled off my t-shirt. I whipped off her own, lifted her high by her waist, and latched on tight to a nipple. The texture and taste of her was a double assault on my senses, making my cock throb and ache. I was so hard it was actually fucking painful.

Moaning, she threaded her hands in my hair, tugging as I suckled and bit hard enough to sting. I switched my attention to her other breast, licking, nipping, and drawing the taut bud deep into my mouth. As the scent of her need swirled around me, a growl rumbled up my chest. "I love how you smell." I needed to be inside her. Right. Fucking. Now.

Snapping off her panties, I slid a finger through her folds and plunged it inside her, finding her slick and ready. "I want to fuck you deep and fast, baby." Withdrawing my finger, I tore open my fly and dropped her hard on my cock.

She gasped, curling her legs around my hips. "Salem…"

"So fucking good." Wanting the last few inches buried inside her, I slowly withdrew and then slammed home. "That's it." Cupping her ass, I pounded into her and she took it, arching into each thrust and clawing my back as she urged me on. It was wild and greedy and primal. The sounds she made fed the sexual thirst flaring through me.

I slid my hand between us and parted her folds so that my pelvis hit her clit with every forceful, possessive thrust. A voice in my head said I was being too rough, to slow down. But I couldn't. Too many feelings were battering at me, demanding an outlet. It wasn't just jealousy, wasn't just anger at the insecurities she had. It was the frustration that I couldn't make her see how important she was to me; every frantic thrust was an attempt to drive it home.

"Salem, I need to come," she panted.

I would have told her to hang on, that I wasn't done with her yet, and maybe she knew that…because she sank her teeth into my throat. I pounded harder, faster, and she screamed as she came, clenching and rippling around my cock. That and her Sv/enté saliva sent me hurtling over the edge. I rammed into her one final time as everything I had burst out of me, filling her.

As if every ounce of energy left her body, she slumped in my arms, panting. Still shuddering with aftershocks, I cupped her face and brought it to mine. "Did I hurt you?" She was no shrinking violet, but she was still small.

Her eyes flickered open. "Only in a good way."

Relieved, I carried her to the bathroom, took off the rest of my clothes, and then carried her into the shower stall. I didn't put her down as we stood under the spray. There was just something satisfying about carrying her, about the fact that she let herself lean on me. This strong female who kicked ass and had a core of steel let herself be vulnerable around me. It was a balm to my protective streak, and it showed a deep trust that humbled me.

Now if only she'd trust in everything I said…

Soaping her down, I spoke into her ear. "You have to stop underestimating your importance to me." When she went to speak, I put my finger to her mouth. "I know why you do it, but I'm not like those bastards. Stop expecting me to suddenly reject you."

She snorted. "Says the person who's keeping shit from me because he fears I'll do the same to him."

She said it with a small smile, but there was a glint of sadness in her eyes. That was when I realised… "It hurts you that I haven't told you everything." Jared had predicted as much, and it galled me to admit – even to myself – that the cocky bastard was right.

"Does it hurt that I've bared my soul and you haven't? Yes. Because it means you don't trust me."

"I do fucking trust you. Never say that." She was the only person I trusted completely.

She shook her head sadly as she struggled to get down and then rinsed off the soap. "If you trusted me, you'd tell me everything, because you'd trust that I'd stay with you no matter what."

Turning off the spray, I stepped out of the stall and grabbed two towels. "It isn't about trust."

"Yes, it is," she stated firmly, accepting the towel I offered her and wrapping it around herself. "You say I underestimate my importance to you. You do exactly the same thing."

I hadn't thought of it that way before. But she was right. The fact that I expected her to leave indicated that I didn't sense my importance to her. But then, I'd never really expected to *be* important to her.

Following me into the bedroom, she continued. "That you think I'll reject you hurts, just like it hurts you that I worry *you'll* reject *me*."

I whirled on her. "Baby, why *wouldn't* you reject me? I'm selfish. I'm aggressive, and pushy, and rude, and short-tempered. Not to mention possessive and jealous when it comes to you."

"You're also loyal, hard-working, protective, trustworthy, and a damn good soldier. Although you're an interfering bastard at times, you're also considerate and attentive; I don't care if that's only with me – it's still a side of you that exists."

Her words both warmed and hurt. Warmed because she saw good in me when I was pretty sure few else did. And hurt because I knew I could destroy the good she saw in just one conversation if she pushed for me to tell her everything.

"If you're so certain I'll turn away from you, wouldn't you rather find out sooner instead of later?"

No, because that would mean her leaving sooner instead of later. Keeping the towel wrapped around my waist, I lay on the bed and stared up at the ceiling. A 'fuck off' vibe had to be radiating from me. But of course Ava ignored that. She joined me on the bed and nestled against my side.

"Will you tell me a little about your mom?"

The gentle question took me by surprise. Honestly, I didn't want to talk about my mother, didn't want to remember what had happened to her. But better that than the other shit. "She was like you in some ways. Kind. Empathetic. But she wasn't strong. She saw good in everyone, but it was her downfall at times."

"What do you mean?"

I sighed. "It made her a shitty judge of character, especially when it came to men. My biological father was the worst. Hard. Cold. There was something missing in him. A conscience, maybe." I shrugged. "He was unfaithful and he saw no reason to hide it. He…hurt her. Beat her. A lot." I'd felt weak, powerless, and guilty that I couldn't protect her. "He left when I was seven, and I couldn't have been happier about it."

"Your stepdad was better?"

"He was good to her. They had a baby. My mother devoted practically all of her attention to Josh. Like she was determined to get it right second time round. I always felt on the fringe of the family, but I wasn't jealous. I knew she never meant to make me feel that way and it would have devastated her if she'd known."

"So you never told her."

"No."

Ava lightly ran her fingers over my chest. "See, it's not so hard to share stuff."

Knowing what she was getting at, I met her gaze. "You really want to know the rest?"

"I think it's time we got it out in the open so you finally realise I'm not going to leave."

Oh, she'd leave for sure. But if I persisted in keeping this from her, I'd drive her away anyway. What was the difference?

I returned my gaze to the ceiling, unable to look at her while shame and guilt rode me. "When I was in the last year of high school, I was with this girl, Sandra. I liked her, but she always did weird shit for attention, and tried to make me jealous. I had no time for mind games or people who wanted to play them. So I broke it off with her.

"Honestly, I didn't think it would bother her much." I still wasn't sure why it did. "But she took it badly. She'd call in the middle of the night, crying. She'd post crazy letters through my door. Hang around my house. Then the middle-of-the-night calls became bad; she'd call when her mother was at work, threatening to kill herself if I didn't go to her."

Ava inhaled sharply and kissed my shoulder. "It's okay. You don't have to say anymore."

I could have accepted that, left Ava to believe her suspicion was correct, and taken the easy way out. But that had never been my style. "Time and time again, I went round there, talked her down. She'd cry, ask why I didn't love her. I tried talking to her mother, telling her that Sandra needed some fucking help, but she didn't take it seriously." In fact, her mother had insisted that I was exaggerating.

"One night, Sandra called again. Said she thought there was someone in the house; that her mother was at work, and she wanted me to come over and check." I swallowed hard, fisting my hand in Ava's hair. "I didn't believe her. I found out the next day that an intruder had raped and killed her."

Cursing under her breath, Ava curled her arm tight around my waist. "It's a sad story, Salem. But you have to know that it's not your fault."

My gaze whipped to hers, filled with disbelief. "I didn't believe her, Ava. I hung up on her. Because of that, she's dead."

"You don't know that you could have stopped it, Salem." There was an understanding in Ava's voice that I hadn't expected. There was also pure steel – she wasn't budging on this. "Even if you had gone to her house, it could have been too late to help her." Bracing her weight on her elbow, Ava propped her chin on her hand. "Did she call the police too that night?"

"Yeah. After she called me."

"If they didn't get there on time, why would you believe that you could have?"

I knew there was a bitter curve to my mouth. "She lived at the corner of my street. It was a long street, sure, but it still wouldn't have taken me more than a minute to get there." But I hadn't bothered my ass to check. I'd dismissed Sandra's fear and gone back to bed.

"It's still not your fault," Ava maintained, still as fiercely adamant as before. "The blame belongs to the killer. Any ounce of responsibility you attempt to claim for his actions absolves him a little of what he did."

Not having thought of it that way before, it took me a minute to respond. "I still could have stopped it."

"Or you could have been killed too. Have you thought of that?"

No, I hadn't. And now I found myself staring curiously at Ava. The last thing I'd expected from her was this. Not only had a young girl gone through a horribly traumatic experience, she'd been murdered. That would undoubtedly sicken Ava. I could have stopped those things from happening, and I hadn't. Yet, there was no horror or judgement on her face.

She was infuriated. Infuriated because I didn't see things her way.

Just in case she wasn't getting the point…"A young girl died that night. Just like my mother and stepdad did all those years later. That's three people I didn't protect."

She slapped my chest. "Why do you insist on torturing yourself for things you had no control over?" Now she was *seriously* pissed at me. "You didn't light that fire. You didn't break into that girl's house, assault and kill her. None of those people died at *your* hands. Shitty things happen every fucking day, and you can't shoulder the weight of those things. You just can't. I won't let you."

A touch of amusement slithered through me. "You won't let me?"

"No. I refuse to let you torture yourself. Give yourself a fucking break." She sighed. "No wonder you don't connect with people. You basically withdrew from life. For you, connecting with people meant losing them. I can even understand why Gina suited you. She was never going to want you to love her, never going to claim she loved you. She was too wrapped up in herself. And you were sure you'd never come to care for someone like her, so it wouldn't matter if you lost her. That was why you stayed with her. How cowardly of you," she teased.

She was *teasing* me? This female was baffling at times. I toyed with the chocolate-brown strands dangling around her face. "You amaze me. You cling to the good, let it outweigh the bad. You accept people for who they are." Probably because she knew what it was like to be rejected for being nothing other than herself. "And you accept me, despite everything." She wasn't judging me, wasn't pulling away. I dragged her on top of me and kissed her hard. "You're a surprise, Ava Sanchez. And you're mine."

"Yours."

"There's something you need to understand. If this had been too much for you to accept, I'd have respected that and left you alone." Maybe. Probably not. "But you chose to stay, which means you just sealed your own fate. I won't let you go." It came out sounding like a warning of danger. Maybe it was.

She just smiled. "No, you won't. And I won't let you go either. Deal with it, big guy, because I'm here for good. And so are my cushions."

No one else on the planet could have made me want to smile right then, but she somehow managed it. "Give me your mouth. I want you again."

She released a long-suffering sigh. "Oh, all right."

CHAPTER THIRTEEN

(Ava)

Thanks to Salem's rigorous round of sex, which lasted a few hours, I was late for movie night. As I needed to first pick up some bottles of red wine-flavoured NSTs, Salem was just about to escort me to the store when we found Sam and Jared outside our apartment building.

She was staring at her mate, looking fierce and ready to burn shit down. "Where did he put the bastard?"

Head cocked slightly, Jared held up a finger. I realised he was conversing telepathically with someone.

Salem arched a questioning 'Is everything okay?' brow at Sam.

"Evan managed to track down one of the two remaining suppliers – the bloke's alive."

"He's in a containment cell," Jared told Sam.

"Then let's get going. Sorry, Ava, but I'm giving movie night a miss. There's no way I'll be able to relax with the girls when I know I'm so close to getting some answers."

I sighed. "I don't blame you. To be honest, I'm feeling the same."

"Fancy coming along, then?"

My smile probably took over my face. "Oh yeah. Watching you at work is better than any movie. Or are you using Ryder to get your answers?"

"I'd rather not call on him. He's exhausted with all the work he's been doing; it's causing his control over his bloodlust to waver."

"This bastard isn't worth making it worse for Ryder," interjected Jared, "he needs a rest."

"Besides, considering all the charges that lay at our captive's feet and considering what went on in that brothel, I think he deserves a little pain."

Maybe it was wrong to be in full agreement with that, but I was. "Shall I contact the other girls or the rest of the squad?"

"No," replied Sam. "Let them all have some time to wind down. They need it."

Jared looked at his mate. "Ready to go?" At her nod, he then teleported us all to the prison beneath the mansion. Inside was a row of containment cells that were constructed of unbreakable glass. A short distance away was Evan and one of the prison guards, Alec. We headed straight for them and tracked their gazes to a Mexican-looking Keja who was bound to a metal chair in one of the cells.

Jared patted his twin on the back in a 'well done' gesture before turning a dark glare on the Keja.

Evan handed a sheet of paper to Sam that had a photograph attached. I was guessing it was the personal profile of this particular supplier that had been compiled by The Hollow's researchers. He then arched a brow at Sam. "I take it you don't need me for this?"

She shook her head. "You've done well and you must be knackered. Go rest." Once Evan and Alec were gone, she turned to Jared. "Ready?"

"Definitely." He fitted his hand into one of the two imprints that were situated on the door of the cell – one imprint was for him, and the other was for Sam. The door made a hissing sound as it unlocked. Jared opened it wide, letting Sam, Salem, and I enter before walking inside.

Sam consulted the sheet of paper in her hand. "Vinnie G, isn't it? Seventy-three years old, human and vampire years combined. Originally from Mexico. Your vampiric gift: an ability to immobilize things. Favourite pastime: kidnapping innocent people and selling them like frozen goods with three of your best mates. Occupation: total and utter prick." She looked up at him. "Did I miss anything?" He didn't say a word.

I leaned into Salem, who had his arms folded across his chest. "Not very talkative, is he?"

Sam sighed. "At least he's not faking respect. It's such a nice change."

Jared stepped forward. "Okay, here's the situation, Vinnie. We know that you dabble in human and preternatural trafficking. We have testimonies to that effect from the survivors and the keeper of a brothel that was recently shut down. There is no escaping the fate that lies ahead of you. It's no secret that my mate and I are a little rough when it comes to punishments. We believe in making unforgettable statements that certain things won't be tolerated. Trafficking is one of them. So I'm guessing you know you're in for a world of pain."

As if to prove that, Sam conjured her silvery-blue energy whip, and threaded it through her fingers. Vinnie's eyes followed the movement and his entire body stiffened, bracing itself for the pain.

Jared smiled at him. "But there's good news. You see, we have some questions. If you answer them truthfully, we'll give you a swift execution – which is much more than you deserve. If you don't…well, things are going to go downhill from here for you."

Vinnie still didn't speak, but his eyes darted repeatedly from the whip to Salem…as if sensing the danger he presented, and expecting him to lunge at Vinnie any second. Salem's stillness was in fact scary. Not to mention the way his glare was locked on Vinnie with lethal intent.

"Not interested in our offer?" Sam smiled brightly. "Fabulous. That means I get to play."

I clapped a little. "This is going to be *sweet*."

"Actually, Ava, why don't you join me? I said I'd give you some pointers for the process of interrogation. No time like the present. And we're in no rush." Sam looked at Jared. "You don't mind sitting out for a while, do you?"

Jared frowned. "Just for the first hour. I like to play too." He backed off, planting himself next to Salem.

I knew that this was all psychological warfare, but I still happily skipped forward; adopting my airhead act, since it tended to make people underestimate me.

"Now, Ava, it's important that the captive is scared. Does he look scared to you?"

I studied his expression. "Not a lot. Which is kind of stupid. Maybe he's just dense."

"Even dense people have a sense of self-preservation."

"True enough."

"So, like I said, we need to be sure he's scared." With that practical tone, she could have been reciting the ingredients of a cake recipe. "That's where my whip comes in handy." She cracked it at Vinnie, splitting open his bottom lip and startling a guttural groan from him. "Or my energy balls." Moulding her whip into a ball, she flung it at Vinnie's abdomen; he would have keeled over if a rope wasn't wrapped around his middle, pinning him in place. "Sometimes, I even burn them for a little while." Flames sprouted from one palm and engulfed Vinnie's shoes. "Depends what mood I'm in, really." A splash of water from Sam's other palm killed the fire.

Vinnie sagged, but he hardly made a sound – clearly unwilling to give us the satisfaction of hearing him cry out. "Ooh, he's a quiet one. How awesome. Screamers are too much to take."

"Hard on the ears," agreed Sam. "Right, your turn. Any special skills?"

I turned to fully face her, as if Vinnie's presence was of no consequence and Sam and I were having a gossiping session. "Well, when I used to work for my brother, he asked me to help with some of his interrogations. He's not squeamish, but he hates the sound of bones cracking. I can't say that's ever bothered me. So I always stepped in."

"Do you go for the fingers?"

"No, not painful enough. I go for the thigh – breaking the femur bone is supposed to be fucking agonising. The ankles too, since the ligaments tear at the same time; that's bad. The heel bone is a good one too. Hey, did you know that a calcaneal fracture is also called 'Don Juan fracture'?" I shook my head. "I never did find out why. Anyway, I used to go for the cheekbone because I'm told that's real freaking painful. But they always used to pass out from that, which was *really* annoying, so I—"

"Just get it over with!" Vinnie shouted, suddenly looking extremely nervous.

"Ooh, it talks."

"That's handy," said Sam, "because we have some questions for him."

He snickered. "You can't seriously think I'll talk. It will gain me nothing."

"Wrong," interrupted Jared, "it will gain you a swift execution. Trust me when I say that if you turn down that offer, you'll wish you hadn't. But it will be too late by then. It's kind of hard to stop my mate when she's fully at work. And I'd rather not watch Ava sulk if she has to back off."

"I won't give up the others!"

"We don't need you to. We already found two of them. They were both dead by the time we got to them, though – demon casualties, apparently." Jared shrugged when Vinnie gawked. "Yeah, kidnapping a demon wasn't the brightest idea. The fourth of your little group will soon be found by either us or the demons, depending on who gets there first."

"I do hope it's us." Sam puffed. "The demons are spoiling my fun."

I bounced on the spot. "Back to *this* round of fun…he looks a little uneasy now. Is that enough?"

"It'll do. So, you say breaking bones is your preferred method of torture?"

"Yeah. I'm not bad with a knife. I just find slicing and dicing a little slow and messy. And I don't want my new dress to get stained. It wasn't cheap, but I got a good deal on it."

"For Christ's sake, *will you just be done with it*!" bellowed Vinnie.

Sam stared at him, confused. "Well, no. I would have done if you'd agreed to truthfully answer our questions, but you didn't. So I figure we'll play with you for a little while and then tomorrow night I'll have one of my vampires scan your mind." She turned back to me and waved a hand toward Vinnie. "Take the floor."

"Yay!" I cocked my head at Vinnie, giving him a winning smile. "This is really going to hurt. Hope for your sake you have a masochistic streak."

"You're just a Sventé. You can't hurt me. You *won't*." But he didn't sound so confident of that.

"The last person who said that to me sobbed like a baby when I rammed his broken index finger up his rectum. Your finger is a similar size. But I'm guessing that if you touch me with any of your fingers, your gift will immobilise me. So I'll skip that."

"You going straight for the femur?" asked Sam.

"No, I like to start with something simple. Something that doesn't cause *too* much pain. I always find when it comes to breaking bones that it's best to take it easy at first and let the pain escalate." I grabbed his balled-up hand and abruptly wrenched it backwards. The sharp crack mingled with a throaty sound of pain that slipped between his grinding teeth.

Sam took a good look at the break. "That was quick and clean."

I smiled impishly. "It's not my first time."

"What next? The other wrist?"

"Nah. I like to mix it up a little or it gets tedious." Squatting, I gripped his ankle. "Shame we don't have a hammer or we could have done a Kathy Bates on him. No matter. I'll just hit the joint hard with my fist – it'll have the same effect." I did just that, and again he did his best to muffle his cry of agony as his foot snapped to the side at an unnatural angle.

Inwardly, I winced. Causing pain wasn't truly something I enjoyed doing. But while the images of what I'd found in the attic of that brothel – of the awful state the female demon had been in – was flashing in my mind, I found that I couldn't be sorry for what I was doing. He deserved so much worse.

"Sounds like the bones in his wrist are reknitting."

I just shrugged, turning my attention to his other ankle.

"You're not going to do anything about it?"

"No. I find that it's best, and more entertaining, to let their injuries fully heal and then start all over again after I've—"

"What do you want to know?"

Sam tilted her head at Vinnie. "You're reconsidering our offer?"

"Just keep *her* away from me!" He jerked his chin at me.

I gasped, but inside I was smiling in satisfaction. "How rude."

(Salem)

I never thought I'd say this, but my little Ava could be seriously scary. She wasn't fierce and threatening in her approach like Jared. Nor was she direct and insulting in her approach like Sam. In fact, Ava barely addressed the prisoner at all. She didn't look at him like he was a person. There was no hate, no rage, and no desperation for vengeance in her eyes. She was indifferent to and dismissive of Vinnie and his pain – breaking his bones while smiling merrily and chatting with Sam.

Instead of being sharp, offensive, and confrontational, she came across as empty-headed, dippy, and flip; completely uninterested in the prisoner as anything other than a form of entertainment. That made her confusing, unpredictable, and seemingly insane. There was no way of bracing yourself for what came next with someone like that, because there was no way of knowing what they would do next.

Prisoners tended to reason that all they had to do was block out the pain and hold onto their resolve because their interrogators would eventually get bored. Especially if they didn't satisfy them with cries of pain or answers to their questions. But Ava wasn't presenting herself as someone who had any interest in whether or not he screamed or in anything at all that he had to say. She also didn't look like there was any chance of her getting bored sometime soon. She was perfectly happy to go at her own pace...as if she had no goal other than to make him suffer.

Of course, I knew that wasn't the real Ava. Not at all. My Ava *was* capable of harming another, but she wasn't someone who did it for shits and giggles. A part of her would be balking at what she was doing, and another part of her would be silencing that judgmental voice by reminding it just what this bastard had done; how many lives he'd ruined.

This here and now was mostly psychological warfare – and it was fucking good. If I hadn't known her so well, I'd be thinking the exact same thing that Vinnie was currently shouting: "Get Homicidal Barbie away from me! The bitch is fucking crazy!"

I'm so glad Ava came along, chuckled Jared telepathically. *She's spiced up the interrogation and managed to crack the fucker without much torture.*

Huffing, Ava came to stand beside me, crossing her arms over her chest and pouting – the image of petulance. "I didn't even get to break his femur bone!"

I spoke in a voice that a parent might use to calm a child on the verge of a tantrum. "I'm sure Sam will let you continue if Vinnie doesn't give us the information we want. Right, Coach?"

Sam nodded reassuringly at Ava. "Of course."

Jared stepped toward Vinnie. "My first question is...are there any more brothels out there? Don't bother lying to us, Vinnie. We've interrogated enough people to know a lie when we hear one. And for every time you lie, Ava will break another bone."

Vinnie flinched, casting Ava a wary look. "I don't know if there are more brothels. I didn't even know about the last one until I saw the announcement on V-Tube and heard Marge's name. I don't ask questions. I just deliver the goods."

"They weren't 'goods', Vinnie," snapped Sam, "they were people."

"All the survivors from the brothel are now awake," Jared told him. "Each one believes their Sire sold them. Is that how it always worked?"

Vinnie nodded. "We couldn't afford to have nests tracking us down – four Kejas aren't much good against entire nests of vampires – so we bought them."

"What about the other preternaturals? Were they sold too?"

"No. We usually never went near anyone outside of our species. But the woman who came with Marge – I don't know her name – promised us big money if we got our hands on some other species."

"How long have you been working in this trade?" Sam asked him.

His eyes briefly slid to Ava, and I wondered if he was considering lying but then thought better of it. "Four years."

Sam raised a brow. "I take it Marge and her friend weren't your only buyers, then?"

"No, but we only worked for five others. Like I said, there's only four in our group. Or there *was*. We didn't have the means or resources to take the business any further."

Jared gave him a pointed look. "I'm going to want the name of every one of those buyers, Vinnie. And their location."

"I'll tell you what I know."

Then he did.

By the end of the interrogation – during which Ava's assistance wasn't again required, to her disappointment – we had five more names to add to the soon-to-be-assassinated list, in addition to the bastards' locations.

Sitting in one of Antonio's parlours a few hours later, we repeated everything we'd heard to him, Lucy, and Luther. Having been a ruler for an eternally long time, Antonio was as good at giving advice as Luther. Currently, Sam and Jared were torn on what to do about what they now knew: Did they reveal the identities of those who had bought other vampires? Or did they simply send out squads to eliminate them and hopefully retrieve their captives?

"I say we name and shame them on V-Tube either before or after we've dealt with them," proposed Jared.

"It is indeed what they deserve," said Antonio. "But you must consider that if you do such a thing, you will also bring shame to their nests."

"It is also worth noting that people may accuse their nests of being involved," Luther warned.

Jared considered that for a moment. "We could make it very clear that they don't share the blame."

Luther inclined his head. "Yes, but take into account that many people will be enraged by what has occurred. Families of the trafficking victims will want blood. If they are unable to get their hands on the vampires who bought and abused their loved ones, they may attack their nests in lieu of them."

I rested a possessive hand on Ava's thigh. "You think that if Coach and Jared publically reveal the identities of the vampires involved in the trafficking ring, innocents could die?"

"It is a strong possibility," replied Luther.

Lucy frowned. "You revealed Marge's identity and those of the suppliers but nothing happened to their nests, right?"

"No, nothing happened to them," Sam verified.

"But you have not yet revealed the names of the survivors of the brothel," Antonio pointed out. "Once their loved ones become aware of what has happened to them – and that their Sires were involved – trouble will undoubtedly break out. It is hardly likely that you will need to step in, since lines are permitted to deal with their own issues. But there *will* be violence of some sort. Innocents could get caught in the crossfire."

"You could execute the buyers publically," suggested Ava. When all eyes fixed on her, she continued. "If you were to, for instance, show their execution on V-Tube, it would satisfy the bloodlust of any enraged vampires."

I was impressed by that idea. "And it would be a solid statement of the consequences of any such trafficking in the future."

Ava nodded and then looked at Sam. "You could include Vinnie in the public executions too."

Sam's mouth curved into a wicked smile. "I like it."

"It could in fact work." Luther shrugged. "After all, it is one thing to *know* that justice has been served. It is another thing to *see* it with your own eyes. Those that are bloodthirsty enough to need to see it will have the option of doing so. Again and again, in fact, since the recording will remain on V-Tube."

"Think on it a little more," advised Antonio. "There is no great rush, since you have until the squads return with the felons and Diane is in your hands before you need to decide."

"In the meantime, we need to concentrate on ensuring my female squad members are totally prepared for the inevitable battle that lies ahead." Sam smiled at Ava. "You certainly have the art of interrogation down. Now you just need to get a handle on the rest."

CHAPTER FOURTEEN

(Ava)

As always, the training session was brutal and tiring. When Sam and Jared led both the male squad and female squad to the tactical training field after lunch, I'd expected more rounds of paintballing. But rather than taking us to the supply hut to retrieve camo gear and weapons, they halted near the base camp – a little detached house – just a few feet away.

"Sorry to disappoint," began Jared as he slowly paced in front of us, "but there'll be no paintballing tonight. This session will be a practice run for the upcoming battle. How can we do a practice run when we don't know what we'll be facing? It's not really that difficult. We know the likelihood is that wherever Giles sends us will in fact be a trap. We know vampires will be waiting both inside and outside the building to attack and kill us. And we know our goal is to avoid being killed."

Sam spoke then. "For the purpose of this exercise, we're going to pretend that the 'B and B' is where our targets are waiting for us."

The 'B and B' was the tallest of the buildings and situated in the centre of the tactical training field, which looked much like an abandoned village. From what I'd heard, the field had been a surprise Binding gift from Evan for Sam and Jared. Evan had designed it, and the entire legion had then come together to help him build it. The buildings were all constructed of plywood. Gas drums and piles of tyres were sporadically placed along every 'street'. In addition, several vehicles – including a bus – lined the streets. There was also a base camp on either side of the field and a 'dead zone' for when squad members received what would have been fatal injuries in a real situation.

"As Jared said, we'll be walking into a trap – and we'll be doing it voluntarily simply because it's the only way we can get to Diane."

Chico cocked his head. "What makes you so sure Diane will be there, Coach?"

"Giles told us that she's infuriated with me and Jared. We burned down her business, we're losing her money, we're picking off her employees, and we're forcing her to go into hiding. One thing we know about her character is that she likes revenge. She won't miss a chance at getting her hands on us. She'll plan an attack, forcing her nest to participate, and she'll coax Giles and his vampires into joining her. It won't be difficult to get him involved, since she's his vampire and he obviously wants to protect her."

"We're too powerful as a whole," Jared pointed out. "It would be practically impossible to take us all out in one hit, and they'll know that. If the situation was reversed, what would you do in such a situation?"

"Kill them one at a time," I said without hesitation.

"Yes. They'll attempt to pick us off – leaving only Sam and I alive, since it's very likely that Diane will want to get up close and personal with us. First, they'll lure us to a building of their choosing. I doubt it will be Giles' club, since he won't want his business being destroyed. But whatever it is, every entrance will be covered by guards who are ready and waiting to attack.

"In my opinion, though, the entrances won't *look* covered. They'll have vampires positioned close enough to pick us off but not close enough for us to easily sense them; they won't want to tip us off that it's a trap. So they'll spread themselves around, but they'll lurk nearby."

"As such, objective number one will be eliminating their 'marksmen' – vampires like David who can kill from afar. Three other squads, including Evan's, will take care of the marksmen." Sam turned to Alora. "Evan's going to find it hard being away from you in a battle. Likewise, you'll find it hard being away from him. As much as I sympathise, I can't send you with him."

Alora nodded in understanding. "He needs to get used to the fact that I'm part of the legion now."

"Yes. And you need to stick close to your partner, which is Maya. If it wasn't for the fact that Ava doesn't yet have a partner, I'd be having the same conversation with her and Salem."

Beside me, arms folded, Salem just grunted. I giggled, which earned me a deep frown from him.

Jared stopped pacing. "While Evan and his squad are busy getting rid of the marksmen, Denny and Stuart will do their usual thing."

"Search the perimeter, find out how many exits there are and how well they're guarded," muttered Denny.

"Correct. Once Evan contacts me" – Jared tapped his temple, indicating he would use his telepathy – "with news that he's destroyed the marksmen, we'll be going in. We'll split up, enter through every door and pick off everyone inside one by one, until we've circled the main party – which will most likely consist of Diane, Giles, and their personal guards."

"What will Evan and his squad be doing then?" Butch asked Jared.

"Guarding the perimeter with the other squad in case more vampires show up or anyone tries to leave. We don't want any surprises; we need all bases covered."

"Usually, there are two ways to get in or out of every building – windows not included," said Sam. "But we need every side plus the roof covered, even if that means entering through windows. Every floor needs to be searched. As such, we'll split up into six groups."

Jared resumed his pacing. "As practice, your objective tonight is to enter the 'B and B' as quickly and silently as possible. It shouldn't take more than three minutes at most to get inside."

"Sounds simple enough," said Damien with a shrug.

Jared smiled. "It would be…if the entrances weren't currently being guarded, and if some people weren't already waiting inside."

Sam chuckled at our surprised expressions. "Yes, we've invited along two squads to participate in this session – both of which will be accompanying us on this assignment. One is on guard, the other is inside. Just like Diane and Giles will be on the night of the battle, the squads will be expecting us to show up any minute now. And they'll be watching and listening, searching for any indication that we're close by."

"Now it's time to split up. David and Butch will come with me – we'll take out any guards on the roof before exploring the first floor. By the time we've made our way downstairs, you should all have taken care of the guards on the ground floor so we can circle our targets."

"I'll take Damien, Cassie, and Jude," announced Sam. "We'll enter through the front. Salem, Max, Stuart, and Ava will go through the back. Paige, Imani, Harvey, and Reuben will enter through the left side of the building, and Chico, Denny, Alora, and Maya will enter through the right side."

Jared's expression turned serious. "Right now, you need to imagine that we're merely yards away from the building wherein Diane and Giles are waiting. Imagine I've just received confirmation from Evan that the marksmen are now out of the equation and the area is secure. Imagine that Denny and Stuart have each already scouted the perimeter and revealed that each side of the building is being guarded by three vampires. That would mean there's no time to waste. But before we begin, Reuben needs to weaken some of your gifts."

After Reuben had done so, Sam tipped her head in the direction of the 'B and B'. "Let's move, people."

We all quickly scattered; each group heading in different directions in order to circle the building. Moving at vampire speed, Max, Stuart, and I followed Salem as he passed the first three streets, and then scurried down the fourth. He stopped at a particular 'house', urging us inside without a word. We then followed him to the back door, where he signalled for us to crouch.

Salem scanned the immediate area before turning to Stuart. "That 'house' opposite us is positioned at the rear of the 'B and B'. I want you to check the house, see if it's empty and safe to use for cover."

Instantly, Stuart exploded into molecules and disappeared out of a window.

"You went the long way around to be sure that the three guards weren't waiting inside another building," Max then understood.

"Jared said that there were three guards covering the rear of the 'B and B'. He didn't say they would be in plain sight. I want to know exactly where they are before we chance getting closer."

Good plan, I thought.

Mere seconds later, Stuart reformed in front of us. "One guard is in the house, like you suspected. He's positioned on the first-floor balcony that faces the 'B and B'. The other two guards are pacing outside the back door of the 'B and B'."

"Then we take out the guard on the balcony first," said Max simply.

Salem held his hand up. "Wait. There's something we need to consider."

I frowned. "What?"

"If we take him out, the other two will clearly see it. They'll know we're close and they'll be ready – might even alert the vampires inside."

"And vice versa," I noted, to which Salem nodded.

"Then we need to take them all out at the same time," stated Stuart.

Salem nodded again. "It's the only way to get inside undetected."

"Me and Stuart could take out the two guards covering the door," I proposed. "When he shreds into molecules, he can move as fast as me."

"I could use my gift on them first," offered Max. "That would stop them from alarming anyone – including the guy on the balcony." He looked at Salem. "Then you'd be able to take him out at the same time."

Salem's eyes settled on me, clearly torn. He didn't want to send me ahead of him, even though this was only a practice run – it went against his protective instincts.

"I can do this. You have to trust me."

"I trust you." It was an agreement of the plan.

Again, we travelled at vampire speed – silent and stealthy – as we entered the house. Salem darted up the stairs just as Max, Stuart, and I rushed out of the front door. Max paralysed the senses of the two guards, giving them no time to cry out before Stuart and I were behind them; our hands cradling their heads as if to snap their necks. I looked up at the balcony to see that the third guard was cradling his jaw, courtesy of a psychic slap from Salem.

It was obvious that the three guards wanted to loudly grumble and march off as they headed to the 'dead zone', but they resisted; knowing it wouldn't be fair to give away our presence. The moment Salem joined us, he turned to Stuart. "You know what to do once we get inside." Then he opened the door wide enough for us all to slip through. I exhaled a relieved breath when it didn't creak.

In molecule form, Stuart entered first, quickly followed by Max. Salem signalled for me to go in before him, but he stayed close to me once the door was shut behind us. I could hear voices coming from another room, recognised them as belonging to another squad.

Suddenly, Stuart was once again before us. He held up two fingers, mouthed 'kitchen' and then 'alert'. The three guys made a series of gestures I didn't have a hope in hell of understanding, which had me feeling like I'd been ranked as unimportant. There was no way Salem was leaving me out of this. It wasn't something he could afford to do on a real assignment, so there was *no* way I'd allow him to get away with it now.

I elbowed him, pointed at my chest, and then gave him a 'what about me?' look. He gestured for me to stay behind him. The bastard was protecting me, even during practice! I would have pressed him to involve me if Stuart and Max hadn't chosen that moment to quietly advance toward the kitchen.

This wasn't the time to argue, I reminded myself. But I'd definitely give Salem a verbal rollicking when the session was over.

In the kitchen, the boys attacked much the same as before: Max paralysed the guards' senses, Salem gave one a psychic slap, and Stuart threatened to snap the neck of the other. Off the guards went to the 'dead zone'. It might have all been very simple...if another guard hadn't then began to creep up behind me. I heard him before I saw him; swiftly I twisted my upper body and rammed my elbow into his throat. Then I knocked him unconscious with a blow to the jaw. I caught him before he could hit the floor with a thud, carefully placing him on the ground.

Standing, I found Salem glaring at me...like it was all my fault and I'd *asked* the guard to try to attack me. He made some kind of signal with his hands that I didn't understand. So I gave him a signal of my own: I flipped him off. Max was shaking with silent laughter, but Salem wasn't at all amused. Noting that Stuart was missing, I gathered he'd shredded to check for other guards. When he reappeared a moment later, he put his thumb up.

Led by Stuart, we exited the kitchen and walked down a long hallway that I guessed would take us to the living room. We almost crashed into Paige, Imani, and Harvey when we reached a junction. I mouthed, 'Reuben?' Paige shook her head sadly, meaning he was in the 'dead zone'. *Crap*. I then mouthed, 'Guards?' Paige slashed her throat with her hand, indicating the guards on her side had been taken care of. Good.

Salem held a hand up for us all to remain in position and tapped his heart twice. I knew what he meant this time: if we went any further, the vampires in the living room would hear our heartbeats. He wanted us to wait there.

I went to mouth, 'For what?' when I picked up movement in my peripheral vision. Jared, David, and Butch were coming down the stairs just as Chico and Maya rounded a corner and headed straight for us. If Alora and Denny were absent, that meant they were also in the 'dead zone'. Just the thought that Alora might have been dead if this session was real made me shudder inwardly.

The guys all began communicating in hand signals again, making me once again feel left out. Paige, Imani, and Maya looked at me questioningly, and – frustrated beyond belief – I gave the sign for 'wankers'. The trio struggled to hold in a laugh. I looked back at the guys to find them all scowling at me. Yep, they'd seen me. I lifted my chin and sniffed haughtily.

Sam, Damien, and Jude are in the lounge, Jared told me, and I knew he'd also informed the others. *The room is up ahead and adjacent to the living area, but far enough away that no one has sensed them. Get ready to move.*

Jared then held up three fingers and pointed toward the living room. Understanding, I nodded. He put one finger down, another, and then finally the third finger. At that, we all dashed at vampire momentum into the living room just as Sam, Damien, and Jude raced inside and instantly attacked. A battle then began.

It was absolute mayhem. Poisonous darts and energy balls were flying around; bolts of lightning were zapping people; psychic slaps were repeatedly rippling through the air; a black jaguar was launching itself at people, going for the jugular but not delivering a fatal bite. We all did our best to kick ass, but the opposition was good too. Strangling us with unseen hands, firing red-hot arrows, encasing people in a circle of flames, causing hallucinations, making skin feel feverish. No wonder these guys had earned spots in the legion.

By the time it was over, more of our people were injured. Some of the injuries would have been fatal. The other squads suffered more injuries than ours, meaning we won. Still, though, if this had been real we would have been mourning Chico, Damien, Reuben, Cassie, Denny, Alora, and Jude now. It was a reminder that Sam was right: no matter how powerful you were, all it took to be killed was to be faced with someone whose gift could combat yours.

"You all did good," Sam told us once the other squads had left.

"Did good? I would have been *dead* now." Chico looked more embarrassed than upset.

"Yeah, and that would have been right after Jude was 'killed'. That distracted you and made you pissed. Am I right? This is part of why I wanted you all to train together. You can't afford to let yourselves be distracted or fight in anger. If something bad happens to any of you – even if it's to someone you care about – you take that rage and you use it as fuel. Then later, after the battle is over, you can cry and rant and break shit. Until then, you shelve it all. If you don't, you risk not only *your life*, but the lives of those who are relying on you to watch their backs."

"Consider it a learning experience," Jared suggested.

Just as Sam was about to signal for us to leave, I said, "I don't think I should be partnered with Salem for the battle."

Salem rounded on me. *"What?"*

Ignoring him, I continued. "This was only a practice session, and yet he wanted to hold me back. He even kept me at the rear at one point, trying to keep me safe, which almost caused me to be attacked from behind."

He growled. "I let you go ahead with Max and Stuart to get rid of the guards, didn't I?"

"Two things about that statement proves my point. Not only did you use the word 'let' – which suggests you don't see us as a partnership at all – but I was only forty feet in front of you at the time with Max and Stuart as back up. If I remember rightly, you *still* hesitated to 'let' me do that, even though this was only practice."

He growled again, holding my gaze as if he was trying to stare me down.

Sam cleared her throat. "Maybe we *should* partner you with someone else, Ava."

His head whipped round to face Sam. "Don't even think it, Coach."

"Salem, every single person here is important to this battle. If you're acting in ways that stop Ava from being the asset that she is – which will also distract you and piss her off – then you're better off apart."

"Try it," he snarled.

She just rolled her eyes, sighing. "Salem, don't be bloody awkward."

"And watch your tone," warned Jared.

There was a short silence. "Me and Ava need to talk." Salem fisted his hand in my t-shirt and lifted me.

"Put me down!" But he didn't. He moved at vampire momentum, stopping halfway through the rainforest. When he released me, I snarled at him. "That really has to stop."

"Do you really want to be partnered with someone else, Ava? Or did you just say that to make me as pissed off as you are?"

"I truly want it. The fact that it pisses you off is just a bonus."

"You want to be away from me during the battle, not knowing where I am or if I'm alive?" That seemed to actually hurt him, which wasn't my intention, even though he *had* agitated the shit out of me.

"Don't you get it? If we're distracted by each other, we *will* get hurt."

"It doesn't work that way for Coach and Jared."

"Because they work as a team. Oh, I'm sure it galls him that they have to, and I'm sure there have been plenty of occasions when he's tried to protect her even though she doesn't need him to. But they still consider themselves a team. They trust each other to watch the other's back. You see me as someone you need to protect. You don't see me as someone who can kick ass as good as you, who can defend myself or protect you if necessary."

"I *know* you're deadly. I've *seen* you fight."

"Yet you insist on treating me like I can't protect myself." I sounded sad even to me.

He was still and silent, but he wasn't calming. "I couldn't protect them, Ava."

He meant his family and Sandra, I knew.

"I couldn't even save myself, in the end, which is why I'm here now. But I'll be damned if I ever let anything happen to *you*."

So much freaking guilt. "You didn't fail them, Salem. That's how you feel, and I can even understand why. Grief isn't logical. It makes us feel things we don't *need* to feel. We punish ourselves because the idea of letting it go and moving on makes us feel guilty. I get it. But you didn't let them down. What happened to them was *not* your fault. And if something ever happened to me—"

"It fucking won't."

"—it wouldn't be your fault either. It's just the way of the world."

"So you want another partner?" It was a total dismissal of everything I'd just said. He simply wasn't listening.

"Unless you can see us as a team, I don't see any other option."

He said nothing, just looked at me blankly. Then he turned and walked away. I got my answer.

(Salem)

"You do realise you have fucked up *big time*, don't you?"

I didn't look at Sam. Just kept my gaze on the ocean as I sprawled on the same lounger that I'd once rested on with Ava.

Ava. I hated that we'd fought. Physical fights were nothing to me – something I'd engaged in on a regular basis for a very long time. But emotional fights…they were alien to me. I was in unfamiliar territory; I didn't really know what to do now. I felt out of my element, unsure.

Did I find her and try to talk things through?

Did I give her time to herself?

Did I give her the space to think?

I didn't like the latter idea. She had a habit of overthinking stuff. We'd be okay…right?

Pulling me out of my thoughts, Sam sat on the lounger beside mine. "You know, I'd kind of understand you being such a knob if you hadn't been helping me train Ava; if you thought she might be one of those people who runs off to be the heroine rather than sticking with the plan and being a team player. But you know how strong she is, you know she's getting even stronger, and you know that she can be trusted to follow orders. So why the fuck would you behave like such a daft prick?"

I could have explained the truth of why I was so overprotective, but I didn't trust anyone with as much of my past as I'd told Ava. "It's between me and Ava."

Sam snorted. "If you're lucky."

That made me look at her. "What's that supposed to mean?"

"Ava has always had people undervalue her. It's what made her undervalue herself."

Yeah, I knew that. And it pissed me off.

"You've just gone and done the same thing. Do you really think she'll stick around for you to keep making her feel like shit?"

That wasn't what I'd done, and Ava would know that because she knew me better than anyone. Again, though, I wasn't about to spill the truth to Sam or anyone else. "Like I said, it's between me and Ava."

"Well...Clearly you know her better than me." Every word rung with sarcasm. "Clearly I'm wrong and she's not going to be absolutely heartbroken right now that someone she cares about doesn't see her as his equal. And clearly I'm wrong and she's not going to be exceptionally pissed that you made it clear to everyone that you don't believe she's capable of taking care of herself."

No wonder Sam was so pissed if that was how the situation looked to outsiders. Although her suppositions weren't entirely accurate, three things could probably be true: Ava might be heartbroken, and she might be pissed, and she might genuinely believe I failed to see her strength. Which meant finding and talking to her soon was definitely important.

"If you two are to be partners, you have to trust in her ability to—"

"It's easy for you. You have the Binding link." She had the reassurance that she'd know instantly if Jared needed her.

"I didn't have it until after we shut down the baby snatching operation and took care of the Trent brothers. Before then, I was in the same position as you: going into danger with someone I care about — and *don't* deny that you care about Ava or I *will* hurt you — knowing they could be killed and I wouldn't even be aware of it until it was too late."

That right there was my biggest fear: failing to protect her.

"Even now, Binding link or not, I have to trust Jared to take care of himself. It's hard, but it's the only way to make our working and personal relationship work. You have to do the same with Ava. If you don't, you'll keep on hurting her — which I truly believe you hate doing." Sam got to her feet. "She's in the Tiki Bar with the girls. Fix it, Salem."

(Ava)

Stirring my cocktail with the straw, I wondered if I could sneak away without the others noticing. As much as I appreciated that they had brought me here in the hope of cheering me up, there was really no chance of that happening. The fact that Salem and I were at odds left a lead weight in the pit of my stomach. I felt sick and anxious, unsure what to do next, and wondering what was currently going on in Salem's confusing head.

Maya hopped onto a nearby stool. "You shouldn't take what he did personally. He's a guy. Guys are stupid." She said it so simply that I had to smile.

"I don't think he meant to hurt you," soothed Alora. "He cares about you, Ava. He really does. He's just terrified of anything happening to you. That's no excuse, I know that. Just like I know the overprotectiveness isn't easy to deal with. Evan drives me insane sometimes."

"Chico can be just as bad," said Jude.

"So can Butch." Imani's eyes widened when all our attention fixed on her. "Don't ask me why, because I don't have a clue."

Paige looked pensive. "Yeah, it's hard to read sociopaths."

Imani seemed offended on Butch's behalf. "He's not a sociopath."

"Oh, I'm sorry. Do you prefer 'deranged killer'?"

I had to laugh at that.

Smiling, Imani snorted at me. "Like Salem's much better."

Just hearing his name was enough to make my amusement evaporate. *Bleh.*

"Don't let him get you down," begged Cassie, patting my knee.

Curling an arm around my shoulders, Alora sighed. "I hate him. He broke you."

"Can I stab him?" Jude looked totally serious.

I giggled, but it was a sad sound. "No, you can't. He has issues, and I want to be understanding but...I just don't want to suffer for what his past has done to him." I had no intention of elaborating on just what that past was, and thankfully nobody asked.

"That's reasonable," said Alora. "Just explain that to him when you guys talk."

Cassie blinked. "Salem talks?"

I rolled my eyes. "He's not *that* bad."

"Only during training," Cassie insisted.

"I'll bet he talks dirty." Maya smiled devilishly, crossing one slim leg over the other. "The quiet ones are always the chattiest in bed."

"Oh, would you look at that blush!" chuckled Paige as my face heated. "You must be right, Maya."

I cast the chuckling group a disgusted look. "I hate you bitches."

"Stop teasing her!" Alora admonished, but she was still laughing. "We're supposed to be cheering her up, which means *not* talking about the asshole and his insistence on being ridiculously overprotective."

"Well of course he's overprotective of you," laughed a *very* unwelcome voice. Gina kind of slinked her way into the group, making them all stiffen and gather closer to me, on guard. Later, I'd probably smile about it.

Gina gave me a pitying look. "You're no doubt in constant danger, since you probably annoy everyone you meet – which is a substantial talent, I have to say. And, well, you're not exactly *sturdy*, are you, child?" The implication was that I was helpless and weak.

I sighed. I didn't have the energy or patience to deal with the demented heifer. "Is there a reason you're tainting my air?"

"Such anger. He really has upset you, hasn't he? You should never let a man have this kind of power over you." She sounded genuinely sympathetic, which was of course a total act. "Although I can understand why him being overprotective would get tedious after a while. But if it's any consolation, it won't last much longer. Salem will quickly get bored with a damsel."

"Hmm. Well, thanks for bringing that to my attention. Here." I handed her my straw. "Go suck the joy out of your own evening and leave me to enjoy mine."

Gina flushed. "You think he'll stay with you, don't you? Why? Oh, you're not going to say he loves you, are you?" She sneered, as if the concept of love was utterly ridiculous.

The fact was that, no, I didn't think he loved me. I wasn't sure Salem – being as emotionally stunted and messed up as he was – would even be able to connect with someone on a level that deep. But I had no wish to share that with Gina, or any intention of letting her see how much she could get to me. No. I'd seriously had enough of this bitch. And I was going to have fun while I pissed her off.

Knowing it grated on her nerves, I brought back the airhead tone as I clapped a little. "Ooh, is this another game of 'trying to make Ava leave Salem'?" I let my shoulders sag. "But we play that one all the time. We need to think of another game. Hey, how about we play 'Ava kicks Gina's skanky ass'?"

Gina's flush deepened. Ooh, how special. "That particular *game* wouldn't end well for you, child. Or for your little friends here, if they were thinking of *playing* with us."

Faking a Scottish accent, I spoke in a theatrical voice. "You may take our lives. But you'll never take...our free—" Suddenly a mountain was wedged between us. "Ah, Salem, I was having fun."

A growl rumbled out of him as he faced Gina. "Didn't I warn you to stay away from Ava?" The danger in his voice sent a shiver down my spine.

"We were just talking, weren't we, child?" Her mocking tone didn't quite conceal the nervous tremor in her voice.

"Don't look at Ava, look at me. This is the last time I'll tell you, Gina. Leave. Ava. Alone."

"What will you do if I don't?" she snickered.

"It's not me you need to worry about." The dark humour in Salem's voice made me frown. My frown deepened when he stepped aside, clearing my path to Gina. He cast me a quick glance. "Go ahead, Ava."

I knew then what he was doing. In his own weird way, Salem was apologising. Was making a statement that *he* did trust in my ability to take care of myself, and that he *could* and *would* step aside when I needed him to. I almost laughed at the soppy 'How sweet is that?' look on Alora's face. You'd think he'd proposed marriage or something.

I slipped off the stool, my eyes fixed on Gina. "You sure you want to do this?"

She smirked and braced herself, inviting me forward with a flick of her fingers. "Let's dance."

I snorted. "Who says that?" Then I punched her breast. As she yowled – there was no other word for the noise that came out of her mouth – and folded over slightly in pain, I dealt her a blow to the jaw...and down she went. Unconscious before she even hit the floor. Well that was disappointing. "Huh. I was kind of hoping for a decent fight."

"Yeah, me too." Jude twirled her knife on her finger as she stared down at Gina. "Would it be terribly bad to carve something creative on her forehead?"

Alora regarded Jude with a smile. "You know, Chico's good for you."

Jude blinked. "Why do you say that?"

"He's taught you to think before you act. A few months ago, you might have already scrawled 'I am a hoebag' into her flesh."

Imani's face lit up. "That would be amazing!"

"But immoral – she's out cold," said Alora, the voice of reason for once.

Imani shrugged. "So?"

Leaving the girls to explore the ethics of carving into an unconscious woman, I turned to Salem. "Most people just say 'sorry'. But handing over your ex for painful handling was *so* much better."

His mouth curved as he pulled me close. "So we're okay?" Concern and uncertainty clouded his eyes. It was odd seeing such a confident male feel unsure. But the fact was that he wasn't any better at relationships than I was.

"We're okay…providing you can agree on us being a team."

He inhaled deeply. "Being a team would be good." He engulfed my hand in his. "Home."

No sooner had he shut the front door of the apartment behind us than he was on me. But he wasn't rough. His hands moved over me gently and slowly while his mouth sipped at mine. Still, though, there was desperation and intensity in every purposeful touch and in every sensual flick of his tongue.

He teased me in bed for what could have been hours before finally thrusting inside me. He kept the pace slow yet intense, his eyes locked with mine the entire time. He was reassuring himself that everything was fine, reconnecting in the only way that someone as unromantic as Salem would know how to do.

Afterwards, he curled himself around me, his hold tighter than usual, and fell asleep with his face almost buried in my hair. I smiled. We'd be okay. All was good.

CHAPTER FIFTEEN

(Ava)

All was not good. Not when I had the Dynamic Dumb-assed Duo standing in front of me.

This evening's training had taken place in the arena and, like always, it had been gruelling but invaluable. Everyone had been seriously determined to work hard and do well, since Giles had only one final night after this to contact Sam and Jared. If he didn't, we'd be paying him a visit at his club, which wouldn't at all be friendly.

After the training session, Sam and Jared congratulated us all on our progress before ordering us to go wind down and mentally prepare ourselves for the upcoming battle. But I sensed it was more than that. She wanted quality time with Jared, conscious that it was possible that one of them could be terribly hurt in a battle. Just the same, I wanted that time with Salem, and I was more than happy to have it.

The female squad was sent out of the arena first, since Sam and Jared wished to have a short private chat with the guys. That was when I'd found Will and Blythe waiting outside, which kind of shit on my good mood. The fact that they were glaring daggers at me indicated it was *me* they had come to see, not Salem. That was actually a relief, because I really was pissed at Will's insistence on taking out all his envy and spite on Salem.

Conscious that Salem would soon follow me outside, I figured it was best to get it over with. I spoke in a flat voice. "Can I help you?

Please say no." The girls gathered around me, snickering at the duo.

Blythe shook her head at me, as if she was marvelling over something. "You don't feel even an ounce of shame or remorse for what you did last night, do you?"

"Ah, we're discussing Gina."

"We're discussing how you attacked her," spat Will.

I tilted my head. "'Attacked' is such a strong word."

"But fitting," he insisted, "since you punched her hard enough to render her unconscious. Maybe you can explain to me why you believe this to be acceptable."

"Sure. Got any crayons?"

Stiffening, Will drew to his full height. "We'll see how amusing you find this when I've spoken to the Grand High Pair about your behaviour."

I double-blinked in surprise at what he seemed to think was a threat that should have me quivering. I must have missed something. "You want to complain to Sam and Jared?"

Imani leaned into me. "Where's he going with this? I truly fail to understand exactly what he thinks that will achieve." So it wasn't just me, then.

Will sniffed at Imani. "I'm sure they have strict rules on their legion members using their skills outside of training or battle." His narrow-eyed gaze switched back to me. "You shall face the consequences."

I had to wonder if he honestly believed there would be any consequences. It was quite probable that he simply wanted to do something – anything – that would incense Salem. He had nothing better to do? How sad. "You know, I'm pretty sure they sell lives in one of the stores over there. I suggest you buy one and butt out of Salem's."

Blythe looked like she truly wanted to gut me. "Do not think that angering us will make us walk away. We will not tolerate what you did to Gina."

"What Gina did to herself, you mean. She was warned several times to keep her distance from me. She chose to not only harass me twice, but to try and cause shit between me and Salem. I have witnesses to confirm that, if you're interested. The fact is that she brought this situation on herself. And I'm sure she's very aware of that, which is why she isn't standing with you. She knows that if anyone will be facing consequences, it will be her."

That was when I heard Sam, Jared, and the guys all filing out of the arena. I didn't move my eyes from the duo, though. The crowd must have parted to allow Sam and Salem to come through, because they were suddenly flanking me.

"What's going on?" demanded Salem, his arm brushing mine.

"Is there a problem here?" Sam's voice was cold.

Will lifted his chin as he addressed Sam. "Your squad member assaulted my vampire."

Sam studied Blythe from head to toe. "She looks fine to me."

Will appeared to be grinding his teeth. "I'm referring to Gina. *She*" – he stabbed his finger in my direction, earning himself a growl from Salem – "attacked her in a bar last night."

"Is that true, Ava?" Jared asked from behind me.

"Yep. And I'll do it again if she doesn't back off."

"Gina provoked her on two separate occasions," interjected Alora, "spouting petty little insults, and saying stuff like Salem will soon leave Ava, and that Gina could easily have him under her thrall because he secretly wants her."

Salem snorted at that, clutching my hand in his.

"She was trying to make Ava doubt Salem," deduced Sam.

"Yes." Alora smiled as she then added, "Gina even said she could have Jared under her thrall, if she wanted." Jared actually laughed at that.

Sam's expression hardened as her brow arched. "She did, did she?" There was a promise of repercussions in her voice.

"Gina would never say such a thing," Blythe declared, resolute.

"Oh, but that was exactly what she said," contradicted Alora, still smiling – taking utter joy in stirring some shit.

Maya spoke then. "She even invited Ava to fight with her in the bar – said something pathetic like 'let's dance'."

"All things considered," began Jude, "I'm honestly confused about why Gina thought she wouldn't get hurt at some point."

Cassie nodded. "Personally, I think Gina's lucky that all Ava did was knock her out."

After a brief moment of silence, Sam shrugged at Will. "Sounds to me, then, that Gina knew exactly what she was risking by provoking Ava again and again."

Will's eyes bulged. "You will let this go unpunished?"

"Taking Gina's 'let's dance' comment into account, it's clear that she didn't protest to the duel; she actually welcomed it," stated Jared. "We won't punish Ava for the fact that she won."

A flush crept up Will's neck and face. "She should not be allowed to use her abilities outside of the legion! She is exploiting her training!"

The chuckle that came out of Sam was empty of humour. She looked at Will with pity. "Oh, Will...Don't you get it? Every single member of this legion is trained to destroy their opponents with minimal effort. If Ava had truly wanted to cause Gina any major harm, your vampire would be recovering – very, very slowly – in the infirmary right now. So enough with the dramatics, all right."

With that, Sam walked away. The others followed, casting very unfriendly glances at Will and Blythe, until only Salem and I remained.

Clearly irate, Will glared at Salem. "You find it perfectly acceptable that *she* – someone you have known for only a short length of time – attacked a member of your own line? A member who you have known for so much longer, who you have been intimate with, who helped you learn the control you have?"

"Even if I didn't find it acceptable, my loyalty lies with Ava. Not with my line."

That made me smile. It made Blythe gasp in horror and a dose of shock. Shock? Um...why? Will might be Salem's Sire, but loyalty had to be earned. If Will had ever truly earned it, Salem would never have left to join the legion.

Shaking his head in what seemed to be both disappointment and anger, Will claimed, "You have changed, Salem. I never thought I'd see the day—"

"Night," I corrected.

"—that you betrayed me and your line so wholeheartedly. To leave us to become a member of the legion was bad enough. But to side with someone outside your own line, someone who *attacked*—"

"I was there, Will," Salem interrupted. "Or did Gina not tell you that? I was at the bar last night, I witnessed her bait Ava. I warned her away from Ava *yet again*. But she stayed. She wanted a fight, and she got one."

"But I don't think any of that matters to you," I said to Will. "Not really. I don't think you honestly care about what happened to Gina. You saw an excuse to confront me, to cause shit, and you took it."

"How could you let this *child* come between us, Salem? How could you turn from me this way?" Will's face was so red by that point that

Blythe was starting to look worried. "I am your Sire."

Salem sighed. "Yeah, you keep saying that. What's your point?"

I raised my hand high, like I was a kid in a classroom. Well, if they were going to call me a child, I'd give them one. "Ooh, I know, I know!"

Salem's mouth twitched. "Then share it with the class."

"Well, at first I thought his problem was that he felt you *owed* him your obedience and respect. But it's not." I looked at Will. "Having authority over people makes you feel good, doesn't it? It's a way for you to feel superior to them. The fact that you've lost what authority you had over Salem was bad enough. But he also has more than you've ever had. And you just can't stand that."

Will didn't respond.

"I'd say that I can't understand why you won't just put all your personal issues aside and make the most out of the new life you now have here. But I *do* understand why. I've met hypercompetitive people before. They measure themselves against others, against what others have. They never admit defeat, and they'll do anything to win.

"You feel like you come up short compared to Salem; it's something that eats at your pride. And the only way it'll all feel balanced again – the only way you can help maintain your self-worth – is if you either get what he has...or you make him lose it. You tried the first, but it didn't work. So now you're hoping to try the latter. You knew that if everybody turned against me tonight for attacking Gina, Salem would then turn against them. Again, though, your plan failed." I smiled. "Bet that rankles."

Blythe tried to pull her mate away. "Let's leave them both with their own idiocy."

He shook her off as an ugly smirk darkened his features. "If only Ava knew the entire truth about you, Salem. I sincerely doubt she would have such adoration for you if she did. That's right, I looked into your past. I know it all."

"Actually, I doubt that you do." Salem shrugged. "Not that it matters. Ava knows everything. You have nothing to hold over my head, Will. No authority over me. If I were you, I'd let all this go. I'd make some attempt to live peacefully here. For your mate's sake, if nothing else. Or things could get very, very bad for you."

"Is that a threat?" Will sniggered. "You cannot touch me, Salem. I made an agreement with Sam and Jared. Information for—"

"Residence here," finished Salem. "But no one said you'd live long."

As the implication hit Will, his expression was almost comical.

"It's true that they won't banish you from the island without good cause. They don't go back on their word. But that doesn't mean you're untouchable while you're here." Salem tugged on my hand. "Come on, baby."

I happily let him lead me away, leaning into him. I wasn't prepared to allow the duo to steal any more of my quality time with Salem.

We hadn't been home for more than twenty seconds when Salem quite expectedly brought up the subject I didn't want to discuss. "You didn't tell me that Gina had confronted you a few nights ago."

Retrieving a cola-flavoured NST out of the fridge, I confirmed, "Nope."

"Why?"

I shrugged, unscrewing the lid off my bottle. "It wasn't important."

"Repeat that." His voice was low, vibrated with annoyance.

"It wasn't important."

He advanced on me, arms folded. "It wasn't important that she said things to hurt you?"

As the NST eased the small tickle of thirst in the back of my throat, I sighed. "I didn't want to spend our time together talking about her. That would have been like letting her in our bed with us."

His face scrunched up in revulsion. "*Nothing* would be like letting her in our bed."

Major eye roll. "You know what I mean. I didn't want us to spend our time talking about her or the poison she gets a kick out of spewing."

He grunted, appearing dissatisfied with my response.

"She was probably hoping I'd take it out on you and that, like Sam said, I'd doubt you."

"Gina was wrong in everything she said. Tell me you know that."

"I know." He'd have been castrated by now if I thought differently. He grunted again. "Good."

"What did Sam and Jared want to talk to you and the guys in private about?"

"They were warning us one more time not to turn all overprotective with your squad tomorrow night; reminding us that we're supposed to watch your backs, not try to shield you and become distracted. What are you doing?"

I dialled a familiar number using my cell phone. "Calling for pizza."

"Pizza?"

"And some wedges and stuff." Knowing what Salem liked, I quickly placed our order and ended the call with a satisfied sigh. "Tonight we're going to relax, eat junk, and have some alone time."

Heat flared in his eyes; he'd no doubt interpreted 'alone time' to mean 'sex'. Typical male. "Sounds good."

"First, I have to change. Reuben tore my jeans during training, the fucker."

"He's still sour that you bruised his ego." Now that Salem had gotten past his annoyance over my spar with Reuben, he was nothing but proud of the fact that I'd won.

By the time the food arrived, I'd slid into a red dress – one that was casual yet racy – that Fletcher had chosen for me. Salem had reacted just as Fletcher predicted: he'd tried to rip it off. Only once I'd promised he could remove it later was he happy to settle on the balcony. We placed all the boxes on the glass table, and each claimed a deck chair.

It was when we were almost done eating that Salem said, "You never told me how you became a vampire."

Sitting cross-legged, I swallowed down my last wedge before responding. "My Sire, Victor, wanted to create himself a sizeable nest, so he went around attacking humans, leaving them for dead, and then 'saving' them. He Turned Cristiano and me on the same night, but it took us a while to realise he'd also been the one who attacked us."

"How did you adjust to being immortal?"

"After I got a hold on my bloodlust, I took well to this life. It felt like a fresh start. And I had a cool gift, so that went a long way into making me happy with being a vampire. Cristiano...he had a harder time adjusting."

Salem claimed the last slice of pizza, the asshole. "Why?"

"He has a son. Poor kid was the product of a one-night stand, but Cristiano was still part of his life. Spent time with him on weekends and stuff. It hurts Cristiano to stay away from him, and he hates that his son will grow up believing that he'd abandoned him. It makes him feel guilty." Remembering the mini version of my brother, I smiled. "He's such a sweet kid."

"Is there anything you miss about that life?"

"I miss vodka – it's just not the same when it's in an NST or running through the veins of a human. I miss playing with my nephew. And I miss my dream of one day being a mom – it's not a dream I can have anymore."

"You'd have made a good mother." The glint of sympathy in his eyes was at total contrast to his apathetic tone. "I'm sorry you'll never have that."

I was pretty sure Salem and I would have made pretty babies. "What do you miss about being human?"

A shrug. "Nothing."

"Come on, there must be *something*."

It wasn't until he'd eaten the last of his pizza that he answered. "Okay. I miss being able to be thirsty without feeling edgy, agitated, and like my stomach's on fire."

Yeah, that would totally suck.

Having used one of the wet wipes to wipe away the grease from his skin, he leaned back in his seat. "You done?"

Bloated, I nodded and cleaned myself up with another of the wipes. "All done."

"Good. Come here." He held out his hand, and I stood and took it with a smile. He pulled me onto his lap, so that I was straddling him, and skimmed his nose along my neck. "Hmmm. I love that this scent is all over my skin and fills our apartment. But it smells a lot better coming directly from the source." He licked my bottom lip. "I always did like black liquorice."

I slid my hands under his t-shirt, wanting to feel his solid, defined chest. "You have to take care of this body for me tomorrow night."

He began running his fingers through my hair. "You worried about the battle?"

"Of course. Aren't you?"

"Am I worried about the battle? No. Am I worried that *you'll* be part of the battle? Yes. Doesn't matter that I know how strong and capable you are. I'll always worry. When I'd see Jared panicking on assignments about Sam's safety, I never understood why he let himself get so stressed about it – she's strong and powerful, so what's the big deal? But now I get it. He has something very important to lose. I never had that before."

I scowled at him. "Your *life* is important." If he hadn't thought that way before, he'd better freaking start thinking that way now.

A teensy smile warmed his expression. "Glad you think so." Abruptly, he wrapped my hair around his fist and snatched my head back, giving himself perfect access to my throat. His other hand cinched around my waist, tugging me closer and tilting my hips to grind me against his cock. His mouth tormented every inch of my neck – licking, nipping, sucking, and raking his teeth along my skin. One hand closed over my breast, kneading and clutching, and then thumbing my nipple.

"Are you wet for me yet, Ava?"

What a dumb question. I'd been wet since the first flick of his tongue on my neck.

His hand snaked beneath my dress with an urgency that told me I'd have lost my panties with one sharp tug...if I'd been wearing any. He froze, eyes flaring with hunger. "You're not wearing any panties." The words came out strangled.

In less than a millisecond, my *brand new dress* was on the floor, his mouth was devastating mine, and a finger was thrusting inside me. He swallowed my moan as my body clamped around his finger. I pulled back, gasping. "What if someone sees?" The side walls of the balcony were too high for the neighbours to see anything, but there were many apartments.

Completely undeterred, he continued driving his finger in and out. "We're too near to the balcony door for anyone above or below to see."

True, but..."People might hear us."

"Well yes, yes they might." And the weird bastard seemed to be turned on by that. "Which means you'll have to be very quiet."

I bit my lip, doing my best to hold back every moan, gasp, whimper, and groan as his finger plunged, swirled, and twisted. When his teeth sank down hard into my neck just as his thumb circled my clit, a wave of pure bliss swept me under, and I helplessly cried out his name. He continued feeding from me, drawing out my climax until I was shaking.

As I lay slumped against him, eyes closed, I distantly registered some fumbling and the sounds of buttons snapping open.

"Take me inside you, Ava."

Was he kidding? I could hardly move...*and we were still outside.* But when I felt his cock slap my navel I realised that, no, he wasn't kidding at all. I might have told him to give me a few minutes to recover from my orgasm, but I was very much aware of an ache inside me – an ache only having his cock deep within me could satisfy.

He lifted me by my waist, positioning me just right. "Slow," he ordered.

Placing my hands on his now bare chest – where did his t-shirt go? – I sank down on him. His size stretched and burned, and I wanted more. It took two downward thrusts before I was totally impaled on him. We both groaned, and his hands slid down to cup my ass.

I took a minute to just enjoy the feeling of being so amazingly full. Salem, however, wasn't much interested in letting me 'bask' in the moment; his hands squeezed my ass, hinting for me to move. Eyes locked with his, I slowly rose until just the head of his cock was inside me. Then, just as slowly, I sank back down. I'd expected him to soon urge me to pick up my pace, but he didn't. He was content to watch me ride him slowly, taking in every inch of his cock over and over.

But me? I wasn't so content with 'slow' anymore. I attempted to move faster, and his hands stilled me.

"Slow."

I didn't want to go slow, I wanted to come. And I knew just how to make him lose control. I went to lean forward and bite into his shoulder, but the bastard collared my throat and held me back.

"Tut, tut, tut. That's cheating, Ava."

"You got to feed. Now it's my turn."

The hand on my throat urged me to keep riding him, guiding my movements. "Oh, you'll feed. Just not right this second."

"Why?" I practically whined.

He nipped my bottom lip just as he pinched my nipple. "Be patient."

I pouted, speaking in what I hoped was a sensual purr. "Don't you want to come inside me? Don't you want to feel me come around you?"

His hand flexed around my throat. "No games, Ava."

"Not. Fair."

He arched a brow. "You need it that bad?"

"Duh." In a blur of movement, he scooped me up, took me to the bedroom, and positioned me on my hands and knees on the bed. One thing I loved about sex with Salem was that he never made me beg. He worked to give me exactly what I wanted, even if he took his time about it.

"Head down, baby. That's it." Without any preamble, he slammed home; burying his entire length inside me with one smooth stroke. I gasped, fisting my hands in the covers. His body folded completely over mine, trapping me beneath him.

He flexed his cock inside me as he rocked forward, as if to show me just how deep he was. "Now I'm ready to fuck." He powered in and out of me – it was hard, fast, and fierce.

And I loved it.

His pace was frenzied and merciless, and every frantic slam of his cock was a stab of pleasure/pain. I wanted to rear back to meet each thrust, but I couldn't move while his body blanketed mine. I was pinned in place, forced to take everything he gave.

He thrust his arm in front of me. "Feed."

Without hesitation, I sank my teeth into his wrist and sucked hard. I felt his cock pulse inside me as he came, and my own release thundered through me so intensely that I almost passed out.

Thankfully, Salem tipped us onto our sides rather than collapsing on top of me. With his hand gently stroking my stomach and my body humming with sexual satisfaction, it was easy to let my eyes slide shut while I began to drift off to –

"When we Bind, can we scrap the party?"

My eyes snapped open and my entire body stiffened. I *had* to have heard him wrong. "Um, what?" My voice came out sharp, almost shrill.

He sighed in disappointment. "I guess we could have one if you really, *really* want it."

"Slow down." I twisted in his arms. "What are you talking about? Where did this come from?"

"Why do you look so surprised?"

If this was a joke, I really couldn't guess the punchline. "Binding is an emotional connection that's practically soul-deep and doesn't allow for privacy. And you are a guarded, reserved, distant individual who treasures privacy."

"What's your point?" He seemed genuinely confused.

Nowhere near as confused as I was, however. "You're serious?"

"Would I say it if I wasn't?"

No, Salem didn't waste words or say anything he didn't mean, but…"If you truly want this, then you want it for the wrong reasons."

"No, I don't," he stated firmly. It was of course important to bear in mind that as long as something made sense to *him*, it was perfectly reasonable in Salem's world.

"You want to trap me. Keep me stuck to you. And have a link that gives you peace of mind during assignments. They're not reasons to Bind with someone. You have to care about that person."

He looked affronted. "I care."

I arched a dubious brow.

"So, what, because I can kill without remorse I can't feel something for someone?"

"That's not what I meant," I said impatiently. "But Binding is a humungous thing."

He narrowed his eyes, annoyed. "Are we back to that 'we shouldn't rush things' conversation?"

"No." Because Sam had been right in the things she'd said to me: Time comes to mean something different when it's not running out...When it comes to making decisions about taking huge steps, there's no timescale to measure against. It forces you to rely on your instincts. My instincts told me that Salem was mine, that what we had was deep and real. "I can't Bind with someone I love who doesn't feel the same way."

His eyes and expression softened, but his voice was gruff. "You love me?" Seeing the relief and contentment on his face, I realised that he actually did care.

I smiled. "Why else would I cope with your unreasonably intense possessiveness?"

"I warned you I'd hold you tight to me."

That made me think of something else Sam had said: We're predators now. Predators possess and guard what's theirs. "And I'll hold you tight to me. But I won't Bind with you for the wrong reasons, even though I'm happy to hear that you care."

"I do care," he asserted. "I feel sort of...calm when you're with me. And I think about you constantly when you're not." It was spoken with his usual apathetic tone. "I trust you, and I want you to have everything you want, even those goddamn cushions. And I feel...good. But vulnerable, because you know me better than anyone. And I feel panic. Because whenever I stop to think about just how much you could hurt me, I'm suddenly fucking terrified. It's like a physical hurt. An ache. I know that losing you would hurt worse than anything. And it scares me how much I've come to need you just to be okay, and just how much you – this one little person – is important to me."

I had to swallow past a lump in my throat. "That's love, Salem."

"Then I guess I love you, don't I? Why are you crying?" His arm wrapped around me, pulling me close. Of course Salem would never understand that his words could possibly have any emotional impact. To him, it was actions that spoke. "Stop it. I hate it when you cry."

I smiled, trying to blink away the tears. "Okay, stop freaking out."

"Does this mean you'll Bind with me?"

"Yes, and we don't have to have a party." I had to giggle at the relief that crossed his face. Bindings were week-long events of entertainment that culminated in a ceremony. Being a host and the centre of attention would literally kill him. "We'll just skip straight to the ceremony, and then have a little after-party. Okay?"

He inhaled deeply. "I can do that."

"You do understand that we can't have it until after this assignment is over, don't you? You'll have to walk into that battle without a Binding link."

"I know. And I trust that you'll keep yourself safe for me."

That made my smile widen. "Just like I trust that you'll keep yourself alive for me."

His expression turned fierce. "But I won't go on any other assignment after this until we're Bound."

"You're really adorable when you get all growly."

Ooh, he was offended. "Only you would ever describe me as stuff like adorable, or warm, or cuddly. And I'm betting you only do it to drive me crazy."

"Is it working?"

Growling, he rolled me onto my back, hooked my leg around his hip, and drove himself deep. "Yes. And I have no idea why I like it."

CHAPTER SIXTEEN

(Ava)

Okay, so when everyone was prepared to leave for Giles' club at dusk, the plan had been simple enough: pay him a visit, offer him one final chance to give up Diane. If he refused to do so, we would then give him two options.

Option A: return with us to The Hollow so that Ryder could do his thing, and Giles and his nest would then be spared.

Option B: let his entire nest die by engaging in a battle with us they had no hope of winning, and then we'd take him with us anyway.

However, two things fucked up that plan. The first was that Sam and Jared received a call from Giles an hour before we were ready to leave. He gave them Diane's current location in exchange for escaping punishment. The second thing was that Sebastian arrived at The Hollow merely three minutes after Sam and Jared's call with Giles had ended. Sebastian's news had not been welcome.

Sam frowned, leaning forward in her seat at the conference table. "She has something I want? What does that mean?"

Sebastian shook his head. "I have no idea. But I managed to track her to the abandoned warehouse where Giles claims she's hiding. I overheard her discussing the matter." As with Jared, Antonio had given Sebastian additional power as a reward, allowing him to develop a second gift. As such, in addition to having the ability to teleport,

Sebastian was able to create a mental shield that prevented him from being sensed.

"At least we know he's telling the truth about her location," said Chico.

Sebastian continued speaking to Sam. "He is with her, willing to fight alongside her, as you predicted. She does not believe it will come to a fight; she is sure that her marksmen will eliminate your squad. She also believes that when you see what she has in her possession, you will give her what she wants."

"What *does* she want?" asked Sam.

"She didn't say. This 'something' she has will soon be planted in the abandoned building adjacent to the warehouse."

"If it's not there yet," began Jared, "it could mean this is all just bullshit; that she intends to call our bluff."

"It is a possibility," allowed Sebastian. "But I doubt it – she seems too smug."

"It could be that she wants immunity for her crimes," suggested Butch.

Max's mouth twisted. "Or maybe she wants The Hollow."

"I'm quite sure we can cross the latter off the list of possibilities," replied Sebastian. "When Giles asked if she would demand The Hollow, she scoffed at the idea. She is perfectly aware that we would never leave The Hollow unguarded; that we would never bring the entire legion to any assignment. As such, she's certain that the moment she and Giles stepped on the island, they would be killed. She says she has no intention of dying, and what she wants from Sam is much more significant."

"She honestly believes that she has something important to me?" Sam shook her head, seemingly baffled. "The only things or people important to me are on this island."

"She was extremely vague about her plan to Giles. She either does not trust him, or she is simply enjoying his irritation and confusion."

"Maybe it's a bit of both," said Jude.

Jared sighed. "Okay, so we know she plans to place this 'something' in the building adjacent to the warehouse. Will it arrive before we do?"

"Yes," replied Sebastian. "She believes it will be in place by then."

"Then we'll have Evan and his squad retrieve it while Donnie and his squad remains on the lookout," said Sam. "You'll all do exactly what you were trained to do: split into five groups, invade the warehouse after the marksmen are dead, and then pick off whatever guards lurk inside so that you can circle the group that awaits us.

"At the same time, Evan and his squad will invade the other building. We'll have to trust that they'll have retrieved what's inside before Diane has the chance to try and use it against us."

Jared nodded his agreement with that plan. "Is the building guarded, Sebastian?"

"No. The warehouse is, however. But I did not stay long enough to get an accurate number of guards – I wanted to quickly relay the information I'd gathered."

"It was the right thing to do." Jared exhaled heavily. "Okay, we do just as Sam said."

"You don't want to take more squads with us?" Damien asked Sam and Jared.

She shook her head. "No, especially not when two of the other squads are still hunting clients. The Hollow needs to be protected – it's been invaded too many times for us to take its safety for granted."

Salem spoke then. "When do we leave?"

It was Jared who answered. "Giles told us that Diane intends to leave the warehouse sometime in the next two hours – which is clearly his way of getting us to arrive in a timeframe that suits them and prevents us from taking them by surprise. We'll have to leave very soon."

"Sebastian, I'd like you to return to the warehouse now," Sam told him. "We just need to have a quick chat with the other two squads first to let them know of the changes to our plan before we leave. My hope is that Diane may have this 'something' transported to the other building by then."

With a nod, Sebastian teleported away.

The rest of us met with the other two squads at the rear of the mansion. As Sam and Jared quickly debriefed them, Salem turned to me. "Remember: keep yourself safe for me and stay close. That's what teams do, right?"

I smiled at that. He was trusting me with not only my safety, but his. "Right," I confirmed. "Same to you. I don't want to see a single scratch on your body. Got it?"

His mouth twitched. "Got it."

(Salem)

It wasn't until Reuben had strengthened certain gifts that the squads were teleported to a desolate building a short distance away from the warehouse. Once all thirty of us were gathered there, Jared summoned Sebastian telepathically. Moments later, the Keja appeared at Sam's side.

"Please tell me you know what's inside the—" Sam stopped mid-sentence as she took in his grim expression. "I'm not going to like this, am I?"

"The 'something' she referred to…" Sebastian cast Ava a brief glance before continuing. "She has your old nest."

Ava tensed, inhaling sharply. I took her hand in mine, but she was like stone – I wasn't sure whether it was anger or shock that had her in its jaws.

Sam gaped. "The entire nest?"

"I'm not sure if it is all of them. There are thirty-three inside."

"Including my brother?" Ava's voice was like ice. Sebastian's nod didn't gain a response; her body remained stiff as a board. Seriously, it was like rigor fucking mortis had set in or something. Had to be shock.

"Thirty-three isn't a big number for a nest," remarked Harvey.

"A lot of vampires left the nest when Victor was alive," said Ava tonelessly, her expression distant, "so it's not as big as it once was." The girls supportively gathered close to her, but she didn't react in any way.

David puffed out a long breath. "I did not see that coming." Murmurs of agreement rang throughout the large crowd of vampires.

"They were brought here in a large van only minutes ago," Sebastian told us. "They are all unconscious – I'm guessing as a result of some kind of psychic attack. None of them seem close to waking. I was just about to follow the vampires inside the building to see where they placed the nest when Jared contacted me."

"Well, fuck a duck." Sam began pacing as a concerned Jared watched her closely, as if he feared she'd run off in a rage and try to burn down both buildings.

"Odd that she'd expect you to care about them though, Coach, since you're not a big fan of your old nest," said Damien.

"I was never a fan of my deceased Sire, but I never had an issue with most of the others. Ava's brother is in there." Sam knotted a hand in her own hair. *"Shit."*

Jared's voice was sharp. "Those of you who are our best spies, go."

Stuart, Denny, and three others disappeared instantly.

"I have to get him out of there," stated Ava, her voice still arctic-cold. "I have to get to Cristiano."

"We will get him out, Ava. I swear to you," vowed Jared. "First, we need to find out if the building is guarded. If it isn't, this could be a straightforward retrieval job."

But when the 'spies' returned a few minutes later, it was to tell us that the building was as heavily guarded as the warehouse; two guards covered the roof and all four sides.

Jared turned to the commanders of the other two squads. "Evan, Donnie – your roles remain the same." The two commanders and their squads dispersed, ready to target the marksmen. "As much as I hate to do this, we're going to have to split into two units. It's vital that we get into both buildings. Evan and his squad can help, but they wouldn't be able to take on the retrieval job alone. Not with how well guarded it is, and especially since there is a nest of vampires to retrieve. If we add him and his squad to our number then that gives us thirty people."

Sam nodded, visibly gathering herself. "Half can concentrate on infiltrating the warehouse, and the other half can concentrate on rescuing the nest. Other than that minor change, everything remains the same: we split up into small groups, invade whatever building we're assigned to from the upstairs and all sides, and then kill any guards inside. Meanwhile, Donnie and his squad will be on the lookout."

"How are we dividing?" asked Cassie, clearly anxious at just the idea of separating. I'd seen that look on David's face dozens of times; he never liked it when the squad split. Although I hadn't judged him for that, I'd never understood his anxiety. Now that I had Ava, I finally got it. David felt at ease and self-possessed when with his team, with those he trusted. The only times I ever felt truly at ease and level-headed was around Ava, the only person I completely trusted.

Jared turned to Sebastian. "I want you to go with Evan and his squad. You can teleport, and we're going to need that ability to relocate the unconscious nest to The Hollow. Between you and the teleporter in Evan's squad, you should be able to get the nest out of there pretty quickly."

Chico spoke then. "Which of us will accompany Evan, his squad, and Sebastian?"

Jared ran his gaze along all of us, lingering on Ava. *If I don't send her with them to retrieve her nest, will she go postal?* he asked me.

No, she'll follow your orders. But she'll be thinking about her brother, wishing she could rush in and help him, just like you would if it was Evan.

After a moment of silence, Jared said, "Ava, Salem, and Max – you'll go with Evan, his squad, and Sebastian to find and move the nest to safety."

It was the right decision, in my opinion. Ava relaxed *ever* so slightly.

"That will then mean fifteen vampires are working on retrieving the nest while the remaining fifteen of us concentrate on getting to Diane and Giles."

Sam scanned those who would be accompanying her and Jared. "We'll all split up much the same as we did during training." She then separated all fifteen of them into five groups of three.

"What about the second squad we brought with us?" probed Maya. "Can't they help us?"

"Unless totally necessary, I don't want them shifting their attention from guarding the perimeter," replied Sam. "Up until now, Diane has been very careful, and very well-prepared. She's resourceful and cunning. We can't afford to be suddenly surrounded by more vampires or let Diane and Giles escape; if she realises she's losing, she'll do a runner. Donnie and his squad can ensure both of those scenarios don't happen."

Jared stiffened, cocking his head, and I guessed he was speaking to someone telepathically. "That was Evan. The marksmen are out of the equation. Time to move. Ava, Salem, and Max – you enter through the front of the building that's holding the nest. Sebastian, you need to meet Evan and one of his squad members at the rear of the building; you three will cover the back exit. The remaining nine of Evan's squad has been divided into threes that will enter the building from the upstairs and the sides. They're ready when you are."

Each of the girls hugged the breath out of Ava, instructing her to take care of herself, just as she did the same with a forced smile.

Sebastian turned to me. "Before I meet Evan, I can teleport you, Ava, and Max to a spot that's a little closer to the front of the building." I nodded in appreciation.

Sam spoke to Ava; both females looked totally fierce. "Get them back for us."

Ava's smile – which was now a little malevolent – wasn't forced this time. "You can fucking count on it."

In a blink, I found myself in an old, crumbling building that smelled of mildew, mould, and ash. The charred walls were adorned in graffiti, and I wondered if it had once been the victim of a fire. Going by the machinery, it was an abandoned factory.

Careful to remain concealed by the shadows, Sebastian peeked out of the window and gestured to the six-floored, L-shaped building opposite the factory. "That is where you will find the nest. Good luck."

Max nodded. "You too."

Then Sebastian was gone. Just as he had done, we used the cover of the shadows to glance out of the window. Two Pagori guards were near the main entrance of the abandoned building, which seemed to lack a door.

"They're alert, which is disappointing." Max sighed.

"I recognise them from Giles' club," said Ava.

"Yep, they're his vampires," I confirmed.

"Which means it will be more fun to kill them, because that bastard led us into a fucking trap, and those two assholes down there are apparently okay with that." There was no real anger coming from Max. More like anticipation for vengeance.

"Where do you think they'll have hidden the nest?" asked Ava, her voice still flat and glacial.

"Hard to say," replied Max. "The building's pretty big."

"If it was me, I'd hide them in the centre."

"Why?" I asked her.

"Because it would mean that if anyone infiltrated the place, they wouldn't find it simple to locate the nest no matter where they entered. Diane probably doesn't believe we'd even know the nest are here, but she's paranoid. Like Sam pointed out, the bitch likes back-up plans and covering her ass. She'll account for this possibility just in case."

"I agree. So we'll assume the nest is on the third floor, but we'll be sure to search each area as we go."

Max seemed happy with that. "Same drill as last time?"

I nodded before turning to Ava. For once, she seemed just as eager as I was on assignments. "Ready?"

"Ready."

With the simple act of closing his hand, Max had deprived the guards of their senses. We didn't give the two Pagoris time to react. Without moving from the factory, I took out one with a lethal psychic punch. Ava literally appeared behind the other guard – she'd moved so fast, it was more like she'd teleported there – and mercilessly snapped his neck.

Max and I quickly joined her in hunkering down in front of one of the smashed windows near the main door, scanning the interior. The room seemed to have once been a large reception area, going by the overturned desk and the papers strewn all over the floor.

"Can't see or hear any guards," whispered Ava.

"There'll be some further inside," predicted Max.

"Let's find out." I slipped in through the front entry, avoiding stepping on the papers or anything else that would make a sound. Behind me, Ava and Max moved just as stealthily. Like the factory, it smelled of must and mildew, and also of an ammonia-like scent that was distinctive to mouse urine. I sure hoped Ava wasn't one of those people who got freaked out by the squeaky little shits. The last thing we needed was her squealing.

Both she and Max followed me through the arched entry of the reception area, which led to a long hallway. Still, I couldn't sense any guards. Sticking close to the wall, we silently advanced down the hall – pausing each time we came to a room, peeking through the open doors. Nothing.

As we neared a junction deep inside the building, I heard the slight scuffling of feet. Halting abruptly, I held up a hand, listening hard. More scuffling, followed by a gusty sigh.

We were too far away for me to pick up the vampire's scent and be sure it wasn't one of our own – it wasn't likely, but it was possible. As such, my gift wasn't the best to use or I could accidentally kill one of ours. I turned to Max and mouthed, "You move on three." Then I looked at Ava, mouthing, "You on four."

She seemed surprised but gave me a curt nod. I held up four fingers and then slowly began the countdown. The instant I dropped my third finger, Max acted, stripping the vampire's senses. Once I dropped the fourth finger, Ava seemed to fucking vanish. Hearing the tell-tale snapping sound, I knew the vampire hadn't been one from The Hollow. I rounded the corner, Max close behind me.

Ava was staring down at a pile of ashes in a way that said 'good riddance'. "He was covering the stairs. Now he can't."

Moving as silently as before and staying close to the wall, we scurried up the stairs until we reached the first floor. I stopped dead on reaching the doorway, causing the others to halt behind me. There were two piles of ashes on the wooden floor.

Peeking around me, Ava whispered, "They must have been guards. If they were ours, there would have been some kind of uproar."

She was right. If the guards had found and destroyed intruders, they would have loudly alerted the others, and guards would be searching the place far and wide for more of us.

"If vampires are guarding the stairwell, maybe it's because the nest is on a higher level," mused Max.

"My thoughts exactly." I continued up the next set of stairs with Ava and Max again behind me, heading to the second floor. Abruptly, I froze at the sound of harsh panting. Someone was in pain and trying hard to breathe through it. Then there were running footsteps nearing the stairwell.

"I'll get you out, just hang on," said a familiar voice.

I rocketed up the stairs, finding Evan's teleporter, Ian, scooping up one of his squad members – whose leg was broken in at least three places. Max winced.

"He got hurt fighting the guards. I'm taking him to The Hollow, and then I'll be back. I haven't yet found the nest, but I can tell you they're not on this floor." Ian then teleported away, knowing better than to waste time chatting.

"Then we keep going up." I'd only advanced a few steps when suddenly Sebastian appeared right in front of me. "Christ, I almost fucking killed you," I whispered abrasively. He didn't seem to care.

"We have a problem."

"Another one?" mocked Max.

Sebastian ignored that. "We have found the nest, but it is not going to be easy to reach them. There is a bomb – a psychic bomb."

"What's a psychic bomb?" Ava demanded, echoing my own thoughts.

Sebastian didn't answer until he'd teleported the three of us to a large room where Evan and one of his squad, Trent, were waiting. A loud gasp flew out of Ava as she noticed her nest slumped all over one another, unconscious. Surrounding them was a thin blue ring that occasionally flickered and produced a low hum.

She swallowed hard. "What the hell is that?"

"It's a rare gift, but it's a fucking good one," replied Evan. "It allows the vampire to surround something with what's referred to as a 'detonating ring'. As you can see, the ring is slightly visible, but it's a psychic construct. One that's linked to the vampire who made it. It acts as a sort of tripwire. If something crosses the ring, he'll know, and then he can cause whatever is inside of it to instantly explode."

Max skimmed a hand over his head. "Well, shit."

"We still have to get to my nest," insisted Ava. "There has to be some way to do it." I placed a hand on her shoulder, squeezing it comfortingly.

Sebastian pulled his cell phone from his Armani pants – he always dressed well, even for assignments. To be fair to him, he probably hadn't anticipated that Sam and Jared would ask him to partake in it beyond spying on Diane. "If you will excuse me for a moment, I must contact someone."

"Who?" asked Ava.

"One of The Hollow's researchers. They have been gathering information about gifts for centuries. If there is a way around this gift, they will know."

I held Ava to my side as she watched Sebastian closely, most likely trying to eavesdrop on his conversation. I wanted to tell her that everything would be okay, that she didn't need to worry, but I didn't want to lie to her. The fact was that this could be really, really bad.

The second Sebastian ended the call, she burst out, "What did they say?"

"The only way to deactivate the ring would be to kill the vampire who created it. If someone in the warehouse manages to kill him or her, that would work, but I would rather not wait around in the hope that this will happen soon. The researchers believe that although it is not possible to cross the ring without alerting its creator, it may be possible to teleport *inside* it without his or her knowledge."

Ava stiffened. "*May* be possible?"

"It is a risk. It could be that an attempt to teleport inside the ring actually alerts it's creator. And the nest would then be destroyed before your very eyes."

Horror flashed across her face as she again swallowed hard, casting a longing gaze at her brother.

"Ava, if we don't take the risk, Diane will use them against Sam," Evan pointed out, his voice sensitive. "We still don't know what she wants. But even if Sam gives it to her, I'm betting Diane won't hand over the nest. She wants Sam to suffer. The best chance these vampires here have at surviving this is if Sebastian tries to save them."

He was right. Had it been me, I would have immediately told them to take that chance. But Ava wasn't like me. For one thing, she had a heart. For another, she would hesitate at just the very thought of anything happening to them – particularly to her brother. "Ava, Evan's right," I said. "Diane will be planning to kill the nest no matter what happens. You know it, I know it. What's more, Sam knows it. You know what that means."

She nodded. "It means Sam won't agree to whatever Diane's request is, because she'll know there's no point since it won't save them."

"Sebastian really is their best chance, baby."

After a long moment, she looked at Sebastian. "Do it."

He inhaled deeply, closed his eyes, teleported away...and appeared inside the ring.

"It worked." Max grinned. "It fucking worked."

Ian and five of his fellow squad members appeared in front of Evan, their backs to the ring. "I took our injured to The Hollow and then gathered these five together to...What are you all looking at?" Ian pivoted. "Shit, is that a detonation ring?"

Sebastian teleported back to us. "Yes, it is. There is not much space inside the ring for me to move, and I do not want to risk alerting its creator by tripping it from the inside. I could probably teleport two people into the circle with me at a time. We can each scoop up a vampire, and then I will teleport us all to The Hollow."

"I can help," said Ian. "Once you've gone, I'll do the same – we'll alternate."

"That would help immensely," Sebastian told him. "It will take us some time, but we can hopefully have the entire nest out of here before a confrontation occurs between Sam and Diane." Sebastian teleported Evan and Trent inside the circle. He first scooped up Cristiano, to what was likely Ava's utter fucking relief, while Evan and Trent each gathered another. Once they were gone, Ian and two of Evan's squad then teleported inside and did the same.

After three runs, Evan called out to us from inside the circle, "Maybe you three should join Sam and Jared, since you can't do much here. They could probably use your help. When I contacted Jared to let him know we've found the nest, he said the interior of the warehouse was more heavily guarded than they'd expected, and quite a few have been injured, but Diane doesn't seem aware of their presence."

I definitely wanted to be part of the fight, but leaving these guys alone didn't sit too well with me. "We should stay and stand guard here."

"The other squad is patrolling outside. If they see anyone attempting to enter the building, they'll let us know. If we need help, I'll contact Jared and ask him to send or teleport some back-up here. You guys just—"

A pain slammed into my head as a strange 'bong' sound seemed to drown out all else, and I – to my fucking embarrassment – swayed on my feet. I shook my head, trying to focus. And that was when I saw that everyone else was doing the same.

Max had his hands slapped over his ears. "What the fuck was that?"

My instincts told me the answer. "That was some kind of psychic blast, and we caught the tail end of it. I'd say Diane knows she has company."

"A psychic blast that almost knocked *us* out when we're way over here?"

Ava gasped. "If it almost did that to us, imagine what it's done to them."

A growl rumbled out of Evan. "I have to get to Alora." He was gone before anyone could say a word.

"It's okay," said Ian. "One of the others can take Evan's place here. They need you over there. Go."

Moving at vampire momentum, we sped out of the building and over to the warehouse, where we crouched beneath a window. Reuben, Damien, and Stuart were sprawled on the floor inside, clearly unconscious. Thankfully, they weren't piles of ashes.

"Looks like it's been a psychic blast that's a little like your punch, but on a grander scale," said Max.

200

"If the gift *is* like mine, they'll wake after a few hours or once the vampire who released the blast is destroyed."

"Do you think it's affected the squad that's on the lookout?" asked Ava.

Considering they were closer to the warehouse than we had been…"I'd say so."

She frowned. "I can't sense Evan close by."

Neither could I, but I was confident that the last thing Evan would do was anything stupid. All he would be concentrating on was getting to Alora and getting her out of the warehouse. Had I been in his position, I would have done the same.

We crept further along the building, following the sound of a woman's maniacal laugh. Pausing in the shadows near another window, we slowly stood and saw Giles, Diane, and four male Pagoris glaring at Sam, Imani, and Jared, who were cocooned inside Sam's energy shield. Unfortunately, it seemed that Jared was unconscious.

Max grimaced. "Coach will be pissed that she didn't expand her shield in time to protect him from the blast."

"Going by the mercury glow to her irises," began Ava, "I'd say you're right."

"I'm thinking we do the same as before. I'll paralyse their senses and you guys attack them before any have a chance to retaliate."

Ava gave a weak smile. "There's a huge problem with that plan."

"What?"

"One of the Pagoris must have acted as some kind of psychic shield if the six vampires in there were unaffected by the blast. That same shield would protect them from your gift and Salem's. Any attempt to harm them by us would be instantly sensed, and then we'll be unconscious too. We're going to have to rethink that plan and—" Ava froze at the exact moment that myself and Max did…which meant we'd all sensed the two presences behind us.

We instantly spun. All at once, I growled, Max cursed, and Ava sighed as she said, "This has been a really shit day."

CHAPTER SEVENTEEN

(Ava)

"If you kill us, I'll be totally pissed."

Knox Thorne's dark eyes glinted with amusement. "Our fight isn't with you or yours, Miss Sanchez. You know who we're here for. My question is...why are you three out here instead of in there, helping your Grand High Pair?"

"We were about to think up a plan for getting inside without being placed in a coma when you two showed up." I eyed Knox and his friend suspiciously. "How long have you been here?" Neither demon answered. "See, I'm thinking you guys watched and waited until the vampires inside were vulnerable. And I think you did it for two reasons. One, it saved you some time and energy. Two, it meant there weren't many people to interfere with *your* plans."

Knox's mouth kicked up in one corner. "You should have been a demon, Miss Sanchez. You think like one."

Salem sighed. "We get that you want vengeance, but if you do anything—"

"It could begin a war between our species and yours," finished Knox, seeming unconcerned. "What you fail to understand is that we're demons; demons always get even. Do we like war? Not really." He actually sounded bored by the prospect. "We have better things to do than fight people we have no issue with, so it will be a shame if our species go to war with each other. But demons never let a wrong go unpunished."

"Speaking of 'wrong'," I began, "it was shitty of you to psychically 'tap' one of our legion so you knew what he knew." Ryder had found the evidence of demon interference a few hours ago; the legion member had been devastated to find he'd been involuntarily leaking information.

Knox simply shrugged. "I told you that we demons have our ways of getting information." At Salem's growl, he added, "We aren't here for you. But if any of you or your other vampires attack us, we'll retaliate."

"They're not really in a position to attack you," I pointed out. "They're unconscious."

Knox's friend, who I recognised from the hotel – if I was right, he'd been one of the doormen – peered inside the window. "How did that happen?"

"One of the vampires with Diane seems to have the power to release a powerful psychic blast. As if that doesn't give us enough of a problem, another of the vampires can create a psychic shield – that shield is currently surrounding all six of those asshole vampires that are awake."

"That won't be a problem for us," stated Knox, totally confident.

I frowned. "Why?"

He shrugged. "It just won't."

"Will you all shush," said Max, his eyes on what was going on inside the warehouse. "I'm trying to listen here. Coach seems to be doing her best to buy us some time so the nest can get to safety."

I peered through the window and watched as Diane went to stand before Sam, Imani, and a still unconscious Jared. In the background, Giles was exchanging smirks of triumph with the four Pagoris behind him.

"It's disappointing how easy it was to bring you down." Diane studied Sam from head to toe. "You're smaller than I expected. I must say, the females were a surprise. I take it these are from the brothel and they've come for their revenge." It pissed me off that her victims were so insignificant to her that she wouldn't even recognise one if they stood right before her.

"A little like you, you mean?" asked Sam. "That's what the brothel was all about, wasn't it? Buying the girls, forcing them to work at your brothel, blackmailing the clients…It was about getting revenge on men like those who forced you to do the very same thing once-upon-a-time."

Diane licked her teeth, as if savouring the idea of biting into Sam's throat and tearing it out. Apparently she didn't like to be reminded of her past. Not that I could blame her. "Someone did their homework, I see," she said with a sneer. "Well, so did I, little hybrid. I learned much about you. About your first years as a vampire. About the rumour that you killed your own Sire."

"Good for you." Sam sounded bored.

"Your nest was a well of information. Especially the new leader. He didn't want to talk at first, but Fritz" – she flicked a smile at one of the Pagoris – "*persuaded* him to answer our questions." If I hadn't seen for myself that Cristiano hadn't been beaten, I'd be panicking right now.

Imani leaned into Sam. "I once had a dog called Fritz."

Brows raised, Sam looked at Imani. "Yeah? What breed was he?"

"I'm sure you have bigger things to worry about than *pets*," Diane ground out.

"Of course," placated Sam. "Do continue. Or is this the part where you're hoping to kill us? I say 'hoping', because it would be a delusional idea."

Giles snickered. "You say that…yet here you are, without the protection of your squad." Yes, it was easy to look all smug and brave when he had four guards at his back.

"You cannot attack us from inside your shield," Diane said to Sam. "I learned that from the new leader of your nest." I doubted that Cristiano had told her a single thing about Sam. Considering how many assignments Sam had been on, it would be easy to find out about her gifts. I wondered if Diane was hoping that mentioning the nest would prod Sam into asking when Diane had spoken to them so that she could then smugly reveal that she had them in her possession.

"Yeah, I believe you already mentioned that you'd spoken with him. I'm tired of that subject now. How about we discuss your surrender instead?"

A loud laugh burst out of Giles. "And why would we surrender?"

"Because you'll die if you don't." It was said with such certainty that both Giles and Diane's confidence seemed to falter. But only for a moment.

"You can't hurt us from inside your shield," Diane maintained.

It was true that Sam couldn't, but I was betting that Imani could. While Diane and her crew were psychically shielded, however, Imani couldn't harm them with her gift.

"Your back-up has been disabled," continued Diane. "You have only your friend here."

Sam cocked her head. "You don't think the vampires in this building were the only back-up I brought along, do you?"

"No, which is why I have some back-up of my own."

"Oh, you mean the vampires you sporadically placed around the warehouse? The marksmen? Yeah, they're dead."

Diane's eyes narrowed. "You lie."

"You're cunning, devious, and calculated – I'll grant you that. But Diane, I've been up against people much more cunning and dangerous than you. People who put you more in the league of a rabid squirrel. Did you really think I wouldn't be prepared for whatever you threw at us? You honestly believe that more of my legion won't be swarming this place any minute now?"

"We'll see how prepared you really are. I have something you'll want."

"I hope it's the new Call of Duty game," Sam said to Imani.

With a nod, Imani spoke in an excited whisper. "Fingers crossed."

I heard Knox's friend snort with laughter behind me.

"I'd leave you to try and guess what it is, but you never will." Diane's chin lifted as a superior smirk surfaced on her face. "I have your nest."

Sam just blinked. "I don't have a nest."

Diane rolled her eyes. "Your old nest, then. I have them all."

"So?"

That had Diane doing a double-take. "So if you want them to live, you'll give me exactly what I want."

"Oh, you think you can use them as leverage. It won't work. But out of interest, what is it you intended to ask for?"

"It's simple, really." Diane shrugged. "I want your blood."

Sam's brows arched. "Say again?" Giles looked just as shocked. Apparently Diane hadn't shared her plans with him until now.

"Just enough blood to Turn a few humans. Those newborn vampires can then Turn others for me, and so on and so on."

"You hope to create a hybrid army for yourself?" asked Imani.

"Wars are not my thing. But if I was to open a brothel containing a multitude of hybrids...now *that* would earn me big money. Many would pay to drink from a hybrid." The red tint to Diane's irises glowed as her gaze locked on Sam. "And you owe me. I lost a lot of money and business because of you. I had to give up my homes because of you. I've been in hiding because of you." Like she had been falsely accused of something and forced to go on the run.

Sam made a 'hmmm' sound. "You're missing a few things."

"Such as?"

"If my blood was used to Turn any humans, it would make me their Maker. That would mean you would have no way of concealing them from me. I would find them, find you."

"Yes, but all I need is to take some of their blood – just like I intend to take some of yours. Any hybrids created from their blood would have no blood-link to you. You would be unable to find them. As soon as I have the blood of your 'babies', I can destroy them before you have a chance to locate them. We both know in that moment you will be in no state to track them down, not when the breaking of a blood-link is excruciating. To suffer the breaking of several blood-links at one time might even kill you." That was probably true. Christ, what a bitch.

Sam pursed her lips. "It's a good plan."

"I think so."

"There is a big problem with it, though."

"And that is...?"

"Well, I have no intention of giving you my blood. Guess that fucks up everything."

"You would let your old nest *die?*" Diane's expression said 'doubtful'.

"Yep. If you were thinking I had some kind of emotional tie to them, you clearly didn't do your homework well enough."

I almost jumped when Sebastian appeared beside me. "Shitting hell," I hissed.

"My apologies. I simply wished to let you know the nest has been moved."

I went to introduce him to Knox and his friend. "Fuck, where did they go?" I swiftly spun and returned my attention to the happenings going on inside the warehouse. There were no signs of the demons in there.

Diane clenched her fists. "How can you not care about the nest? You're the Grand High Bitch—"

"Oh, I like that title." Sam smiled at Imani.

"—which means every single vampire is your responsibility!"

"Yeah, I get that. And I really do care about the safety of every vampire in existence. But the thing is, the last time I risked my life to save others, Jared got *really* pissed about it and made me promise not to do it again." She made a huffing 'What an overreaction!' sound. "And then there's the fact that if I die, he dies, since we're mated. So, yeah, there's just no chance I'll give you what you want. And I can't regret that, considering what you would have done with any blood I gave you. No good whatsoever would come out of it."

Eyes diamond hard, Diane announced, "Then the nest dies." When Sam didn't react, Diane gave a nod to the vampire on Giles' far right, who I was guessing was the creator of the detonation ring.

After a few seconds, he gruffly told Diane, "It's done."

The image of self-satisfaction, Diane switched her focus back to Sam. "Now maybe I'll move on to all these squad members of yours just lying around the building. Maybe that will make a difference to you."

"No, it will just make your death more painful."

Diane laughed. "I doubt that."

"You really shouldn't." Knox stepped out of the shadows on Sam's left. At the exact same moment, four demons emerged out of the shadows behind the four Pagoris at Giles' back...and then suddenly those four Pagoris were ashes. I didn't even see what the demons had done to them.

Giles pivoted, clearly terrified – his gaze darted from the demons to Diane to Knox and to Sam...Did he expect her to protect him? What a fucking idiot.

Sam shrugged at Giles. "I did warn you the demons would come for you at some point if you didn't give her up."

A terrified Diane made a move to run, but in a blink Knox was in front of her, shaking his head.

"Imani," said Sam, "show Diane and Giles what happens when they don't have a psychic shield." With a wide grin, Imani did exactly that. Diane and Giles both dropped to their knees, crying out in pain.

"What is she doing to them?" one of the demons asked, appearing both curious and approving.

"Playing a tune on their blood-link," answered Sam.

Another demon then came out of the shadows; it was one I recognised. "She's the one we found in the attic," I said to Salem, who nodded.

Knox raised a brow at the she-demon. "Is that her?"

The she-demon studied Diane. "That's her. When I try to get an image of her face in my mind, I can't see it. But I *know* that's her."

Knox glared down at Diane. "Then you'll be coming with us." He cast Giles an uninterested glance before turning to Sam. "Do what you want with him. But she's ours."

Sam, holding the hand of a now conscious Jared, frowned thoughtfully at Knox. Her eyes then darted briefly to the she-demon, her expression torn.

It was Jared who replied to Knox. "Just make sure she suffers for what she did."

"That I can do," Knox drawled.

Sebastian was officially my fucking hero. If it wasn't for him, my brother might have been a pile of ashes right now. Instead, Cristiano was here in my apartment with me – alive and well…and pacing in front of my sofa, purple-faced and agitated.

Sitting cross-legged, I stared at him curiously. "You were kidnapped, knocked unconscious, and would probably have died along with the nest if it hadn't been for Sebastian…but *this* pisses you off?"

"You're my baby sister," he growled.

"And?"

"And he's a few mental steps away from a fucking psychopath."

"Don't judge."

It was a good thing that I'd asked Salem to give me some time alone with my brother. I'd wanted to tell Cristiano about the upcoming Binding ceremony in private – particularly since I'd worried that he might not be too pleased. I hadn't wanted him and Salem arguing. In actual fact, I hadn't even gotten to the subject of the Binding yet. The moment Cristiano realised that I'd moved in with Salem, he'd exploded.

"You seemed to have accepted the relationship when we last spoke on the phone." After his little chat with Salem.

"Of course I hadn't accepted it," he scoffed. "I just knew that fighting you on it would have made you stay with him just to be fucking contrary." Yeah, it probably would have. "I figured it would be better to let you see your mistake yourself. I should have known better. No, *you* should have known better. He's wrong for you."

I sighed tiredly. Any other time, I might have engaged in a shouting match with him over this, irritated by his interference. But my relief at Cristiano being alive kept my anger in check. Besides, I knew that his real problem wasn't Salem, it was that Cristiano was too overprotective to ever be comfortable with any male so much as *touching* his sister. "You never liked any of the guys I dated."

Cristiano stopped in front of me. "But at least they didn't have *psychosis.*"

"I won't deny Salem has issues—"

"That's putting it lightly."

"—but that's not why you disapprove. No, you're just latching onto that as an excuse to rant and rave, and justify being an interfering shit." I leaned forward, my face imploring. "Don't you want me to be happy?"

"You can't say with total honesty that that miserable bastard makes you happy."

"He does. He's sweet and funny."

Cristiano regarded me with astonishment and disbelief. "Sweet? Funny?"

"My point is he's not the one-dimensional psycho you seem to think he is."

"This really is serious for you, isn't it?" Cristiano cursed, looking helpless. "You're honestly thinking of staying with him."

It wasn't a question, but I confirmed, "Yes. I love him."

Closing his eyes, Cristiano inhaled deeply, and I got the feeling he was counting to ten in his head. It was something he often did when I was around – how fun. "Ava…you're sweet, and caring, and good." At my raised brow, he admitted, "All right, you can also be a bit of a bitch. But you're still too good for someone like him."

Truly fed up now, I waved a dismissive hand. "Whatever."

"I mean it, Ava."

"Oh, I know you do…which is why your opinions will now be redirected to '1-800-I-fail-to-give-a-flying-fuck'."

"Ava." With a sigh of resignation, he flopped on the sofa, looking sulky and worried. And that was when something occurred to me, and I was amazed that I hadn't seen it before. This wasn't simply him being overprotective. He was feeling like his nose was being pushed out. Like his role of protector and the most significant person in my life was now threatened. He worried he was losing me.

I twisted to face him. "Cris, I love you. You're important to me, and you always will be. Salem isn't replacing you. He's just sharing the burden that is me."

"You're not a burden."

"Two people can be important to me at one time, right?"

His face softened, and a smile tugged at his mouth. Then it quickly vanished, replaced by a petulant frown. "No."

I laughed, hugging him. "Let's look at it another way. You'll now have peace of mind that while we're countries apart, there's someone looking out for me."

He grumbled something unintelligible under his breath, but I could hear the defeat in his tone.

Pulling back, I smiled. "Does this mean you'll come to the Binding ceremony?" I almost laughed again when his eyes fairly bulged out of his head.

"You're *Binding* with him?"

"Yep." Ignoring the disapproval once more radiating from my brother, I confessed, "I'm still pretty shocked that he asked. I didn't think it was something he'd ever want."

"It was his idea?" Cristiano calmed a little at my nod. "He said he cares for you?"

I nodded again, and it surprised me that Cristiano didn't snort. "You believe he meant it?"

"I learned some things about Salem when I was last here. One was that he doesn't say anything he doesn't mean." He paused. "Another was that he can kill without remorse. Which is a psychopathic tendency and further supports my 'he's not right for you' case, but we'll ignore that."

I chuckled. "Thanks."

"Maybe being around you will make the miserable bastard more sociable."

"Let's not expect miracles, okay."

That made him smile. "And you're happy here? Being part of the legion?"

"Very. Please be happy for me."

His shoulders slumped, but his smile remained. "I still say you're fucking clueless for getting involved with him. But if he's what you want, I'll back off." He awkwardly patted my back when I again wrapped my arms around him. "Now let's talk about something else, get my blood pressure down. What's going to happen to Giles?"

Returning my gaze to his, I replied, "Sam and Jared will be executing him on V-Tube, along with the others who were involved. I'm guessing the survivors of the brothel will be glad to hear that."

He frowned. "They haven't returned home yet?"

"Their Sires sold them, so they don't know who they can trust in their nests."

His expression turned pensive. "I don't mind taking some back to our nest. Thanks to Victor, our numbers dwindled. But even if it wasn't now punishable by death, I wouldn't want to be like him – going around Turning humans against their will so I can increase my numbers."

See, Cristiano wasn't a total pain in the ass. "I could ask them, but I'm not sure if they'll be keen to go with you. They're pretty distrustful of everyone right now."

"Understandable. But it might make them feel better to know I'm tightly connected to you – one of the legion members – and that Sam was once a part of our nest. She'd vouch for me. Just don't ask for a character reference from Jared."

I smiled. "It's your own fault that he seethes at the very sight of you."

Cristiano shrugged, unrepentant. "I better get going. The nest will be eager to get home."

"But you'll come back for the Binding ceremony?"

"I'd never miss that," he assured me. "Even if you are planning to spend your immortal life with a complete nutter."

"It's so cute that you two have pet names for each other."

He snorted. "What is it exactly that he calls me?"

"My personal favourite is 'fuck-faced bag of shit'. But mostly he just refers to you as 'that asshole'."

"I think Jared does, too." It was said with smugness. He liked the affect he had on Jared.

"Tell me you're going to stop winding him up now that he rules our kind."

Cristiano grinned. "Where would be the fun in that?"

I rolled my eyes. "They're right. You are an asshole." He just laughed.

CHAPTER EIGHTEEN

(Ava)

Once Cristiano left, I decided to take a shower, knowing Salem – who had agreed to wait until my brother had left before coming home – would walk through the front door any minute and probably join me. But it was at least twenty minutes after I'd dried myself off and changed into fresh clothes that he appeared in the doorway of the bedroom.

I smiled. "Hey. Cristiano wasn't too happy to hear our news at first, but after a little—" I frowned as a familiar and offensive scent reached me.

That was when Gina stepped up behind Salem. "Hello, child." Her grin was arrogant and superior. "Look who I bumped into outside."

Returning my gaze to Salem, I found him staring hard at me. There was no emotion there, no sense of recognition. My stomach sank. No, no, no, no, no – this just wasn't happening. I leapt from the bed, intending to charge at the bitch.

"I wouldn't do anything hasty, if I were you. My protector here wouldn't like it."

Protector?

"He's my puppet now, just like I told you he would be." She stroked his hair as she pressed up against his side. His gaze moved to her, stayed there. "The adrenalin crash made him susceptible to me." She'd spoken as though she, as a woman, had seduced him as opposed to him being under her thrall.

"Susceptible to your *gift*. Not to you." I licked my lips nervously. "Salem?" No response – not even the flicker of an eyelid. "Salem, come here." Still no response; he just continued to gaze down at Gina, as though she was all there was.

"There's no point in calling to him."

Ignoring her, I repeated, "Salem, come here. Come to me." But he didn't. It hurt that I couldn't get through to him, even though I knew it wasn't his fault. I'd always suspected Gina would seek him out at a moment when he was weak. It hadn't occurred to me that the after-effects of a battle could make him vulnerable to her gift unless they were injuries.

"Why do this?" I demanded. "You don't want him. Not really."

She leaned her head on his shoulder, rubbing one hand up and down his arm. "You're right. I don't. But he betrayed me. And I can't allow that."

"Betrayed you?" Maybe if I kept her talking, it would give the thrall time to wear off.

"He left me. And then he chose you over me."

"But if you don't want him, what does it matter? Is it an ego-thing? You want to fuck him to shine your ego?"

She laughed. "Oh child, I don't want him to fuck me. Originally, it *was* my plan. But then I came to realise a few things as I watched you two together. You'd forgive him, wouldn't you? If he fucked me right now, it would hurt you, but you'd forgive him."

Yes, I would. It would devastate me if he touched her that way, but I'd forgive him.

"You'd blame me. And he'd blame me. It would achieve nothing. But...if I made him hurt you, if I made him kill you – someone whose life he actually seems to care about – that would give me exactly what I want. You would be dead, and he would be punished for betraying me."

And that really would hurt him. He'd already lost the people closest to him, and he blamed himself for their deaths. If I was to literally die at his hands, it would be a torment like no other for him. "It's a good idea. In theory."

Picking up on my scepticism, she prodded, "In theory?"

"You forgot one very important thing. The moment Salem realised he'd hurt me, he'd turn on you. Then you'd be dead too."

"Oh, I'm quite aware that he'll be hungry for vengeance. Salem always is. But in the moment that a vampire surfaces from a thrall, they're disorientated and weak. It will be all the opening I need to leave."

"He'd hunt you down. He wouldn't rest until he found and destroyed you."

Gina didn't seem concerned about it. But then, spoilt kids never thought much on their punishments. "Then maybe I'll kill him while he's staring down at your ashes, trapped in misery on realising what he's done to you."

"Salem would never hurt me."

"As much as it annoys me, you're right. But child, that isn't Salem you're looking at. No. My pheromones call to the predator within, bring our primal selves to the surface." She smiled up at him, grazing his chin with one nail. "Predators are elemental at their core – they want to feed and fuck. That is what you see in front of you. His human characteristics, his personality…it's all buried deep. He's been stripped of everything other than his predatory instincts. And he will do exactly as I tell him to."

Well, shit.

Gina skimmed the tips of her fingers down his chest, earning a sensual growl from him. "You can have me…as soon as you kill her." She pointed at me, and his eyes latched onto me like a snake latches on prey. Then he took a single step forward, snarling.

This really wasn't good. "Salem…" It wasn't the best idea to back away from a predator, but I didn't want to look challenging. I didn't want to hurt him, and I didn't want him to hurt me. Not just because he was a tough bastard who could easily end me, but because Salem would never forgive himself if he came out of the thrall to find that he'd killed me. He carried enough damn guilt.

His eyes narrowed the slightest bit – something I'd learned during training was one of Salem's 'tells'. So I expected the subsequent swing of his fist, and I instantly ducked, avoiding the psychic hit. A growl of irritation rumbled out of him.

"Salem, listen to me, you have to stop," I implored. I considered screaming for help, but it would do no good. The walls were all vampire-soundproof.

His fingers twitched – another 'tell'. Then his hand again clenched into a fist and swung. I jerked to the side, evading the psychic impact.

Again, he growled. He began prowling toward me, seemingly pissed. With each step he took forward, I took a step back, keeping a fair distance between us. I didn't want it to come to hand-to-hand combat, as things would then get truly messy. So I stayed away, forcing him to fall back on his gift. Again and again he aimed psychic blows at me; again and again I eluded him.

Dodging another punch, I shouted, "Salem, stop!"

"I told you, child: calling out to him is pointless. He's under my control now. He'll do absolutely anything for me."

Really? Well then she might just come in handy. As another psychic punch came my way, I ducked, rolled to the side, and came up behind Gina – all in the space of a single second. Arm wrapped tight around her throat in a constricting hold, I hissed, "You'd better tell him to stop, bitch. As you've seen, I'm fast enough to move before his punches make contact. You're not."

She didn't hesitate. "Salem, halt."

Instantly, he did; his eyes once again focused on Gina.

"Now, release him from the thrall."

"I can't." She futilely tried to free herself from my grip.

I just tightened my hold on her. "Do it!"

"That's not how it works. The thrall won't wear off until he's fucked me."

"I don't believe you." I didn't *want* to believe it.

"Look, he's hard – probably to the point of pain." A single glance at his crotch told me she was right. "Until he fucks me, he'll stay that way, which means the only way I can free him is if you step aside so he and I can have some fun."

Well there wasn't even the slightest chance that I was going to do that. "Salem, snap out of it!"

"He won't. His will is tuned in to my voice."

Her voice…That gave me an idea. "Tell him he can't have me."

"What?" Total confusion coated the word.

"Tell him he can't have Ava. Say it."

"You do understand that at this moment the only person he wants is me, don't you?"

"Then you'll have no problem repeating it. So do it." If there was one thing I knew about Salem, it was that he was a stubborn bastard who didn't like anyone telling him what he could or couldn't have; it was almost like he had an elemental reflex to challenge authority. He'd sure as hell never liked anyone attempting to come between us. He was darkly possessive, Fletcher had said. Maybe prickling that possessive instinct would appeal to something inside him and get through to the predator, maybe it wouldn't. But it was worth a damn shot. "Tell him."

"You can't have Ava."

He growled, clenching his fists. That was promising, right?

"Say it again."

"What's the point? He doesn't want you."

"Say it again."

A bored sigh. "You can't have Ava."

He growled again, louder this time.

"Tell him Ava doesn't belong to him. Now, Gina!"

"Ava doesn't belong to you."

His growl sounded more like a boat motor this time. His irises began to glow as his hands again balled into fists. Still, though, he only had eyes for Gina. It occurred to me then that he could be simply impatient to fuck her as opposed to affected by her words.

"Tell him he has to let someone else have Ava."

She snorted. "Gladly. You have to let someone else have Ava. Now help me, Salem! Pull her away from me!"

He stalked forward, eyes locked on Gina. The closer he came, the more I panicked. Sure, I could hold him off. Sure, I could fight him. But then I'd hurt him, and he'd hurt me. I didn't doubt for one minute that he could take me in a duel, if it came down to that. A big reason I'd lose was that I'd never be able to bring myself to kill him – not even in self-defence. So when he finally reached us, I shoved Gina at him. Yes, he'd fuck her, and yes, it would wreck me. But it was better than either of us being dead.

His hand gently slipped around Gina's throat, collaring her, as his eyes fixed on her like lasers. "Mine."

Fucking ouch.

She gave him a sultry smile. "Yes, I'm yours."

His head lowered, and I closed my eyes, unable to watch him kiss her. I seriously needed to get out of this fucking room. There was simply no way I could—

Crack.

My eyes flipped open…just in time to watch Gina, whose head was hanging at an unnatural angle, burst into ashes. "Oh, thank God." I rushed toward Salem, whose gaze then flew to mine. I instantly froze.

Because it wasn't Salem. It was still the predator. And he was totally pissed; probably because I'd repeatedly thwarted his attempts to harm me. As if to confirm that, he snarled. *Uh-oh.*

Slowly, I raised my hands in a gesture of peace as I backed up. The gesture didn't appear to work. Not in the least bit placated, he followed me out of the bedroom. *Shit.* Clearly, he still intended to obey Gina's order to kill me. "Wait. Salem." I gulped, admittedly terrified at the rage now emanating from him. "Salem, you have to come back now."

Another snarl. He made a grab for me, but I quickly backpedalled again. Maybe if I made a run for it and fled from the apartment...? No. He would surely follow me, and I couldn't be certain that people wouldn't attack him in an attempt to save me.

"*Salem.* Snap. The. Fuck. Out. Of. It!"

He dived at me, shackling my wrist in a harsh grip. But I easily broke free of his hold and retreated. Every muscle of his body seemed tense with fury as he advanced on me again.

Finding myself in the kitchen, I glimpsed the knife block in my peripheral vision. Out of any *useful* ideas, I snatched the chef knife and held it in front of me. I didn't think it would, for even a fraction of a second, scare him. But I was hoping that the threat might pierce his daze, make his resolve falter for even a moment. It didn't. He spared the knife the briefest glance, dismissing it, as he continued to stalk me around the kitchen.

"Don't make me use this, Salem." Like I ever could.

He lunged. Cursing, I leapt to the side and turned to make a dash for the living area. That attempt was hampered by the arm that looped around me, pulling me back against his chest. His fingers wrestled the knife out of my hand, and he slung it somewhere behind us. I kicked and punched, trying to get free despite that I was tired of running and trying to talk him out of a thrall – which, in hindsight, was ridiculous.

Suddenly I was twisted in his grip so that I was facing him; his irises were glowing red as he glared at me. "Ava," he rumbled. "My Ava."

"What?" The word rung with shock.

"You ran from me." He bit down hard on my neck, no warning or finesse. Helplessly, I moaned. The breath slammed out of my lungs as he backed me into the counter, grinding against my stomach. What was it Gina had said? *Predators are elemental at their core – they want to feed and fuck.* Apparently, she was right. His hand dove down my shorts, his finger circled and flicked my clit until I was squirming. The circumstances of the moment didn't matter; my body was trained to respond to him. It always would, it knew what he could give me, and it readied itself for him.

His teeth released my neck just as he tore off my shorts and panties. He plopped me on the counter, and unsnapped his fly. Without any preamble, he rammed into me so hard I almost yelped. I locked my arms and legs around him as he fucked in and out of me so deeply and ruthlessly that I knew I'd be aching afterwards. But I didn't care. Because even under a thrall it was *me* who he'd come to, it was *my* body he was craving and taking.

He nipped my earlobe hard. "Mine, Ava."

I would have agreed but his cock was hitting a really delicious spot inside me and his pelvis was teasing my clit with every thrust, and all I could do was moan and scratch at his back.

"Come all over my cock, Ava. Do it."

A particularly hard slam of his cock sent my climax barrelling into me, tearing a scream from my throat. I felt as my body constricted and rippled around him, felt as he came deep inside me, biting out a harsh curse into my neck.

When he brought his face to mine, the rage was gone. It was Salem looking at me, disorientated and lost. It seemed that now his body had the relief it needed, the thrall had worn off. "It's okay." I wrapped myself around him again, comforting him this time. "It's okay."

(Salem)

What the fuck had happened?

The last clear memory I had was of standing outside the apartment building. I'd scented Gina, knew she was coming up behind me, and I'd intended to chase her off. Then nothing. There was this huge gap; it was like I'd gone into some kind of deep sleep. Most of it had been dreamless, but then I'd heard a voice saying Ava's name. That same voice had told me I couldn't have Ava, had wanted to keep me from what was mine, pissing off every instinct I had.

It had made me push for control, push to surface from the dream. Little by little, I'd then become aware of things around me. Saw I was face-to-face with a woman who I vaguely remembered – Gina, I now realised – and that same woman was saying Ava's name, saying Ava didn't belong to me. I'd wanted to argue, shout, and demand to know where Ava was. But my body hadn't responded to me. Like I wasn't behind the wheel right then, and still yet not completely out of the 'dream'.

I'd then found my hand wrapped around that annoying woman's throat. I'd wanted to growl my satisfaction, insist that Ava belonged to me. The only word, however, that had come out of my mouth was 'Mine' just before I'd snapped who I now knew was Gina's neck. Then, suddenly, there was Ava…but she was backing away from me, denying me what belonged to me. Worse, she'd had fear in her eyes – like I'd ever fucking hurt her. All I could think about doing was grabbing her, biting her, and fucking her. *But she was backing away.* So I'd been pissed-the-fuck-off.

And then her blood was on my tongue, her skin was under my hands, and I could feel her wrapped around my cock. The more I'd fucked her, the more I'd rose from that 'dream', until I'd exploded inside her and then – just like that – I was awake.

It didn't take a fucking genius to work out I'd been under Gina's thrall. Considering I'd just fucked Ava like a damn animal, it was clear that Gina hadn't forced me to cheat on Ava. So what *had* she made me do? An insidious suspicion crept into my mind as I recalled the fear that had earlier stained Ava's eyes. I cupped her face. "Tell me I didn't hurt you."

"You didn't hurt me."

Something in her expression clued me in. "But I tried to, didn't I?"

Ava rested her forehead against mine. "That wasn't you. At that moment, you were a puppet – an extension of *her.* You didn't recognise me or my voice."

"Tell me exactly what happened." Being in the dark was giving me room to imagine all kinds of fucked up shit. I'd rather have the truth, no matter how horrible a truth it was. Taking a deep breath, Ava then filled in the gaps. Guilt, anger, and horror trickled through me; my stomach knotted at the thought of what *could* have happened if she hadn't been so damn smart. I fisted my hands in her hair. "Baby, I'm so fucking sorry."

She smacked my chest – and it actually hurt. "No, you don't get to feel guilty about this! Dammit, that wasn't your fault! And you fought it, Salem. You were stripped to nothing but basic instincts. But even then, once you realised who I was, your instinct was to protect me." She shot me a little smile as she added, "And fuck me silly."

I smoothed my hands along her thighs, wincing inwardly. "I'm sorry I was rough." I'd been *beyond* rough. More like violent. That in mind, I lifted her off the counter, carried her through the apartment and into the bathroom – pointedly ignoring the pile of ashes on the bedroom floor. When I started filling the tub, she sighed.

"This isn't necessary, I'm fine."

"Ava, don't lie to me. I vaguely remember shoving myself balls-deep in one thrust without much foreplay involved."

"All I cared about was that it was *me* you were fucking, not her. That we're both alive." She kissed me gently. "So stop torturing yourself. I want my cuddly bear back."

I narrowed my eyes. "You're calling me cuddly? I tried to kill you ten minutes ago."

"Stop dwelling on old shit."

With a grunt, I gently set her on her feet and carefully undressed her. Trying to apologise with every soft touch. Intellectually, I understood that she was right; the guilt was needless. But I still felt like complete shit. The thing I'd wanted to do from minute one was protect her. I'd almost fucking killed her.

By the time I was done undressing her, the tub was ready. I gently settled her into the Jacuzzi before turning on the jets.

She released a sigh of pleasure. "Why aren't you joining me?"

I crouched beside the tub. "This is for you." I skimmed my hand up her leg, unable to *not* touch her.

"Stop brooding."

I frowned. "I don't brood."

She snorted, sinking deeper into the water. "My conversation with Cristiano didn't go so good, at first. But when I told him I was happy and that I loved you, he calmed down. He'll come to the Binding."

I knew she was trying to distract me from what just happened, and I was willing to let her if it made her relax. "Good." If that asshole had refused, it would have upset her. Then I'd have had to kick his useless ass, which wouldn't have gone down well with Ava. "It must have been hard for you on the assignment, knowing he was close and in danger. But you didn't lose your shit. I'm proud of how well you handled it."

She glanced at me sideways, smiling shyly. "Thank you."

"I can't say I'd have been thinking straight if it had been you in that detonation ring."

"You think I'd have handled it just as well if it had been you and not Cristiano?" She got to her knees and faced me. "Salem, part of why I didn't lose my shit was that I had you with me. It helped me stay calm."

That got to me. I was used to making people feel nervous, never calm. My squad members might trust me with their lives, but I would bet none of them would claim I had a way of keeping them calm…particularly if I'd tried to kill them. "I'd never deliberately hurt you. You know that, don't you?"

"Of course I know that. Stop feeling guilty."

"I can't help hating what I did." Harming her went against everything in me.

"If the situation had been reversed, would you have blamed me?"

I didn't say 'obviously not', but it must have been evident in my expression because her smile was very self-satisfied. Sliding my hands into her hair, I drank in every detail of her face. I never would have thought that anything could be this important to me, and I didn't know how to handle it. I just knew I had no intention of losing it. "As long as you know I'd never purposely hurt you."

"I know you wouldn't."

"And that I love you." The words were gruff, but her smile was so bright that it might have knocked me on my ass if I'd been standing.

"I know you do." She didn't return the words, and I could tell by the teasing glint in her eyes that she was playing with me.

"Ava."

"Yep?"

"You have something to say."

She cocked her head. "Really? Like what?"

I bit her bottom lip hard enough to sting but without drawing blood. "*Ava.*"

She giggled. "Okay, I love you."

I grunted, which for some reason made her giggle again. I was just about to bite that lip once more, maybe break the skin this time, when a loud thud came from the living area – a thud that sounded suspiciously like the front door crashing open.

I zoomed through the apartment, and released a menacing growl at the sight of Will staggering inside looking pale and weak with an anxious Blythe in tow. "What the fuck do you think you're doing?" I moved to charge at the bastard, but Blythe slipped in front of him.

She started to quickly explain, "Don't harm him, Salem, he's upset and he wants to know how—"

"Get out," I snarled.

"He's upset!"

"You're mistaking me for someone who gives a shit."

"I felt my blood-link with Gina break!" Will burst out. "I *know* she's dead!" Which explained why he was in a bad state. The breaking of a blood-link was painful and draining. No doubt he would have come sooner if he hadn't been folded over in agony.

"What's going on?" demanded Ava as she sidled up to me, having thrown on a vest and pair of shorts.

Will locked on her like a pit bull might lock on something that moved too fast. His rage was evident through our link. "It was you, wasn't it? You did it."

"You'll have to be more specific," she said acerbically.

"It was you! You killed Gina!"

Ava snorted. "I wish."

"It was me."

Will gaped at me. "You?" Distress rippled along our link, and I understood why. It was natural for Sires to be distressed when their vampires fought amongst themselves – it was a little like a parent might be distraught if their children turned on each other. People took shit from their siblings that they wouldn't take from others, and the same often applied to vampires and those within their lines. But Gina had pushed too many buttons, and we all knew it.

"Me," I confirmed, sighing when I saw that the neighbours – all of whom were members of the legion – were gathering around the wide open front door.

Blythe put a hand to her chest. "You killed Gina?"

"I killed the vampire who put me under her thrall and tried forcing me to kill Ava." When Blythe shook her head in denial, I arched an impatient brow. "Are you really going to pretend she didn't have the nerve to do that?"

"I'll admit that it wouldn't have surprised me to hear that Gina tried to put you under her thrall in the hope of making you betray Ava. But to make you kill Ava?" Blythe shook her head again. "And if she *had*, surely Ava wouldn't be standing here now!"

"Ava snapped me out of the thrall, in a roundabout way."

"That isn't possible," claimed Will.

"Obviously it is. And now I'm done talking." I stalked over to him, grabbed him by his collar, and dragged him to the door. He struggled against my grip, hurling profanities. The vampires at the door parted for me, and I threw Will against the hallway wall. "Get the fuck out of here. And don't even *think* of barging inside my home again – unless of course you want to be as dead as that stupid bitch."

He righted himself, ignoring Blythe's fussing. "How dare you speak of her that way! Gina was *my* vampire! *My* firstborn! She was—"

"A spiteful bitch with a sense of entitlement that always got her in shit. This wasn't the first time she did something stupid because her ego got thrashed. You know that, just like you knew Gina would eventually do *something*. And you knew through your link that she was seething, plotting. Maybe you didn't know exactly what she was plotting, but you'd have sensed her frame of mind. Yet, you did nothing."

"One could go as far as to say it's partly your fault that she's dead," mused Ava, leaning against the doorjamb.

Confused and sad, Blythe spoke. "Gina tried putting you under her thrall countless times, Salem, but it never worked. I don't see how it could have worked now."

"My guess is that *she*" – Will snarled at Ava, who smiled brightly – "killed Gina in a jealous rage, and you're covering for her. Or maybe it really was you, Salem; maybe you set a trap for Gina because you wanted vengeance after she baited Ava."

I looked at him curiously. "You don't see it at all, do you? Gina saw it, and that was part of why she couldn't let it go."

"See what?" asked Blythe.

"I'm fucking happy," I said simply, not caring that I had an audience. "I have Ava. I have my position in the legion. I have the loyalty of good people." None of which I would ever take for granted. "The last thing on my mind was vengeance." My mind hadn't been preoccupied with thoughts of hurting someone, but of keeping someone safe. "The only way Gina could have been more than an irritating blip on my radar was if she did something huge. She realised that, and she acted on it."

Blythe went to speak, but then made a startled 'gah' sound as Sam and Jared suddenly appeared next to her. Neither of the pair looked surprised by the tension or the presence of Will and Blythe, so I had to conclude that someone from the small audience had called them.

"If someone could tell me what the bloody hell is going on, that'd be great," said Sam impatiently.

It was Ava who explained, fingers flying over the keypad of her cell phone. "Short version: Gina put Salem under her thrall, tried to make him kill me, but it didn't work and now she's sobbing in hell." I went to ask Ava who she was texting, but then Sam and Jared were speaking to me at once.

Jared growled, "She did *what?*"

Sam's eyebrows flew up. "She tried to make you *kill Ava?*" The mercury glint to her irises flared.

"I refuse to accept it," snarled Will. "They set Gina up. They wanted her dead, and they made it happen." He jabbed a finger at Ava. "She hated Gina—"

Ava gasped, returning her cell to her pocket. "How long have you been sitting on this information?"

"—so she got rid of her. And now they're trying to justify her actions by falsely accusing Gina of this."

Rolling her eyes, Ava pushed away from the doorjamb. "Why do you keep trying to pit us all against one another? This isn't one of your fight clubs. You're not going to turn Sam and Jared against me or Salem, which means you won't manage to turn us against them. Just the same, you won't make Salem lose his position."

"Lose his position?" repeated Jared.

"Will doesn't like that one of his vampires has succeeded in achieving more than he ever has. When he couldn't match Salem's success—"

"He tried to take Salem's success away from him," deduced Sam, clenching her fists.

Will sneered. "He wouldn't have his position if it wasn't for me! I'm the one who Turned him and trained him."

"No, *we* trained him," objected Sam, gesturing to both her and Jared. "You laid the foundations, but it was us who helped him earn the strengths he has now. I say 'helped', because he could never have the control and skills he can now boast of without his own determination and focus."

Jared nodded. "Salem earned his position. You didn't earn it for him."

SUZANNE WRIGHT

"And now I really am tired of listening to your grievances," said Sam with a sigh. "In fact, even the sound of your voice pisses me off at this stage, Will. As for your insistence on making life hard for two members of the legion…that's not something that can be overlooked. It's not something we'll allow, which means you're no longer welcome here. But Jared and I gave our word that you could stay, and we don't break our promises."

I understood that. The Grand High Pair wouldn't have the confidence, trust, and loyalty of vampirekind if they were known for going back on their word.

"So that leaves you with two options, Will," continued Sam. "Option one: you and your mate can voluntarily leave, thereby escaping punishment for harassing two legion members—"

"I did not harass them!"

"—and for not warning us that your firstborn was scheming, which is something your blood-link would have helped you sense. Option two: you can hold me and Jared to our word and remain here, but you'll have to accept punishment for your actions."

"P-punishment?" stuttered Blythe nervously.

Sam regarded her with an analytical gaze. "I doubt you're guilty of anything more than blindly following your mate, but you will of course share any pain he feels through your bond; there's no way of getting around that."

Will spluttered. "You cannot be serious!"

"Let me assure you I'm *very* serious."

"I have—"

"Will, maybe we should agree to leave," interrupted Blythe, apprehensive.

"I will not be run off!"

"Don't let your pride get in the way," she begged quietly.

He ignored that. "I am guilty of nothing other than voicing my opinions!"

"You have repeatedly made accusations against Ava," began Sam. "Accusations that would have led to her being harshly punished if we had believed your bollocks."

"I see the real her, just like Gina did," growled Will. "She has even turned Salem against me – his own Sire."

Ava gave a soft groan. "Here we go again. *Annoying*," she added in a singsong voice.

226

That got a few chuckles from the bystanders, who were all glaring at Will with a mixture of anger and pity. And that was what did it, what knocked Will over the edge and sent a pounding need to *hurt* through his system; I felt it through our blood-link, *knew* exactly what he was going to do. So I was ready when, with a battle cry worthy of a highlander, he launched himself at Ava.

Several things happened at once – all under the space of a second. The legion members in our audience moved to plant themselves between Will and Ava; Sam conjured her whip, most likely intending to curl it around Will; Jared raised a hand, his fingers trickling with electricity; I raised my fist, ready to hurl a psychic punch at the motherfucker.

But then we all froze, because it became clear that none of us had been quick enough to keep her and Will apart. Having moved faster than all of us, Ava was now latched onto his back like a spider monkey. Her hands were tightly gripping his head, showing him that with just one minor move, his head would be hanging from his body. Shock alone had Will freezing, wide-eyed.

"Don't think I won't do it," she snarled at him. "I don't like that it would put Salem in physical pain. But I know as well as you do that you've just signed your death warrant. If I don't kill you tonight, someone else will." But Ava didn't want it to be me who killed him, I quickly realised as her expressive eyes landed on me. She didn't want me to be responsible for killing my own Sire, even if said Sire was a complete prick. Because prick or not, he was still my creator – family, in a sense. She worried that my killing him would pile more guilt on my shoulders, so she'd intervened.

It was sweet, but…"Ava, move. The bastard's mine." But Jared got in my way.

"Don't hurt him," pleaded Blythe.

"He tried to attack a member of the legion," interjected Jared. "There's a penalty for that, and he'll pay it."

"Excuse me," a familiar voice called out. The crowd parted, allowing Imani through. "Thanks." She laughed at the sight of Ava on Will's back. "I got your message…Can't say I expected to find you like this when I got here."

I arched a brow questioningly. "Message?"

"She's here to sever your blood-link with Will," Ava told me. "If Imani does it, it will cause you only a brief moment of pain."

Will's brows knitted together. "Break the link?"

"Ava, come here." I wanted her back with me, away from the fucker who'd tried to hurt her.

She pouted. "But I'm comfy here."

I jerked my head. "Come here, baby."

With an extremely put-out sigh that made Imani chuckle again, Ava hopped down and came to my side. "Happy now?"

"Yes." I curled an arm around her, holding her close as I glared at a still seething Will.

Sam turned to Blythe. "You have a choice to make. Will is going to die tonight. As you're Bound, if he dies, you die. But I don't believe in making people pay for what others do. You're no fluffy bunny, but you don't deserve to share in his punishment. Imani here can sever your Bond before Will is punished, which will save your life. Or you can die with him. It's your choice."

Blythe and Will both stared at Imani in shock before then turning to face one-another. They didn't say a word, but their emotions were clear in their expressions. Blythe was torn and confused. Will was pissed that she would even consider Sam's offer, warning Blythe with his eyes not to betray him and accept that offer. Which just demonstrated how much of a bastard he truly was. If I'd been in his position, I'd have insisted that Ava accept that offer and *live*. I wouldn't have seen that acceptance as betrayal, wouldn't have cared what she did as long as it kept her alive.

"We need an answer, Blythe," prompted Jared.

She shook her head, though she still seemed torn. "I don't want to live without him."

"Fair enough."

Ava looked at her friend and squad member. "Imani?"

All business, the short brunette turned to face me. "I'm told it's a similar feeling to when Ryder goes surfing inside your brain. The only difference is I'm not searching through what's there. I'll only find and touch the blood-link."

Imani closed her eyes, and then I felt it: a tiny hand treading through my brain. But it wasn't an invasive feeling because the pads of those psychic fingers were simply skimming the surface as opposed to digging.

When the hand stilled, I knew she'd found the link. One finger lightly flicked the taut thread, sending reverberations through my head.

I flinched, involuntarily clutching Ava tighter to me. Shit, no wonder Butch had been in agony when Imani had strummed his link like a guitar string. Then two fingers seized the link and pulled hard. The 'snap' echoed through my brain, left me feeling like I'd taken a hard blow to the skull. I winced, grinding my teeth against the pain, as I grabbed my head. I distantly registered that Will was doing the same.

"Done," announced Imani with a smile.

Ava rubbed my arm soothingly. "Is the pain easing?"

I took a deep breath. "Yeah." It had hurt like a bitch, but it would no doubt have been worse to *feel* Will die.

Will glared at me. "You're going to let them kill me?"

"You tried to attack my mate." Didn't make any difference to me that we weren't yet Bound – it was only a matter of time. "No one hurts her."

Ava's arms constricted around me. "Sam and Jared will take care of his punishment."

I glanced down at her. "The last thing I'd feel is guilt if I took care of it."

"You took care of Gina. Why should you get to have *all* the fun?"

"He tried to attack a member of the legion," said Jared. "His punishment is therefore mine and Sam's."

Sam nodded. "Now go play with Ava or something." With that, Sam and Jared teleported away with Will and Blythe.

"You okay?"

I knew what Ava was asking: Was I at all upset that my Sire was due to die? "He tried to hurt you. He deserves exactly what's coming to him."

Seemingly satisfied by that answer, she said with a little clap, "Come on. Let's go vacuum Gina's ashes." Ava sounded so delighted by the idea that I felt a slither of amusement. Life would never be boring with this woman.

CHAPTER NINETEEN

(Salem)

"You don't need to be nervous." Jared clapped me on the shoulder. "I can tell you from personal experience that the ceremony moves pretty fast. And there's no chance that Ava will stand you up."

"I know that." She and I had exchanged a few text messages, although they had been mostly to remind me just how pissed she'd be if I started anything with her asshole of a brother. The same asshole who had last night said, 'If you ever hurt her, psycho Sid, I'll kill you.' Naturally, I'd replied by dangling him over the balcony until he begged me to pull him back up. It had been kind of fun.

"Don't tell me you're having second thoughts."

I threw Jared a look of disgust. I wasn't going to credit that dumb question with an answer. I wasn't afraid of this. Wasn't scared of the depth of commitment I was about to make. No one would ever fit me the way Ava did. Nobody. She accepted me just as I was, broken and all. Everything – even the fights – were good with Ava. And I knew that no matter what happened in the future, it would be a better one with her in it.

Also, after tonight, there was no way she could ever doubt how important she was to me. Nothing said 'I love you' like Binding every part of yourself to someone for your immortal life, did it?

Keeping to her word, Ava had rejected Sam and Jared's offer to hold a week-long celebration for the Binding. Call me miserable, but parties really weren't my thing, particularly if I was supposed to be the host and the focus of any attention. Also, I personally found the formalities and traditions that went with Bindings plain weird; I wasn't much interested in throwing a celebration that was suited to everybody else. Thankfully Chico and Jude, who had asked to hold their own Binding in the same ceremony, were in total accord with me on that.

Much like me, Chico hadn't really involved himself in the planning of the event. In fact, it would be fair to say that I'd actively avoided taking part. Maybe there were many guys out there who found it fun to choose flowers, balloons, table decorations, and fonts for banners, but I just wasn't one of them. I wanted few things from tonight. One, to be Bound with Ava. Two, to have beer-flavoured NSTs at the – in my opinion unnecessary – after-party. Three, to have Ava revert back to the woman I adored…as opposed to the stressed out psycho of the past three weeks.

She had agonised over every minor detail to the point that she'd exploded on two occasions, and I'd hated that it was causing her stress. Particularly since, to me, a small ceremony was more meaningful than a showy production. I didn't want the meaning behind the Binding to be muddied by colours, fonts, and styles. But when I'd – most reluctantly – offered to help in the hope of easing the burden a little, she had smiled and assured me, "It's fine; me, Fletcher, and Jude have got this."

Maybe she'd correctly sensed that allowing me to join in planning the event would have led to a very different evening. Instead, she'd told me: "I'll give you the time, date, outfit, and sort out all the details. All you need to do is dress and turn up on time." Was it any wonder that I loved her?

"*Relax,*" said Jared. It was only then that I realised I'd started to pace.

I couldn't relax, and for a very good reason. "They're going to do something," I muttered, tipping my head toward where my squad was whispering among themselves in the second row seats. White covers and pink bows had been attached to each chair, as Ava had requested.

Jared frowned, confused. "What do you mean?"

"They're going to pull some kind of prank." I could see it in their oh-so-innocent eyes.

Arching a brow, Jared snorted. "What, you mean like they – *you included* – did at *my* ceremony?"

Well, yeah.

Standing under the floral arch, the Prelate – the same one who had performed Sam and Jared's Binding – *hmphed* at me. The uptight vampire hadn't been at all impressed by the pranks, and he clearly remembered them. Not only had we all pinned 'Run' signs on our shirts and flashed them at Sam, but we had attached a 'Help Me' sign to the back of Jared's shirt.

"I think they call this kind of thing 'karma', right?" Jared smirked, the prick.

Just then, Chico came to stand at my other side in a similar get up as me – open necked shirt and pants. He cast the rest of our squad a quick, distrustful glance. "They're going to do something."

"Yep," I agreed.

He fiddled with the collar of his white shirt. "I have a feeling Harvey's speech is what we need to worry about." As it was tradition for a friend of the couple to do a speech during the feast, both my squad and Ava's had put their names into a hat. Harvey's name had been drawn out, and we all knew that he would take absolute delight in making the entire thing painful at our expense. He could be a dick like that.

Movement in my peripheral vision caught my attention: Fletcher was exiting the back door of the mansion – the very same door that Ava was due to step out of any minute now. Moving at vampire speed, he past the bat pool and advanced across the beach; not stopping until he reached the end of the aisle.

With a smile, he did some kind of weird curtsy. "The girls are ready, they look fabulous, and they're on their way with Sam." For Sam to escort Ava and Jude was a symbol that the Grand High Pair approved of and blessed both Bindings. "Big smiles," he encouraged before skipping over to his seat. It was odd watching someone skip on sand.

"Now both of you relax," Jared told us. Chico nodded, blowing out a long breath, while I just grunted.

Resisting the urge to fidget with the anticipation rushing through me, I fixed my gaze on the open doors at the rear of the mansion. Moments later, Ava, Sam, and Jude finally stepped out into the warm evening, hand in hand. The very second Ava's eyes locked with mine, a bright smile lit her face; just like that, my body and mind relaxed. I knew I had a similar smile on my own face.

How could I not smile right now? Fletcher's 'fabulous' comment was an understatement. She looked amazing, captivating, and enchanting in her white strapless gown that I was guessing was satin. While the skirt was ruffled and long, it was knee-length at the front, showcasing those legs I loved. Her gorgeous hair, which always made me think of melted chocolate, was loose around her shoulders and curled slightly at the ends. I was pretty sure I'd never felt more proud or satisfied than I was in that moment.

Soft music began to play and the guests rose. The three women followed the trail of white and pink petals, pausing only to remove their high-heeled shoes at the fringe of the beach. Ava's eyes didn't leave mine as she advanced up the aisle, and her smile didn't once falter. But her stride did when the soft music suddenly spluttered and was replaced by 'Macarena'.

Not even the slightest bit amused, the three women halted. In unison, their heads swivelled to glare at my squad, who were all looking deceptively innocent. Behind them, Ava's squad leaned forward and whacked the guys over the head, making them flinch and whine. Jared cleared his throat to disguise a chuckle. Glancing at the other guests, I saw that he wasn't the only one entertained.

"I'll kill them," Chico ground out.

"You'll try, but I'll get there first."

Thankfully Fletcher acted quickly, and soon the soft music was playing again. The women blew out a calming breath and then continued making their way down the aisle. When they finally stopped, Sam placed Jude's hand in Chico's and then Ava's hand in mine.

"Hey," Ava whispered simply. Her smile had returned in full force.

It took everything I had not to yank her to me and take that mouth. I was about to tell her how amazing she looked when Jared clapped me on the shoulder once again before kissing Ava's cheek. As he then went with Sam to take their seats on the front row, I turned back to Ava. Quietly, I spoke. "You look—"

I froze as two farting sounds split the air. I looked at Sam and Jared only to find that they were both scowling as they pulled out whoopee cushions from under the white chair covers. Knowing exactly who was responsible, I shot the guys – all of whom were shaking with silent laughter – a snarl. That was when they smiled, revealing blackened teeth.

A loud giggle popped out of Ava, which acted as a catalyst. Suddenly everyone, even the damn Prelate, was laughing...other than myself and Chico.

"They're dead," he mouthed to me, to which I nodded in agreement.

Irritated and eager to get started, I turned my glare on the Prelate. With a sheepish look, he pulled himself together and cleared his throat.

"Stop scowling, you're scaring him," Ava teased loud enough for only me to hear. I cast her a mock glare that made her giggle again.

Signalling for both couples to face him, the Prelate then began. As the ceremonial words were all spoken in Latin, Luther had explained the gist of the speech to us beforehand: that for vampires, our human-death was not the end, but the start of something new; that we should never take for granted this gift of finding someone to spend our immortal life with.

When the Prelate gestured for us to link hands, Ava and I turned to look at each other. Having joined our palms together, we then spread our fingers wide, and threaded them through each other's – forming a 'V'. Ava once again gave me a beaming smile that made me want to kiss her until she couldn't breathe. Instead, I listened as the Prelate spoke a string of Latin to me.

Thanks to Luther having told me beforehand, I knew the Prelate was asking if I agreed to love, protect, treasure, comfort, support, and laugh with Ava, and to forsake all others, in good times and in bad. *Well, obviously.* So I responded, "Ita vero." When Ava then did the same with no hesitation, a sense of self-satisfaction warmed me from the inside out.

Eager to pull her close and finally taste her, I waited damn impatiently as the Prelate had Chico and Jude exchange the same vows.

"Stop scowling," Ava whispered. "You can't scowl at our Binding." But she was on the verge of laughing. I made an effort to soften my expression, but I wasn't sure I succeeded.

Finally the Prelate signalled for us to exchange blood. Leaning down, I kissed Ava deeply before biting her bottom lip and licking away the rich blood that seeped to the surface. Ava copied the move, wearing the sultriest smile. *Minx.* As I'd expected, a small wind suddenly built, whipping around us, causing Ava's hair to lift slightly.

I almost jumped as I felt it: what I could only describe as a 'psychic bridge' came into place with a sharp snap.

Just as Jared had once described, the pathway was almost like having an additional sense. This bond tied me to Ava so completely that I could sense not just her current state of mind, but her heartbeat, her thirst-level, her location, her energy-level. It was both strange and reassuring, gave me a soul-deep fulfilment that I'd never before known. I would now always be linked to this person that meant more to me than anything else.

I didn't have much time to marvel over the bond before heat seemed to engulf my third finger, and there was an odd sensation – much like a sharp nail was scratching at the base of the digit. That was when a black, intricate, Celtic-like pattern formed exactly where a wedding ring might have been: a Binding knot. It wasn't a *dull* black. Not something subtle or easily missed. It seemed to glimmer and *demand* attention.

Seeing an identical knot forming on Ava's third finger, I smiled inwardly. I knew that Binding knots varied for each pair, which meant that Ava's knot would match only mine, just as mine would only match hers.

That knot showed the world that she was taken, that she belonged to me. It let people know there was someone who would go to deadly lengths to keep her and protect her from any external harm. It was also a sign that she wanted to be mine just as much as I wanted her to be – and that in itself was an absolute fucking phenomenon in my eyes.

"I love it," Ava murmured. "You're stuck with me now."

I kissed her again, just because. "Then I have what I want."

Once Chico and Jude completed their Binding, the Prelate gestured for the guests to rise. At that, they all got to their feet and clapped just as Sam announced, "Let's eat, I'm bloody starving." Diplomatic, as ever.

(Ava)

"Does it tingle?"

Salem blinked. "Tingle?" He cast his groin a glance, and I giggled.

235

"I meant your knot." I lowered my voice so the rest of the table couldn't hear. "When I touch mine, it sends a little shiver through me."

His mouth curved just as his face took on a speculative look. "Does it now? Interesting." I didn't like the roguish glint in his eyes. "You look beautiful," he said gruffly. I could feel his sincerity and admiration through our bond. The connection was so much deeper than I'd expected, so amazing and comforting.

I fingered his shirt. "And you look rather dazzling." Honestly, when I'd seen him standing near the floral arch with Chico, Jared, and the Prelate, I'd almost groaned at how mouth-wateringly masculine and sexy he looked.

"Dazzling?" He sounded offended.

"Sorry, not manly enough for you?"

Lifting one of my hands, he traced the intricate vine pattern on the back. I could sense his confusion.

"It's one of the prenuptial rituals for Bindings." After being covered in exotic-smelling oils and given a full-body massage, I'd enjoyed a spicy wrap treatment. Then I'd been given a milk bath, followed by having my hands and feet painted with a glistening ink. I'd actually kind of liked the rituals, but the ever-so-impatient Jude hadn't found any of it relaxing.

As his finger began to trace my Binding Knot, I gasped. And the bastard's eyes lit with mischief and smugness. "Not here," I hissed.

"You're right. Let's go."

Knowing he was totally serious, I placed my hand on his thigh to stay him. "Not yet."

"Then when?"

His pained expression made me giggle. "Soon, but not yet."

"Why?"

"We haven't even eaten, for one thing." As tradition, the feast was taking place in the grand garden at the back of the mansion, which was adorned with butterfly lights, candles, torches, and banners. We were seated at the 'head table' with Jude, Chico, Sam, Jared, Luther, and Sebastian. "I spent a lot of time planning this menu, and I intend to taste it." When his pained expression deepened, I guessed, "You don't want to stay for Harvey's speech, do you?"

"No." Salem leaned closer, speaking matter-of-factly. "There's also the little issue that having a great view of your legs makes me want them wrapped around me while I'm buried inside you." He took the hand I'd placed on his thigh and laid it over the hard bulge in his pants.

Heat and need rushed through me, making me swallow hard. "Soon," I promised again, giving his cock a gentle squeeze.

When Jared got to his feet, a respectful silence descended. "Before we eat and kick this party off, Harvey and I would like to say a few words. Before we do that, though, I have to thank Fletcher and his crew of very creative people who worked hard to organise the ceremony and after-party. Secondly, thanks to everyone for coming to witness and celebrate the two Bindings that occurred tonight."

Jared looked down at me, Salem, Chico, and Jude as he continued. "All four of these vampires have dedicated their immortal lives to serve and protect their kind, and that's no small thing. They deserve the happiness they've found." He lifted a champagne chute. "Please raise your glasses and join me in blessing this Binding and wishing these vampires well." Once everyone had taken a sip of their champagne-flavoured NSTs, he took his seat. "The floor's yours, Harvey."

As Harvey stood wearing a superior grin, I felt Salem's tension and unease understandably increase. He and Chico were right: Harvey would take utter delight in giving a speech that embarrassed all four of us and undoubtedly featured a few pranks.

"As a good friend of both couples, I'd like to say—" He flinched as a series of loud popping sounds practically deafened us all and colourful streamers rocketed into the air. Only Salem, Chico, and Harvey were confused by the fact that every guest except for those on our table were setting off party poppers. Jude, Sam, and I exchanged a knowing grin that made Salem arch a brow at me.

Harvey cleared his throat. "I'd like to say—" Once more, numerous popping sounds split the air, bringing an angry flush to his cheeks. Raising his voice, he tried again. "I'd like to say congratulations to both couples and—" More loud popping sounds. "Oh, fuck it." He slumped in his seat, sulking. Laughter spread around the tables that circled the man-made dance floor.

Salem narrowed his eyes at me, amused. "That was your idea, wasn't it?"

"I wasn't going to let him make you even more uncomfortable than you already do at our Binding."

"I'll love you forever for that alone."

I laughed, straightening in my seat as a plate of food was set in front of me. Clearly the feast had now began. During all four of the delicious courses that followed, Salem insisted on turning eating into a sensual act. He lifted food to my mouth using either his fork or fingers, licked off any sauce or cream from my lips, and even fed me ice cream by taking a spoonful into his own mouth and then kissing me. The whole time, he never stopped touching me – whether it was to caress my nape, stroke my knee, or trace my ear. He was also sure to trace my Binding knot from time to time, the teasing bastard.

"*Must* you torment me?" I hissed, flushed with need.

"Yes, because if I can't be alone with you, I'm going to at least make sure I have all of your attention." He kissed me, swallowing my chuckle. "Besides, you taste *so* fucking good. How am I supposed to sit here and not take a little lick?" He swiped his tongue over my bottom lip. "Or a bite?" He nipped that same lip just as his hand cupped the back of my neck. God, I was so damn turned on right now it wasn't even funny.

Hearing a throat clear, I looked up to find my brother sneering at Salem. "Can you stop mauling my sister?"

Salem glared at him. "No, I won't stop touching *my mate*." That had Cristiano scowling.

"Boys, boys," I interjected, "this is a *celebration*. No arguing."

Cristiano shot Salem a withering glare before flashing me a smile. "I came to ask you for a dance."

"She can't right now, she's busy," Salem answered for me. I rolled my eyes.

"You can't expect her not to have at least *one* dance at her own Binding." Cristiano smirked. "Let's face it, it's not like *you'll* give her that dance."

Well, that was probably true enough so…Wait, why were we standing?

"Your brother's right, baby. You should get to dance at our Binding." His reluctance was clear in his tone. But apparently he was more unwilling to part with me than he was to dance, because sure enough he escorted me onto the very crowded dance floor.

Considering how reluctant he was to get up there, I'd expected him to totally lack in rhythm. Big mistake on my part. He held me just right as we swayed: his left hand kept my hand over his heart, his right hand rested on my lower back, and he tucked my head beneath his chin.

Feeling his hard cock brushing against my stomach was like a promise of what was to come. It was also sheer torment, because I was already hot with need after his sensual torture during the meal. Deep inside, I felt *empty*. And I knew that only he could take that emptiness away by thrusting inside me.

When the song ended, Salem lowered his mouth to my ear and nipped the lobe. "Please tell me we can go now."

I swallowed hard, more than ready to be alone with him. "We can go now. But discreetly," I stressed, pulling him towards the shadows.

Sam had warned me that it was tradition when the couple was leaving for the guests to line up and not only shake their hands, but for the guys to kiss 'the bride' and the women to kiss 'the groom'. *Not a chance* was I letting that happen. I doubted Salem would like it any more than I would.

Creeping around was pretty simple when you had a member of the Grand High Pair's personal squad in the lead. Obviously all his training had paid off. Entering our apartment, he moved to pull me to him. Shaking my head, I backed up.

"Come here," he rumbled, his face a mask of intensity.

I wagged my finger. "This is our Binding night. We are going to celebrate it in the bedroom." If I went to him now, let him touch me just once, we'd undoubtedly end up fucking on the floor or against the wall. Not that those were necessarily bad options at all. But for this night, I wanted a bed.

"If that's what you want." Moving so fast I had no time to react, Salem scooped me up and carried me through the apartment, not setting me down until we reached the foot of the bed. His stare was so predatory and so piercing it burned my skin and hardened my nipples. Humming low in his throat, he breezed his mouth over mine. Instead of kissing me, he lifted my hand and admired the Binding knot once again, eyes glinting with both satisfaction and arousal. Then, holding my gaze, he sucked my finger into his mouth and swirled his tongue around the knot.

My knees actually buckled. "Shit." The smug curve to his mouth was nothing but irritating right then. Taking him by surprise, I retrieved my hand and smoothly tackled his fly; smiling when his cock bobbed out of its confines. "All mine," I whispered, fisting him and sweeping my thumb over the head. Keeping my grip firm, I pumped him; wrenching a thick groan of need from his throat.

"Harder."

Instead, I knelt at his feet, peeled down his pants, and helped him step out of them. His cock was hard, thick, and long, and I wanted it inside me. But first…Cupping his balls, I lifted them slightly and then very slowly licked from his perineum, over his balls, right to the head of his cock. His hands bunched my hair as a growl rumbled out of him. Again and again, I licked him like a lollipop; his grip on my hair tightened to the point of pain.

"Open your mouth, Ava." The instant I did, he surged inside. Rather than withdrawing and thrusting again, he stilled. "I love looking at you with my cock in your mouth." I swirled my tongue around him, and he groaned. "Here's what's going to happen next. I'm going to take this mouth. Going to come down your throat, and you're going to swallow every drop. Then I'm going to taste you until you come all over my tongue. After that, I'm going to fuck you so hard, you'll never forget how I feel inside you." He smoothly pulled back and then thrust back in. "You want that, don't you?"

Well, duh. I nodded as much as his grip would allow.

"Good." Then he did as he promised and fucked my mouth. I held onto his thighs, and alternated between digging my fingers into the skin and lightly raking him with my nails. Despite how rough he was, he looked at me the entire time like I was all that mattered.

"Every drop, Ava," he reminded me. Then he stilled and came with a guttural groan, watching as I swallowed it all. With his hold on my hair, he urged me to stand and kissed me hard. "I think you deserve a reward for that." He backed me into the open closet door, crushing me against my silk robe. Spotting it, a devious gleam entered his eyes that made me a little nervous.

"What?"

He pulled the tie free of the robe. "Hands above your head."

Well now. Holding his heated gaze, I slowly did as he asked.

He bound my wrists together with the tie and then attached it to the hook. "Very nice." He brushed his nose along my neck, inhaling deeply. "Don't move." Then he dropped to his knees, and his hands shackled my ankles gently. "I've been thinking about doing this all fucking night," he said as his hands slowly and smoothly slid up my legs, forcing the front of my dress to hike up around my waist. Arousal flashed across his face as he saw my white lacy, silk panties.

Seeing his intention in his eyes, I quickly told him, "You don't need to rip them off. There's a ribbon on each side."

"Is that so?" He slowly unravelled one knot. "Like my very own present." Then he unfastened the other ribbon; watching, content, as the barrier slid away. "So pretty." His tongue flicked out and lashed my clit, startling a low gasp from me.

Grabbing my hips, he tilted me slightly. "Put one leg over my shoulder, baby." The moment I did, he dived in – there was really no other term for it. His seriously wicked tongue licked, lapped, swirled, and stabbed, hitting all kinds of nerves and buttons. The more he tasted and teased, the more pronounced the ache inside me became…until it was just too much.

"No more." I moaned as he began to suckle on my clit. "Salem, get up here." A finger plunged inside me, followed swiftly by another. Again and again, he drove them into me – all the while playing with my clit and working me into a frenzy. Honestly unable to take it any longer, I lifted my leg from over his shoulder and tried pushing him away with my foot. Unaffected, he grabbed my leg, hiked it high, and rammed his fingers inside, curving them just right. I exploded.

"That's what I was waiting for." Getting to his feet, he lightly kissed my neck as he freed my hands and gently skimmed his own over me, as if soothing me.

"Now I want what *I've* been waiting for." I shoved him toward the bed so hard he stumbled, and he did something I never would have expected. He laughed. It was a low, throaty sound that made my stomach clench and caused me to blink in surprise. "I'm glad you don't laugh a lot in public, because I think I just came."

(Salem)

"I don't want you coming again until I'm in you." Yanking her to me, I lifted her up and dumped her on the bed.

She landed on her back with a bounce, giggling. "Ooh, I like the direction things are moving in." The little tease raised her knees and then slowly parted her legs, giving me a perfect view of what I wanted most.

I took a moment to drink in the sight of her – eyes shining with arousal, face flushed, legs spread invitingly, folds swollen and glistening. Shedding my shirt, I knelt between her thighs and hooked her legs over my shoulders. "Look at me." When her gaze locked with mine, I slammed home, and her body clamped tight around me; she was so damn wet I was balls-deep in just one thrust. "You feel too fucking good around me."

"No more teasing, Salem," she ordered, panting.

"No more," I agreed. "Because now I'm going to fuck you." I scooped her breasts out of her dress and drew a nipple into my mouth just as I started pumping in and out of her. Nothing tasted, smelled, or felt better than Ava. Add in the amazing little sounds she made and her hands threading through my hair, and I was already close to coming.

"Harder, Salem."

I gave her what she wanted, pounding hard, fast, and deep; relishing every moan of my name. Needing to taste more of her, I licked and sucked at her pulse, letting her know what was to come. Then I bit hard, groaning as her rich blood flooded my mouth. Sliding one hand under her head, I lifted it – hinting at what I wanted. She didn't hesitate to return the bite; the pleasure/pain had me feverishly hammering into her.

She screamed my name as her climax hit. Feeling her blood on my tongue, her teeth in my shoulder, her nails raking my arms, and her body rippling around me as she came was too much – I jammed my cock deep as I erupted inside her, filling her.

Not wanting to crush her, I rolled onto my back, dragging her on top of me.

As I lifted her hand to look at her Binding knot, she smiled. "The bond is pretty awesome, huh."

"Now you can't ever again feel lonely."

"And neither can you."

"Even better, you can't ever again be insecure in how I feel. Can't ever again stupidly wonder if I'm getting tired of you."

"Never again," she vowed.

"Just know that there's no get-out clause, Ava. Don't think having Imani around means this isn't exactly what it's supposed to be – *binding*. This is forever. If I fuck up, if I hurt you, if there's something that needs changing, we talk about it and I'll fix it."

She pressed a reassuring kiss to my jaw. "I would never have Bound myself to you if I'd first needed to be secure in the knowledge that I had a way out. I would never have formed such a connection with you, let you so deep inside my soul, unless this was forever for me." She held up a finger. "Having said that, if you ever cheat on me or some shit like that—"

"That's never going to fucking happen," I snapped.

"—I will definitely be seeking Imani's help." She smiled sweetly. "And then I'll kill you."

My mouth twitched. "You'll never have to, because I'd never betray you. You're all I want."

"Just like I'll never betray you. There's never going to be anyone else for me. I love my warm, cuddly bear too much." She patted my chest. "Ooh, here comes the lethal scowl."

"You just had to do it, didn't you?" She just had to start the whole 'cuddly bear' thing again.

Ava shrugged one shoulder innocently. "Maybe I just want you to prove how *not* cuddly you are by fucking me silly a second time."

"And maybe you just enjoy driving me insane."

"How am I doing?"

"You know."

"Ooh, you're getting all growly again." She gave a shiver of delight. "I think you're just mad because there are Hello Kitty curtains in the living area."

I frowned. "There aren't Hello Kitty curtains in the living area."

"There will be if you don't fuck me silly again."

I shook my head, torn between annoyance and amusement. "Well then I guess I better get to work."

"I always said you were smart."

EPILOGUE

(Jared)

It was really no surprise to me that Sam had found herself a dark corner. Much like Salem, she wasn't a fan of formal events. To her credit, she'd lasted two whole hours before hiding. But there was no way that my mate could ever hide from me. Walking right into her personal space, I pressed a light – and somewhat teasing – kiss on her mouth. "You're looking very smug, baby."

She shrugged innocently, but her self-satisfied grin remained. "I'm just happy for Ava and Salem."

I snaked my arms around her waist and pulled her to me, aligning that perfect body to mine. "And I'm sure your happiness has nothing to do with how your matchmaking skills got them together."

Another innocent shrug as she lightly raked my nape with her nails. "I just gave them nudges in the right direction."

"Nudges?" Oh, what an understatement. "You lied that Ava was in Luther's vision so that you could take her along to the brothel, making she and Salem spend time together."

"Only because Ava needed some work experience."

"You threatened that if anyone dared to come between Ava and Salem, their efforts would be met with bodily harm."

"Only because I was looking out for her."

"And you were chatting to Ava about Binding, planting the seed of the idea in her head."

"How do you know that?" Sam gaped, eyes wide.

I smiled. "I know *you*. I know how your mind works." Nuzzling her neck, I slid my hands down to cup her ass. "And I know how to make this body melt for me."

"Cocky bastard," she muttered.

I pulled back. "Are you saying I can't? Because that sounds like a challenge, and you know I'd have no choice but to accept it. Macho-guy pride insists on it."

She rolled her eyes in exasperation. "Any excuse to have a tumble."

Well, of course. "Let's go. We don't need to stick around, Ava and Salem have already left."

"Snuck away, did they?" And now that smug grin was back.

"I take it you're not done with matchmaking yet."

"Definitely not. This is fun."

I nipped her bottom lip. "Who's next?"

She spoke against my mouth. "I'll tell you...right after you've made me come so hard I can't move."

Yep, that was a halo hanging over her head. "Have I mentioned that I love you?"

"Never hurts to hear it again."

I held that aquamarine gaze, knowing that everything I'd ever wanted was staring back at me. "Then I love you, Sam Parker."

"Good, because I love you, Jared Michaels."

"I like it better when you scream it."

An affronted look. "I don't scream."

"Yes, you do." I teleported us to our bedroom. "And you're about to do it again."

ACKNOWLEDGMENTS

Super big thank you to my family for their support and for being so amazing as to forgive me for going off in my 'zone' so often. I know it's got to be weird living with someone who hears voices in her head, so thank you for pretending it's not.

As always, a massive thank you to my Beta reader, Andrea Ashby – she's fabulous, and she never lets me down, no matter how much she's got going on in her own life, and I truly appreciate it.

Finally, a gigantic thank you to all my readers. You're all seriously amazing. The support for the series has helped it go from a standalone to a series, and I will never forget that.

If for any reason you would like to contact me, whether it's about the book or you're considering self-publishing and have any questions, please feel free to e-mail me at suzanne_e_wright@live.co.uk.

Take care,

Suzanne Wright

TITLES BY SUZANNE WRIGHT

The Deep in Your Veins Series

Here Be Sexist Vampires
The Bite That Binds
Taste of Torment
Consumed

✥

The Phoenix Pack Series

Feral Sins
Wicked Cravings
Carnal Secrets
Dark Instincts

✥

The Mercury Pack Series
Spiral of Need

✥

The Dark in You Series
Burn

✥

Standalones
From Rags

ABOUT THE AUTHOR

Suzanne Wright lives in England with her husband and her two children. When she's not spending time with her family, she's writing, reading, or doing her version of housework – sweeping the house with a look.

Website: www.suzannewright.co.uk
Blog: www.suzannewrightsblog.blogspot.co.uk
Twitter: twitter.com/suz_wright
Facebook: www.facebook.com/suzannewrightfanpage

74257264R00141

Made in the USA
Middletown, DE
22 May 2018